The Fortress of Faltryn

The Token Bearers — Book Two

Books by Derin Attwood

The Token Bearers Series

Book One: The Caves of Kirym

Book Two: The Fortress of Faltryn

Book Three: The Trail to Churnyg

The Fortress of Faltryn

Read & dream.

Derin Attwood

The Fortress of Faltryn

A Wordly Press Publication
Ashhurst, New Zealand
Phone 64 6 326 8066

First published by Wordly Press in 2014

Copyright © Derin Attwood 2014

All rights reserved. No part of this publication may be reproduced, stored in a retrieval system, or transmitted in any form or by any means, electronic, mechanical, including photocopying, recording or otherwise without prior written permission from the author.

This book is a work of fiction and is the product of the authors imagination. Any resemblance to any persons living or dead is entirely coincidental.

The author asserts her moral right to be identified as the author of this work.

Cover Art Copyright © Llyvonne Barber

Set in 12/18/24 Adobe Garamond Pro
This text uses English (UK) spelling.

ISBN 978-0-9941108-1-7

A catalogue record for this book is available from the National Library of New Zealand.

Wordly Press
www.wordlypress.com

For Ron
who encouraged me to
reach for the stars

ACKNOWLEDGEMENTS

Many friends have supported me as I wrote this book. They read, laughed, cried and critiqued as necessary. You know who you are, my darlings.

Suzanne Main, Stuart Lee, Mark Brady, Jess Copping, Karen Pearson and Julie Scott, for support and encouragement through some very difficult times.

My children, Llyvonne and Garreth, who accept that the family in my head are as real to me as they are, and understand when I remember the characters names as readily (or more) as theirs.

Last but not least my husband, Ron, whose unswerving belief in me has given me the strength to continue Kirym's adventures.

Characters on this Adventure

Name		Relationship
Arbreu	M	Token brother to Kirym, Teema and Bokum
Bildon	F	Orphan
Bokim	M	Joined to Zephrah, Papa to Sarel and Trayum
Danth	M	Joined to Jinda, Tarjin's Papa
Findlow	M	Kirym's uncle, Lyndym's papa
Jinda	F	Joined to Danth, Tarjin's papa
Kirym	F	Veld and Loul's daughter, Aligned to Teema, Arbreu and Bokum
Lyndym	F	Kirym's cousin, daughter to Findlow
Mekrar	F	Kirym's sister, Twin to Mekroe
Mekroe	M	Kirym's brother, Twin to Mekrar
Sundas	M	Aligned to Findlow
Tarjin	M	Mekroe's best friend. Danth and Jinda's son
Teema	M	Aligned to Kirym, Arbreu and Bokum
Veld	M	Headman, Kirym, Mekrar and Mekroe's papa

It was the blackest of nights; the crescent moon had long since set. The stars looked remote and cold.

A star shot across the sky dimming all of those around it. In moments, it had covered half the sky shooting into the north-east. Then it exploded. Six fragments altered their path and fell earthward, hissing as they disappeared. The core of the star continued north east, breaking in two just before it vanished from my sight in an exploding flash.

I woke. The full moon shone brightly on the western horizon. One star glowed near it, the rest lost in the reflected light. A small star shot across the sky, vanishing as it reached the Dragon-star.

1

Kirym Speaks

We had never quite decided what created the canyon. It sat in the centre of a massive hill, accessed by a single curved path. A deep gash marred the northern edge of the rim. The best guess was that it had been a vast cave in the hill; the gouge in the rim was the entrance, and at some time in the past the roof had fallen in. What worried me about that theory was the absence of debris on the floor of the canyon. However the trips we made there were always exciting. The two or three days we took to get there was part of the celebration.

Late in the spring, our third since we had discovered this land and the canyon, we had celebrated late into the night, this time to acknowledge the naming of Bokum's son, Trayum.

We had had a wonderful day, and the singing and dancing continued until the moon was falling back towards the western horizon. Now our fires lit up the canyon, casting strange shapes and shadows on the walls, the deep gash on the northern wall a dark void. Guards patrolled the entrance and watched over the sleeping family.

I was in charge of the middle watch that night, starting just after midnight as the celebration began to wind down. My shift was uneventful and in the dark time just before dawn, Teema joined me as I handed over to Arbreu.

We were quietly discussing the earlier ceremonies when the tunnel leading into the token cave lit up, and not with the glow of candlelight.

I sprinted towards it, hearing Teema and Arbreu thundering behind me. The light went ahead of me, drawing me through the tunnel and into the cave. Arbreu and Teema were right on my heels.

The large tokens sat on a flat rock in the centre of the cave. They glowed warmly, but what was surprising and different was the many small tokens shining from the walls and ceiling.

"What does it mean, Kirym?" Teema asked.

I shook my head. "Just watch." The lights went out and we stood in the darkness for a long long moment. Then the large blue token glowed, followed by the green and the yellow. They pulsed gently for a short time until with a flash, the rainbow token lit up. Its colours seemed to reach out, the blue, green and yellow connecting to the large tokens there. The other colours, purple, red and orange, spiralled away in different directions, searching for connections and bathing the cave in soft colours.

The small tokens in the ceiling glowed and began to pulse, and the tokens we wore took up the rhythm. Soon the whole cave was a vibration of pulsing light and colour. Slowly a white ray arched from the rainbow token to the other large tokens. It blazed and connected to the small tokens, seeming to draw the colour from them. A shimmer of light joined

Kirym Speaks

the blue, green and yellow tokens and then connected also to the tokens we wore.

The lights again went out and we stood in the darkness. Then the large tokens started vibrating, but this time they all flashed one colour.

Red!

"We're in danger here," I said, and even as I spoke the colours faded, leaving just the blue stone glowing. I frowned, trying to understand what it meant.

"Is the danger to the settlement?" I asked. Nothing changed.

"Is there danger here in the canyon?"

The red light was almost blinding, and the tokens thrummed.

"Is it close?"

The colour and the noise intensified.

"Will we be safe when we leave?"

They steadied, although there was still a vibration in the air.

"Can we travel straight back to the settlement?"

The tokens screamed.

"Is the hill safe?"

Silence!

"Can we use the ridge to get to the settlement?" The tokens vibrated gently, retaining their usual colours.

I couldn't think of anything else to ask. "Thank you for the warning."

As I turned to leave, the tokens called again, although this sound was different. It diminished as I returned and settled when I picked up the blue token, followed by the green one, the glowing rainbow token and the yellow. As I picked up the last token, the lights suddenly went out. We stood in the darkness for a moment and then the blue token lit up again. I slipped the tokens into the pocket I carried at my waist and grabbed Arbreu's hand. "We have to warn everyone and get them out of the canyon." I followed him and Teema towards the tunnel, but paused and turned back.

"Will we return?"

High in the roof of the cave, a circle of tokens glowed. At the same time the ground beneath them heaved and roiled into a shape, but before I was even sure I had seen it, it was gone. The tokens continued to vibrate in the pocket, although faintly.

I was worried.

2

Kirym Speaks

Once out of the cave, I raced over to the shelter and shook Papa awake.

Despite being disoriented with sleep, he quickly understood the essentials of the danger, exploding into action and calling in the guards.

"Waken everyone! Move out, fast! Where do we go, Kirym?"

"The hill is safe. Climb high," I said.

By now people were awake and grabbing cloaks and footwear.

Papa calmly issued orders. "Grenin, Raff, lead the way. Take those who are ready. Go now!"

Holding lamps and carrying children, they calmly ushered young and old towards the ravine. Lyndym and Bildon grabbed a triangular hauling frame, still holding possessions from the trip to the canyon, and piled extra items on it.

"Teema, Arbreu, walk at the rear. Ensure everyone leaves

the canyon!" Papa barked.

"Always amazes me," said Arbreu. "There's no panic. They trust Veld to know what's going on and guide them. No arguments, no questions."

He's right, I thought, watching everyone quietly gather their families together and move quickly towards the ravine. *Perfect trust.*

Findlow, Arbreu and Teema were the last to leave the canyon, with me just in front of them. Dawn was breaking, although it was still dark in the ravine.

Most people followed the left hand side of the ravine wall to climb the gentler slope, although they had to go further along the path to reach the base of the hill.

We were approaching the entrance when I realised I was running through water.

"Arb, where did this water come from?" gasped Teema.

Arbreu looked back and grunted.

The water flowed past us in the direction we travelled, getting markedly deeper with every step we took. We sprinted to catch up with Findlow who had powered ahead.

"Run, man, run!" Teema yelled.

A stronger wave hit us and he staggered, struggling to keep upright. It knocked me over and as I fell I lost hold of my pack. I made a frantic grab at it, but missed, although I managed to grasp a pouch sticking out of it. Together, Arbreu and Teema picked me up under my arms and dragged me with them as they raced after Findlow.

As we reached the entrance to the ravine, the water rose past my waist. We turned west, struggling to climb the steep hill. Waves of water swamped us, occasionally reaching my shoulders, and we struggled to keep our footing. Teema pushed me up the hill ahead of him and finally he and Arbreu pulled themselves out of the water.

In the strengthening light I sought to find out who was

Kirym Speaks

with us, but saw only ghostly figures flitting through the trees. There was a bellow from the other side of the ravine — Papa urging everyone to climb higher.

Teema grabbed Arbreu's arm, pulling him up to join Findlow and Sundas. "What happened? Where did all the water come from?"

Arbreu shook his head. "No idea, Teema. That was the weirdest thing."

I helped him up a small vertical section of the hill. "Come on, there's one way to find out. We go to the top and look into the canyon."

He pulled back. "Wait, Kirym, dry off first or you'll get sick."

Rugs and towels were handed out while we searched our packs for dry clothing. Footwear was a big problem, but the hill was grassy and although it was still cool, our feet weren't cold once we'd dried off.

Everything was too big for me. I ended up wearing Findlow's short tunic and belt. With the sleeves rolled up I had far more freedom, and it really was a huge improvement for tackling the hill.

It was a hard climb. The slope was steep and there weren't a lot of handholds. The sun peeked over the horizon, and I wasn't surprised to see Papa and the family on the other side of the ravine, climbing through the trees towards the top. As I tried to identify them, there was a roar from the ravine and the land shook. I looked back and down, stopping with amazement.

Water streamed out of the ravine, shooting out with such force, it was like a horizontal waterfall. The hill vibrated with the power of the water. The noise was deafening.

I looked up. Everyone stared at the water, their faces strained and white. Teema ushered me ahead, and we quickly caught up to Mekrar, Bildon and Lyndym, who still stared,

The Fortress of Faltryn

awestruck, at the water gushing from the canyon.

"Oh, Arbreu!" gasped Mekrar. "How did Kirym know? There was no water in the canyon. Where did it come from?"

He squeezed her hand. "It's enough that she found out, and in time to get us to safety." He pulled her on up the hill. "Come on. Let's see what's happening in the canyon."

No one spoke as we climbed. The hill was steep enough for us to want to save our breath, but my mind was numb and I had trouble putting thoughts together. I couldn't take in what I'd just seen. The force of the water leaving the ravine was staggering.

The sun was a hand span from the horizon when a strange thing happened. A rainbow arched across the hill and a damp haze settled over us. I began to feel quite chilled. There were no clouds in the sky, and it didn't feel like fog. The mystery unsettled me even more.

Soon afterwards, we caught up with those who had climbed the hill ahead of us. It felt better all being together, and we needed a short rest and something to eat. Mekroe and Tarjin wrestled as they waited. Bokum watched on, ensuring the play didn't get overly enthusiastic. Zeprah and Mekrar fussed over Trayum. A sour faced Danth sat apart and glowered at everyone. There were fourteen on this side of the ravine. It was a mixed group.

Packs were opened and food set out. Findlow collected his portion of twice baked bread and dried fruit and asked what had happened in the cave. He listened quietly as I told him.

Danth snorted. "Stuff and nonsense," he said. "You pander to her, Findlow, just like everyone else. She'll do anything to get the limelight."

"Are you suggesting she did that?" Teema asked, pointing down at the water.

Kirym Speaks

Findlow waved Danth aside. "What do we do now, Kirym?"

I shrugged. "The settlement isn't in danger, and we can use the low ridge to get there."

"And what do you think, Teema?" Findlow asked.

He frowned. "I make no claim to read the cave or the tokens, but I saw their response when Kirym asked questions. Understanding what I saw and heard, and seeing what's happened since then, leads me to believe that Kirym has it absolutely right." He took a deep breath. "I'm happy to be guided by her. We should do as she says. Look into the canyon, isolate the source of the water, and then join the others and go home. I guess it'll be a matter of time until we can return here."

Lyndym shuddered. "We can't come back. What if this happens again?"

"There was time to get to safety, Lyndym," I said. "What makes you think the tokens would stop caring for us?"

3

Kirym Speaks

The sun had reached the meridian when we arrived at the top of the hill and looked over the edge. It took me a while to understand what I was looking at.

The bottom of the canyon was a mass of water. It frothed and foamed around the walls, straining to leave through the narrow ravine.

Glancing around the hill, I now understood the gash that had marred the perfect circle. Not a cave entrance, as had been thought, but a river bed.

The water rushed over the lip, falling in a massive waterfall. The force was amazing, and I was mesmerised by the absolute power of the flow. Water thundered over the edge, deep blue as it left the river bed, but changing to varying shades of turquoise, violet, green and white as it boiled down into the canyon.

I could feel the spray even at this distance — and now I understood the fine mist I had felt lower on the hill. Here

Kirym Speaks

it was thicker and more penetrating. We already were quite damp.

I watched, fascinated by the force of nature. Far below, our shelters had disappeared and only the top of the cave entrances showed above the swirling surface. The water was still rising as more rushed in than was able to get out.

I watched for a long time and then turned to look at those on the other side of the ravine. Papa raised his shoulders in a shrug of resignation.

"Is there anything to write on?" I asked.

"I've got some parchment," said Arbreu, turning out his pack. "There's probably a pack of it on the frame as well."

"We need to let Papa know what they should do and what we'll be doing. We can't walk around to meet them as planned, but they need to know the settlement is safe and that they can get there safely."

"We can cross the ravine here," said Danth. "Make a rope bridge. Veld did it over the river back in the old land."

"It's too dangerous," said Arbreu. 'I used that bridge, and I'd not ..."

"Danth, there's nothing to attach the rope to. Back there it worked because of the rock outcrops at the edge of the gorge. Even then it was dangerous. The land here is different. Nothing solid enough stands near the ravine to anchor the ropes," I said.

"Anyway we don't have rope long and thick enough to do it. Kirym's idea of walking along the ridge is much safer," said Findlow.

"So no idea is considered unless it comes from Kirym," snarled Danth.

"We did consider it," Sundas interrupted. "It's just not practical." He picked up the hauling frame, and with help from Teema and Mekroe created a sheltered area to protect the parchment from the dampness in the air, and ensure the ink wasn't smudged or washed away before it dried. The message was wrapped around an arrow shaft and Teema shot it over. While the sun moved a hand-span across the sky, messages passed to and fro as decisions were made.

Papa stood at the edge of the ravine smiling broadly as he shot an arrow bringing the last messages.

Findlow handed them out and read Papa's message to us all. "Take care in your travels and return to us soon. Map the land and come back with exciting stories — next winter will be shorter because of them. We will think of you often." He looked up from the parchment. "We need someone to lead us, make decisions on the trip. I think Kirym should do it. It's because of her we've made it this far."

"No damn way!" objected Danth. "I'll not take orders from her. She's the youngest here, and the least experienced." He rounded on Findlow. "And don't say it's because she's Veld's daughter. She has older siblings here."

"I don't want the responsibility," said Mekroe. "Kirym's decisions are always better than mine."

"Me neither," interrupted Mekrar. "She's welcome to it. If anyone in our family's destined to be headman, it's her."

"That's not the point!" Danth yelled. "Veld would choose me; well, me or Teema."

Findlow shook his head. "No. In fact, he does choose Kirym. Kirym, he says you have the ability. You should use the skills of your people. He has confidence you will do well."

"We have some say in this," snarled Danth. "Leadership isn't a birthright. Veld can't pass it on as he wishes just to indulge a spoilt child."

"That's the headman's position, Danth — a different thing again," said Bokum. "Anyway, I'm happy to follow Kirym."

From around the group, there were nods and sounds of agreement.

Danth shook his head in disgust. "Tarjin and I won't."

Kirym Speaks

"I will, Papa," said Tarjin quietly. "If it hadn't been for Kirym, we'd be dead. You should give her a chance."

Danth turned away, muttering under his breath.

Teema sat beside me. "Are you all right?" he asked.

I nodded. "I'm used to Danth's attitude. I can't let it affect what I do or how I act. He's part of the family."

"I don't like him," he muttered.

"You don't have to. But he is allowed to say what he thinks. And it should always be considered."

We ate again, and watched Papa lead the family away. With them gone, it was easier to leave.

There were animal trails near the edge of the canyon, paths for us to follow. The hill got steeper and the hauling frame kept slipping sideways down the hill, making it difficult to pull. Finally Mekroe and Teema hoisted it to their shoulders and, with difficulty, carried it aloft. As tempting as it was to leave it behind, what was on the frame was almost all we had, and would have to be carried one way or another. Those items would be vital in the days that followed.

It was slow going. The hill was steep, rough and covered with scrub and rocks. Occasionally someone would push through the scrubby bush to the rim of the canyon to see if anything had changed.

Late in the afternoon I decided to go and look. The cave entrances were completely covered. The water still swirled around the walls and struggled out through the ravine. High in the canyon wall, set at an angle was a cave. I called out and everyone rushed to look. This was a surprise. We had no idea it was there.

"I wonder if the water ever gets high enough to flood it?" asked Lyndym.

Teema pointed to the canyon wall. "I don't think so. Look, from this angle you can see lines on the walls. If that's where previous floods reached, none went anywhere near the cave."

"Would it be possible to make a path to it when we return to the canyon?" asked Bildon. "It could be somewhere safe for us to go if we got caught during another flood."

"I'm not sure," I said. "It's good to know it's there, but we can't do anything until we return."

We spent the night in the lee of a massive rock. While still damp, it was drier than the surrounding area. However, we were in for a cold wet night.

Teema, Mekroe, and Tarjin collected wood, while Arbreu dug under leaf-fall to get dry kindling for starting the fire. Most of the wood was superficially wet and difficult to ignite although, once lit, it burned well.

Zeprah, looking pale and drawn, sat down to care for an unsettled, damp and fractious Trayum. It had been a stressful day for her. She'd coped well, but once she relaxed, she burst into tears.

Everyone except Danth gathered around to comfort and reassure her.

She was being well cared for. I could do nothing that wasn't already being done, so I started to sort through the gear we carried in the packs and on the hauling frame.

Teema left Arbreu feeding the fire and came to help me. "Is Zeprah all right?"

"She will be. It's just reaction. Trayum's birth wasn't the easiest I've seen. And now she's having to deal with the flood. Sarel is with Mama and this is the first time Zeprah has been separated from her." I paused. "Teema, I need to know how much harkii we have. Other remedies also. Zeprah left her medicine pouch in the canyon and Lyndym didn't bring hers. Bildon's was used up yesterday and I don't know what happened to mine. It may have been in the pack I lost in the flood."

Teema helped me take everything out of the packs and off the hauling frame and the work went quicker when Findlow and Sundas came to help.

I squealed with delight when I found my medicine pouch along with the larger family pack. I handed them to Mekrar with instructions to grind some harkii for Zeprah.

Near the bottom of the hauling frame I came across one of the old sails from our boat, Dragon Quest. "Wonderful. This will mean a lot less work each day," I said. "Teema, get Sundas, Bokum and Danth to help erect it, please."

I continued sorting the packs, dividing everything into smaller loads that could be carried with ease. What was left, including the sail, would be carried on the now much lighter frame.

With the shelter erected, I hung the wet clothes at the back to dry overnight and helped prepare a meal.

The morning was misty, but I thought that was because of the waterfall. There were hints the day would be hot. The top of the sail was wet with drift, and the air was moist and cold. Clothes were still damp and wouldn't dry until we were away from the waterfall. Fortunately, our boots had been placed at the back of the shelter and they had dried enough to be worn.

We ate the remains of last night's dinner, folded the shelter and loaded it onto the frame.

Then we shouldered our packs and began our journey.

"It's a shame we never explored this area before now," said Findlow. "It'd be nice to know where we're going."

"Papa did the important things first. The area close to the

settlement was checked for people and to choose the best place for crops," I said. "He planned to explore to the north this summer, but even then we probably wouldn't have come up here."

Teema nodded. "The decision's been made for us, but I wish I'd checked the hill earlier. I never even realised it was the end of a ridge. If I'd looked, I might have realised that was a river bed." He shook his head. "Always, I've tried to look ahead. Then the first thing I do is close my eyes and avoid dealing with things that are important. We all could have died because of my stupidity."

"No one's at fault, Teema," I said. "We all had the responsibility, I as much as you. But what if we had come up here last summer or even last winter? We'd have seen an old dry river bed. There has been no water in it for a long time. We'd have felt at ease with it. We mightn't even have recognised it for what it was. It was hard to get to. The hill is dangerously steep and slippery. That was one of the reasons we forbade the boys access to it. Anyway, who'd think of a river bed on the top of a ridge?"

Arbreu nudged Teema's shoulder. "The plant growth in the canyon was old. We've no idea where the water came from, or why for that matter. Why now and not over winter? And why not every spring?"

Findlow chuckled. "I'm as surprised as you to learn the canyon isn't just a hollow hill. The river must run the length of the ridge. Would we have explored it had we known? Other things were important, so probably not. Even if we had, what would we have learned?"

The sun was a hand-width above the horizon when we walked past the top of the waterfall. We watched for a while, fascinated by the power and sound. It was mesmerising. I could feel vibrations through the ground. When I stood still my legs felt quite weak. It was the strangest feeling. The

Kirym Speaks

water ran deep and swiftly, but the drift from it was like rain here. The trees dripped constantly and although I could have stayed watching all day, there was restless movement behind me. No one would move on until I did.

The path was muddy and slippery, but there were plenty of handholds to ensure our safety and we didn't go too near the edge.

Now we could see along the ridge. I was glad we were walking along this side of it. Not that what we were using was a path, but it was flat and wide enough for us to feel safe. The far side was much rougher and the paths were scarily narrow.

The ridge appeared to rise gradually into the distance, but I could see no indication of hills beyond to give such a run-off of water. It was as if somewhere ahead, everything stopped.

Findlow stared ahead and frowned. "It must be an illusion. Maybe heat haze stops us seeing what's ahead."

"It's too early for heat haze, but it makes little difference," I said. "We have to travel the length of the river until we find a bridge or ford. The volume of water in the river indicates there's a massive area of run-off. It must be below the horizon. We've a long walk ahead."

By midday the water drift was well behind us. The path had widened enough for us to walk comfortably, but there was no shade and the side of the ridge was too steep for us to go lower.

It was good to get beyond the waterfall. It was noisy, and the spray ensured we were damp all the time. Looking behind, I could see the rainbows in the water droplets.

Late in the day I found an area that was wide enough to set up the shelter. The little bit of shade made a huge difference and the fire, hot water and food were of great comfort. We had come a long way and were all tired.

4

Kirym Speaks

We started travelling early to get as far as possible before the heat of the day. The path widened and we were able to walk in companionable groups. By mid-morning each day, we were strung out along the path. Teema and I went ahead, checking the route while Arbreu and Findlow walked at the back to ensure no one fell behind.

On the third day the trees grew to the edge of the path, giving us shade in the afternoon. However, the path became rockier and occasionally we had to climb over and around boulders. It was a hard day.

Late in the afternoon when we set up the shelter, we had to lever rocks away to give us enough clear room to lie down. The ridge ahead still seemed endless.

From the path we could see the expansive valley floor to the east. It was really different from anything I had ever seen before. It appeared flat for almost as far as I could see. Then there was another massive hill, much like the one we were on. In the middle of the flat area was a gigantic rock. It towered above the land around it, an outsize object that didn't fit into the landscape. A river snaked through the land, being fed by others it met. It widened and disappeared to the south east. There were clumps of trees, lakes and open meadows. There were no low hills leading up to higher hills as we were used to back in our old land. Here, everything seemed to be horizontal or vertical.

On our sixth day of walking beside the river, the view changed. Ahead was a grove of trees and I decided we'd stop there for the night, and maybe spend a few days. We had been walking for most of each day and had covered a good distance. Zeprah was tired and Trayum unsettled. She needed to relax, but I felt we could all use a rest.

The trees were huge and we approached them in the early afternoon eager to get to the shade they promised. I dropped my packs onto the path, loosened my knife and grabbed my bow and arrows. There was a small waterfall here, the water splashed over rocks beside the path, although the deep blue showed the depth of the water in the centre of the flow.

The path to the trees was steep and covered with small flat stones that slipped as I walked on them. I climbed quickly and stepped thankfully into the shade. Allowing some moments for my eyes to adjust, I followed the watercourse through the trees.

With Bildon behind me, the bird song and insect noise dropped as we advanced through them. I walked around a large tree and stopped in amazement.

Bildon bumped into me as she came up behind. I heard her exclamation of bewilderment. "Wha — what is it, Kirym?"

"It's the beginning," I said. "The beginning of the river.

It's a fountainhead."

The water gushed out of the ground with such force it rolled up to almost shoulder height over a wide area. It spilled over and ran down to the river bed.

Bildon dipped her fingers in it and squealed. "It's freezing."

"It must come from deep in the ground," I said.

We waited until everyone joined us, and walked further into the grove. A small overflow from the fountainhead ran north, ending in a wide circular bowl. Beyond that was an outcrop of ivy covered rock that curved away to the northeast as it rose to shoulder height.

Sitting clear of the water in the centre of the bowl was a large grey token.

Danth stretched over the water, trying to grab it.

"Don't touch it, Danth!" I called sharply.

Findlow pulled him away from the edge of the pool. "You know better than that. If it's a token, the women handle it."

"Don't tell me what to do," Danth snapped. "It's just a stone. Even if it was a token, which it isn't, it's dead."

"Large tokens are never dead," I said, "but this one isn't glowing for some reason. It won't hurt to wait a while and think about it. Let's check this area before anything else."

Danth stamped away. Findlow grabbed his bow and followed. By now, everyone had their weapons at hand and I divided the area to ensure it was fully checked. The grove of trees wasn't big, but parts of the undergrowth were thick.

To the east of the bowl was a large clearing and after we had thoroughly checked the whole area, we erected the shelter there. Zeprah settled to care for Trayum, firewood was collected and we began to relax. A meal was prepared and we sat back and talked.

"We'll stay here for a few days," I said. "We know we can

Kirym Speaks

get home in eight or nine days. There's not the urgency there was."

"Maybe not for you," interrupted Danth, "Me an' Tarjin, we're leaving in the morning. I'll not let Jinda worry needlessly about him."

"Zeprah needs to rest, Danth. We've travelled fast, and that's not good for a nursing mother."

"I don't need you. We can travel by ourselves. At first light we're gone."

"It's safer to stay together."

"There is no danger!" he said. "If you don't want us going off alone you can always follow us. Anyway, we won't be alone. There are two of us."

"I'd like you both to stay."

"Don't order me around!" he yelled, instantly angry.

Everyone was tense. We had all known it would come to this. I couldn't make Danth stay with us, but I wanted him to. It would be better for everyone.

"I'm not going, Papa," said Tarjin. "I'd like a rest and this is a nice place. It's the right decision and the best for everyone. Anyway, Kirym's in charge. We should respect her position."

"You should respect me. I decide for my family. I'm not about to let some silly little girl take over."

"It's nothing to do with that, Papa. It shouldn't matter who's in charge, it's the position we should honour."

Danth snorted and stormed off into the trees.

I felt uneasy, restless, and it was something other than the confrontation with Danth.

I started to sort out the items on the frame and in the packs. The sun was beginning to set and the rays hit the surface of the small pool, making it gleam like copper. The token also appeared to glow. The air quivered, and as I grabbed the pocket containing the other tokens, I felt a vibration on my forehead.

Now everyone was aware that something was happening, and they followed me towards the pool.

Danth raced past me.

"Don't!" Teema's warning shout came too late.

Danth stepped into the pool, and disappeared from sight.

Sundas raced forward, threw himself on his stomach and reached down into the water. Danth emerged coughing and screaming. Sundas had him by the hair. He grabbed Danth's tunic, lifting him bodily from the water.

Danth was shaken. "It's bottomless," he gasped. He grabbed Lyndym's cloak from her shoulders, wiped his face and head, and settled it around his neck.

"No one's gonna get that token," he said smugly.

The vibrations from the tokens increased. I walked around the pool to a flat rock on the far side. In the centre of it were shadows in the rock — six of them around a slight depression. It looked as if a pattern or painting that had existed there in the past had worn off.

The blue token fitted in the southernmost shadow, and I moved the others around it until they seemed to fit. There was nowhere for the rainbow token. The depression in the centre was far too big, but not having any other place to put it, I placed it there anyway.

The setting sun glowed on the tokens. A beam of light from the rainbow token connected to the others, including the one in the pool, creating a shadow on the water. It looked like a path. I stepped onto it, sure it was exactly that, a path.

The water was warmer than I had thought it would be. It took three steps to get to the centre and retrieve the token. Bringing it back, I sat it in the next space on the rock. It connected to the rainbow token and the colour changed subtly to a coppery orange. I stared at them — five stones

Kirym Speaks

and the two empty spaces.

"There are more out there, aren't there, Kirym?" Zeprah stroked the new token. Its light flashed around the rocks and then dimmed.

"I think so, and each one leads us to the next. There must be a hint here, some indication of where to look."

Danth snorted. "Oh, a new theory! Let's thrust you into the limelight again. What utter nonsense!"

I ignored him.

"It's more than just tokens, Zeprah. Tokens align with people. Large tokens generally represent a family, so this means more families and some connection between them all."

"The land is empty," she said. "Could it be the families who lived here before?"

"I don't know," I said, collecting the tokens and putting them back in my pocket. "The tokens glow; they glow for people. The land we've looked at is empty, but there's a lot more land out there."

5

Kirym Speaks

It was wonderful not to be travelling. I spent the early morning making notes about the land I had seen on the trip, and drawing the area around the fountainhead. We always carried parchment with us when we travelled for this reason.

The weather was lovely and I wandered through the trees gathering flowers and herbs. High in one tree were fruits I'd never seen before, and I was determined to collect some. Most of the trees were big and old, the bottom branches well out of reach, but a few had lower limbs and one or two were very accessible. Soon I was high in the branches and working my way from one tree to another. I collected the fruit, storing them in my collecting basket along with birds' eggs, leaves, bark and creepers. The solid branches were like a path among the trees; one led to another and so on. I was able to work my way around the grove quite easily.

Kirym Speaks

Late in the morning I found myself in a tree above the pool. I leaned forward on the branch and looked down. From here, I could see the whole pool, the dark depths where Danth had jumped in and a lighter area where the rock bottom was nearer the surface and connected to the plinth that had held the token. Most of the water was black, deep, dark and foreboding. Less than an eighth of the pool was shallow enough to use as a path.

The rock wall curved away, covered with creepers and vines. One corner far out to the east was exposed, being less protected from the weather. From where I sat on the branch, I could see the squared edges. Very squared. Manmade, I thought and I urgently wanted a closer look.

I worked my way back along the branches until I could climb down. It took a frustratingly long time.

I raced over to the wall, only to be thwarted by a call to lunch.

As soon as was decently possible after the meal, I was back at the wall, carefully stripping the greenery away. Soon, Teema, Arbreu, Mekrar, Lyndym and Bildon arrived to help.

The wall was man-made; the top and sides were square although exposed parts were crumbling away. As Teema pointed out, it had been made a long time ago.

We continued to clear it through the afternoon, and near the centre we found an ancient engraving. I was reminded of Findlow's relief carving, although this was far more primitive and it was hard to see. The seasons had left it stained and discoloured and parts of it appeared worn.

I ran my fingers over it, feeling more detail than I could see. Reluctantly, we left it as the sun set. I fell asleep wondering how I could make the detail clear. By morning, I had an idea.

Everyone looked more refreshed with the day's rest and

they were mostly happy to stay longer.

After eating, I took a number of sheets of parchment from the pack and carefully joined them together into one large piece with the white of one of the eggs I had collected. Then I gummed them to the wall over the carving with the last of it, and used charcoal from the fire to take a rubbing of the engraving.

I was delighted with the detail. I carefully took the parchment from the wall and laid it down to study it. The charcoal had a tendency to smudge and Findlow suggested I copy it using ink. It was exacting work.

In the evening we studied it. There were lines, circles, dots, a crescent and things that looked like trees and a triangle. Some of the lines were so spidery, I thought they may be fractures in the rock, but when I checked there seemed to be no others and I finally accepted them as part of the pattern. I was fascinated.

We talked far into the night. Initially we chatted about the engraving, who had done it and why, but soon began to focus on continuing our journey.

"What route do we take?" asked Findlow.

"Well, that's obvious," spat Danth. "We follow the eastern side of the river. We know where it leads, and we'll meet up with the family on the hill."

"A safer way," I said, "would be to climb down the hill and travel on the valley floor. It will be faster too."

Danth argued. "We need to get to where we last saw the family. We don't know this hill, but it's steep. It'll be safer to go the route we've seen," he said.

"We've seen the path on the eastern side of the ridge. It's rough, narrow and crumbling," I said. "We'd not be able to stop overnight, and it'd be too dangerous to travel in the dark. The valley floor will be safer in the long run."

"Anyway," said Mekroe. "They won't be waiting for us on

Kirym Speaks

the hill. They'd already started back to the settlement when we left."

Danth was neither convinced nor pleased, but when we broke camp in the morning we started down the hill. It was a difficult path.

Many tracks led to sheer drops and some petered out.

We marked and mapped the route so we could use it with more ease next time. As the afternoon wore on it became easier and we moved faster.

Once on the valley floor, we made our way to a grove of trees and set up the shelter. It had been a trying day.

Our next two days of travel were uneventful, but while the terrain was flat, it was rough, and a swampy area meant we had to detour to the east.

We camped on the high banks of an oxbow lake I had seen from the ridge above. It was cold and the evening sky promised a band of unsettled weather coming. If it was raining in the morning we would stay for the day.

We had a quiet evening, and soon after dark we settled for the night.

I woke with a sudden start, Tarjin whispering urgently in my ear: "Kirym! There are strange noises all around us. It sounds like something big! It's coming from two directions. I can't check both at once."

I shook Teema and Arbreu as I grabbed my knife, bow and arrows. I glanced at the fire, noting an absence of glowing embers.

Teema woke Findlow and Sundas. *Enough*, I thought. I whispered quick instructions to them and drew Tarjin to the eastern outskirts of the camp. Something was crashing through the wooded area some distance away.

We slipped into the shadows beside the lake, and I bent low to get a view of the horizon against the stars.

Breasting a rise to the east were five deer. They slid down

the bank and splashed into the water, followed almost immediately by a large boar. The deer raced through the water and away from it. The boar snorted loudly and followed them along the shore.

"The pig must have spooked them, Tarjin. Let's see what Teema has found."

We scooted back through camp and out to the west, spying Teema and Arbreu moving into the dark of a tree.

"Where's Findlow?" I asked quietly.

"He and Sundas are circling around. There's something big out there, quite a few of them, I think." Teema pointed towards a grove of trees. "Whatever they are, they're over there."

I stared intently. With no moon it was hard to see.

Suddenly a chilling scream rent the air and pandemonium broke out. Sundas yelled, and there was the glint of starlight on a knife blade.

6

Kirym Speaks

Beside me I heard Arbreu's knife hiss as he pulled it from its sheath; mine was already in my hand. We sprinted towards the trees.

"Gerr'off me, ya great lump!"

I lunged forward and grabbed Arbreu's arm. "Light! Give us some light!"

A number of lamps flashed through the trees. For a moment shadows wavered, evolving into people. Many people.

Sundas sat on someone's chest. Findlow rolled on the ground laughing fit to bust. I grabbed Arbreu's lamp and raised it. A familiar face stepped into the light.

"Papa!" I exclaimed. "What are you doing here?"

Sundas was hauled off Armos, who was helped up. Findlow staggered to his feet, still laughing. Everyone was now awake. Those in the camp were alert, weapons at the ready.

It took a while to coax life into the dead embers of the

fire. I straightened up from putting water on to boil to see Papa watching me.

I formally welcomed everyone and settled in front of him. "Papa, why were you travelling at night? If we hadn't heard you, you would have been far past us by morning."

"We made camp in the wrong spot. Attacked!" He shrugged. "Those insects had a nasty bite," he said, smiling. Then he looked around speculatively. "You've a lot of guards awake, Kirym. Is there a problem?"

Instead of answering his question, I asked another. "Are you taking over as leader, Papa?"

He shook his head. "Not yet. This is your camp and I'd like to hear everything before I make decisions."

"It's late," I said. "We can discuss it in the morning. It's going to rain and I thought we'd stay here for the day." I glanced around. "Teema, Sundas, can you start your guard-duty? The rest of you should get some sleep."

Papa raised his eyebrow, but then smiled and helped Findlow, Bokum and Arbreu to extend the shelter. The ten people he had with him found somewhere to place their rugs, and they soon slept. I banked the fire and listened as everyone's breathing settled. Then I walked out to talk to Tarjin.

"Danth is supposed to share your guard duty, Tarjin. Where is he?"

Tarjin was close to tears. "I don't know. He doesn't follow a set pattern when he's on guard. I rarely see him after I start my shift. I've always woken Teema for him and seen to the fire. I missed the fire tonight because of the noises. What will you do?"

"I'm not sure yet. I'm disappointed in you, though. I understand you have a loyalty to Danth, but what about the rest of us? If you couldn't tell me what was going on, you could have asked me to change your place on the roster.

Kirym Speaks

Danth need never have known."

"He told me his was a better way of watching. If I couldn't see him, no enemy could. He said Veld told him to do it this way, but he never saw the need for sentries anyway. That it was a good way to oversee and that other experienced men did the same thing. Deep down I wondered, and last night I searched for him. When I couldn't find him, I didn't know what to do. I should have come to you straight away."

"Tarjin," I said. "This is important. If there was ever any change in the way we do sentry duty, Papa would call a meeting and tell everyone. This time we were lucky, but it could easily have been a disaster. It's unfair of Danth to do this to you, but it won't ever happen again. I'll make sure of that."

"Veld will have noticed. Will he put me before a Judicial Council?"

"That's not his decision, Tarjin. I'm leader at the moment. But he will probably ask."

7

Kirym Speaks

Papa studied the pattern I had copied from the wall. Everyone waited with bated breath. Eventually he looked up. "Well, what does it mean?"

"Childish nonsense," said Danth. "Stupid scribble, and a waste of time. We squandered days until Kirym finished playing her silly little games."

There was a long silence. I reached out and smoothed the surface of the parchment. "It's a map."

Danth snorted derisively. "Map? Maps are nothing like that. That bit of scribble is just Kirym's time-wasting nonsense!"

Papa took a deep breath. "Well, Danth," he said. "Different people, different styles. Carving in stone would be less subtle than drawing on parchment. If it is a map, Kirym, what's it depicting?"

"When I look at your maps, Papa, I feel I'm looking at the land as the birds do. This is different, it includes the

Kirym Speaks

sky." I pointed to the two circles on the lower left of the parchment. "If the larger is the canyon and the smaller is the fountainhead, then the line between them is the river. Therefore the rest must map the land to the north. Maybe it leads to the owners of the token."

"Blunt scrapes in rock," said Danth contemptuously. "An animal could have done it. A total waste o' time. Days and days she held us up for this nonsense. It was irresponsible. Everyone back at the settlement would have been worried sick about us, needlessly worried while she played her self-indulgent childish games."

"Zephra needed the rest, Danth," said Arbreu angrily. "The few days' rest meant Trayum could get his strength up."

"Absolute rubbish!" Danth interrupted. "The brat was carried, and anyway it was more important for those in the settlement to know we were safe. It was foolish time wasting."

"But ..." spluttered Arbreu.

"If we're discussing reckless behaviour, Danth ..."

Danth swung around. "What are you accusing me of? You troublemaking little upstart! How dare ..."

"Danth!" Veld's voice was steely. "Kirym is the leader here. Respect her as such."

"It's time to change the guard. Would you take your turn now, Danth?" I stared him in the eye and, to everyone's amazement, he stamped out into the rain.

I moved the map back in front of Papa and pointed to the thin crescent above the fountainhead. "That's the moon just after moon dark. The other circle could well be the full moon." I pointed to the ten dots. "These are interesting."

"They don't seem right as stars, Kirym. None sit in a line like that," said Zeprah.

"Could there have been an alignment like that in the past?" asked Bokum. "Perhaps this commemorates that."

33

The Fortress of Faltryn

"There's nothing like that in written history or in the myths, and it's so unusual, I'm sure there would have been. Assuming these are moons," I touched the crescent and the adjacent circle, "and there are about fourteen days between moon dark and full moon, maybe the dots imply a period of time, ten days or nights. We know that that part of the map is land because of the trees. The triangle to the north could be a hill. Possibly the dots are the time we need to travel towards it."

"What about these interconnecting circles before you get to the hill?" asked Mekrar. "Are they part of the sky or land?"

"There's only one way to find out. Go there."

There was a long silence. Then Papa laughed. "Well it does seem to be the next step. But why should I allow this trip? It's a long way into the unknown."

"Because the token glowed, Papa. Because maybe there are people out there. And we sorely need more people."

8

Kirym Speaks

There had been a heated argument over who should travel with us.

Teema, Findlow, Sundas and Arbreu almost fell over themselves in being the first to volunteer.

Tarjin wanted to come, and despite his parent's objections, Papa agreed he could join us. Danth, although he argued against the trip in general, declared initially that he and Jinda would join us, but after a short private conversation with Papa, they decided they would return to the settlement.

Mekroe, Mekrar and Bildon all chose to continue the adventure. Bokum wished to join us, but saw sense in Zeprah's arguments to return home.

"The trip may not resolve the secrets of the map," I pointed out. "Time will have altered the land and the map details are obscure. What we search for might no longer be there. Even if it is, the late start could mean we miss the full moon and have to wait for the next one."

"Is it a waste of time then?" asked Bildon.

"Oh no," I said. "But we shouldn't expect to find anything other than possibly a hill, and we will certainly do our best to meet the deadline. That means we start moving as soon as it's light, and continue until dark on most days. The hill must be significant to be on the map, but it will be impossible to explore the whole area in the time we have."

I led them past the base of fountainhead hill mid-afternoon, two days later. We travelled fast and needed to. Moon-dark had passed the night Papa arrived and we were running to a tight schedule.

Still, the weather was pleasant, the terrain easy and we made good time. We had been able to raid Papa's supply of stores and were well set up for an extended trip.

Then we entered a forest.

It was unlike any forest we had seen before. The ground was covered with grass and white flowers. The tree trunks were silver, tall and straight. High above us was a lush growth that hid the sky. It was easy to walk through, the trees weren't particularly close and we could see a long way in all directions, but it was a strange area and I felt the lack of sunshine. It wasn't long before we could no longer see the sunlight at the edge of the trees.

Night fell quickly, faster than I expected. That was a problem with the lack of sunshine. The next day was the same, and everyone seemed to be tired when we stopped in the late-afternoon.

"I'm glad we have the fire," said Arbreu, putting a large branch onto the flames. "Cheerful." He was quiet for a while. "Kirym, can we find our way back? I don't think it's a good idea to go on."

Kirym Speaks

"Why?"

"It's confusing in here. There's no point of focus. I just feel lost."

"We're fine, as long as we keep travelling north. We have stores and there's enough game, herbs and roots in here to ensure we don't starve."

"How can you be sure we're travelling north?" said Bildon. "I can't tell what direction we're going in."

I pointed back the way we'd come. "The tree trunks that way are lighter than they are in front of us. As long as we keep the darker tone in front, we're travelling north." I looked at the sceptical faces. "The sun bleaches the north face of the trunks more than the south. Back between the gorges, there was moss on the southern side of tree trunks, none on the north.

Obviously in here, the winters aren't as damp as they were back there. The trees are further apart. No moss, but the sun still affects them."

"But the sun doesn't shine in here," noted Lyndym.

"The light gets in, enough to make a difference. It's happened over a long time."

Lyndym nodded. "I should have asked sooner. I felt hopelessly lost and scared. It's amazing what knowledge can do. It already looks brighter in here."

"I'm embarrassed," Arbreu said with a short laugh. "I didn't pick up on the subtleties of the growth. I should have raised my concerns much sooner. I did look for moss, and when I didn't find it, I just carried on. Stupid!"

"Don't blame yourself. I felt ill at ease too, and I did nothing either," said Findlow.

Everyone was a lot more light-hearted in the morning. There was more chatter and laughter as we travelled. I realised how much they had felt the strangeness when a glimpse of sunshine brought a rousing cheer from Arbreu,

The Fortress of Faltryn

Mekroe and Tarjin.

Good training kept them alongside me. I knew they wanted to race ahead. Every face I looked at was smiling. We took our last steps through the trees and out into the sunshine.

"Oh. It's only a clearing," said Arbreu. "I um, I ..."

"Me too. I hoped it was the end," said Findlow, slapping him on the shoulder. He looked at the sky, analysing the distance the sun was from the horizon. "Do we carry on, Kirym?"

It was good to soak up the late-afternoon sun, and because of that, I agreed to an early stop. We set up the shelter, ate and fell into an exhausted sleep.

"I'm surprised at how well rested I feel," said Arbreu as he dawdled over breakfast. When I began to place rugs and packs onto the hauling frame, Mekroe objected. "It won't hurt to have an extra day here, Kirym. We have until full moon. Why not spend the spare days here?"

"Where'd you get the idea we have days to spare?"

"Um, fourteen days between moon dark and full moon and it'll only take us ten to get there," he said.

"Ten days to get where?" I asked. "Mek, we don't know how long this trip took. Whoever did it in the past had information we don't have. When we get near the hill, if it is a hill, we may have to search for something. There's so much we don't know, we need to be early to be sure. What if something else holds us up? The ten days was counted from the fountainhead and that may be very important. I don't want to wait until the next full moon unless I really have to."

There were grunts and comments of acknowledgement and the work to break camp moved faster.

We walked until dark before stopping for the night, attempting to recover the time wasted in the morning. Through the night it rained heavily and the next day was

Kirym Speaks

miserable. Normally, we wouldn't have travelled in such weather, but with my comments in mind, the shelter was dismantled without complaint.

It seemed even gloomier under the trees in the rain.

At dusk I suggested a ground oven, and that we add a collar around the fire to protect it from the wind.

"There is no wind," said Arbreu quietly.

Teema leaned forward. "You've been on edge all day. What is it?"

I shrugged. "Nothing I can put my finger on. But a feeling is a feeling, so I'd like to increase the number of guards overnight."

"All right, and one of us needs to be awake and part of the group on guard," said Teema.

The rain was heavier in the morning, but we broke camp and continued on our way. It made no difference when the rain stopped, the sodden trees dripped and we got just as wet. I was surprised at the marked trail we made through the grass and flowers.

With more overnight rain, the next day was the same. Arbreu walked behind me watching the ground. He didn't notice when I stopped, and walked into me.

"Look," I said, interrupting his apologies. Ahead, far ahead, was the glow of sunshine.

"Is it another clearing?" he asked. "It's got to be."

The edge of the trees showed open land that stretched ahead. The grass was a different green. There were bright spring flowers, and best of all we could see the sky. It didn't matter that the sun sat behind wispy clouds.

On the far horizon was the hill, although it was not so much a hill as a mountain. A perfect triangle, it was exactly as drawn on the map. The top was covered with snow and the lower slopes were blue, indicating the distance needing to be covered before we reached it.

39

It was so good to be in sunlight, the distance wasn't at all daunting.

The next morning it seemed a little more overwhelming. The day's walk appeared to take us no closer. The mid-afternoon stop for a hot drink gave Arbreu the opportunity to question our ability to reach even the lower slopes in the six days before full moon, let alone the two making up the dots on the map. Others voiced their concern also.

I took a different point of view. "The mountain isn't our aim. If we have it right, it'll take ten days. I figure we've lost time due to weather and leaving late, although we have no idea of the speed we should be going. The trip is the adventure. Maybe we will find something, maybe not."

"We've got a visitor, Kirym," called Sundas, who was watching the path behind us.

I sent Findlow and Bildon to support Mekrar who was watching the path ahead, and with weapons in hand, the rest of us joined Sundas.

Arbreu and Teema stood just behind me as we watched the figure stumbling towards us. He walked with his head down, concentrating on the path rather than his surroundings.

I gasped when I recognised him. "It's Bokum!" I dropped my bow and raced towards him.

Bokum stopped as I shouted. He looked up, his face ragged with fatigue. "I thought I'd never catch up with you," he said when I reached him. "That forest was weird. I'm glad you left such a trail, I'd never have made it through otherwise."

Welcomed, he settled back and closed his eyes while we made him a hot drink. "Ah, that's so good," he said, sitting with his hands around the flask. "I've had nothing hot since I started north. Kirym, Veld sent me to tell you that Danth and Jinda disappeared. He thinks they're following you. He's worried. They had half a night on me — you were a day gone before that. I think I crossed their trail in the forest, although I'm not sure. They may have turned back." He suddenly looked tense. "Danth threatened you and Trayum. He talked about taking life for his stolen son." He frowned. "Veld wants you to think carefully before you go further on this trip. He's most concerned."

I leaned forward and clicked his token.

"Papa will protect Trayum and Zeprah. They'll be safe. For us, well we need to know what the map means. We lose so much if we turn back now and anyway, the trip has to be made at some stage." I paused, frowning. "Tarjin, what will happen if we postpone it for a few seasons?"

"It'll be exactly the same. A delay, that's all. Everything's a conspiracy to him. He dislikes everyone. He thinks you're all against him. When people talk out of his hearing, he's sure it's about him. If someone laughs, he thinks they're laughing at him. He resents not being leader, and not just on trips. He'd make a claim to be headman if he wasn't so scared of Veld."

"If they turn up, would it help if we asked them to join us?" Kirym asked.

Tarjin shook his head. "He'd think it was a plot. No matter what you do, it won't be right. He'll assume you're planning something behind his back. You know what he's like, Kirym. He dislikes people and he can't make decisions. You think the map may lead us to new tribes. He'll insult them. There's every possibility he'd start a war. But if you go back now, he'll assume you found something and you're hiding it from him."

I nodded. "Well, we don't know where they are at the moment so we'll carry on. We must be close to the circles on the map if they are still there. I'd like to know what they are at least. Do you have enough energy to carry on, Bokum?"

He nodded.

"I'll carry your pack," said Sundas.

We quickly repacked everything, doused the fire and continued on.

I discussed all of the possibilities with Bokum. I was amused to hear Arbreu's loud whisper. "We'll have to watch her carefully, Teema. Guard her without her knowing."

I turned to see Teema's eyes crinkled with amusement. "You think she'd let us do that? Nothing gets past her. We'll do it openly. Then at least there's less chance of her objecting. I'll talk to Findlow and Sundas. Everyone will help," he said, trying to stare me down. I shook my head, and he laughed.

The day became hotter as we travelled. We were relieved when our path took us into a shady wood. Early in the afternoon, when we stepped out of the trees, we saw a strange cluster of rocks ahead of us.

"We're just over nine days from the fountainhead. This may be our goal," I said.

Mekroe snorted. "It's a mess of rocks, Sis. It isn't mentioned on the map."

"We don't know what it is, Mek, but because it's so unusual it's definitely worth a look."

I directed them to set up camp to the west, where a stream widened to become a small pond. Then we wandered over to look at the rocks.

9

Kirym Speaks

I'd never seen anything like it. Standing stones. Well, some of them were. Others were carved in a similar manner to Raff's stellon, although Raff's has been made of wood. The rest were tall poles. Some had patterns or figures of animals and people carved on them, and many had slits and holes cut through them. All stood tall except one which leaned over, pointing to the south. On the western side of the stones was a large arch.

Evening came far too quickly and I couldn't continue exploring. It was frustrating. When morning arrived I went to have a better look, carrying a sheet of parchment. I paced out distances and angles, noting them down. Eventually, I returned to the shelter. Everyone was there and food was laid out for us.

"What do we do now, Sis? It's interesting, but ..." Mekroe shrugged.

"Have you studied them, Mek? There is so much

information in them — it would take many seasons to understand it all."

"But we can't stay here. We have to find the circles on the map."

"We won't have to stay too long. There's a simple brainteaser. We just solve that. The rest can wait."

I dug through our extra gear and pulled out a package of parchment. Again I carefully joined some sheets together and drew in the pattern of the stones. It took most of the afternoon. I continually had to go back to the stones to check on measurements and angles.

While the evening meal was being dished, I gathered a pile of small stones, twigs and rock shards. Using the parchment pattern as a guide, I made a representation of the stones: three intertwining circles. They were made up of twelve standing stones, twelve carved poles, six stellons and one other stone.

I was concentrating on it when Arbreu finished guard duty. I heard his startled intake of breath as he came up behind me. "What is it, Arbreu?"

"I've seen this. When we were leaving the cave, you asked if we'd return. There was a circle of tokens in the ceiling and underneath I saw a pattern on the floor. I wasn't sure what it was then, but now, well, this is it. Isn't it? Did you see it?"

I nodded. "It's not quite the same though. I'm hoping the full moon will show us something else."

"I don't know if the arch is part of the circles or not," said Mekroe, "but I guess you should include it." He handed me a small arch shape he had whittled from a scrap of firewood, then took it back and placed it to the west of the circles. "I suppose you know that if you look through the holes you always see another stone thingy."

I nodded.

"Thought so," he said with exaggerated gloom. "I never

Kirym Speaks

think of anything first."

Teema patted him on the back. "Never mind, you did think to make the arch. No one else did."

"Really?" Mekroe grabbed me around the waist and lifted me off the rug I was sitting on. He grabbed it and shook it out.

I struggled to regain my footing and snatched it back. "Fool," I said laughing. "I was comfortable."

Amid general laughter, he apologised and with great care and exaggeration, refolded the rug and set it down for me to sit on. "I was sure you were hiding an arch in there," he said.

I laughed again, but sat down quickly as the small arch I'd made of willow twigs threatened to slip from the bodice of my dress. I dropped it into the fire later when no one was watching.

As we ate, we talked about what we would do next. I agonised over whether to continue or return home. I was worried about Danth and Jinda. They hadn't appeared, although I was sure they would have had no trouble in tracking us.

We slept early, not knowing how long we would need to be awake on the night of the full moon.

Danth and Jinda arrived soon after dawn.

10

Kirym Speaks

Findlow woke me when Danth and Jinda were first spotted. Everyone else was awake and alert as they drew near. I asked Arbreu and Mekroe to discreetly circle around to see where they had come from.

Danth ignored everyone. He dropped his pack beside the shelter and helped himself to a large platter of the stew bubbling away on the fire. He sat down and started eating.

He'd timed his approach badly. That meal was being prepared for the evening and had not long been cooking. It was tough and unpalatable. He spat out the mouthful he'd taken back into the pot, and dumped the platter on the fire.

"Not very hospitable, are you?" he said to no one in particular.

"Hrumph!" snorted Findlow, retrieving the platter before it caught alight. "Hospitality follows manners. If you'd waited, we'd have offered you food — when it was cooked."

Kirym Speaks

"So where are these people you're searching for? A little hard to find, are they?" asked Danth smugly.

"We didn't come to find people," I said. "We followed a map, as did you."

"I followed no such nonsense," he said harshly. "I tracked my son. I'll take him and I'm gone."

"All right, Papa. I'll return to the settlement with you. As soon as we eat, we can leave."

"I'll come too, Tarjin," said Lyndym. "I want to get back to Mama, but I didn't want to go by myself. It'll be nice having someone to travel with."

"Me too. I hadn't planned to stay this long." Bokum sounded casual, but the tension in his stance belied that.

"Can't wait to push us out, can you?" said Danth. "Well, you'll have to. Jinda's exhausted. We travelled all night to rescue my son. We'll leave later, maybe tomorrow."

The water was hot and drinks were handed around as Bildon dished up a fruit and grain loaf we'd prepared overnight in a ground oven.

Mekroe arrived back and handed Mekrar a gutted rabbit. "Hey, skin this, Sis."

She screwed up her nose, but accepted the body. "If it's not gutted properly, you're getting it back," she said, pulling the skin away and inspecting the body.

Sometime later, Arbreu arrived from the direction of the stones and dropped a handful of herbs in my lap. "I think I got it right this time. Is this what you are looking for?"

"Taste one."

He dubiously nibbled a leaf. "Oh, horrid! It's bitter," he said, screwing up his face and spitting it out.

I dug two dried leaves from my medicine pouch. "They're similar, and different from anything else you'll find. If you enjoy eating it, it's good for salads. If it's bitter, I use it for healing."

Now Danth had lost interest and took Jinda off to a corner of the shelter. Settling her on Bokum's bed, he took Mekrar's, Bildon's and Findlow's rugs and hung them across the corner to give them extra privacy.

Mekrar bristled, but subsided when I shook my head. "Handle it later," I said quietly.

Arbreu accepted a large hunk of the loaf and sat beside me. "They camped in the middle of the grove last night. They were there overnight. Tracks show them coming to the tree edge three or four times."

Mekroe sat down opposite me. "They obviously planned to arrive here this morning. They've left a disgusting mess. I'll clean it up later. I'd be embarrassed to leave it."

We tidied up after our meal, and did the necessary chores to keep our clothes and other possessions clean. In preparation for the full moon, I changed into my festival dress. I had an everyday dress, hunting trousers and tunic, all of which I washed, hanging them over lavender bushes to dry.

We walked out to the stones and studied them further. This time, I concentrated on the carvings. These were different to the stellon Raff had on the hill above his settlement, in the hills north of The Land Between the Gorges. Some had abstract lines, chevrons, squiggles, spirals and arrows. Others had exotic creatures and weirdly proportioned people carved onto them.

Danth joined us and wandered around, casually looking at the stones. He turned to Findlow. "You're a fool wasting your time here," he said.

"The moon rises when it's ready," said Findlow amiably.

"That's ridiculous. I know where the path is. Why act as stupid as you look because the moon isn't going to help you." He walked to the arch and looked through it to the west. He held out his arm in a rough alignment to the angled pole and took a few steps north. "If you stand here and look

Kirym Speaks

through the arch, you can see the path. We can save time by leaving now."

"We could be here for something else entirely," said Mekrar. "Not a path and conceivably nothing to do with the arch. The moon will tell us more."

Mekroe snorted. He stood three steps south of Danth. "Anyway, if you stand here, you can see a different path. In fact, if you turn around and look towards the rising sun, you can see a path there also."

"Idiot boy! What would you know? It has to be through the arch, like out at sea."

Mekroe frowned briefly. "Oh, you mean Kirym's Arch?"

"THE SEA ARCH!" Danth roared. "It fits together. An arch there, an arch here! Anyway, I'm going. You can follow along when the moon tells you I'm right."

He walked back to the camp, and returned a while later with Jinda and his packs. "Come on, Tarjin. We're going."

"Not me," said Tarjin.

Jinda looked alarmed. "Jinjin, you said you'd come with us. We should do this together as a family."

"I said I'd go home with you, Mama. I'm not following him into the unknown to have him abuse my friends every step of the way."

"You ungrateful ..."

Danth lunged at Tarjin with his hand raised. Everyone reacted. There was a lot of shouting.

I stepped between Tarjin and Danth. "Don't!"

He hesitated, made a fist and struck. The impact knocked me off my feet and into Sundas. I saw stars, and everything went black.

49

11

Kirym Speaks

When I opened my eyes, I was lying on the ground. A sea of concerned faces peered at me. Teema helped me to sit. The world swam for a few moments. I felt nauseous, and my head and jaw throbbed. I took a deep breath and struggled to my feet, pushing my way through the crowd. Danth stood very still, knives and arrows close to his throat.

"Lower your weapons," I said.

I faced Danth. "You are no longer welcome here. Leave now!"

"You don't tell me what to do," he said. "I wouldn't stay here if you begged me to." He grabbed his packs, thrust them into Jinda's arms and turned away.

"Stay with me, Mama," said Tarjin. "I'll look after you."

Jinda looked forlornly at Tarjin. "Come with us, Jinjin. It's better if you're with us."

"He's dangerous, Mama. Don't go, please. Please!"

"We'd like you to stay, Jinda," I said.

Kirym Speaks

"Jinda!" Danth yelled. "Here! Now!"

She clutched the packs to her chest and scuttled after him. He walked through the arch and took one of the paths.

"Are you all right, Tarjin?" I asked quietly.

He nodded. "I only hope she is."

"Does he hit you often?"

Tarjin shook his head. "No, but she has lots of bruises. More lately. She hides them though."

"I wish I'd known. I might have been able to help."

"You couldn't," he said. "You can't help those who don't want to be helped. We've both protected him, Mama and me. She didn't want anyone to know and she would have denied it if asked. I guess for a long time it wasn't too bad, but he's getting worse. I should have made her talk to someone." He paused. "Nah, she wouldn't have done it and it wouldn't have stopped him."

We walked back to the camp. The cooking containers had been kicked over, our meal strewn across the ground. The stone shards, twigs and pebbles making up the pattern of the circles had been stamped into the ground. Our packs had been emptied and thrown around. All of my possessions, including my spare clothing, cloak and rugs were blazing on the fire.

Tarjin pulled off what he could and stamped out the flames, but it was burned beyond use. "I'm so sorry, Kirym. He's a mongrel. Wear my cloak until I replace yours."

I looked at Tarjin towering above me and imagined wearing his cloak. Tripping over his cloak. Falling on my face in his cloak. I started to laugh hysterically.

Mekrar hugged me close, patting my back and making comforting sounds. Sundas muttered and growled incomprehensibly. I was aware of the others all hovering around us.

"I'm fine, really," I assured them.

I knew I was suffering from shock. I'd never been hit like that before. My face was swollen and tender, and my thoughts skittered all over the place. My head ached. I moved my jaw experimentally. It wasn't broken, but would be sore for a few days. I chose a few calming herbs from my pouch. Arbreu brought me a hot sweet drink to steep them in, and Teema picked and mashed some water weed, then wrapped it in a cloth to hold against my jaw to reduce the swelling.

"Oh my stars," gasped Mekrar. "Where are the tokens?"

"They're safe," I said. I pulled the pocket holding them from inside my skirt. I moved over beside Tarjin. "Are you all right?"

He nodded.

"Do you want us to go after her?"

"No. She won't leave him and it'd give him power if we followed him. The best thing is to carry on with what we're doing. He'll come back. Because you don't follow him, he'll suspect he has it wrong. He'll be sitting just out of sight, watching to see what we do."

While everyone tidied up, I settled back and closed my eyes. I must have slept, because next thing I knew, it was mid-afternoon and I felt a little better.

We returned to look at the stones. This time, I concentrated on the standing stones. There were twelve of them, and they were huge. They were rough-hewn, but seven were smooth on an edge or partially on the back. Some were carved, although they were not as complicated as those on the stellons and poles. It was a lot to take in.

Late in the afternoon, we returned to the camp to eat and prepare for the evening. I wore Tarjin's cloak. He had asked Mekrar and Bildon to stitch the hem up for me, insisting I

Kirym Speaks

use it while he used a rug. The cloak was too big around the neck and shoulders, and it sagged annoyingly, but it was a lovely thought. Bildon had spread it over a lavender bush when they finished stitching it. The fragrance mixed with Tarjin's smell. It wasn't unpleasant, but I knew it would permeate my clothes until I washed them.

I collected a hooded lamp and a hank of fibre to take with me. As we ate, I explained what I wanted to do through the evening. Because Danth was probably still close, I wanted the camp to be guarded while we were away.

Tarjin volunteered to do it and Sundas stayed there with him. "But you all call me if Danth turns up," he ordered.

As the sun went down, we walked out to the stones. "This shouldn't take long. I want us back in camp as quickly as possible."

"I guess we'll take as long as it needs, Kirym," said Arbreu. He turned and peered through the gloom at me. "What do you know that I don't?"

I laughed. "We'll see."

The darkness seemed heavy as we waited. The lamps were kept hooded — no one wanted to mar the effect when the moon rose. Mainly we concentrated on the leaning pole, although there were other stones and poles I wanted watched. I placed people in areas where I felt they would be most useful.

The moon's glow reflected against the sky and then it peeped over the horizon, shining onto the stones. In moments, a shadow from the leaning pole raced across the open circle and shone on one of the tall poles. Then, as the moon rose further, the shadow shortened.

I reached the pole just after Teema. He had his hand on it just above his head. "It came up to this hole."

I handed him a strand of fibre and asked him to tie it through the hole. The moon shone on the stones around us,

53

creating areas of light and dark. It was strangely eerie.

"That's all we have to do tonight," I said.

"What?" Mekroe sounded surprised. "But we haven't found the path."

"Danth said it was a path, and possibly that's what we'll find. I want the secret of the stones. We've started, but it's too dark to do more. The real search starts tomorrow."

We built up the fire and talked as we ate supper. I doubled the guard and enlarged the area we watched to include the stones.

12

Kirym Speaks

The sun was only just above the horizon when we returned to the circles. Mekroe and Tarjin rushed ahead and Tarjin legged Mek up to peer through the hole.

"Oh," he said. "This one doesn't look at anything. Did we get it wrong?"

"Don't assume," I said.

Teema grabbed the end of the fibre strand. "What do we do with this?"

"Take it off and study the pole," I said. "The hole must be relevant."

From the hole, a line spiralled down to the bottom and turned back across itself, to stop at a narrow hole just over an arm's length from the ground. Teema knelt and peered through the hole.

"Aha, that stellon over there." He pointed to the far side of the circle.

Everyone rushed over to look at it.

"Oh." Mekroe sounded so disappointed. "You must be wrong. There's no hole. A dead end already."

"It's not always holes, Mek. That'd be too simple. Again, what do you see?"

The top part of the pole had deep diagonal lines carved into it. The bottom quarter was mostly smooth but for a small section of crosshatching. Where the two patterns met, the lines created an arrow that pointed to a carved pole. Many of the figures on this pole were only roughly engraved, but one was fully finished and its tongue, sticking out of the side of its mouth, pointed to a standing stone. There, the tip of a shadowy leaf indicated another pole and so we worked our way around the stones, stellon and poles. Many of the stones had multiple clues and some of them were obscure. I worried we would get them wrong, but we all enjoyed ourselves. At midday we stopped for a rest, eating our meal there among the stones.

"What gave you the idea to read the stones this way, Kirym?" asked Findlow.

"I told you there were lots of messages here. That was one of them. I'll show you."

I took him to one of the carved poles on the northern side of the circle. It was made up of people and creatures standing one on top of the other. The bottom figure was human like, short and stocky, and the details were only obliquely hinted at. The next figure was more obviously a person with finer features. The face was particularly well done. On his head stood a strange figure, human, but barely dressed. The three fingers of one hand sat knitted together, with four on his other hand above his rotund belly. His feet, likewise, had only seven toes between them. Perched on his head were the finely cloven hooves of an animal we had only occasionally seen. With short legs, a stocky body and a long neck, it stared across the circle to the south. This figure was

Kirym Speaks

also very lifelike.

The carving I pointed to was on the belly of the middle figure. It sat below his interlinked fingers: three large circles with lines zigzagging through them. Above and to the right was a sun.

"This told me we had to do it during the day. The rest was obvious when I realised many of the holes looked at something, and when I followed those signs, I learned all sorts of things."

"And I thought it was just decoration," said Bildon in wonder.

Late in the afternoon, a clue took us to the arch. Everyone gathered around, searching for a carving or some other hint.

Mekroe sighed deeply. "Nothing here," he said. "Was Danth right after all?"

"There's a big picture, Mek," I said. "We were led here by the tokens, so that must be relevant here. Remember the puzzles Mama gave us when we were children? We needed all of the pieces to get the final answer, and we were never given them all at once. We had to search, and some of the pieces needed to be used more than once. It's the same here. We have to look at all of the clues, because one alone could lead us in the wrong direction."

I took him to one of the massive standing stones. A shape was inscribed into the back of it: an arch-like shape with a small irregular lump on the top. Lines radiated from one side of the lump.

Everyone jostled to study it. "Are there others we haven't found?"

"Possibly. There's such a lot here and we may never understand it all. I hope we have enough for now." I pointed to the carving. "Could that be a token sitting on an arch? If so, which token is it?"

The Fortress of Faltryn

Everyone had a suggestion, each as likely as the others. Slowly, they petered out.

"What do you think, Kirym?" said Arbreu softly. "You know the tokens better than we do."

"The orange one guided us here. Perhaps it'll tell us what to do next. Teema, get on top and see if there's a place for it."

Sundas gave Teema a leg up. Once astride the arch, he brushed off the dirt that had accumulated over the seasons. "There's a shape carved into the top here."

More debris showered down as he cleared it. I handed up the token and he placed it there, rotating it until it fitted.

"Perfect," he said. "But what now?"

"We wait."

The sun lowered in the sky. It touched the horizon and continued to sink. Just before it disappeared from our sight, the token caught the sun's rays. For an instant they seemed trapped inside, and then a beam of light shone onto the trees and undergrowth to the north of us.

The sun disappeared.

Teema handed down the token and joined us on the ground. Having very little time before the light disappeared, we raced over to look at the final clue.

In the past, the trees here had been felled. The new growth was tall and thick, impossible for us to force our way through.

"We'll check more thoroughly in the morning," I said, but I knew it would be more work than we had time for. It seemed we had reached a dead end.

Back in camp, I pulled out the map I had made from the carving by the fountainhead pool. I knew now that the fine lines I had thought were fractures in the rock were the paths that radiated from the stone area. There was no track, or in fact anything, in the area indicated by the token. So the

Kirym Speaks

token shining there had to mean something else.

I studied the map, wondering what could be there and how we could find it. I had a sleepless night, pondering over the problem.

In the dark time just before dawn, something occurred to me.

13

Kirym Speaks

As soon as it was light, I checked the map again. Beyond the area of the stones, there was a jagged line of dots. If the undergrowth hadn't been there, it would have taken about a day and a half to reach them. It would take a long time to chop our way through, but — the stream went in that direction. It didn't go right to where the dots were, but close enough and it was worth a try.

"It'll take a few days," I said when I explained my plan, "and more if it leads somewhere. I think we have to try it, because if we don't, we'll always wonder."

Findlow frowned, shifting to look over the camp area. "It's a good idea, and of course you have to do it. But I'm going to stay here. I'll wait a few days to see if Danth returns. I want to be sure he doesn't make trouble for you."

"I don't know when we'll return, Findlow. I really don't want anyone to be alone," I said. "It could be dangerous."

"He won't be," Bokum said quietly. "I'll stay and we can

return home together in a few days. It's time I got back to Zeprah and Trayum."

"I'll stay too," said Lyndym. "I meant it when I said I was missing Mama."

While I was reluctant to split the group, I could see the sense in having someone watching our backs. Bokum desperately wanted to get back to his family, and this was a sensible way to allow him to do so while ensuring he wasn't alone. Eventually I agreed.

Everyone else was enthusiastic, and we hurried our meal and packed the hauling frame.

We followed the banks of the stream. By mid-morning the trees and undergrowth had closed in, encroaching onto the path. There was no choice but to remove our boots and step into the water. It was cool but not deep, and we were able to splash along happily. Although the trees grew to the edge of the water, there were frequent clearings and we could leave the water often. As the sun crept towards the horizon, we set up a temporary shelter, cooked food and heated water.

I was surprisingly tired, but with eight of us, there were plenty to guard the camp while allowing each of us plenty of sleep.

The morning dawned bright, although there was a cool wind blowing. Today's journey through the water wouldn't be quite as pleasant as yesterday's.

We started early. Soon the trees closed in above us, creating a tunnel. The water deepened and I held my skirts high to keep them dry. A clearing we found late in the morning gave us an opportunity to climb out, dry off, rest and warm up. The clearing was small, and we had trouble fitting everyone on it out of the water. Our stop was short.

"If we pile everything onto the hauling frame," suggested Teema, "Mek, Tarjin and I can carry it. The water is getting a bit deeper, so it'll keep everything dry."

The Fortress of Faltryn

"It's a good idea," said Mekrar. "Bildon and I can help too, but with the water growing higher, we need to change our clothes."

She sent the men upstream to wait while we looked through the packs. Mekrar had clothes similar to Mekroe's, garments she used when hunting. Bildon pounced on Mekroe's spare trousers and tunic, but for me nothing was small enough. Earlier in the trip, I had used Findlow's other tunic, but Danth had thrown it on the fire along with my other clothes. All I had was my festival dress, petticoats and shift — the clothing I had been wearing when the rest were destroyed.

In the end, I removed my petticoats, put them in my pack and tied my skirt and shift as high as I could.

Then we joined the men.

14

Arbreu

Arbreu loved travelling with Kirym. This journey was different to others he had done. Orphaned when his family were buried under a landslide, he had been captured and enslaved. The slaver, Slynd, wanted to kill him.

If it hadn't been for Kirym, he would have succeeded.

Kirym had done more than save Arbreu's life. She had brought him into her family. That was cemented with a token: green, matching hers. Teema and Bokum each wore an identical token, making them his token brothers.

However, Kirym was special. Arbreu still felt he owed her his life. He had resolved to spend forever paying her back, protecting her and keeping her out of danger. The problem was, she was fiercely independent, and on the occasions he had tried, she had been particularly scathing. It didn't stop him wanting to, though.

Arbreu enjoyed walking through the stream. It was sandy underfoot and what rocks there were, were smooth. For most

The Fortress of Faltryn

of the day it didn't get much above his thighs, although having to push against the strong flow became tiring.

As the afternoon wore on, the stream narrowed, deepened, and the water became very rough. They struggled through this with the sun moving two hand-spans towards the horizon. With the roar of rapids ahead and the river deepening again, they knew they had come to the end of this particular path.

Kirym directed them towards dry ground, and they struggled up the steep slippery bank.

"It's too far to return to the last clearing," she said wearily. "Let's clear an area here to spend the night. We'll start back in the morning." Although tired and wet, she began to hack out the small trees and bushes to create an open space for them to rest in.

The undergrowth was thick, as thick as that back at the stones, and the area cleared was small. The growth and ground were damp; it would be an uncomfortable night.

Even with Sundas' muscle, some of the stumps could not be removed, and they curled around them trying to get comfortable. Arbreu thought of lighting a fire, but the wood was wet, and when it came down to it, he was too tired. He decided to rest awhile and do it later.

Kirym sorted through the hauling frame and handed everyone fruit and drinks.

Arbreu was annoyed with himself. He was so tired, he hadn't even thought of it. He knew Kirym had had a harder trip than any of them. She was so much smaller than them in stature and she was wet to her shoulders. When she left the water, her face was blue and yet she had been uncomplaining.

Now they were out of the water the humidity was affecting them, and as night approached they were inundated with clouds of insects that bred along the bank of the stream.

Arbreu

Arbreu idly watched Kirym tie the end of a rope to one of the trees and wondered why she chose that particular tree.

He looked around, trying to figure the best place to tie the two ends if she wanted to fence off the water. *Certainly not where Kirym tied it*, he thought. He closed his eyes tiredly.

When he opened them, she had disappeared.

He jumped to his feet, suddenly concerned. "Where's she gone?" he demanded.

Teema jumped up. "Who?" he asked, looking round. "Damn her! Why does she do this? Where was she last?"

Arbreu leapt over people and packs to where he had last seen Kirym. "Over here." The rope led into the undergrowth. He grabbed it and forced his way past the first bushes. Once away from the stream, the bush thinned and the trees sat further apart. Then Teema was on his heels, and he could hear Sundas muttering darkly as he followed too.

The rope Kirym had chosen was long and she'd tied two others to it. Arbreu followed it for just over two hundred steps before he saw her returning.

"What are you doing here?" she asked.

"Why'd you go off alone?"

"I was checking the area." She slipped past them, ignoring their comments and complaints.

They stepped into a cloud of midges at the water's edge, and Arbreu realised she hadn't brought the other end of the rope with her.

Teema rounded on Kirym, ready to tear strips off her. She held up her hand, stopping him. "There's a clearing nearby. Grassy, no insects and we'll be far more comfortable overnight than here. I've tied the other end of the rope there to guide us."

She picked up two large packs and slipped into the trees. There was a mad dash to collect everything and follow her. The further they travelled, the easier it was, and then suddenly they were in the clearing.

Kirym hadn't told them how big it was. Nor had she mentioned the avenue of standing stones.

"It struck me that the undergrowth was thicker at the water's edge than it had been further south," she said. "That implied it had been cleared at some stage in the past. I thought if we had to stop about where we stopped, maybe there was something close by to lead us further."

"Yoohoo hoo!" crowed Mekroe. "We're going on, aren't we?"

Teema rounded on Kirym. "Don't do that again! I was so worried."

Kirym smiled sweetly. "Are you challenging my leadership?"

"Good leaders tell their people what they're doing. What if you'd gotten lost? I may never have found you again."

"You could have followed the rope."

They faced each, faces darkened in anger. Mekrar giggled. It was infectious and soon everyone was laughing. Teema's lips twitched, and the tension quickly disappeared.

Kirym took a line on the standing stones, aiming to go in the same direction, more north than west. The forest opened up and they moved fast.

By late-afternoon two days later, the trees had thinned and they walked through open countryside. The lower slopes of the mountain they had seen from the stone circles were off to the right now, and the ridge the fountainhead was on continued far to their left.

Every now and again, they would find a large standing stone or a cairn which she took as indication they were on the right track, although Arbreu wondered if she was reading

Arbreu

their finds correctly.

Kirym was more philosophical. "They're not a natural occurrence here. Someone has placed them as markers, so they must lead to a place or thing. Each of them is within half a day of the last one, and they are pretty much in a straight line."

Six days passed, and if it hadn't been for the stones, Arbreu would have assumed no one had ever been here before and they were on a wild goose chase, but Kirym seemed sure and it was a pleasant journey. The land was rich, and hunting was never a problem. Kirym was experienced in foraging, but each of them found food to add to the meals they shared.

Suddenly there were no more stones. They passed the last one late-afternoon on the sixth day. Despite checking in all directions, they could find nothing to take them further in their journey. At midday the following day they stopped to make some decisions, although mainly they questioned their thoughts and beliefs of the last six days.

"Maybe we were chasing a dream after all," said Tarjin.

Arbreu sighed deeply. "Could the stones have been placed to lead people to the stream? Maybe we're looking at it the wrong way."

"Maybe there aren't any other people in the land," interrupted Mekroe. "Is it time we returned home and accepted that?"

Sundas had been lying on the ground, his head on his pack, giving the impression of being asleep. In the despondent silence he grunted. "Aye, maybe you're right, but there is one thing none of you lads has thought of," he said.

There was an extended silence while they waited in expectation. Sundas milked it for all it was worth. He yawned, stretched and sat up, scratching his beard and head. Finally he picked up a flask and drank deeply. "You've not asked the person with the brains," he stated, smacking his

The Fortress of Faltryn

lips and turning to Kirym. "I know you've been thinking, lass, and you wouldn't be walking with no plan. Now you can tell them. They need their spirits raised a wee bit."

She laughed. "We assumed the stones were there to lead us somewhere or to something. If we were right, then when they end there must be something else that's obvious. So what do you see?"

"There's nothing out here," said Tarjin. "We've looked. We'd have found a fallen cairn if it was there. We've been pretty thorough."

Kirym waved the comment aside. "The problem could be we've been looking for more of the same. Maybe from here the destination was so obvious they didn't need markers to indicate the path. There was something else they could see."

The tree clad ridge to the west had stopped abruptly earlier in the day. Beyond it was a sheer cliff rising to red arid rocks. The massive hills to the east were blued by distance. Northeast of them, the mountain towered closer now than ever.

"The mountain!" exclaimed Mekroe. "Is that where we're headed? It'll take us ages to get there, and then what?"

"I don't think it's the mountain," said Kirym. "We could see it from the avenue of stones. Why bring us in this direction if that was the goal? That's the path I'd have chosen had the stones not directed us here. Why would they even build the cairns if that was the direction? No, it's something else, something less obvious."

"Unless they're there specifically to lead us in the wrong direction," said Mekroe.

Kirym shook her head. "There are too many for that to be so," she said, "and the line is too precise. Look there." She pointed to the north.

It was almost invisible, a tiny black nub on the otherwise

flat northern horizon, sitting just to the east of the western cliffs.

Despite some scepticism, they travelled towards it with renewed vigour. The land appeared flat, although deep narrow valleys appeared with a suddenness that was frightening. Most of these couldn't be crossed, so they detoured as necessary. The land was otherwise featureless, with few trees and little obvious water. The grasses were lush though and hunting, when necessary, was easy. As usual, Kirym foraged as she travelled, and she kept them moving from first light until almost dark each day. As they travelled, the nights became cooler, and after two days, they found the fire they built each night to cook their food became a necessity.

"It's weird," said Sundas. "When I was a child it was always warmer to the north. Even the winters there were warm. Why is it so different here? It doesn't make sense."

"The land is rising," said Kirym. "It's subtle, but it's consistent. Even though it appears flat, it rises from the shore line. I think we are now higher above the sea than even the top of the canyon."

She waited until the sceptical comments stopped. "Back in the old land, it was always far colder above the waterfall. We understood that because we climbed the cliff. Here it's much more gradual, but the rate of rise has increased over the last few days. Have you noticed we've all been slightly more tired and breathless when we're due for our usual stops through the days?"

Sundas chuckled. "I thought it was because you were making us walk faster, Kirym."

After three days, the nub had become a triangle of stony rock on the horizon. Thin and tall, it seemed to wedge itself into the land between the cliff to the west and the flat land to the east. Five more days of travel took them to the foot of it, a rough craggy peak that towered massively above them, dwarfing the standing stones they'd seen on the way. The land here seemed to be either vertical or horizontal, but all of it was rough. The cliff to the west had reduced abruptly two days earlier, although still high. A river separated it from the rocky crag they were aiming for.

Arbreu looked across the land. "Going northeast would be easier. Northwest, well, it's just a rocky gorge. There's nothing there but cliffs and water. Surely if there were people, they'd live in rolling countryside where the hunting is easy and the land is rich?"

With nods and grunts of agreement from Mekroe and Tarjin, he discussed the merits of the easier landscape.

Wordless, Kirym walked on to the pointed face of the rock.

The standing stone was camouflaged and dwarfed by the cliff it stood beside. From between it and the cliff, Arbreu could see past the nearby trees up a river valley — a rocky flood plain that stretched into the distance. The river was wide, dividing into many crisscrossing channels. The islands created by them were sprinkled with spindly trees. Beyond the river, the cliff rose, steep but mostly green. The cliffs showed damage wrought by recent flooding.

They were pleased to spend the night there; Kirym had set a fast pace over the days since they left the stream.

They walked across rock, the sheer cliff rising massively to their right, the river to their left. Early in the morning it was cold; the sun wouldn't shine past the cliff until later in the day. Far ahead a waterfall dropped down the cliff hitting

Arbreu

a ledge half way down and falling further to ground level where it ran shallowly across their path and joined the river. The river twisted and turned. The rough untamed beauty amazed them. It was stark and wild.

During the afternoon, they looked for somewhere to spend the night. Kirym found a ledge sitting high above the water. She clearly wanted to be on the cliff so that in the event of a flash flood they would be safe.

There was plenty of driftwood scattered along the river's edge, an indication of both the obvious flooding and forests further upstream.

The setting sun washed over the cliff, colouring the black rock a deep red. As the last of the sun's rays waned, they lit a fire and settled for the night. A wall of rock was built around the fire to protect it from the wind and to make it less obvious from the river plain below. Kirym double-checked, not overly happy with the flame's reflection on the dark walls behind them, but realised this was the best they could do in the circumstances. She doubled the guard, and when asked why, had no real explanation except that it was unknown land and as strangers, they were at a disadvantage.

"It'll be very dark here tonight, and a difficult place to escape from if there is a problem," she said.

However, the night passed quietly, and as the icy morning dawned they ate the hot meal she'd had prepared. The cold seemed worse as the sky lightened, and they were eager to get moving. After dousing the fire they continued on their way.

The second day was a repetition of the first. The scenery was stark and wild. The cliffs towered above them. There was little growth along the path they took. Kirym was unable to forage, although she eyed the river and suggested they try to get a fish from there for their evening meal.

Again, she began to look for an accessible ledge during the

The Fortress of Faltryn

afternoon. As they rounded a corner looking for an easy way up the cliff, Arbreu was distracted when Kirym, who was leading, suddenly whirled around and retraced her steps. At the same time, he heard a sound, something he didn't instantly identify.

15

Arbreu

"I knew you'd come."

Kirym whirled around, her knife instantly in her hand.

There was no one in sight. Arbreu almost thought he had dreamt it, but everyone else looked wary. "What was that?" he asked.

He caught a small movement above them and looked up in time to see something light blue flash past a space between two rocks. Kirym followed it back. There was an occasional glimpse of the blue between the rocks.

A pair of dark blue felt boots stepped onto a ledge at about eye level.

"You travelled very fast." The voice was soft, but strong. "Help me down, dear." She extended her hand to Kirym.

They saw her clearly as she bent to avoid a low outcrop. She was old, older than anyone Arbreu had ever seen before.

"Come on, help me down, dear. You won't need the knife. Well, not yet, anyway. I'm quite harmless."

The Fortress of Faltryn

Kirym reached up and grasped her hand. The old lady stepped onto a small ledge, then a narrow projection, another ledge and jumped lightly to the ground. For all she was old, she was agile.

Once she was on the ground, Arbreu realised how tiny she was, smaller even than Kirym. Her face was wrinkled beyond belief, but her eyes shone, bright and intelligent. Her long robe was sky blue, while the felt hat matched the darker hue of her boots.

"You came sooner than I thought you could. And you travelled fast." She nodded as she spoke, her smile showing tiny worn teeth. "It's a long time since the dwellers of The Green Valley visited us. Token wearers, too — we are doubly blessed."

She sounded a little awed, and that surprised Arbreu. He doubted much would astonish this lady.

They stared at her, open-mouthed. Then Kirym remembered her manners and introduced everyone. "How did you know we were coming? Even we didn't know that."

She laughed. "I am Wind Runner. As you see, I no longer run as the wind, but the knowledge I gained when I could, remains with me. The stories telling of your arrival have been passed down from our ancestors." She paused. "We'd talk more comfortably if you were rested and able to wash away the rigors of your long journey." She turned away, beckoning them to follow. Kirym shrugged and hoisted her pack to her shoulder.

Wind Runner led them along the base of the cliff. They walked a long way and she walked very fast, too fast for them to question her further. It was getting dark when they rounded a sharp corner. The sight ahead was amazing.

The dwelling was built into the cliff and it was huge. Tall battlements towered over them and lines of dark windows stared down on the river valley. A narrow path, starting in a

Arbreu

large shallow depression in the cliff, zigzagged its way to a fortified gate half way up the cliff.

Wind Runner took them past the path into what seemed to be a narrow crack in the rock. Once inside, a stone gate thudded shut behind them and they followed a line of lamps to a shaft running straight up the hill.

"This path is easier," she said. "Safer too."

Easier it may have been, but unlike Wind Runner they were all out of breath by the time they stepped onto a massive fortified ledge. Another solid gate thumped shut behind them and Arbreu was able to look over the battlements to the valley floor far below.

"This is incredible, Wind Runner. Are you expecting an attack?" Arbreu hoped the amazement he felt wasn't obvious in his voice.

"No, but if one has defences and fails to use them, then one is a fool, and there is always a panic when they're needed," she said. "Attacks stopped long ago. Nevertheless, we remain vigilant."

The sun had set as they climbed to the ledge, but bright welcoming lights now shone from a wide double door. The brightness made it difficult to see the dwelling up close.

Wind Runner pointed to a small roofed area against the wall. "Leave your things here, they'll be quite safe."

Mekroe and Tarjin placed the hauling frame near the door and stacked their packs on it, although the tokens remained hidden under Kirym's skirt, her herb pouch tied to her waist.

Wind Runner seemed all right, but Arbreu didn't trust her yet and safe didn't mean their possessions wouldn't be searched.

The walls in the large hall were covered with hangings, reaching from the ceiling to the floor. The only areas exposed were three enormous doors, one to each side and one ahead.

A wide staircase wound around the wall to a landing high above and four doors led off that. Wind Runner picked up a lamp, opened the door to the left, and directed them along a short passage with three doors opening off it. She ushered them through the first into a large room, lit other lamps and placed the one she was holding on a low table.

"You'll feel better when you've washed and eaten. I'll organise water and something to tide you over until a meal is ready." She disappeared, shutting the door behind her.

The room was large, set up with comfortable seats and tables. The stone floor was hidden under skins and thick felt rugs. Two of the walls were covered with shelves reaching above Sundas' head. These were packed with strange narrow oblongs of different colours and sizes, sitting together in long lines. The rest of the room was draped with hangings.

The walls, which Kirym checked, were generally made of large squared stone, although one wall was obviously solid natural rock. She looked at each of the hangings, checking behind them. Two long panels of wood were inset into the outer wall. They pivoted easily at one edge, swinging out to expose tall narrow windows.

"It looks over the ledge where the guards are, but it's too dark to see anything," she said. A second door sat in the right hand wall. A large bolt closed it. Teema double checked, but didn't attempt to open it.

Next, Kirym investigated the shelves. The oblong things were made mainly of well-cured leather, although a few were of felt and one was made of a thin fibre Arbreu didn't know. Kirym took one down. On one side was a small engraving of a flower and the word Herbs. It opened, revealing a pile of parchment leaves joined on one side and attached to the back of the leather. Arbreu studied it over her shoulder. The spelling was a little different, but it was readable. Made up of notes on the use of various herbs in cooking and healing,

Arbreu

with sketches of the plants, it was very interesting.

Kirym placed it back and took another. This one had notes, and drawings of dragons. The next book recorded a winter storm and subsequent flood. "Oh," she said, "it's about a boy who fell off the ledge into the river and drowned. They searched for the body but never found it. These are like our memory book. I wonder how they know where in their history the tale belongs." She frowned. "If it's their history, why is the dragon story there? And why put them with notes on herbs?" She chose another of the oblongs. "This one talks of the stars. So interesting."

Arbreau stared at the diagrams over her shoulder, beginning to enjoy it, when the door opened and a large man walked in. "Put that down," he snapped. "They're not toys."

Kirym looked up, alarmed. "I'm sorry, I've been very careful. They're interesting. Is this how you keep your history?"

"You can read?" He sounded surprised.

To assume Kirym couldn't was insulting. "Of course, can't everyone?" she asked coolly. She held up the item in her hand. "What do you call these? Our writings and memories are stored differently."

"They're books. They hold more than memories. Only those versed in the arts are able to understand them." He took it from her and placed it reverently back on the shelf. Then he frowned, and shook his head impatiently. "Why are you spying on us?"

They were suddenly wary, stiffening in surprise.

"If we were spies," Kirym said, "we'd not have approached you openly. We didn't know you existed until Wind Runner spoke to us."

He waved her aside and turned to Sundas. "Perhaps we should discuss this without the children interrupting."

Mekroe started to laugh, but turned it into a cough when

Kirym nudged his shin firmly with her boot. "You should talk to our leader," he said. "This is Kirym."

"Can't you control them?" the man asked Sundas. "I'm surprised you allow them to travel with you."

Sundas gestured towards Kirym. "Our leader, Kirym. Born in the land that lies between the gorges, and traveller of the great ocean. Kirym, daughter of Veld, son of Parve, son of Vauld, son of Vald, son of Arabos, son of Arbros, son of Tarj, son of Varl. Would you like me to continue? Kirym is our leader. Who are you?"

The man looked uncomfortable. "You follow a child?"

"She's small, but scarcely a child and yes, she is our chosen leader."

"Who chose her?"

"We did."

"You know who I am," Kirym interrupted. "Who are you?"

He turned back to Sundas. "Let's talk privately, just you and me."

Sundas growled, sounding menacing.

The stranger took a step back.

"If you don't wish to speak to me, why did you come in here?" Kirym asked.

Sundas stood and the stranger's eyes opened wide when he realised that as big as he might be, Sundas was bigger. "In our society, it is manners to acknowledge a leader," Sundas said. "We respect other cultures, and we expect you to accept ours. You have no choice. Speak to Kirym."

"Right," the stranger snapped. "Stay here until I decide what to do with you." He was backing towards the door when it opened and Wind Runner entered, followed by four women carrying bowls of water and one carrying a large basket.

She glanced around. "Ah, you've met my grandson, Storm."

Arbreu

"Is Storm your leader, Wind Runner?" Teema asked.

She looked at him with shrewd eyes. "Storm is one of our family heads. The rest are gathering and will welcome you presently." She indicated the bowls of water being placed on one of the tables. "I thought you'd like to freshen up before we eat." She stepped back to the door. "Storm, would you join me please?"

He followed her reluctantly.

One young woman emptied a large basket of soap, herbs, oils and towels next to the water bowls. "I'll ensure someone is nearby at all times. If there's anything you need, please ask them. They will let me know. I'm Starshine."

She left and they fell on the water, eager to clean up. It was warm, and the soaps smelled of roses and lavender. They were all pleased to be clean — there was only so much one could do with cold water and sand, and although they had found soap-nuts and soap root occasionally, this was so much better than bathing in an icy river or stream.

Mekrar's face was pink and shining from the scrubbing she'd given it. She rubbed a dirt stain on her dress. "Kirym, do you think we'd be able to get our festival clothes from the packs? It'd be nice to wear something fresh and it would make a better impression."

Arbreu and Teema followed Kirym into the empty passage and through the door at the end. Starshine was shutting the big doors at the front.

Kirym explained what she wanted. "It'd be easier to get them rather than bring everything in."

Starshine smiled agreement, opened the door again and picked up two lamps, handing one to Teema.

Outside, the packs had been stacked neatly in the back of the lean-to.

"I don't think they've been opened," Kirym murmured, untying the frame and pulling out clothes as she came across them. Teema held the lamp for her.

Arbreu took the opportunity to look around. The gate was guarded by four men, who watched them with interest. Although they had no weapons in sight, an area behind them was in darkness and could have held anything, including, Arbreu felt, quite a few more men. The building above him was, like the rest of the area, in darkness.

Back in the room, everyone swooped on the clean items, shaking them out as best they could. The clothes were wrinkled, but at least they were clean.

"I'll put lamps through here to give you more room," said Starshine, opening the bolted door.

Clean clothes made a big difference and these were the finest they owned. Kirym had brought in what jewellery they had, along with combs and ribbons. Everyone began to look somewhat more decorous than the bedraggled dusty group who had entered the room.

"This will make a better impression," Mekrar said.

Kirym brushed the knots from her hair, shook the dust from her skirts, and tried to rub away the worst of the dirt. It was all she could do. "I wish I had something to change into," she said.

She had worn the dress constantly since leaving the three circles, and there had been few opportunities to clean it and none to repair it. The delicate material had not been designed to be treated so harshly. Days in the sun had bleached it of colour, the hem was tattered, the sleeves and bodice had worn thin and the lace and embroidery were ripped and shabby. It looked dusty, and there were blood stains where a rabbit she had gutted bled on her.

"What can I do to make it more acceptable," she murmured as she ripped off some of the fraying mangled ribbons.

Starshine entered again, this time bringing a platter of food. "Something to tide you over until the meal is served."

Arbreu

She eyed Mekrar's clothes with interest. "Is there anything I can get you, anything you don't have? It's hard to bring everything you need when you travel."

"Do you have something for Kirym to wear tonight? Just until we've washed and mended her dress. Between a flood and a fire, all she has is what she's wearing." Mekrar took in Kirym's frosty stare and looked defiantly back. "You haven't seen yourself," she hissed.

Starshine nodded and smiled.

16

Kirym Speaks

I looked at the garments Starshine brought in. She had guessed my size correctly, but the clothes were very different to those I was used to. I checked through each garment, trying to work out the sequence in which they should be put on.

Loose trousers were covered by a long chemise, split to mid-thigh and laced from shoulder to wrist. That was covered by a single wide-sleeved garment that tied on the opposite side. A similar garment for the other arm — the sleeves were intricately jewelled. All of this was covered with a sheer shift that came under my right arm and tied on my left shoulder. This too was jewelled and embroidered.

It felt different. I didn't recognise the fibre used for the material. The garments were light, but surprisingly warm in the cooler night air.

I picked up my pouch of healing remedies. My dress had been designed to carry the herbs and the tokens, accessible,

Kirym Speaks

but hidden from sight. These garments made that impossible. Tying the pouches over the tunic looked wrong, but I didn't want to leave them behind.

Mekrar was sorting through a basket of accessories Starshine had brought in. In it were a number of silk-like bags containing fragrant herbs. I took one, emptied it and placed small packs of my most important remedies in it. I tied a ribbon around the top and slipped it around my neck. There was nowhere for the tokens, but Mekrar offered to carry them for me.

Moments later, the men joined us and swooped on the food Starshine had brought.

Arbreu paused, mid-bite. "You look different," he said to me. "Sort of smaller."

"Oh that's all I need." I sighed. "To look even more insignificant. Storm already considers me a child."

Teema hastened to reassure me. "No no, not like that. It makes you look rather regal, magnificent. Storm can't overlook you. You have a delicate air about you, but stunning. Quite amazing."

"Anyway, what now, Kirym?" asked Sundas.

"We wait and see what happens. Wind Runner has made us welcome, but be careful what you say. Tell them nothing until we know what they want. In the meantime, keep your knives handy, but hidden, and above all, don't go off alone."

It was some time before Starshine returned. She apologised for taking so long. "Everyone wishes to meet you, but Wind Runner felt that bringing them all together would be overwhelming. So she has arranged for the family heads to join us and everyone else can meet you tomorrow night."

She led us through the hallway and up two staircases, ushering us along a series of passages and into to a large room. As with the other rooms, the walls were covered with rich hangings. There were lamps hanging from the ceiling and others sitting on the table.

Wind Runner sat at the head of a wide table laden with platters, beakers and candles. She welcomed us and introduced the men and women who were dining with us.

We were conducted to seats, Storm trying to sit Sundas between himself and Wind Runner with Teema to his right. But Wind Runner took me firmly by the arm and sat me on her right, calling Sundas to sit on her left.

Storm reluctantly sat between Mekrar and me. He spent the meal ignoring us, talking to a man called Spire who sat opposite.

The talk was light as platters of food were placed on the table. Most of the food was recognisable, although the flavours were slightly different. Some of the herbs used were unknown to my palette. There were one or two foods that were totally foreign, but everything was appetising, and some were delectable. For a quickly assembled meal, they did us proud.

Wind Runner was an interesting dinner partner. Her conversation ranged widely as we ate.

As my hunger was assuaged, I sat back and studied those we ate with. Most were older with a presence of authority. They were richly dressed, but many looked weathered. They talked of crops, hunting, fishing and the seasons. These were hunters and farmers.

As the sweet dishes were taken away and replaced with breads and cheese, Arbreu, sitting further down the table, leaned forward. "You live in a bleak place, Wind Runner. Why here, and not on the eastern side of the hill where the land is more inviting?"

"This is our home and we've lived here for many generations. We have access to some of the green plains to the south and east, but responsibilities have kept us here ..."

Kirym Speaks

"Wind Runner!" Storm was on his feet even before he finished calling her name. His chair crashed to the floor. He strode over to her and whispered angrily.

She listened, waved him away and turned to our dinner companions. "Does anyone doubt the prophecy?"

There was silence, and a few sidelong glances at Storm.

"We've waited for hundreds of seasons for this time," she continued. "If we now ignore it, what has been the point? Our young visitor is right; we could have been more comfortable living in many other places. But we've remained here because of the prophecies. Now when it seems they are about to come true, are you having doubts?"

"What if we have it wrong?" asked Storm.

"What if we haven't?" she snapped. "We can only be guided by what we know."

"The prophecy speaks of a great warrior," Storm interjected. "These are children."

"The prophecy began with a great warrior. There is nothing that says we still need one."

"Of course we do. Who'd follow a child?"

Wind Runner sighed. "We will discuss it further, but if we leave it too long, we may lose any opportunity to bring peace to the land."

"We've had peace," Storm yelled. "Peace stops when people arrive. Soon, they want our game, our possessions and our land. Then it's back to war."

Wind Runner slowly got to her feet. Though she was only about half his height, Storm backed away, muttering.

"Peace in an empty land is not peace," she said. "It's existence. The land needs new people. We need new people, new blood. Our visitors have asked for nothing, they are our neighbours whether we like or not. We have never warred with the Green Valley folk. Why would they want our bleak barren land? And they've brought the tokens back."

The Fortress of Faltryn

"Brought them back!" Storm bellowed. "They have chips of coloured stone. Tokens? No one knows what the tokens are, but whatever they are, this child doesn't have them. We waste our time and endanger everything we've tried to build here." He glared around the room and walked out, slamming the door as he went.

Wind Runner resumed her seat. "Does anyone else feel threatened by our guests?"

There were a few embarrassed laughs, but one of the men stood. "Not so much these visitors, Wind Runner, but what of their people? Are they close and planning an attack? We don't know! These," he said, pointing dramatically around the room, "could be a decoy."

The discussions went on. Wind Runner was impressive. She neither apologised nor justified the arguments in the dining room. They continued back and forth for some time, until Wind Runner visibly wilted and was helped away.

Starshine ushered us downstairs soon afterwards, leaving the others arguing loudly. Someone had laid out more food and drinks for us. A small brazier glowed, taking away any chill in the air.

Mekrar handed me the pocket of tokens. "I don't know how you can carry them all the time," she said. "I've never noticed it before, but they seem to take over your awareness of everything else. It's such a huge responsibility. I'm sure they wanted to be with you."

I pulled the pocket close and accepted a drink. "The tokens seem to be vital to what's happening here. They're active, but I don't know why. It's different. I want to know what this prophecy is. It's obvious Storm disagrees with Wind Runner's understanding of it. There are divisions within this family, and we need to be careful we aren't endangered by it. We need to know what influence Storm has. Can he take over? If he can, then we may be vulnerable. What

Kirym Speaks

power does Wind Runner have? If she supports us, will her influence diminish?"

Before anyone could comment, there was a soft knock at the door and Wind Runner entered, followed closely by Starshine and two others who had dined with us.

Wind Runner reintroduced Cloud and Oak. Arbreu and Teema brought seats over for them. I poured a beaker of hot water and opened my herb pouch, choosing pinches of herbs and dried powdered fruit, which I sprinkled into the water. I handed it to Wind Runner.

Cloud's eyes opened wide. "Wind Runner, do you think ...?"

I laughed. "Cloud, why would I hurt Wind Runner when it could so soon be brought back to me? Young I may be, but foolish I'm not." I turned to Wind Runner. "It's just for energy, although you don't really look as if you need it. Now, what is this prophecy? How does it affect us and why is Storm so frightened?"

Wind Runner sipped her drink, savouring the flavours, and made herself comfortable. "Our summers here number into the hundreds and thousands. We call our settlement 'Faltryn', but its full name from our history is 'The Place of Faltryn's Tears'. Some books call it, 'The Place of the Dragon's Tears'. The prophecy comes from a legend. It tells of seven tokens. Owned by The Green Valley, they were supposed to bring peace to the tribes. That is the beginning of the prophecy, and this is Starshine's story to tell."

"It happened this way," said Starshine. "The land we lived in was lush but hilly, and the tribes argued constantly about territory and hunting. One summer, the dwellers of the desert attacked the cave people. They called on those who lived in the trees for help and there was great bloodshed. The huge carrion birds of Empeat came to view the battle. They darkened the sky as they flew in giant circles, calling to each other, cheering and laughing at the carnage.

They disturbed the dragon who sunned himself on the hill tops. Annoyed at the noise, he took the news to those in the Green Valley.

The warriors of the Green Valley came down in a great rage, but the tribes hid in the hills and didn't allow them to approach.

In his anger, the massive leader of the Green Valley pushed the hills apart, creating a wide plain so the tribes couldn't hide. He demanded they meet and end the aggression.

But the tribes were reluctant. In fairness, each of them was scared the blame would be laid at their feet and that there would be a harsh price to pay.

The leader of the Green Valley created the seven great tokens to assist with tribal unity. He dedicated one each to the waters, the vegetation, the lights that glow in the sky, fire, flowers and fruit, and the bright stones that hide deep in the ground."

She counted them off on her fingers as she recited them. "The seventh was for the people and peace. He explained that all were needed for us to be whole. None made sense in isolation.

Everyone was called to the celebration, a big feast in the centre of the great plain, and the sound of joy drove away the carrion birds. But the dragon flew through the night sky seething, because he had not personally been invited to join them.

As dawn broke, he swooped down and seized four of the tokens: the peace stone, and three others. But the leader was fast. He grabbed a rope and threw a noose around the dragon's neck. The dragon flew away, but the man clung to the end of the rope.

The dragon bucked and kicked, swooped and soared, and in his fight he lost three of the tokens. As they fell to the

Kirym Speaks

earth, the land grew up around them, protecting the tokens and ensuring the dragon could not return for them.

The battle raged through the day, with neither man nor dragon gaining the upper hand. Towards evening, a young one from the valley came to the top of the hill. The child climbed up the tallest tree and managed to grab the end of the peace token as the dragon swooped past.

The dragon was angry that help had come for the warrior. He slashed with his tail, but missed and gouged a long channel along the length of the high ridge. As he tried again to rise into the sky, the youth called on the trees for help and they looped their branches around the rope to hold the dragon tight.

The dragon dug his tail into the ground and pushed and pushed. His tail bored deep into the earth, creating a huge hole. As his tail sank, the rope slackened and he was able to slash at it with his claws and pull free of the trees.

The warrior saw that the dragon would fly off with the youth, so he leapt high and managed to grab the child. The token they held broke in two, half staying with the youth and half remaining with the dragon.

The dragon was furious he'd lost part of the jewel. He flew up in a great circle and lunged towards the warrior and his young helper. The dragon roared — a sound that was heard throughout the land. He flew towards them, planning to incinerate them with his fiery breath.

The two humans stood on the lip of the deep hole made by the dragon's tail. As the beast approached them, the youth called on the lakes and rivers of the earth to aid them.

A huge column of water rose from the hole. It hit the dragon, dousing the fire he breathed, but it also extinguished the fire he held in his belly, ensuring he could never make fire again. Laden with water, he was unable to fly far, so he glided north and found a cave to crawl into.

The Fortress of Faltryn

His heart became like ice and his breath, too, was chilled, now he could no longer make fire. He breathed on anyone entering the cave, his icy breath penetrating deep into their hearts and driving them away.

The warrior and his young companion returned to the great plain, but now there was no celebration. Everyone mourned the loss of the stones. The half token held by the youth, white when it was whole, now called to the elements of the other tokens. Each of them sent a small amount of themselves and the token stored it deep inside, a rainbow connection of colour to all of the other tokens.

The warriors of the tribes raced off to find the lost stones, and so intent were they on the search that they no longer cared for their families. The winter came. Hunger and great sickness entered the land.

Again, those of the Green Valley came to help them. They worked hard to care for the sick, but there was another great death, and the land mourned.

Each of the tribes gathered those they had left of their families and went off to seek out their own peace. Many of the tribes disappeared without trace, leaving their land dead and empty.

The people of the Green Valley returned to their home, but time passed and they were lonely. They decided to search for the tribes and bring them back to the land, for they felt there would be no healing until the people and the land were reunited.

On a day in early spring, they prepared to leave. They left the token that held sun and moon, the sky a beacon to summon them back should the need arise. The remaining tokens would go with them. But as they set off, the broken remains of peace flew away and made its home in a land far far away.

The people of the Green Valley followed, searching for the

Kirym Speaks

token, the land, and the people. Soon they too were lost in the mists of time."

Starshine sighed. "The story has come down to us through the generations. Eager to blame something else for the deaths in their families, a rumour was spread that the sickness was caused by the theft of the tokens, and threats were made against the dragon.

We, the People of the Caves had lost our home, for Faltryn now used them. So we built our fortress high in the cliffs above his home. It was written, and this is the prophecy: When they return who wear the tokens, the tribes will gather and the land will become whole again."

Wind Runner had been lost in the story told by Starshine, but as it ended, she placed her beaker on the table. "You wear tokens and you come from The Green Valley. This must be the beginning."

17

Kirym Speaks

"You were expecting us, Wind Runner. How did you know we were coming?" asked Kirym.

"The dragon fears the return of the other tokens, for he knows he will lose what he has when they return. We were told he would weep when they come near and his tears would fill a pool deep in a special cave. I visit there every full moon, following the habit of my ancestors. The pool has been dry for as long back as the stories tell, but the last full moon of the spring showed the pool to be overflowing. I knew you were close. It's strange though. The legend tells of seven stones, and many were lost. Yet I see eight of you here, and you all wear them. Many are green and blue. Have the tokens you hold broken? Or is this what the story meant when it said they were mere shadows of what they had been?"

There was a long silence. They waited for me to answer, for no one else could. The silence lengthened as I tried

Kirym Speaks

to understand the implications of the myth just told me. Eventually I put a few thoughts aside as I had to answer.

"In our settlement," I said, "many wear tokens. We've worn them for as far back as our history relates. There are many colours; indeed, all the colours of the rainbow. The colours tell of alliances, among other things."

"The twins," I indicated Mekrar and Mekroe, "are birth family. My blue token originally matched theirs, but knowledge and circumstances have changed it." I pointed to Teema and Arbreu. "We are family through choice and the decision of the cave that gave us the tokens. Tokens guide us, although always we make our own decisions, for we're responsible for what we do." I pulled my pocket to me and drew out a wrapped bundle. "This guided us to you." I opened it, revealing the orange token.

There was an awed silence. Starshine leaned forward and stroked the stone, gasping as it glowed to her touch. I picked it up and the light flashed around the room, connecting all of the tokens.

Wind Runner sighed. "So this is what a token looks like. It's beyond anything I dreamed of. If you've found the first, then the prophesies are coming true. The dragon's cave hides a secret, but no one can enter to find out what it is. We've tried. He roars, and his icy breath drives us all away. What's the secret, Kirym?"

"What did you see in his cave when you went in?" I asked, avoiding Wind Runner's question.

"I didn't get far. I too was driven out by Faltryn. That cave is a fearsome place."

I frowned. "I don't understand. You said you saw his tears."

"There are two caves. The cave Faltryn lives in is different to the cave of tears," said Starshine. "Faltryn's tears flow from where he lives. No one has entered far enough into

The Fortress of Faltryn

his dwelling to even see him, although many have tried. I wonder if one needs to wear or carry a token to enter."

"The cave of tears is different, and much closer to us here," said Wind Runner. "Every woman in the family must know how to check the well for tears, and most go once or twice in their life time. Few wish to go each full moon, although some of us are born to it.

I went as a child and continued supporting my great-grandmamma. Starshine supports me, being my great-granddaughter. But only a few will do it constantly, for much is unknown and strange things have happened near the well.

We hear Faltryn calling, he roars and rages. I've long felt it meant something, but thought we needed someone with more understanding. A great deal is unknown, and this is what Storm fears.

Our system here is matriarchal and nothing can change that. If something happens to me, Starshine becomes the matriarch, and indeed, as long as a woman exists in this world, our system will remain this way. It is set in our laws. You have a token, and now Storm must accept that you're here to help."

18

Kirym Speaks

"Kirym, wake up," Mekrar whispered in my ear. "Starshine wants to talk to you."

It was dark outside, but already morning. The moon sat low in the western sky. I wrapped my rug around my shoulders and slipped through the door. Oak slept in a corner, wrapped in rugs, his knife on the floor beside him. Teema and Cloud sipped hot drinks, cloaked and alert. Starshine was also cloaked, holding a hooded lamp.

"I'm going to the cave of tears. I thought you may like to join me."

"I'll get dressed."

She shook her head. "I've borrowed something for you. This way, you won't waken the others."

"I'll need my cloak though." I returned to the room. On an impulse, I grabbed two of the large tokens from the table and slipped them into a pocket under my cloak.

Starshine had clothes laid out for me in her room. They

were a simplified version of those I'd worn the previous evening. These were made of the same fibre as before, but a little thicker. There was none of the embroidery or jewels on these garments, and the sleeves were narrow and sensible for every-day use. It was a matter of moments before I was ready.

Starshine took me through large rooms and along passages. Then she turned into a long passage that became more tunnel-like the further we went. She lit an extra lamp from some sitting on a shelf, and handed it to me.

"This is part of the original cave system. Although anyone can visit here, generally few people use these tunnels."

"I thought you only went to the cave on the night of the full moon."

"We always go then, but we can go anytime. A lot of the women choose to go during the day. They feel it's safer, that Faltryn will be asleep then, but I've never felt in any danger from him even when he roars. Occasionally many moons will pass and he's quiet, but eventually he gets restless. Then only Wind Runner and I visit."

The tunnel wound steadily down, opening sometimes to wider spaces. There were chests stacked in some of these areas, filled shelves in others.

"Storage," explained Starshine. "We keep excess crops here, it's better to keep them out of sight, so they aren't relied on. In here they have a protection of sorts, and the cold helps preserve many things."

All around I could hear strange noises; they were not threatening — in fact, they seemed almost friendly. Something rustled, as if someone or something was moving along with us. Occasionally, a cool breeze hit me. On one occasion, it was quite icy, and I pulled my cloak tight around me.

"That's Faltryn," said Starshine. "These are the wisps of

Kirym Speaks

his breath. His cave is much colder and there he roars in anger when anyone ventures close."

I heard the water long before I saw it. It gurgled and splashed, warbled and laughed, sounding almost like a conversation. Starshine was less at ease now.

She lifted her lamp high as we entered the cave. There was the pool in the centre, with a huge stalactite suspended above. The water gurgled up from the ground, similar to the fountainhead we had discovered at the end of the river on the ridge. As we came close, it lowered and then welled up again, quite pulse-like.

Starshine sat the lamp on a large ornate shelf on the wall. "As Faltryn sobs, his tears rise and fall. He's cried a lot of tears. I wonder what will stop his sorrow. It seems he must lose the token he stole. Will that make him unhappier, or will he then become angrier?"

"Is he crying because he wants the tokens, or because he knows stealing them caused great sorrow?" I asked.

"I don't know," she said softly. "I never thought of that. I've always assumed he wanted them all and would do anything to get the rest."

I walked around the pool. I was surprised how small it was, minute compared to the fountainhead, although too wide to step across. The light from the lanterns reflected on the surface of the water. I placed my light on another shelf on the far side of the pool, with the orange token in front of it. I continued back to Starshine, and removed the blue token from my pocket.

"Oh," she breathed, her eyes wide. "You have the water token." She fell silent as I placed it in front of the lamp. The glow from the flames shone through the two stones, casting a purple glow onto the walls of the cave.

It started subtly: a slight trill in the air that got louder and louder. Then the tokens sang. I'd never heard them make

97

this sound before, and I wondered what would happen if they were all together in here.

The sound slowly reduced; just before it disappeared, the water gave a great surge, almost as if something swam through the bottom of the pool. Water spilled across the floor and a vortex of icy air whirled around the cave. The far lantern spluttered and went out, leaving only one dimly illuminating the pool.

I picked up the tokens, wrapped them, and placed them safely in my pocket while Starshine collected the lanterns.

Breakfast was being served when I arrived back at our rooms. Only Mekrar and Teema knew I had gone off with Starshine and neither of them asked questions in front of the others, although I knew they wanted to know what had happened.

Before we finished eating, Wind Runner burst through the door without knocking. "Two tokens?" She was astonished.

"Five actually."

She sank down, stunned. "After all this time it's going to happen. All we have to do is …"

"Kirym!" Tarjin grasped my shoulder, his voice tense. "Kirym, Papa. He's close."

I looked up and our tokens connected. Starshine and Wind Runner gasped.

"Two — three days away." I closed my eyes and thought of Bokum, Findlow and Lyndym. The connection was tenuous, disturbed. I beckoned Tarjin, "What's Jinda thinking?" I clicked his token.

Jinda's thoughts were all over the place. She carried tokens — Findlow's, Bokum's and Lyndym's as well as her own —

Kirym Speaks

and was finding it a heavy load. Her fear of Danth was overpowering. I didn't think she was even aware of Tarjin.

"How did this happen?" I whispered.

I picked up the green token and beckoned Teema and Arbreu to me. We clicked our tokens to the large stone.

There was a flash of light and I looked into Bokum's eyes.

Jinda returned soon after you left, he told me. *She was battered, bruised and starving. She told us that Danth had beaten her and left her when she couldn't keep up. With me on guard, Findlow tended her. Lyndym went to search for extra herbs. Danth grabbed her. He knocked her out and took her token, holding his knife to her throat. Findlow and I had no choice. We handed over our tokens and weapons and then we followed the stream.* Bokum's eyes slid away, and I stared into darkness. He was unconscious.

It was disturbing, but we were forewarned. I explained to Wind Runner the nature of the man approaching, and what she could expect.

"It's very simple. He'll be trespassing on our land. We can deal with him." She called Oak to her and explained what she wanted him to do. 'A wee hunting party', she called it.

Wind Runner showed us the fortress her family had built over the generations. It was massive. Made of stone blocks and built over seven massive levels, they had cleverly incorporated natural ledges and caves to minimise the work. Further away were terraced gardens with a watering system. Water was piped from the river to a large pool on one of the ledges. From there it went to the gardens, laundry, kitchens, and every level of the fortress. The tunnel system to the Cave of Tears wasn't mentioned, nor was Faltryn's cave, but we saw everything else including an old map of the known land.

It confirmed we lived in what Wind Runner called The Green Valley, but the map didn't go as far as the shore of the bay, and it didn't show the canyon or the fountainhead. Maps had always intrigued me, and I decided to come back later and study the lands around The Green Valley and Faltryn's Fortress.

We were watched by Storm, although he kept his distance. If we separated, others watched, but he never let me out of his sight. I wondered why he had such an interest in me if he considered me so insignificant. Perhaps he had rethought his prejudice.

Others though were eager to meet us and show us the areas they cared for. Everyone talked enthusiastically about the night's planned celebration.

We were constantly surrounded by children who wanted to show us what they could do, question and touch us. Sundas' immense size scared them until they realised he was a gentle softie. Within a short time, they were climbing all over him, eager to include him in their games.

Through the day, I was distracted with thoughts of Bokum, Lyndym and Findlow. I knew Zeprah must be worried, and I asked Mekrar and Mekroe to send a message to Papa saying all was in hand.

Sundas was very unsettled, although he wasn't sure why. His connection to Findlow was strong, but he'd not worn his token long enough to know how to read and control it. I spent some time with him in the afternoon to help him understand what was happening. He was more settled after that. Although very angry, he realised Wind Runner and her people had to handle the situation.

As I walked to our rooms in the afternoon to get changed for the celebration, I felt depressed again about the state of

Kirym Speaks

my clothes. I knew my dress looked anything but festive, despite being the best, and at the moment, all I owned.

When I had arrived back from the cave in the morning, Mekrar told me all of our clothes had been taken for cleaning, and I was not allowed to retrieve mine to wash and mend them myself.

"It'll take more than mending to make them look respectable," she said, "so you may as well resign yourself to just looking fresh."

Now everything waited on a seat, the cleanest they'd been since we left the canyon. The ribbons on the bodice of my dress had been replaced and some of the more worn areas were neatly darned. Three areas that had obviously given up and become holes were skilfully patched. The ragged hem had been cut off and a wide strip of material added to neaten it and provide needed length. The sleeves had been carefully removed, they had been too worn to even patch.

My petticoats were also clean and mended. The undershift was worn, but at least now it was spotless and the places where I'd mended it would be hidden by my patched petticoats and dress. The dress looked so much better than before, and the work was done with more expertise than I possessed. However, it still didn't look great and I was despondent about the impression it would give at the feast that night.

I was pleased to get it back though. Wearing other people's clothes made it hard to carry my herbs and the tokens, and I was unhappy giving the responsibility to Mekrar or Bildon. Through the day, I had carried them in my pocket, but I was unable to attach it without it looking strange. It was awkward not having my hands free to do things, and I hated leaving the pocket lying about while I joined in with the activities we were shown.

I dressed and began to look through our spare clothes

The Fortress of Faltryn

for a wrap of some kind. I knew I would be cold with no sleeves. The weather here was colder than I had expected, particularly at night. We owned nothing I could use, and Tarjin's cloak would look even stranger. Even though it had been shortened for me, it was far too big across the shoulders, and tended to slip off unless it was held tight. I was contemplating cutting a strip off one of our rugs when Starshine came in.

"We thought this may help you," she said, handing me some folded material.

It was a sleeved tabard, made to go with my dress. I was overwhelmed at the thought that had gone into it. The neckline was cut low, so the ribbons and beads on my bodice showed to their best. The sides were split to the bodice so I could carry my tokens as usual, and it covered the ragged appearance of my clothes. Starshine was reluctant to accept my thanks, explaining that many people had helped to make it including Mekrar and Bildon, whose idea it had been.

Late in the afternoon, Oak returned. Most of the men who had gone with him had arrived back earlier with a large pig for the celebration. This was already spitted over a huge fire pit in the big hall.

Wind Runner brought Oak over to me when he arrived back.

"Danth and his party are camped north of the standing stone at the mouth of the river canyon," he said.

He looked tired, and considering he had gone almost to the edge of the open plain and back, that was understandable.

I was surprised at how quickly he recovered, going on to have an active part in the evening's entertainment.

19

Kirym Speaks

The celebration was fantastic. Mekroe brought his pipe and Tarjin his drum and they eagerly joined the band, exchanging tunes and rhythms. The people of the fortress had different instruments and Mekroe was soon experimenting with them, to the obvious enjoyment of many young girls who flocked around him.

Everyone had fun, and even Storm seemed happy and relaxed. I enjoyed the evening, although I was slightly distracted by the closeness of my friends.

The evening ended and I was returning to our rooms when I realised I had left my herb pouch on a table in the big hall. I had taken the large pouch with me on impulse, and I had used it a number of times through the evening. One of the boys cut his hand showing off his knife skills. A cook spilt hot gravy on his foot, and there were a few bruises and a black eye when the dancing got a bit boisterous.

I collected the pouch and was leaving the hall when Storm

called to me.

"Wind Runner said you had something to tell me."

I looked at him speculatively. I didn't trust him. Although I knew he'd have to know about the tokens sooner or later, I thought Wind Runner would have talked to me before telling anyone else about them, even one of her close family members.

I smiled sweetly and inclined my head. "So soon? Very well, come with me," and I started back towards our rooms. As I walked, I sent an urgent message to Teema to get Wind Runner or Starshine to our rooms quickly.

I felt his acknowledgment.

To give them time to organise that, I questioned Storm about the hangings that covered the walls. Some were abstract mixes of shapes and colours, but others showed detailed pictures of people and places. He had excellent knowledge and for the first time, I enjoyed being in his company. I could see some of the intelligence and humour so obvious in Wind Runner.

Everyone looked up as we entered. The brazier glowed and the room looked cosy. I couldn't see Wind Runner or Starshine, but the seats had been reorganised in intimate groups and a number of the chairs faced away, the occupants, if any, hidden.

Teema ushered Storm and me to a small group of seats around a low table as Mekrar poured drinks for us.

"Ahhh, I'd hoped we could talk privately," said Storm.

"Nothing is hidden between us and our knowledge is shared. Now, what did Wind Runner tell you?"

"Oh!" He appeared suddenly flustered. "She said you'd tell me everything."

I nodded, trying to figure the best way to handle him. "May I ask what you'd do if the dragon flew again?"

"That'll only happen if there is a dragon," he said. "No

Kirym Speaks

one's ever seen it. You've obviously heard the stories. Well that's what they are. Just stories."

"You've never seen the Green Valley, and yet you believe a great warrior will come from there. Perhaps some things need to be believed in."

"Are you saying you believe in it?" He seemed incredulous.

"I've not seen anything to convince me he's not there. Most myths have a base in truth, although I must admit it's sometimes a very tenuous thread."

"Like tokens? It'll need more than a story to convince me they exist." Storm sat back in his seat, trying to appear relaxed.

I sat opposite him and smiled. The scene was set.

"The people of the Green Valley grew lonely, and in three boats, they went on a great adventure."

"This is part of Wind Runner's dragon story, and none of it's new to me," Storm snorted. "I didn't believe it from her and I'm not about to accept it just because you restate it. The sea is too vast and wild to be crossed."

I continued as if he hadn't spoken. "After hundreds of seasons, two of the boats returned. They came to the great arch that encloses the bay, the doors opened and they again found The Green Valley, settling there to live as their ancestors had."

"In crossing the sea, they had help," said Teema, distracting Storm's attention. When he looked back, the blue token sat on the table.

His eyes widened. "This is a trick," he said. He flicked his fingers. "So you have a pretty coloured stone. It proves nothing."

"Of course, nothing is ever proved to those who wish never to believe."

Storm looked around, shocked when he heard Wind

The Fortress of Faltryn

Runner's voice. "How'd she get in here?"

"I invited her," I said.

Seats were rearranged, everyone except Sundas and Mekroe, who were sharing guard duty, now joining us.

"Storm that is our family token. This token led us to you." I added the orange token to the table.

He looked uncertain as they both glowed and connected.

"We're here to be friends, Storm. Nothing more, although if we can help with your prophecy then so much the better. If the prophecy is nothing but a story to entertain children then there's no need for any antagonism between our families."

He looked at the tokens. "You really believe them, Wind Runner?"

She nodded.

The silence lengthened. Storm took a deep breath, stood up and bowed theatrically in my direction. "When I am wrong, I'll admit it, although it does take me time to get there. What now?"

I added the green token to the table followed by the yellow.

Storm sat down again. "So you've had these all this time. Why didn't you show them on the first night?"

"Perhaps," I said, smiling at him, "I trusted you no more than you trusted me."

He threw back his head and roared with laughter. "You're a canny one, to be sure." He relaxed visibly. "Well, I'll have to go over all of the prophesies with a different mind-set."

"Now, Storm," interrupted Wind Runner. "There's a small problem heading our way."

We explained about Danth, and Storm grasped the situation quickly. "Well, it's probably best not to let him know you're here. Let's invite him to visit and see what happens. Keep it nice and friendly. But I'll not have him mistreating people

Kirym Speaks

in my land. How can I tell which one is him?"

"He's the bully," said Tarjin bitterly.

I rubbed Tarjin's arm. "He'll wear a token, the others may be restrained somehow. Beware though, he's devious."

"What about the woman?"

"I'm not sure. He has a hold over her. She is loyal to him, possibly because she fears being without him. As he gets worse, and he will, she may be willing to accept help."

Storm nodded. "How can we be sure he'll come this way?"

Starshine called Oak in from the hall.

"I deepened the tracks made by the frame Teema hauled with him. Only an idiot would fail to see them," he said.

Storm nodded again and stood. Before he left, he leaned over the table and touched the orange token. It lit up. He jumped and snatched his hand away, laughed and strode through the door.

20

Arbreu

Arbreu was uncomfortable. The clothes he wore fitted well, but they were markedly different to those he was used to. A breechcloth, leggings and boots were the basics of the men's hunting clothes, accompanied by a short, hooded cape covering head and shoulders. Wearing this outfit, with a band tied around his forehead and his token in his pack, he could join Storm on this trip.

Storm was adamant he keep hidden and not let Danth know he was in the group.

Kirym and Storm both forbade Teema joining them. Kirym pointed out that his token contact with Bokum was such that one or both of them may inadvertently give his presence away. Also, his anger at what was happening was so obvious — Danth would possibly feel it and be wary.

Not that Arbreu wasn't as angry or upset, but Danth had never looked on him as part of the family, considering him beneath contempt and therefore invisible.

Arbreu

All except Teema and Kirym had been sent off on other explorations, to keep them occupied until Storm made a decision about Danth and his prisoners. Arbreu was with Storm in case he needed information in a hurry.

They left late in the morning, as Storm laughingly said: "They're coming to us so we'll not exert too much energy travelling south. We'll only have to turn around and walk all the way back."

Oak and his half-brother Ash left while it was still dark to see that Danth had indeed continued to follow the river. They returned early in the afternoon to say he had taken their bait and was following the tracks along the river valley. All three captives were tied tightly, none wore boots and their clothing was minimal.

"They're travelling so slowly, I doubt they'll make it this far by tonight," said Ash. "I think even an extra day won't be enough for them to get anywhere near the fortress."

"We could intercept them sooner," said Oak. "But do we do that immediately, or leave it until tomorrow?"

Storm frowned as he thought about it. "Tomorrow, I think," he said. "Early in the afternoon."

Arbreu was horrified. "Why wait that long?" he asked. "Surely we need to get them away as soon as possible."

He saw the sense when Storm explained his tactics. "Mainly, I don't want us to spend a night out here with Danth and his prisoners. It'll make it too difficult to care for them and keep him at arm's length without his realising it may be a set up," he said.

The time wasn't wasted though. Storm showed Arbreu how they hunted the huge fish that swam through the waters below the cliffs.

"There's always a deep channel running from high in the mountains down to the great lake in The Green Valley. Other channels get low or dry up, but one always remains."

The Fortress of Faltryn

The work of beaching the fish was tremendous. Ten men manned the net, and numerous others helped with gaffs and ropes.

"We take one every season or two," said Storm. "The meat is a welcome change from our usual game and parts of it are prized by the wise women. The skins are valuable also."

Once they had the fish on land, it was gutted, skinned and chopped into sections. The work was done quickly and the resultant meal was wonderful. Arbreu noted that except for a small amount of the meat kept for a meal in the morning, the rest of the beast was returned to the fortress.

The night was spent on three large ledges above the valley floor. Storm confirmed Kirym's comment about flash floods. "None are expected until autumn, but it's best to be careful." He assured Arbreu that guards placed near Danth's group guaranteed Lyndym, Findlow and Bokum's safety in the event of a flood, even if doing so warned Danth.

Over a blazing fire they told tales of other creatures they'd found in their river, the nearby hills and surrounding lands.

"Why didn't you settle in The Green Valley?" Arbreu asked.

"As Wind Runner will tell you," said Storm, "one cannot take what one doesn't own. The land belonged to you and we always believed you'd return to claim it. Every now and then, we'd talk of going to see what was happening down there. We never made it, and there were many reasons why we always returned here, not the least being Wind Runner and her great grandmamma. Two formidable old ladies you crossed at your peril."

There was general laughter at this, but an underlying agreement.

The morning start was relaxed, although Storm and Oak both checked that Arbreu's disguise was secure. He was placed in the centre of the group of men, well surrounded and hidden if need be.

It was getting late when Danth arrived. Storm had it well organised. Danth came around a sharp bluff and found his way blocked by a line of men. He stopped, conferring with Jinda, and as he hesitated, more men filtered down the cliff and in behind him, cutting off his escape. With no other choice, he walked slowly forward.

He held Lyndym close. She was gagged, a rope was tied tightly around her neck, and her hands were fastened securely in front of her. She wore only her shift, and her feet and legs were bruised.

Findlow and Bokum wore only trousers. They too were gagged, their hands tied behind their backs; Arbreu could see the thin ropes cutting into their arms. Bokum hauled a frame, piled high with equipment, the rope tied tightly around his throat. With every step, he had to pause to fight for breath. His face was grey and his lips were blue. He looked terrible.

It was harder to tell Findlow's condition. His dark skin hid most of his wounds, although he left bloody footsteps as he walked.

Arbreu felt a wave of anger wash over him. These were his friends and he felt impotent. He must have started involuntarily, because Blacknight grasped his arm.

"Steady, lad," he whispered. "We'll have 'em away soon."

Storm hissed through his teeth as he stepped forward.

"You venture deep into my land, Stranger."

"Oh," grunted Danth. "We didn't know it was yours. We didn't mean no harm. We'll leave."

He half turned, yanking on the rope around Lyndym's neck

The Fortress of Faltryn

as he went. She stumbled over a rock, falling to her knees.

"We're stopping for a meal," said Storm. "You'll join us."

It wasn't an invitation.

Storm's men crowded forward, giving Danth no choice. Four men picked up the frame Bokum was hauling, relieving the pressure on his neck.

"Why are these people tied up?" asked Storm.

"They attacked us a few days ago. I wasn't prepared to let them do it again."

"What happened to their footwear?"

Danth immediately got angry. "Is this any of your damn business? If you're not happy with us being here, we'll leave."

"I only asked about footwear. You've a right to defend yourself and if they were stupid enough to attack you, well ..."

"Oh," said Danth, somewhat deflated. "Well, they didn't have any. That might ha' been why they attacked us."

"Oh?"

"Well, we have a few supplies," he said, indicating the frame. "They seemed to have nothing."

Storm nodded.

The small party was surrounded and Danth and Jinda found themselves relieved of their packs and jostled away from their captives.

Danth was shrewd though. He pulled Jinda close and quickly retrieved her pack. "She needs this, it's her personal stuff." He thrust the large pack back into her arms.

Oak's voice whispered into Arbreu's ear. "What'll be in the pack?"

"Most of the personal stuff we left with Bokum, I imagine. Four tokens, their boots and clothes. It's big enough for that and more. The rest of their gear will be on the frame."

Oak nodded. "We'll do what we can for your friends. Just

Arbreu

relax. Storm has something in mind. He's angry. He can't abide cruelty." He paused. "Four tokens, three people. Who owns the fourth?"

"Bokum has two, a family token and another that connects him to Kirym, Teema and me."

Water was heated and drinks were handed out. Ash took a beaker over to Bokum and removed his gag, but the tightness of the rope around his neck made it impossible for him to drink. Ash started to cut it off.

Danth's hand was a blur as he flicked the knife from Ash's grasp. "They're my prisoners," he roared. "I'll handle them."

It was the wrong move. He suddenly faced a sea of knives, spears and arrows.

Storm, sitting opposite him, leaned forward. "Everyone is entitled to breathe, eat and drink and you're close to denying all three to these people. I care not what they've done, but on my land, this won't happen."

Danth went red. "You don't know what they've done," he yelled. "They — they — they stole my son. Their leader has him. We haven't seen him for over a moon an' then they came back and tried to take everything else we had."

Storm stiffened. "That's serious. Would they hurt the child?"

Danth shrugged.

"If this is true," said Storm, "they'll pay a high price. But slowly strangling them and depriving them of food and water isn't the way, and it won't help you get your son back. Are you sure it was these people? Your son's obviously not with them."

"Their friends have him. Their leader has wanted my son since he was born. They've hounded us since then."

"Aye, well," said Storm, "let's get to where we can sort this out. Your prisoners can't escape, but I'll not have them mistreated. They can't travel at a speed I'm happy with, so they'll get help — as will you," he added.

The ropes and gags were carefully cut off the prisoners; they were offered drinks, which they thankfully accepted. Only Findlow was able to eat.

They returned to the fortress, Lyndym, Findlow and Bokum on stretchers. Oak walked beside Arbreu near the back of the group. "Where's their son, do you know?"

Arbreu looked at him, amused. "At Faltryn." He laughed quietly at Oak's expression. "Ah, you met him at the feast. Tarjin. Mekroe's mate."

Oak stopped walking. "That great noisy lump with the drum?" Arbreu nodded. Oak laughed quietly. "Oh dear, they're playing with fire. Lying to Storm? He's well named."

Danth's eyes opened wide when he saw the fortress. Even Arbreu was surprised. The walls and ledges were bristling with armed warriors, their weapons trained on the wide path below. The bright sunset stained the walls red. It was a spectacular show.

Storm was at Arbreu's shoulder. "Not much point having it if you don't show it off. Good, yes?"

He strode off laughing and, taking Danth by the elbow, propelled him along the lengthy zigzag path up the cliff.

Arbreu changed clothes. No longer a hunter, he joined the guards on a raised dais at the top of the hall. Again he was there to advise Storm and Wind Runner. Oak stood to his right while Storm lounged just to his left, also hidden, but watching carefully.

There were three large carved seats just in front of Arbreu. The biggest, sumptuously rugged and cushioned, sat in the centre. Between the seats were small tables holding food and drink.

Danth and Jinda were shown into the hall and left to themselves — a solitary guard ensuring they remained isolated. Seats had been placed in groups, and rugs and cushions were scattered around the floor of the great hall. The room slowly filled up.

Danth demanded to speak to Storm and was clearly annoyed by his inability to influence anyone. Jinda scuttled behind him as he swaggered around looking at the furnishings and tableware, nodding approval at the apparent wealth. He ignored all of the people, pushing rudely past without apology if they were in his way.

The buzz of conversation filled the room, but everyone was aware when Wind Runner entered from a side door. She looked ancient and very frail.

Arbreu was amused at how she could use her age and size to create an illusion. Obviously she was known for it, as no one commented or appeared concerned.

When Jinda saw Wind Runner, she visibly jumped — murmuring and gesturing to Danth. She looked terrified.

Danth ignored Wind Runner, even when she took the centre seat on the dais in front of him. He wandered around the hall, helping himself to whatever food caught his fancy and discarding what he didn't like. Jinda followed him closely, her pack clutched in her arms.

After walking twice around the hall, he dragged a chair from a display of ancient seats and placed it in front of Wind Runner.

He sat, filled a goblet and drank deeply.

"I want my prisoners," he demanded loudly, "and I want them now! You have no right to take them away."

The hall was suddenly quiet.

"Dead prisoners go nowhere," Wind Runner said.

"Listen, you old hag! Get your leader now or give me my prisoners and let me get out of here."

There was a shocked intake of breath from around the room, but Wind Runner smiled politely. "Tell me about your travels. Your prisoners, where did they come from?"

Danth snorted. "How would I know?" He shook his head. "I didn't ask them. They never came close enough. I wouldn't even recognise them — except my son. I'd know them because of him."

"They followed you?"

He nodded. He was getting restless.

"How long were they following you?"

He filled the goblet again and drank, ignoring the question.

"With no footwear or clothes?" Wind Runner prompted.

"They attacked at night. I didn't get a good look."

"You must be devastated, losing your son." She motioned for his goblet to be filled again. "I can't imagine how hard that would be. How old is he?"

Danth grabbed his goblet and brought it to his lips, although he now didn't appear to actually swallow. Jinda hadn't touched hers. Another jug was placed on the table.

Danth abruptly stood and hauled Jinda to her feet, pushing her roughly towards the door.

Storm stepped up behind Wind Runner. "You're leaving? Surely not. We haven't feasted together."

"Jinda's not happy. Um — large crowds, doesn't like them. She wants to go."

"Oh, I had no idea. How thoughtless, I didn't intend to make her uncomfortable." Storm gestured to a group of people near Jinda and they quietly left the hall.

"Well, we'll go anyway," said Danth. "Gotta find my son."

Storm nodded. "I understand the urgency, but I can't let

Arbreu

you leave." He paused dramatically. "Not now, anyway."

Startled, Darth began objecting. Storm waved him to silence. "Things have disappeared in the river valley at night. For your safety, you must stay the night."

Danth looked sceptical and then wary, as Storm stepped off the dais and guided him to a dim alcove on the far wall. He pulled aside the curtain covering it and revealed an enormous jaw. Stripped of meat, the jagged teeth glowed greenly in the dim light.

Danth recoiled in horror.

Storm dropped the curtain back and with his arm around Danth's shoulder, he drew him back to the table. "We find their bones along the river bank. It scares the children so we keep it covered, but this is why we are so diligent in guarding our fortress. They must prowl the river banks. As you saw by the teeth, it could devour any one of us without a second thought." He handed Danth the goblet. "We'd be terrible hosts if we allowed you to be consumed so soon after you've eaten." He raised his goblet high. "To the safety of friends," he said. "Now, let us eat."

Storm took a platter of food to Wind Runner, taking the seat beside her.

"What's your son's name?" Wind Runner asked.

"We called him Tarjin."

"The prisoners say they haven't seen a baby," Storm said quietly. "They haven't got one, obviously, but they swear no little one travelled with them."

"Well, they would, wouldn't they?" Danth looked wary. Jinda whispered to him and he smiled. "Ask the big one. Get him to swear on the life of his wife that he hasn't seen a babe in the last season. He won't because he can't."

"He told you about his wife?" Storm sounded surprised.

"Oh ah, I um, I heard them talking. They didn't know I was listening," Danth blustered.

The Fortress of Faltryn

"How long have they been harassing you?"

"A long time, many seasons. Then they grabbed my boy, but that was recent, before last full moon. Brazen! I only looked away for a moment. I chased them, but they got away."

"You've followed them for a long time then. Why come here?"

"We followed tracks. Well, I thought they were theirs."

Storm nodded. "Possible," he said. "Possible." He paused. "They may have been eaten of course, if they came this way, that is. We've seen no babies except our own. Of course if they came through the night — well, things happen in the dark."

Mid-bite, Danth tried to look crestfallen.

"Were they all bootless?"

With his mouth full, Danth nodded.

"And yet, they outran you?"

He spluttered, coughed and took a gulp from the goblet. "There were lots of them, twenty or thirty. I was afraid to approach too close. Then they split up and some circled back towards our camp. I was worried they'd get our stores or threaten Jinda, so I trapped these ones. I planned to trade them for my son."

"You must carry things of great value for them to keep attacking you," Wind Runner interjected.

"No, no, we … um … we collect things we find, but little of value. Our possessions are worn. It was our son they wanted most."

Wind Runner nodded. "And having got him, they attacked you again?" She paused, but got no response. "Well, perhaps we can help you with more supplies. That may make an exchange more likely — if you find them, that is. We can help with repairing and washing your clothes."

Danth shook his head vehemently. "No, no. Jinda does

Arbreu

that. Proud woman, but as I said, there's not much."

"Not much was awfully heavy," Oak said quietly out of the gloom behind Wind Runner. "I helped carry the pack frame being hauled by your prisoner. It was so heavy I couldn't carry it by myself. For someone trying to catch up with others, you managed to travel very slowly."

Danth looked flustered. "Well, well ..." He swallowed, his eyes darting around the room. "Yeah, but I figured they'd come back for their friends."

"Where do you come from?" Wind Runner inquired.

"Far away. We travelled a long way, many seasons."

"Where from originally?" said Storm.

"Somewhere. Um. East. We came from the east."

"And the rest of your people? Where are they?"

"Nah, nah, there's just us. Me an' Jinda." He paused. "And our boy."

"The stones you wear. What are they?" Wind Runner asked.

Danth ignored her. She asked again, louder. "Oh," Danth said. "Jinda found 'em. We just like them."

Arbreu felt his anger rising again. He valued his token, and couldn't understand anyone who wouldn't have the same feeling. Denying a gift from the cave seemed so wrong.

"Hmmm," said Wind Runner. "There was an old story I heard as a child. It spoke of people who wore jewels like that. The stones were supposed to have great power. Do they? Perhaps it was just a myth."

"Um, yeah, there are stories. That may ha' been where we got the idea," said Danth.

"There was a connection to some wealthy land near a great ocean to the south. We really should go and visit."

There was a long pause. "Well," said Danth, "um — we — um. I heard there was death and disease down there. Everyone who goes there dies. It's a bad place."

119

Wind Runner frowned. "But if they died, how did the news return?"

Danth went pale. "I — um — I ..."

Storm patted her hand. "I heard you can't get there anyway. Bad land between here and there."

"Yeah, yeah, that might ha' been it," said Danth, looking relieved. "All sorts of stories, but north or east is better."

"So now you've eaten," said Wind Runner, "let's talk about these prisoners. The girl says no baby travelled with you. She says you attacked them in their camp and threatened to kill her to get the men to cooperate. She said you stole everything they carried."

"She's lying," said Danth bluntly.

"Is there anything else you wish to tell us?" Storm asked. There was a long silence. "In that case we'll hear their side."

"They'll have hatched up something. I bet they're working on it right now."

"I've made a point of keeping them apart. They've not had the chance to talk together since they came into our care," said Storm.

Danth wasn't happy, but there was little he could do.

21

Arbreu

Bokum was brought in first. His feet were bandaged, and he had trouble walking. The loose tunic he wore didn't hide the dressings or the bruises beneath. His neck was visible, raw and bruised above and below the bandages. He was questioned by Storm, with an occasional interjection by Wind Runner.

Danth kept silent, his eyes averted. Jinda whimpered continuously, clutching her pack and rocking to and fro.

Bokum's answers came at a whisper, so damaged was his throat. Occasionally he resorted to writing the answers, his hand bruised and scabbed, but unbandaged. Twig sat beside him as his voice.

Findlow and Lyndym followed, and were each questioned.

Wind Runner frowned as she listened. Finally, she shook her head. "I'm appalled at the inhumanity here. I'm shocked that one human could visit this onto another."

"They're just animals and anyway, they have my son," Danth interjected.

The Fortress of Faltryn

"She," Storm thundered, pointing to Lyndym, "is someone's daughter! A child!" He motioned to the guards. "We'll look at the frame now."

Danth objected loudly. "That stuff's personal. You've no right to touch it."

Storm rose, his face black with anger. "We have every right," he roared, and Danth sank back in his seat. "You're on our land. You've mistreated people beyond what is even thinkable, and there's a challenge over ownership of some items. These people ..." he indicated Findlow, Bokum and Lyndym, "tell me they had boots, clothing and other personal possessions and that even the frame is theirs. So we will check."

The frame was carried over from where it had been lying against the wall. Cloud cut the ropes tying it closed. On top were clothes, cooking gear, food, cloaks and rugs. Under the rugs were a number of large rocks. Cloud strained to pick one up. "Damned heavy," he said.

The hall went silent. Storm looked unimpressed.

"I was protecting my family," yelled Danth, jumping to his feet. "They kept threatening us. I wanted them tired so we'd be safe at night. Anyway, there's nothing to prove that stuff is theirs."

Wind Runner nodded. "There's nothing to indicate ownership of these items, but there's nothing there for a little one either. When I travelled with my children ..."

"They took all that when they raided us."

Wind Runner sighed. "Jinda, what's in your pack?"

Jinda whimpered, her eyes darting wildly as she rocked.

"Leave her alone," snarled Danth. "She's shattered. Her son's been abducted. She's been attacked by them and now imprisoned by you. All she has are her few private things."

"Nevertheless, she will open her pack."

Cloud gently took hold of the pack, but Jinda clung desperately to it, looking frantically at Danth. He ignored

Arbreu

her and slowly she let it slip away.

Cloud emptied the items onto the floor. Most obvious were three pairs of boots and a pile of clothes. He picked up some blue material and shook it out. The dress was obviously far too small to be Jinda's.

Danth shoved her violently. "You scheming witch!" he screamed. "You lied to me. How could you?"

"Stop that!"

Storm was on his feet and three guards moved between Jinda and Danth. One of the healers helped Jinda off the floor, into a chair and sat with her.

Cloud spread everything out. One small package was securely wrapped and tied. He handed it to Wind Runner, who opened it and placed four tokens on the table.

Storm picked up two sitting together in a holder. They glowed faintly. He handed them to Bokum who placed them on his forehead.

Arbreu desperately hoped Bokum wouldn't acknowledge them. Kirym, Teema and the others were close by, and wearing his token, he would know that.

His tokens brightened slightly and Bokum smiled his thanks at Storm.

Findlow and Lyndym eagerly put theirs on. Lyndym turned and clicked Findlow's token.

"What's she doing?" Oak whispered.

"Letting her Mama know they're all right," Arbreu responded.

Danth was pale. "I didn't know wh ..."

"It's a deep hole, Danth," said Storm. "Stop digging."

Danth sat down and picked up his goblet. "They have my son," he said looking smug. "Go on, ask them."

"Your son, yes," said Storm. "Perhaps you can tell me about that, but the whole truth this time."

"Nothing else matters. They have him, well their friends do.

123

The Fortress of Faltryn

Find them, you'll find my son. I was justified in everything I did."

"Really?"

"You'd do anything you had to, to get ya son back. It was necessary."

A door at the back of the hall opened and Kirym, Teema, Starshine and Tarjin slipped in. Danth wasn't aware of them, but Jinda was. She screamed Tarjin's name.

Hearing her, Danth swung around, saw where she was looking and followed her eyes. The colour drained from his face. Jinda jumped up and lunged towards Tarjin. He hugged her.

Danth ignored him, turning back to Storm. "I'll take my family and go."

"It's not quite that easy, Danth. You've broken our laws. Had the worst happened, you would have been responsible for deaths. Taking prisoners in exchange for an abducted baby is one thing, but knowing the abduction never happened, well …"

"They took my son," Danth interjected.

Storm shook his head. "I've talked to the boy. He made his own decisions and he's of an age to do that. He says he made the choice not to stay with you."

"That ill-begotten little witch who leads them ensnared him. She made him say that."

"That happens to young men," said Wind Runner, "and parents have to accept it. However, I've watched them and I don't agree in this situation."

"You're biased," Danth snorted. "You were influenced by them before you'd even heard what I had to say. Jinda and I had no chance at all."

"We looked at the evidence you placed in front of us, Danth. It helps if you don't lie, but putting that aside …"

"I can't be bothered with this nonsense. We're leaving."

Arbreu

Danth moved towards Jinda and Tarjin.

"She's not going with you, Papa," said Tarjin.

"Ya see?" he yelled. "They've poisoned him. I want my family to stay together."

"This isn't about what you want, Danth. Tarjin and Jinda have a choice."

"Listen! I make the decisions for my family, not you, not them!" Danth waved in the vague direction of Bokum, but went white as the guards lifted their weapons.

"Um, my family — well, you'd do anything to keep your family with you. I want mine together, and I don't ... well ..." He looked around suspiciously. "Didn't mean anything," he mumbled. "I was upset. I just want to leave." He moved towards Jinda, but stopped as the guards again raised their weapons.

With his arm around Jinda's shoulder, Tarjin stepped forward and addressed Wind Runner, using her titles as Supreme Leader of the Tribes of the Stone Fortress of Faltryn.

Danth went pale as he listened; he had assumed her to be an unimportant old lady.

"I've seen nineteen summers and I'm old enough to make decisions for my own life. I'd like some time for Mama to rest so I can discuss her future with her."

Wind Runner looked at Jinda. "I'll allow her time, lad, but the other decisions may not be yours to make. Right now, we all need to rest."

There was a brief moment before everybody realised what she had said, followed by a general drift out of the hall.

Storm motioned to the guards and Danth was taken away, screaming his objections.

Jinda was handed over to the healers.

125

22

Kirym Speaks

Bokum, Findlow and Lyndym had been helped to our rooms, and I finally got the chance to check their wounds. All had cuts and grazes on their legs, knees and feet, but the rope cuts on arms, wrists and throats were deeper and more concerning. However, the treatment for their wounds had been started as soon as Storm had them in his care, and they were beginning to heal. Time would be the best thing for all three. Bokum and Lyndym had damage to their necks and throats. Externally it would heal, although I wondered if Bokum would be left with a permanent scar on his neck. The internal bruising was more worrying. I checked what had been given to them for healing the wounds and removed one remedy, added two more and steeped some herbs for a throat wash.

"I meant to ask you, Storm. What are those bones you showed Danth?" I asked when he, Wind Runner and Starshine joined us. "I saw them a few days ago. They're

Kirym Speaks

clever, but they are from different creatures, aren't they."

"You're quick. Most people don't realise," said Storm. "They were collected over many seasons," he added. "We found the jaws after a massive spring flood. A while later, a few of our woodworkers played with them, cut them apart and re-joined them. This was the result. They disguised the joins with dirt and grass stains. It's better in bad light. They caused one death. Old Slab was playing with it and somehow its mouth managed to close over his arm. He died laughing. Mind you, he had seen a hundred and five winters."

"We've seen some of the teeth before," said Arbreu. "Findlow has two of the eye teeth. He told me how he killed the animal. You should ask him sometime. Those jagged triangle teeth look like they came from some massive fish we saw as we left in the boats to come here. They attacked some men in the water. They were vicious."

Kirym nodded. "Not a nice way to die. What about the long side ones?"

"No idea," said Storm. "But they're sharp. It'd be a nasty creature to meet while swimming."

A meal was brought in, soft food and broth for the invalids and a heartier repast for the rest of us. We ate and discussed the future.

"Jinda needs time," said Wind Runner. "We'll help her become less dependent on Danth. It won't be easy or quick. What will the rest of you do in the meantime?"

"Bokum, Findlow and Lyndym need time to heal also. I thought I'd visit Faltryn," I said.

"But, you're here ..." Storm's voice died. "Oh no! No! I will not allow it! I've been in that cave and it nearly killed me. Wind Runner will back me up. This is not open to discussion."

There was an extended silence.

"Will you come with us, Wind Runner?" I asked. Her

The Fortress of Faltryn

answer was drowned in the laughter from Bildon, Mekrar, Mekroe and Tarjin.

"You can't stop her, Storm. She needs to go. It's to do with the tokens." Teema patted his back. "She'll be well protected. Arbreu and I'll go too."

"When Starshine took me to see his tears, I felt his breath, Storm. I know what to expect."

Storm was quite pale. "That's a mere shadow of what you'll meet in his cave. Grown men, warriors, quail at the thought of going in there. Some have actually refused to go anywhere near that cave. What do I tell your Papa when you don't return?"

Storm was genuinely upset at the thought of us going, but I had to. "The tokens will protect us," I said, as I laid them out on the table. "All I want to do is look. I may return with information that tells me about the other tokens. It has to be done, so why wait?"

"I'll help all I can, Kirym," said Wind Runner, "but I'm now too old to enter."

"Will you take all of the tokens with you?" asked Mekrar.

I nodded and laid the rainbow token on the table.

Storm and Starshine gasped. "Oh," said Wind Runner. "You have the other half of the peace token. Yes, you must face Faltryn. Take it with you."

"I'll come too," said Mekrar.

"Me too," said Bildon, her response echoed quietly by Lyndym.

"No, Lyndym." Findlow's concern was echoed around the room.

"Papa," she whispered. "It's my job to represent our family there. If I don't, who will? My feet are fine, I don't need my voice. Kirym will care for me."

"You'll need a guide," said Starshine. "Perhaps I'd be

Kirym Speaks

allowed to join you. Great-grandmamma has told me all she has learnt over the seasons. Most people seem to have similar experiences in there. They enter as far as they dare and are then frightened off by Faltryn."

"What of the different experiences?" I asked.

"They died or went mad," said Storm bluntly.

"The tokens will warn us if there is danger. We'll be safe."

Storm was not reassured.

Wind Runner had been furthest into the cave, although even she hadn't seen Faltryn's lair. She had stayed in the cave from late-afternoon until just after dawn. I hoped we could explore for at least a day and night, and perhaps a second day also, if we were able to find somewhere safe to rest. If we hadn't found something by then, we probably wouldn't — well, not this time, anyway.

Wind Runner mentioned that many people had strange dreams if they slept in the caves, and they were often sick after spending time in there.

I prepared carefully, having questioned everyone I could. Evidently the path was straight forward and only the presence of the dragon made the trip so hard.

It mattered little if we went into the cave during the day or night, but I wanted to enter after a good night's sleep. On previous occasions, the journey started from the fortress during the morning and reaching the cave late in the afternoon, they had continued on into the cave immediately. I wondered if an earlier entry would change things. We travelled there through the day and camped nearby overnight.

We all carried firewood, food and water. Teema and Arbreu were laden with extra torches. They were heavy and smelly, but Storm said they were effective in the cave. We took a hooded lamp and two packs of oil.

The flat area in front of the cave was really too small to camp in, but Wind Runner's people refused to use the cave itself. Crowded though it was, we set up a shelter near the entrance. Just before the moon slipped below the hill opposite us, we were woken by a loud roar from deep in the cave followed by an explosion of icy air. It was eerie.

The noise woke everyone, their faces white in the firelight. Three of the guards packed up and went home.

"Faltryn knows we're here," said Wind Runner. "Are you sure you want to do this?"

I nodded as I added more wood to the fire. "He makes lots of noise, but ..."

"It's not the noise you have to be worried about, girl," Storm said harshly. "It's his breath. I felt like he'd frozen my brain. I couldn't think straight. He breathed over me as I lay on the cave floor trying to decide if I was alive enough to do anything about it. It was mind numbing. It took me ages to move, even when I realised that if I didn't, I'd die. I needed all of my energy just to crawl away," he shuddered. "Then I had to go back and get Oak, and he didn't wake up until we were almost out of the cave. We slept for two days when we got here, too sick to even walk home."

"You were young to enter the cave, Oak," I said.

Storm shook his head. "Oaken. My brother, his papa."

"It was sad really," said Oak. "He never recovered, but I spent a lot of time with him while he was sick. He talked about the cave. He wanted us to move away from here. He thought Faltryn would turn on us one day." He paused, frowning, then shook his head. "He said he wasn't expecting Faltryn to roar like that. The sound hit him between his eyes and knocked him off his feet. He recalled the sound more than anything else. He remembered nothing more until he was back here and Storm was lighting the fire. He had a sore head for days after, and dreamed of rivers of blood. He had nightmares about it for the rest of his life. He'd wake up shaking and screaming. He told me about Faltryn's fire. That was his biggest memory, the heat and the sound of the dragon's roar reverberating through him, right to his core."

"When did the two of you go into the cave, Storm?" I asked.

"Ah well, that'd be over fifteen summers ago. We were young men then. Foolish and indestructible, we thought. There's many like us. Some, like Oaken, are no longer with us."

The cold grey dawn made it easier to step into the cave. The air was chilly. The sun was still below the horizon, and would be hidden by the cliffs above us for a long time yet.

The tunnel sat at the back of the cave. Once inside, a sharp corner into a tunnel ensured the darkness was complete. The light of our torches flickered on the rough walls. I took a flint as a guarantee we would always have a flame, even though we had a hooded lamp. Time seemed to stand still in the cave, and the lamp would give us an idea of how long we'd been in there.

Initially the path went up. Wind Runner had said it was safe while it rose, but when it levelled off we had to take care. Tunnels branched off occasionally, but we stayed in the main tunnel. They had been explored and led nowhere.

We stopped to eat when it was about midday, heating water and food. Most of the food could be eaten cold, but it was comforting to have something hot. Soon after the meal, the path levelled off. What the tunnel lacked in width, it now made up in height, for when the path stopped rising, the ceiling of the cave didn't. Now it soared above us. Our torches couldn't light up that high and, even when

The Fortress of Faltryn

we turned the lamp up fully, the ceiling of the cave was lost in shadows.

Knowing that somewhere ahead we would encounter Faltryn, I opened my pack and pulled out the added safeguards I'd brought. Padded cloths were tied around our foreheads and over our heads. These were covered with warm hoods and cloaks. It was unwieldy, but we needed to use them until after we had met Faltryn's breath, to see what was required.

Most of those who had entered the cave had gone no further than the first blast of the dragon's breath. Starshine and Storm had met the second and Wind Runner had travelled to the third. Beyond that, we had no idea what to expect.

The blast knocked me to my knees. I rounded a sharp corner in the tunnel and what seemed like icy breath hit me with a numbing roar. I was shocked by the suddenness of it. The noise and icy blast came at the same time. There was no warning. As soon as it hit me, it was gone.

Teema dropped his torch and grabbed me under my arms, hauling me back around the corner. Everyone crowded around, checking if I had been hurt, and chatting excitedly about Faltryn. It seemed to be the right time to have a short rest and a drink. My hands were shaking as I took out my flask.

Arbreu took it off me before I dropped it. "Are you all right? We could go back," he said quietly. I shook my head.

Now everyone had quietened down, waiting to see what I wanted to do.

"I was stunned," I said. "I'd expected it, but it was still nothing like I'd ever imagined. The hoods help, but we need to be careful. It's the cold that's so shocking. It was like an avalanche hitting me. Along with the noise, it was almost

Kirym Speaks

solid. Wearing something over our ears to lessen the impact may help."

"So we must keep the padding on our heads and shoulders," said Arbreu.

I nodded. "But it may be totally different next time. The breath is icy, and that's more of a shock because it is now quite warm in here. Have you noticed?"

No one had.

I was surprised to learn that only Teema and I had been aware of the gust. The others, further from the corner in the tunnel, had been shielded from it. All they heard was a faint rumble and Mekrar, who walked last in line, wasn't even aware of that. The icy air wasn't constant, so I felt that we may manage to pass it safely. I wondered, though, if this was the first blast others had met. Starshine wasn't sure. She thought the first blast she had met was nearer the entrance.

"But this wasn't the second I met either," she said. "Faltryn must move around. I do remember this corner. I think I encountered the second blast a little further along. After that, I turned back. It was too much for me."

We approached the corner again with some trepidation, but all passed safely and continued along the tunnel. Being aware of the blast area meant I was able to look at the wall to see what was different there. All I could see was a small hole in the wall high above my head. It seemed harmless, but it had to be significant. It was the only difference.

We met, and safely passed a second blast early in the afternoon. Again, it was sharp and sudden. It hit just after Teema and I had passed, striking Arbreu and Mekrar. It was gone as soon as it came, but Lyndym was aware of it as she walked past, last in line. The only thing I could see that was different was a long crack in the tunnel wall. The third blast came soon after the second. Again I was past it before it hit,

133

The Fortress of Faltryn

and this blast was small compared to the others. Mekrar and Starshine received the worst of it, and they managed to stay on their feet.

I was getting tired and very hot and I had a really bad headache. I noticed a glow far ahead and saw a shadow flow in front of it. There was a faint gasp from behind me.

The blast struck me with terrifying force. Again, it hit my head and was frighteningly cold and loud. I had tucked my cloak in my pack and just wore the padded hood and earplugs. The blast was far more extended here and as with the first gust, it knocked me to the ground. My fingers and nose ached with the cold, but I took in large breaths of fresh cold air.

It cleared my head and I looked up, rapidly realising that something was very very wrong. My head still hurt, I was suddenly more conscious of it. I realised the glow ahead shouldn't be there, and wondered why I had just accepted it before Faltryn's breath hit me.

A freezing gust swamped me again and I felt Teema pulling ineffectively at my arms, trying to drag me away. I got to my knees and looked at him carefully. His face was screwed up with pain and concern. Behind him, Bildon leaned against the wall with her eyes shut. I was shocked at her obvious exhaustion.

I reached up and pulled Teema down to the ground beside me. "The air is poisonous, Teema. The blast is pure. Breathe!"

Again it hit, shockingly cold and sudden. I grabbed Bildon, sitting her in front of me and reached for Starshine. Bildon gasped as she was swamped by the freezing air. After that I was too busy trying to get everyone into the cleansing gust to be aware of what else was happening.

A few deep breaths of cold clean air and my head cleared quickly. Then my stomach rebelled. I staggered out of the

Kirym Speaks

icy air and back along the tunnel a short distance. My stomach heaved and I was violently sick a number of times. I stumbled back to the blast, passing Teema and Arbreu who both looked green in the dim light.

One by one, we all emptied our stomachs and staggered back to the lifesaving air. My head still hurt, but now I was thinking straight and trying to work out what to do. Intermittently, the blast of fresh air hit us. We were safe for now, but I knew we couldn't stay here forever. Again, we were opposite a gap in the wall. This one was quite narrow, starting an arm's length above the floor.

"Kirym, Kirym!" Starshine grasped my sleeve. "I saw Faltryn! Just before you walked into the blast, I saw him!"

"Where was he?"

"There." She pointed further along the tunnel. "Up there, just ahead. I saw him." She frowned. "I'm sure ... well, I think ..." Her voice drifted into uncertainty.

I looked up the tunnel. Beyond the corner was a flickering glow. It did look like something — many things — swooping past whatever was causing the light.

Now though, I faced another problem. The icy blast was chilling; I was already shivering. I grabbed my pack, pulling out cloaks and shawls. I wrapped a cloak around me, thrusting others at Teema and Lyndym, relieved to see Mekrar had had the same idea.

My head throbbed, but I thought that was good. At least I was aware of the pain, and I felt it was lessening slightly. Belatedly, I grabbed my herb pouch and pulled out packets, opening them carefully. I took a few pinches from three of them, mixed them together and shared them out. I swallowed my share and started to feel a little better, although I still had trouble thinking. My mind skittered from one thought to the next, unable to make much sense of anything. Finally, after one prolonged blast of air hit me,

The Fortress of Faltryn

I began to think more rationally about what had happened. My mouth felt furry and I had the bitter taste of vomit in my throat. I opened a packet of seeds from my healing kit and handed them around, biting into one to cleanse my mouth.

"The air is poisoning us," I said, to no one in particular.

Arbreu was in front of me. "The air?" he asked.

I nodded. "It's that glow, I think," I said, motioning towards the flickering light ahead in the tunnel.

He looked up. "Oh, I thought that was our torches." He looked around. Two torches were smouldering on the ground alongside a hooded lamp. He frowned. "Where are the others?"

"We dropped them, I imagine," I said.

He sank down in front of me. "What's happening?" He still looked dazed, as did the others. "Air isn't poisonous. It can't be. We breathe it all the time."

"Not the air," I said. "This air!"

"So we're going to die," he said. He sounded dreamy and I realised he was avoiding breathing the cold air.

I grabbed him and turned him towards the blast. "No, we won't die. Breathe deeply," I said. "Faltryn isn't trying to kill us. He's doing his best to save our lives."

Arbreu gulped down the cold air, then lurched back down the tunnel and vomited again. When he returned, he looked more clearheaded.

With a glimpse of understanding, I checked everyone, turning them towards the blast of clear air. There were moans as the cold air entered aching lungs, but I made them breathe the cold air deep into their lungs. I sat shivering, eyes closed, as my head slowly cleared.

Teema nudged me. "How do we get back?"

"We'll do it, but we need to rest first. The poison's been building up over a long time. Here, we're safe — for now." I

Kirym Speaks

checked on the hooded lamp and added more oil, calculating the time spent here so far. It was just after midnight.

"We need energy," I said to Teema. "Grind some harkii nuts, that'll do it. Then we'll talk." I pulled him close and whispered: "I'm going to see what that light is. Stay here."

Before he could react, I took a deep breath and ran up the tunnel. I peered around the corner, gasping at what I saw. It was the wrong thing to do. My head felt thick and I gagged — turning and lurching back to the clean air from the hole in the wall.

Teema and Arbreu were alert now, turning me into the blast.

"What's causing it?" asked Arbreu.

I closed my eyes, trying to believe what I had seen. "The rock. It's burning."

"Rock doesn't burn!" Teema yelled. "It's rock, for goodness sake."

"Yes, it does," said Arbreu. "Well, it can. I heard about it once, a long time ago, before I left home. A traveller at a gathering told us about it. Everyone thought he was making it up, but he sounded like he knew what he was talking about. Papa invited him back to our lodge and got him to tell us. He said there were two sorts of burning rock. Both can be dangerous, but in different ways. One lot comes from deep inside the earth. Generally, that sort is tied up with mountains, but not always. The rock gets so hot, it melts and moves like a river. It flows until it cools off. It can bubble, like when we cook oats with water. That sort is heated down deep in the earth." He paused, frowning in the effort to remember. "The other is rock that burns. It's black, I think, or brown. He said it can be dug up and put on a fire to keep it going, although I think you need something — heat to start it burning. After that, it keeps going as long as more is added."

It was unbelievable, but I'd heard other stories that were as incredible, and they proved to be true. Arbreu grabbed my arm to get my attention.

"There's something else, Kirym. The burning is good, really hot, but it needs to be vented off. There's something poisonous about it when it burns. Faltryn's breath is probably all that's keeping us alive."

Teema looked at me. "Is it possible?"

I nodded.

"Right," he said. "We've got to get back to the entrance. Tell everyone what's happening here. Could this have any effect on Wind Runner's people?"

"Oh yes."

"Let's go."

"Not yet, Teema."

He looked shocked. "But ... but ... but people could die if we wait. We could die."

I shook my head. "We have time. This has been happening for many seasons. The fresh air seems to come down various tunnels. Maybe that's because of the burning rock. It also explains why people have different visions during their time in here. Maybe their deaths, too. But I want to take some of the rock back, and I still need to find out what the token connection is."

"You can't carry burning rock. It'll kill you on the way back."

"There's a pile of it in there that seems to have fallen from the roof. It's not burning. I'll grab some of that. I don't want much, just enough to show Wind Runner and identify it in daylight."

I grabbed a pack and emptied it, stuffing the items into the other packs. Then, I wet a shawl and wrapped it around my mouth and nose. After breathing deeply, I again dashed up the tunnel and around the corner. It was hot. Staying

Kirym Speaks

close to the ground made breathing easier. I shovelled the rock into the pack and ducked back around the corner. Again, my head hurt and I felt nauseous, but a few deep breaths of fresh air helped. Arbreu thrust a flask of water into my hand. It was warm, but tasted wonderful.

"We should go, Kirym," said Teema. "This place is weird. Faltryn could start another fire between us and the entrance. We'd never escape."

"Faltryn has no fire in him, Teema. Remember his breath is icy."

Teema stared at me, not comprehending. While he was thinking about it, I picked up the pack containing the tokens and opened it. They glowed dully in the low light. Again, the icy blast hit and my fingers tingled with the cold.

"Teema." I nudged him. "Get everyone close and cuddle together under the cloaks. You have to help each other, otherwise it will be the cold that kills us. I'm going to explore the tunnel where the blast is coming from. If I'm not back by the time the lamp needs to be refilled, take everyone back to the entrance."

"You can't go alone," he said.

"I need someone here I can trust. It has to be you. I'll take a rope, you keep the other end. If there's a problem, I'll tug it twice and you can drag me back."

"Take someone with you."

I knew it would be easier to go by myself, but Teema was adamant. Starshine and Arbreu volunteered to join me.

23

Kirym Speaks

I climbed into the crack in the rock. It was narrow, but high enough for me to stand in. After a few steps, it opened up, wide enough for Arbreu and Starshine to slip in beside me. The roof of the tunnel was rough; I had to duck occasionally to avoid hitting my head. I kept the lamp turned away from the blast to protect the flame. The icy wind was strong when it came, and I leaned into it clutching my cloak around me tightly. I realised the narrowing of the tunnel had increased the force of the blast. The further in we went, the wider it was and the less we felt it. Despite that it was still icy cold.

There were strange sounds, whispers and echoes. They filled the air around us, overpowering my thoughts. Even our footsteps sounded far too loud.

Starshine turned in panicked circles, searching for the source of the noises. She gripped my hand so hard that I could feel my bones grind together. I grabbed her, hugging her close.

Kirym Speaks

Arbreu embraced us both. "There, there," he crooned. "Everything's fine, we're all together, we're safe."

"It's just echoes. Small noises echoing and re-echoing," I said.

From under my cloak, I brought out the rainbow token. It glowed, the colours spiralling away. The blue, green, yellow and orange stayed together, enlarging and surrounding us, but the red and purple twirled away in different directions.

"What now?" Arbreu asked.

"We follow the path," I said.

The shadows danced with our movement. We passed two shafts running off the main one, but I had no desire to investigate them. Our tunnel ended in a black chasm. I held the lamp high and moved to the edge.

It was amazing. An ice cave, shapes reaching for the ceiling. Further away, there were ledges, stalagmites and stalactites that glistened as they strained towards each other, and columns where they had already met. The ice was melting and it ran, splashing down the walls and across the floor. Now I understood the noises we were hearing. From across the cavern, I heard a roar and felt the tendrils of cold around me as the wind rushed past. I was beginning to understand Faltryn's breath.

I reached down to feel the depth of the water. Despite looking black and bottomless, it didn't come over the first joint of my fingers. It was freezing.

I stepped into the cave, looking at the wonderful shapes of the melting ice. Arbreu and Starshine splashed down behind me. I handed the rope to Arbreu, and asked him to secure it. I moved further into the room, delighted as the shadows grew and shrank around me. Occasionally the wind gusted past, flinging drops of water from the melting ice around like rain.

The scream echoed around the cave. I turned to see

Starshine, her hand to her mouth pointing behind me, a look of horror on her face. I swung around following her finger and caught the red glow of an eye. Then it was gone. I turned back.

Arbreu grabbed Starshine, a look of disbelief on his face. They both retreated, slowly and carefully. "Kirym! It's Faltryn: he's here in the cave. Let's go." He was pleading. "Now, please. Come on, Kirym. He's just behind you."

I slowly turned, holding the lamp high. The eye twinkled and disappeared again. I moved towards it and it opened, winked and again closed.

Behind me, I heard Starshine's muffled sobbing. I glanced at her and Arbreu.

"Stay with Starshine, Arbreu." I turned back to Faltryn, lifting the lamp higher.

One brilliant red eye watched me — or maybe he was watching the lamp. He wasn't moving towards me — indeed he seemed to be retreating, hiding in the shadows.

I was acutely aware of the sounds around me, but even so I jumped as a stream of water cascaded from an ice shelf. I placed the lantern on a ledge and slipped into the shadows.

The eye didn't stay constant, but I was sure he wasn't looking at me.

"Stay still, Arbreu," I hissed and started to climb.

In melting, the ice left ledges, most of them solid. I climbed quickly from one to another, working my way up towards Faltryn. We looked at each other and I reached out. Suddenly there was a shout from the tunnel.

"Kirym! Come down!" Teema stepped into the cave.

"Hush, don't shout."

My warning was drowned by Teema's yell of, "Now!" and a roar as part of the ice shelf crashed onto the floor.

I stared in horror. My lamp was gone. Teema's lay on the floor, what light it still showed pointing downwards.

142

Kirym Speaks

Although it was dark, the cave now seemed blue, not black as it had been. I could see the darker hole where the tunnel was. A light flashed and the sides of a hooded lantern opened. I watched as Teema walked gingerly over the ice.

Starshine's red cloak looked like a shadow on the ground, but beside her, Arbreu's yellow showed up and both were moving. I knew the blue cloak I was wearing would look like a black shadow and at this stage I was inclined to wait and watch.

The ice shelf I had been reaching for had been part of the collapse. Faltryn was gone, but under my cloak I held his eye. A large red token.

The collapse of the ice shelf had made the cave look quite different. The shadows were indistinct and I had trouble putting a perspective onto what I was looking at. I leaned forward, but Teema grabbed his lamp, turning it up and blinding me.

"Teema, shutter the lamp, please."

"Where are you?" He looked around. "Oh, there. Let's get out of here before we all get crushed."

"Cover the lamp, Teema." I was beginning to get angry. "Teema! Do it!"

He understood my tone and the light disappeared, although his grumble of annoyance was clearly audible.

I allowed my eyes to adapt again to the dark and then moved along the ice shelf, carefully balancing myself against the wall. At the top of the cave was another tunnel, and far down it, I could see a patch of light, much lighter than the tunnel. I moved back to where I could see the large moving shadow of my friends on the cave floor.

"Teema, there's another tunnel here. I'm going to check it. It's short, so I'll be quick." I darted away, hearing his angry objection as I went.

I climbed along a couple of ice ledges and crawled onto

The Fortress of Faltryn

the slick cold rock of the tunnel. It was cramped, but about sixty steps along was the hole and I was able to stretch up. A warm breeze caressed my face and there were earthy smells, soil and plants.

I stared at the dawn sky, the sun about to peep over the horizon.

Reluctantly, I ducked back down and crawled back to where everyone was waiting. Teema had climbed to the tunnel entrance.

"Don't do this, Kirym," he said angrily. "You could have been killed. You can be so self-centred on occasion."

I slipped onto the ice beside him. "It wasn't dangerous, Teema. It's a way out. There are stars out there."

He stretched up and stared at where I pointed. "You could be right, but the cliffs are dangerous. What if we can't get down?"

"Then we come back and go through the tunnel. We have ropes; we'll make it. I don't want to walk through the tunnels if there's another choice. The poisons build up and we don't know how much it would take to harm us. Storm managed to carry Oaken out, but they were both sick for a long time. Storm came right, but Oaken didn't. If there's an alternative, I'd prefer to take it."

He shook his head belligerently. "We don't know the cliffs. It could be even more dangerous than the route we are familiar with. We have a clear way back through the tunnels. We'll just have to walk faster."

"If we walk faster, we breathe heavier. It'd make no difference. Teema, those stars sit in the eastern sky. At worst, we'll climb down and walk south, back to where we first entered the gorge."

He stared at me. "You mean we've come right through the hill?"

24

Teema Speaks

I dreamed.

I sat on a cloud, drifting. The land below me was the map Kirym had found by the fountainhead. As I watched, a blood red dragon flew out of the canyon. He swooped high, saw me and flew towards me, roaring with anger. I could see the sound headed for me, a visible vibration racing ahead of him. I dug my fingers into the cloud, trying to hold on as it leaped and bucked under me.

The vibration shook the cloud apart and I fell. Not the swooping flight of a bird, but the sickening free-fall of a stone. The ground rushed up to meet me. I felt a violent jolt.

I carefully opened one bleary eye to grass and two tiny fragile white flowers.

My heart thumped. I felt nauseous.

The sun was high in the sky. I lay next to Mekrar, my cloak tossed loosely over us. Arbreu rested on the far side of her, his arm protectively across her waist. Both were still asleep. Starshine, Bildon and Lyndym were beyond them, all asleep.

I reached out to caress the flowers. They disintegrated at my touch. I smelled smoke and sat up, remembering — panicking.

A fire glowed nearby. Water was heating in a skin pot. Kirym sat against a tree, watching the valley below. She looked tired.

I felt a pang of guilt. She had obviously stayed awake, guarding us, and I hadn't even thought to offer my assistance once we had climbed out of the tunnel.

"Have you slept at all?" I asked, crawling over beside her.

She shook her head. "You all needed it more than I did. I think you all breathed in more of the poison." She handed me a flask of hot water with dried flower petals floating on the surface, and the dark flakes of some woody mixture in the bottom.

As I sipped the warming mixture, I told her about the dream.

She nodded. "The ground did move. The ice cave collapsed. The ice was holding the cave up and as it melted, its strength went. The tunnel we climbed out of has gone. It must have been covered with ice from the shelf that collapsed. It was melting quite fast. I doubt it would have lasted much longer.

"Why would that happen after all this time? Was it us?"

"The ice was weak and ready to go. Opening up the tunnel to the outside would have made no difference. The fire was getting closer to the ice cave. I touched the wall nearest and it was warm." She paused. "We didn't change anything," she said emphatically.

"What do we do now? Is it safe being here on the hill?"

"I think we're safe enough here, although there are areas

Teema Speaks

on this hill I wouldn't go near. We'll start back as soon as the others waken. We can get down the hill easily enough, but it'll take days to get back to the cave entrance that way. I hope Starshine knows of a quicker, more direct route."

I stared at the fire Kirym was tending, freezing as a horrid thought hit me. "Could that fire make more of the hill burn?"

She smiled. "It's on ordinary rock; I checked. The two types are very different. We're safe." She paused. "What made you follow us last night?"

"I heard a scream." My head throbbed as I remembered the panic I felt while waiting for Kirym. "I thought you must be hurt. The others wouldn't let me leave them, so we all came. You know, Kirym, I didn't believe in Faltryn, but he was there. He was so close to you, looked like he was going to attack. I yelled to distract him, but then he was sort of where you'd been and then the whole wall was moving and the ice fell. I thought you were dead." I paused, trying to think of the best way to put what I wanted to say. "When I saw him, I was so scared, and angry I'd allowed you to put yourself in danger. But for a brief moment you seemed to have a connection with him. It was incredible. I wish I'd kept quiet."

We sat together quietly for a while.

"It was a full moon last night," I said. "I forgot about it. Could that have made a difference?"

"The full moon did nothing. It couldn't have. Sometimes things just happen."

"Why didn't we die, Kirym? We could have, couldn't we?"

She shrugged. "I'm not sure. There are a lot of fissures in the rock. Fresh air was getting in, and that probably helped."

The Fortress of Faltryn

Everyone woke with headaches and nausea, but Kirym was ready with doses of tea, harkii, powders and ground seeds. She made us drink lots of water to flush out the poisons. Other than that, she dealt with whatever symptoms we had.

I was incredibly tired and could see fatigue in the faces of my friends. Other than that, I thought I was fine. My headache was going, but Kirym made another infusion for me.

"To lighten your spirit," she said, laughing. "You've been a real grump lately."

I thought about it. She was right. In the cave I'd been angry with her every time she made a suggestion. Red faced, I apologised.

She brushed it aside. "It was the air in the tunnel," she said. "We all felt the same."

Kirym asked Starshine about the best way back to Wind Runner and Storm. "Wind Runner needs to know about the dangers here before anyone else, so I'd prefer not to go past the fortress unless there is no other way."

Starshine took us north first. "It's quicker, although it'll still mean two nights on the hill," she said."

Kirym said we had spent a day and a night in the tunnels, and I had no reason to doubt her. When I tried to work it out, my mind skittered all over the place and I felt very unsettled.

Kirym reassured me. "I filled the lamp while we were in the cave, and I was far more aware of the passage of time. Perhaps I was wrong in doing it all myself. It's a lesson to keep in mind."

Many seasons later when I tried to think about the time spent underground, my recollection was always distorted.

Teema Speaks

My overriding memory was of a long dark sinuous tunnel, Faltryn's blood red eyes staring at Kirym, stalactites and stalagmites transforming into his teeth.

During the afternoon, we came across areas where the ground smoked. Kirym warned us to avoid it. "It's from the fires in the cave," she said. "And while it's not as poisonous as the fumes underground, too much will affect you."

Late in the afternoon, Starshine guided us to a clearing near the top of the hill, where we made camp.

"If you're right about the time we spent in the cave, Wind Runner will be expecting us back about now," she said. "She'll be devastated when we don't turn up. I envy you the tokens. They make things so easy in situations like this."

"It doesn't always work like that, Starshine," said Kirym. "Thoughts do all sorts of things and often your own fears get in the way."

Mekrar laughed. "Sometimes thinking of mischief can get you into as much trouble as doing it. When Mek and I were little, Mama always knew when we talked about misbehaving. We hardly ever had the fun of being really bad. When we were, we always felt she knew anyway and confessed. Of course, she had a fair idea. It took me ages to figure it out. Then once I understood, I found it impossible to shut her out. It just made it worse."

"So your mama would have been far more worried than Wind Runner over the last two days. I never thought of that," said Starshine.

"Well, probably not," said Kirym. "Mama can't read my token in the same way, and Mekrar hasn't been at all worried or scared, just nauseous."

We woke feeling a lot better. This time, we had shared the guard duty and although I tried to get Kirym to sleep for the whole night, she joined me as I watched over the camp.

I could see pale plumes of smoke oozing out of the hill all

The Fortress of Faltryn

around us and was amazed at how extensive the fires were. When Kirym told me how close they were to the fortress, I felt chills running down my back.

In the morning our path was blocked by an area where the hill had collapsed — the brown and black was harshly obvious against the green around it. We skirted the smoking crater, and I was about to go closer to explore when Kirym suggested that the land around it may also be undermined, and as dangerous as the fumes. The lush side of the hill had less allure to it now.

By mid-morning, we were over the ridge and turning south towards the entrance of the cave where Wind Runner and Storm waited for us. Now I was aware of the deadly fires, I noticed the evidence of them on this side of the hill also, with a number of tell-tale smoke columns rising starkly against the sky.

The sheer cliffs and narrow paths on the western side of the hill slowed us down, and again we camped on a stony ledge. This time we were all far more alert, but I was shocked at how long we had residual effects from our time in the cave.

25

Teema Speaks

Storm and Wind Runner still waited. There was an air of deep gloom around them.

We had a brief glimpse of two dejected people sitting in front of a small fire before Starshine called out.

Wind Runner wiped tears away as she held Starshine close. "I was sure I was dreaming, hearing things," she said. "I really thought none of you would return."

"Faltryn's breath came again just before dawn three days ago," explained Storm. "It was much worse than the one before you entered the cave, worse than any I'd felt before. I assumed we had pushed Faltryn too far, and this was his response."

Kirym explained about the collapse of the ice cave.

"It has to be that," I said. The timing is perfect."

"I think it's happening more and more often," said Kirym. "The ice in the hill is becoming intrinsically weaker, most probably because of the fires."

Wind Runner quickly understood that no one else could safely enter the cave again, but it took longer to make her understand the danger of the fires to the fortress. She was less sceptical once she saw the stone burn.

"Why now?" asked Storm. "We've lived here for more seasons than are written."

"When did the hill start to smoke?" I asked.

Storm frowned. "It's always done that."

"No it hasn't," Wind Runner interjected. "It started the winter you were born, actually the night you were born, Storm. You won't remember the lightning tree?"

Storm shook his head. "I can see it when I close my eyes, but I'm sure it's because the story has been told so many times."

Wind Runner continued as if he hadn't spoken. "There was a huge storm — you were named for it. We'd been out collecting rare spring herbs, and you decided to arrive early. Glade's labour pains were strong, and we were a long way from the fortress. I knew we'd never make it back. We sheltered in a herder's hut to the north of here. Then I realised a storm was going to hit us. Sometimes they creep up with amazing speed, and this one was the worst we'd had in more than twenty winters. There have been few as bad since. Those at the fortress feared for their lives. You were born at midnight in the middle of it. Soon after you arrived, the winds and rain died for a short time and I took you out to see the night sky. A circle of sky was clear above us; we could see the moon and stars but huge black clouds surrounded them.

At that time, I thought the temporary lull in the weather would influence your name, Tranquillity, Placid or maybe Reprieve.

The calm didn't last long, but it was special. I'd never seen the like before, and I've never seen it since. The tempest

Teema Speaks

approached again the wind was just beginning to rattle the twigs on a big old oak tree nearby. The air smelled strange and there was an odd feeling about the night. I was reluctant to go back into the cramped shelter again, although I could feel the tendrils of wind getting stronger.

It happened without warning. The sky split open and lightning flashed to the ground, hitting the ancient tree." Wind Runner smiled as she reminisced. "We were protected from the blast by an outcrop of rock. Even so, it knocked me over. You didn't make a sound. You just stared. It was amazing. The tree had been old when my great-grandmamma was born. It was huge. I could feel the heat from the foliage as it burned. The rain began again and I raced you back to the shelter. We got into the hut and I handed you to your mama, deciding to call you Lightning.

Then the storm really started. Glade, well, she was furious I'd taken you outside. She swore I'd never hold you again. You objected, somewhat strenuously as I remember, and there was something of an impasse. You wouldn't settle, she wouldn't give you up and throughout the night, you never let up. Just before dawn, she handed you back to me. Then you settled.

I still thought Lightning would be an appropriate name, but Glade was adamant and in retrospect, she was right. Storm suited you better.

It was evening of the next day before the storm died, and again I took you outside. The tree was mostly gone, but it still smoked at the roots and deep in the ground the embers glowed. I was amazed it was still burning. The rain had been torrential through the night and most of the day. Since then the hill has smoked and we've become used to it. However, it is moving closer to the fortress. I've noticed a line of smoke quite close to the target practise area."

"How did you know about it, Kirym?" I asked.

153

"When you went off exploring with Twig and Arbreu went fishing with Storm, Starshine and I collected wild herbs. I saw the smoke then and she commented on its closeness to the fortress. When it wafted over, I felt nauseous. In the cave, I wasn't as aware of it. It was different, because it built up slowly. When I went to see what was glowing, I recognised the fumes. The clean air I breathed from the ice cave cleared my head enough for me to put two and two together. Then I understood the danger."

"Didn't you question the smoke when you saw it, Wind Runner?" I asked.

"Well of course I did, Teema. However the old tree had an extensive root system and at the beginning I thought that was burning. I knew too, there had been a lot of old trees on the hill in the past. As I child, I helped collect winter firewood from there. In my great-grandmamma Moon's time, that side of the hill was covered with forest. So many of the trees were dying, branches and trees fell frequently and many of the old trees were cut down for firewood. The root system was left in the ground. Then I thought it was low lying mist and we get a lot of that, particularly in autumn, winter and spring. When I realised it was visible through all seasons and couldn't be mist, I knew I had reached another wrong conclusion.

We got used to the smoke and accepted it, although lately I have been more concerned. I brought it up to the Guild Leaders recently, but," she sighed deeply, "many put it down to Faltryn becoming active and beyond that no one could agree. Of course, we didn't understand the poisonous nature of the smoke."

"How could that be Faltryn?"

Starshine laughed. "Dragons breathe fire, Teema. There's a book about them back at the fortress. It's very descriptive."

"Faltryn's breath was icy though — well, that's what you

Teema Speaks

told us."

"There are conflicting thoughts about Faltryn," said Storm. "Truth to tell, many don't believe in him, but he's an easy excuse if things go wrong. I didn't believe and I'm still not sure I do. If he didn't exist, he couldn't be a danger. To most of us, including me, the smoke has always been there. Whenever the subject was brought up, we dismissed it. We didn't know about the fire, and perhaps if we did, we may have tried to find an answer. But given the fear everyone seems to have of the cave, it's unlikely we'd have discovered it.

I ignored the cave of tears too. I'd been in there, of course; most of us go once or twice just to have a look. I found it strange. It was simple as I got older to dismiss it as a woman's area. When Wind Runner said the well was full, I didn't think anything of it. Truthfully," he said, glancing sideways at her, "I thought she was imagining it, getting a little old and strange. Of course once she mentioned Faltryn's tears, the only other person who'd enter the cave was Starshine. I refused to listen to anything she said about it, and to be honest she didn't say much."

"Did you wonder what caused the icy gusts from the cave?" asked Kirym.

He shook his head. "It was just something that had always happened. I never thought about it. Even now, I can't quite believe it. I mean, how come we never found the ice?"

"Because we never went far enough into the cave," said Wind Runner.

"I remember you telling me a story when I was little," said Starshine. "It was about a monster who made it winter all the time and scared people away with his icy roar. When I thought about it, I assumed it was Faltryn. I only heard the story once. Do you remember it?"

Wind Runner gasped. "My goodness, yes. I'd forgotten

about it. I think I only told it the once too. I heard it from Moon," she explained to the visitors. "The story was extremely old, and yet I think she said it predated Faltryn. It was never written down."

"Predated Faltryn?" questioned Kirym. "Where did he come from?"

"I really don't know. Maybe I remember the story wrong. I can't really recall what she was talking about when she said it. I was young when she died, and like you, I'd assumed Faltryn had always been here." She paused. "It's strange how one comment can suddenly alter your perception."

"One dragon is unlikely," said Kirym. "We only survive as families ..."

"Which really points to it not being a dragon at all," interrupted Storm. "Between the fire and the ice, well I really don't know what to think. But all of that is irrelevant because the big thing is — what do we do now?"

"Evacuate the fortress."

Kirym was adamant. Right through the trip back to the fortress, she insisted there was no other answer.

Wind Runner called the heads of the families and guilds together and explained the problem and Kirym's solution. There were countless objections. Many said it had always been like that. Even when Wind Runner and the other older ones reminded them how the burning started, there was still a lot of scepticism. Showing them how the rock burned wasn't enough to convince some of the danger.

I helped Storm to survey the area and found large deposits of the black rock very close to the fortress. We organised a group of men and observers to bring a load in. With everyone watching, a few lumps were added to the fire in the large

Teema Speaks

hall. Once they were alight Storm shovelled them into a basket. He added them to a pile of wood in the courtyard. The wood quickly caught alight and blazed up. The addition of more rock kept it going for a whole night.

The demonstration did what was intended, and most people accepted the need to leave the fortress. Their acceptance was mainly because they trusted Wind Runner and Storm. Leaving the fortress was a huge job though, but Wind Runner had an evacuation plan and everyone quickly sorted out what to do.

When I asked about it, Oak explained that every tenth summer, they planned a big hunt away from the fortress. Of course, leaving this time was more comprehensive, but with a few variations, they used the plan for the basis of the move.

Packing started at the top of the fortress and worked along one room and one floor at a time. When an area was empty, the occupants relocated to the great hall and slept there. Everyone treated it as one great party. It took only twenty days to clear the fortress from top to bottom and get it all on the carts.

26

Kirym Speaks

A few days after we arrived back from Faltryn's cave, I was summoned to Wind Runner's office. I joined a small group of people waiting to see her. I tried to identify them, although there was one person I had never seen before. Of the others, Oak was with two guards, Blacknight and Twig, Elk the chief healer, and a young healer sporting bruises on her neck and wrists.

Wind Runner joined us and Oak came straight to the point. "Danth escaped."

Wind Runner sat down and placed a piece of parchment in front of her on the desk.

"How?" Her voice was icy as she picked up a quill and mixed some ink.

The guards looked distinctly uncomfortable and there was an extended silence.

"Twig, you start," she said.

Twig was well named. He was tall and thin with a rough

Kirym Speaks

mop of dark brown hair. He took a deep breath. "Well, it's complicated, Mam," he said. "The big problem was that no one was sure who was in charge and when I came to ask, you'd gone to see Faltryn. She said you'd told her to, so I had to agree."

Wind Runner closed her eyes and took a deep breath.

Oak smiled and lowered his head to hide it.

"Perhaps you can explain it all again, Twig," said Wind Runner, "but from the beginning. Danth was under guard, so one presumes the guards were in charge. Now what happened next?"

"Um, we were at the start, but the morning you left, Rabbit said she had to check him. She's always done health checks on those under guard. Danth seemed all right, but later he was sick and she came back. Healers always have precedence, and well, she took over really. She brought his meals and she said we weren't allowed into his room. The next day, she said he needed special treatment and we took him to a room next to the healers annex. Rabbit said he couldn't go in with the other patients because he might be contagious. When I went to get him, she wouldn't let me in. She said he had to stay. He was too sick to move. We guarded there overnight, but in the morning Elk told us to leave. She said we were upsetting other patients. Elk is in charge of the healing area, and you were gone. After that, Elk wouldn't let me anywhere near the healers annex.

Then today, Jinda tried to escape when she went for her walk. Blacknight took her back to the healers and Jinda asked him to get Rabbit for her. He couldn't find her so he called me.

I asked questions and Willow told me Rabbit was caring for Jinda. You said Jinda and Danth shouldn't have contact. I was suspicious and I asked Elk. She said she'd sent Danth back to us. I looked for Rabbit. She's disappeared."

The Fortress of Faltryn

Wind Runner looked to the other man. "Chalk?"

He shook his head. "I've not seen her. She asked me to take Danth's place in his bed, keep my head to the wall and not talk to anyone for a few days. I refused. She was angry, she always is when she doesn't get her own way, but then she seemed to get over it. A few days ago, she sent me to find some black hellebore. She's asked me to get it before, but that was always in winter, and I knew I wouldn't find any this late in the season. The flowers are gone by early spring unless you go way up the river, and even then." He shook his head. "I stayed away for a few days, thought it would convince her I'd searched. I got back this morning. She's taken everything I own. Everything! No one's seen her, I asked around."

Wind Runner sighed deeply and turned to the older healer, Elk. "I specifically told you not to let Rabbit work with sick people. She's manipulative and works to her own interest. Even though I wasn't there, my instructions were specific."

"I haven't sent her to check on prisoners for a long time, Mam," said Elk. "Twig should have double-checked with me first. I did find her in Jinda's room. I told her to leave, but Jinda wanted her to stay. She said Rabbit was her friend. Then she wouldn't let anyone else help her. I watched for a while, and saw no problems. Then I was called away. You do like all of the records kept up to date, Mam."

Wind Runner's face was like thunder. "Blacknight, take Elk to her rooms and make sure she stays there. I will talk to you later, Elk. Then tell Roses to take over at the healer's wing." She turned to the guards. "Have you talked to Jinda's son?"

"He seems to have disappeared too," said Oak.

Wind Runner looked at me, my feelings echoed in her face.

"When did he disappear?" I asked.

Kirym Speaks

"Soon after you left, Mam," said Twig. "I wondered about it. Willow said he'd gone with you."

Wind Runner turned to the younger healer. "How did you know that, Willow?"

Willow was young for a healer, although age often had little to do with ability. She hung her head almost in tears. "Rabbit told me, Mam. She said he had to take a message to his sister. When I asked for more detail, she got angry. She's not one to argue with, Mam. She told me to tell Oak if he asked."

"Let's talk to Jinda," I said rising. As I walked down to the healing area, I tried not to think of the worst, that Danth had somehow convinced Tarjin to go with him. I wondered what Rabbit thought she would get out of this.

Jinda sat in a corner with a guard standing over her. Wind Runner motioned him away.

I took Jinda's hand. "Where's Tarjin, Jinda?"

She looked complacent, showing no concern. "He's with Rabbit. They're waiting for me."

"Who told you he was going with Rabbit?"

"He came to see me. He said we'd be a family now, he'd help me. We could have a new home with no bad memories. Rabbit said she wanted to join us. She said she would help Tarjin look after me. I'd be safe. But when I wanted to meet her, the guard wouldn't let me go."

"Did Rabbit and Tarjin come to see you together?" I asked.

She shook her head. "Rabbit said they didn't want anyone to know yet. It was a secret."

"Did Rabbit bring you a message from Danth?" asked Oak.

She looked away quickly and shook her head. I was sure she was lying.

"Jinda, it's important. Did Rabbit bring Danth here to see

161

you?" I paused. "Tarjin could be in danger. Jinda, I need your help to protect him."

Tears streamed down her face. "She said Danth agreed we should be a family. Rabbit said she liked Tarjin. We could be together, I'd have grandchildren. Rabbit said she'd make Danth treat me right. He agreed."

I walked away and looked out of the window, thinking about Tarjin. I knew he'd never go off with Danth, but I knew little of Rabbit, and young men did strange things if they fancied they were in love.

I felt a little guilty about not taking him with us when we went to see Faltryn. However, he'd been with us when we talked about it, and Mekroe had stayed behind also. I assumed they would be together; generally, they were inseparable. "Ahhh, I may have an answer," I said. "We need to talk to Mekroe. Oak, do you know where he is?"

"No, but I'll find him." He left, taking Twig with him.

"Wind Runner, what's Rabbit like?" I asked quietly.

She drew me back over to the window, out of Jinda's hearing. "As I said, she's manipulative. Sometimes names give wrong impressions. If Danth thinks he's in charge, he should think again."

"Danth is violent, that's how he controls people. How would Rabbit cope with that?"

"Oh, she'd not put up with it. She'd give as good as she gets. I really feel her interest would be in Danth, not Tarjin. I wonder why she would want Jinda with them."

"Nothing like having a compliant slave, someone to humiliate, I guess," I said.

Mekrar burst through the door followed by Oak.

"Mekroe's off fishing," Oak said. "I've sent Twig to get him."

"Is he safe, Mekrar?"

She screwed up her face, concentrating. "Yes, but a little

Kirym Speaks

angry. He'd just caught a fish; then he was distracted by the guards yelling and it escaped."

I had a thought. "Mekrar, do you know where Tarjin is? Is he with Mekroe?"

Again she screwed up her face. "I wish I was better at this. No, he's alone. That's weird. It's night where he is. Someone's laughing or singing."

I leaned forward and clicked her token. Yes, I saw the same blackness and I heard a trilling sound. I'd heard it before. "I know where he is."

I ran out, followed by Oak, Mekrar and Wind Runner. It seemed to take ages to get to the lowest level of the fortress.

As I turned away from the big hall, Oak suddenly realised where we were going. He grabbed my arm. "Hold on, we'll need lights, weapons and guards."

I stopped. "Why?"

"Well, that's one of Faltryn's caves and from what's being said, he's left his home cave. He could be waiting for you."

I laughed. "Tarjin's in no danger. Faltryn isn't there, believe me."

The door was open when Starshine and I went to see the pool, but now it was padlocked and chained. Oak brought out a large ring of keys and started to sort through them.

"This door has never ever been locked," said Wind Runner angrily. "Everyone is allowed free access to the cave."

The wait seemed agonising, as Oak carefully checked each group of keys and then each one of a group. Finally, he grunted and placed one in the lock. It turned with agonising slowness. He put his shoulder to the door and it gradually opened.

Tarjin was curled up on the floor, sound asleep. Mekrar pushed me aside and knelt beside him, gently shaking his shoulder. He woke with a start.

He was hungry, dehydrated and a little disoriented, but as he tucked into a meal, he told us what happened.

"Rabbit asked me to help her clear some stores from the tunnel. As we worked, she talked about Jinda and Danth. She talked about them starting afresh with a new community, her helping to look after Mama. I told her I'd never even consider it. She asked me to get another flask of rose oil and while I was doing that, she shut and locked the door. I knew you'd find me."

27

Kirym Speaks

Wind Runner suddenly looked tired and anxious, and that worried me. I mixed some relaxing oils, made up a tisane and went to visit her.

I had never been in her private rooms before. They were large and richly appointed, with a wall of shelves holding books and keepsakes, some of which were already packed for the trip. The partly-filled open baskets were scattered across the floor. The item that took my attention was a woven wall hanging that covered the entire eastern wall. It was huge: one whole hanging, not many smaller ones as decked the walls elsewhere in the fortress. I recognised it as an expanded version of the map I'd found in one of the lower rooms.

I studied it while waiting for Wind Runner to arrive. The detail was impressive. While most of it was immensely old, a few areas were brighter and obviously recent. Our settlement was there in misty detail, along with the land to the east and west of it. The canyon was depicted as a hill, but the fountainhead was there although portrayed as a deep hole, not a pool. The sea arch was missing. In its place hills surrounded the lake, and the river that ran past Faltryn's Fortress ended there. The western hills were much larger than in reality.

The mountain we had walked towards was there, although not the stone circles. The area between the mountain and the canyon was a mass of greys, dark greens and blacks. It looked quite foreboding. Much of the land north of the mountain was featureless. The river gorge the fortress was built on went far to the north, ending in wild mountains. Westward, the land opposite the fortress appeared barren, and although my view across the river belied that, I realised that could just be the area along the edge of the river.

I turned as Wind Runner entered. For a moment, she was unaware of me and as I looked at her, I realised for the first time how very old she must be. She looked like she remembered every moment of her life.

Then she saw me and drew herself up, instantly looking much younger than her seasons. "It is magnificent, isn't it?" she said, joining me at the map. "I love studying it, and I've been privileged to add to it over my lifetime. I am aware though, that parts are portrayed wrongly."

She drew me away to a seat by the window, accepting the gifts I'd brought. "How lovely," she said. "What occasions this?"

"I'm worried about you."

"Why?" she gasped.

"Because you're troubled. In all the time I've been here, you've been decisive. You've seemed to know the answers before the questions were asked. What's upsetting you?"

Wind Runner sat silently for a while, and I was concerned when a tear slipped down her cheek. "I ... I'm leaving my home," she took a deep sobbing breath, "and I have no

Kirym Speaks

problems with that. It's just, I don't know where to go, where to take my family." She smiled tremulously through the tears. "It isn't me, I could live anywhere, but I need to see them settled."

I gestured towards the map. "But you've a huge choice there. Just pick somewhere."

Wind Runner shook her head. "Our land goes north up the gorge, and it's wild, stark and mountainous. And there's the same threat of the burning rock. I've sent guards up there to check. We have to learn so much that's new, even the building of dwellings. I have no idea how. That knowledge is lost. Before this, we lived in Faltryn's cave. We know nothing else."

"But you can't have lived in the cave, Wind Runner. It's far too small, and other than the entrance area, it's all tunnels. What about moving east?" I asked. "It's rich land. Your family would thrive there. Or you could move west, or south."

"We own the gorge and land within two days walk to the east. We couldn't get far enough away from here to ensure that people wouldn't return when they realised their life would be a lot harder. That would put their lives and the lives of their children in danger. To the west, beyond the green fringes, the land is barren desert. It's a harsh land. No one can survive there for long. The land to the south, well, it belongs to your people. There is little that isn't owned, you know. Taking what belongs to someone else isn't right, even if the owners aren't using it. But even if we had land, we have little knowledge in how to survive beyond here."

"Then come to us in the Green Valley. We can share our knowledge. We know about building without rock. The possibilities there are vast."

"There are many reasons why that wouldn't work, Kirym. Your offer is so generous, and it is what I'd expect, having come to know you. But we can't come to The Green Valley.

The Fortress of Faltryn

I don't think we can even get there. There's an old legend, you need to know it."

Wind Runner went to the wall of shelves that held her special books and after a short search, returned with one of them. There was no title on the cover, but on the front leaf was a picture of three interconnecting circles. Intrigued, I settled down to read it.

'The Legend of the Stone Circles'

On the next page was an explanation.

The old hanging disintegrated with age.
Here I have drawn it as I remember it, and written the story that went with it, as told by generations of storytellers.
Wind Runner
written in the season Glade was born.

The following page had a drawing of the circles, much as I'd drawn them when I first found the stones. Around the edge were copies of some of the carvings and engravings I'd found on them. The next page pictured the arch.

I settled comfortably and started to read.

In the days when my great, great-grandpapa's great-grandpapa was a young man, there was an old story that was told to our children.

It told of two boys, born on the same day, although to different parents. One was the son of the ruler, the other the son of a farmer.

At the time when they were old enough to venture forth by themselves, they met. Both boys were brave and adventurous. They did all the things boys do, and they enjoyed doing them together.

The ruler's son was a bigger lad and he often took the lead in the games they played. But the farmer's son was a thinker, and it was he who solved the problems they faced and got them out of the trouble they got into.

As they grew into young men, they had to part. The ruler's son went into the tutelage of his papa and learned the things a ruler should learn. The farmer's son joined his papa and brothers in caring for their land and animals.

But he was restless, and he remembered the juvenile adventures he had with his friend. So he packed a few things he thought may be useful and went off on a great journey.

He travelled for many seasons, had numerous adventures and learnt countless things.

When he returned, he found that everything had changed. His papa had died, and his older brothers had divided his property between themselves, leaving the lad with no home and no inheritance. Fearing he would challenge this, they drove him away with large sticks and many threats.

He didn't find this particularly worrying though — he had vast experience and had never gone hungry.

Now, as happens in communities, word got around of his return, and his old friend searched him out.

He, too, had lost his papa, and being an only child was now the ruler of his land. When he learnt what had happened to his friend, he grew incensed.

"I will fight them, take their land off them and give it to you," he declared.

"No, please don't do that," said the young man. "They worked the land all the time I was away. Their attachment to it is different to mine. My inheritance was unique. I'm unable to share that with my brothers, and they wouldn't value it anyway. So perhaps this is the best resolution."

"What was left to you?" asked the young ruler suspiciously. "All your papa had was his land."

"Papa gave me the freedom to travel and the ability to think. In my journey, I gathered the things I value: dreams and

knowledge. My brothers couldn't understand this. Leave them with their land. I am more than contented with my life as it is."

Now the young ruler wasn't such a nice person. In the seasons since he had taken over his papa's lands, he had become acquisitive and callous. When he understood that his friend valued something more than his rich family land, he demanded a share.

"It's not something I can give away, my friend. The value of Papa's gift is that the one who wants to hold it must find it themselves."

The ruler was not pleased. "In all the time you've lived in my land, hunted and eaten, you have never paid taxes. You owe me. I demand this knowledge as portion of the repayment."

"It is not something I can give away, Your Honour," the farmer's son said. "I would if I could, but I can't."

The ruler was infuriated. "If you won't pay my tax, then you will work it off. You will not leave this place until you have paid me."

The large circle of land was barren and he knew his friend would be hungry, but he hardened his heart and turned away, ordering his guards to watch, but not assist him.

Every season the young ruler visited to demand his tax. In time, he noticed that things had changed. A dwelling had been erected, a garden planted, and he occasionally glimpsed a woman, although he refused to acknowledge her presence.

Time passed. Now, when he visited, his old friend looked contented. Stone poles bearing strange markings appeared on the barren land. The number increased by the season; one stone became a circle and one circle became three.

The young ruler was inquisitive, but his pride wouldn't allow him to question his old friend. He interrogated the guards, but all they could say was that the stones appeared on the nights of the full moon, and the engravings on them were often found after the darkest nights.

One day after many seasons, when the ruler came again to visit, he found the dwelling had fallen down and the ruins were covered with creepers. He searched through them, but there was no sign of anyone and no hint of what happened.

Now, he regretted his actions over the seasons. He realised he missed his old friend, and he grieved. He was about to walk away when he saw a boy studying the stones. He approached him and asked what he was doing.

"I'm looking at the final clue," said the boy.

"What clue?"

The boy smiled and gave no answer. Instead, he turned and walked away.

The ruler stared at the stone, seeing nothing he would call a clue. Nevertheless, he was inquisitive, so he followed the boy.

He trailed him all through the day and into the night. Eventually, they settled on the ground and slept. In the morning, the boy prepared a meal for them and they continued on their way. They travelled for a long time and the ruler saw many wondrous things.

One day, he realised the boy had grown into a young man, but still they travelled on. They shared things now, preparing meals and setting up camp each night, but when he asked questions about the stones, where they were going or what had happened to his friend, the young man just smiled quietly to himself.

After they had journeyed for many, many seasons, they came to a large clearing in the middle of a wood. In the centre of the clearing sat a man surrounded by many children.

The boy walked up to him and hugged him.

"I did it, Papa. It was a wonderful adventure, and I learned so much."

The ruler watched the scene and felt great regret. He thought of his own family, his wife at home alone, coping with his

The Fortress of Faltryn

responsibilities while he travelled across the land on a whim. He envied the boy's papa.

The boy returned to him and invited him to come, rest and eat. As he came close, he recognised the man. It was his old friend.

"Can you ever forgive me?" he asked. "I envied what you had, but now I realise that what is yours can never be mine. I had all I needed from you — your friendship. And even that, I wasted."

"You were more of a friend than you realise," said the farmer's son. "You provided me with somewhere to live, a place of security for my family to grow, and a place to build a dream. I was able to entice you to follow the dream and now you have all I was given by my papa. You have shared my inheritance, my freedom, adventure, knowledge and experience."

The ruler took back the caring of his land, hoping his friend would now settle close by.

However, his friend's brothers had fallen into misfortune, and he went off to help them. In time, the brothers all died leaving no other family. He inherited the land, more than the young ruler had, and he took his family off to live there.

The ruler constantly looked over to the land owned by his friend. He saw property that was rich and he coveted it. He took an army to demand a share — "just a small tax," he stated to himself, "between friends," — on all that his friend owned. The battle lines were drawn up, but the farmer suggested they meet at the stone circles to talk.

From one full moon until the next they talked, but the ruler just increased his demands until he saw the whole land as being owed to him.

As the full moon rose, the farmer walked to the edge of the circles. "Before this, I've called you friend. I'll not fight with you. I was happy to own what my Papa left me when he died. He gave me freedom and contentment. If you want my land, come and take it. But my family will not work the soil for you, and we will not live on the land if you are there. We will leave, and you can do with it as you will." He turned to walk away.

The ruler was so incensed, he seized his spear and threw it.

The farmer fell to the ground, dead. A great arch grew over the body.

His son came to collect his father's body. He faced the ruler.

"As long as the sun and the moon are able to shine through this arch, I vow this: if you attempt to travel to the land of my father, you will lose the sun and the night sky. You will wander for moons, lost as you were when I was a boy. Even the land will not sustain you."

Then the son and the body vanished.

The arch glowed in the evening sun, a reminder to every one of the treachery that had happened there.

A great forest grew up, and protected the farmer's land, his children and grandchildren. Anyone who tried to go through did indeed lose the sky, and wandered forever lost.

28

Kirym Speaks

"Of course," said Wind Runner as I closed the book, "there must be more to the tale than was written. I always felt the end had been left off. Still, maybe there wasn't one. Occasionally I bring it out and read it to the family, and even as it is, it's an engrossing fable. I haven't thought of it for many seasons, but sometimes it needs to be recounted."

"The stone circles do exist," I said.

"Oh dear, I hoped they didn't," said Wind Runner sadly. "I wanted it to be just a story."

"The stones held the clues that allowed us to find you. Why didn't you want it to be true?"

Wind Runner seemed to be a little embarrassed.

"Did the young ruler own the Green Valley?" I asked quietly.

She shook her head and sighed. "I could live with that more easily. No, he ruled over our land. The farmer's son is your ancestor. You see, Kirym, this is why I'm reluctant

Kirym Speaks

to take my family to your land. If the story is true, then we can't get there. I have no desire to see my family wandering lost for the rest of their lives, to never see the sun again."

"This is different, Wind Runner. If you tried to take our land by force, yes we'd object and there would be repercussions, but you're invited. We'll get you there safely. We know the path. The story is just a myth, and perhaps it shows that coveting what's not yours doesn't bring peace or happiness. But that's not why you're coming to us."

"I doubt such a crowd of strangers will be welcome in your land. You saw how aggressive Storm was when eight of you arrived here. There are more than four hundred of us."

"Papa will welcome you," I said. "He has always encouraged the integration of families. It's healthy for all of us, your family as well as ours. There are too few people in both of our families. Papa says we need new blood, and I think your family does too. It's healthy. Mole was saying you have to be careful of family lines when it comes to marriage."

Wind Runner sipped the tisane I'd brewed for her. "It's a huge thing to do without Veld's personal invitation. If he disagrees, he may find it hard to say no with us all standing there. I could cope with a decision like that, but I'd hate to have to convince my family. Many of your people would feel as Storm felt. How could he refuse, and yet if he's thinking of his people, as headman perhaps he should."

"You showed me the extent of our land. It's massive. There's such a lot we're not using, could never use. Heavens, much of it we've not even seen. There's lots of room. Northeast, there's an area where the river widens out to a lake. The land is rich. You'd be about six days walk from us, although you could easily be closer or further away if you preferred. You'd have the choice of one large settlement or a number of smaller ones. Our family will make you welcome. We've had to find a new home ourselves and we know what it's like to be without one."

"It's such a long trip, Kirym. I'd be reluctant to go so far without knowing we'd be welcome. Veld may say yes solely because you've spent so many summers away from home. That could cause problems later on."

I felt a faint niggle in the back of my mind. Summers? "What route would you take?"

Wind Runner's trail went east around the northern side of the mountain and through the eastern forests, turning south only when they reached the massive hills in the east.

"We left home at the beginning of spring."

"Four seasons! My, you did travel fast. That's incredible. I figured you had taken at least six or seven and if the stories are true, more like eight to ten."

I shook my head. "This spring! It would take longer with a larger group of people, but no more than a season."

Wind Runner's eyes opened wide as I traced the trip we'd made. "It can't be done," she exclaimed. "There are fearsome stories told. People get lost in that land, they just disappear. Others returned and told tales of deep crevasses, forests that grow up or change overnight so you have no knowledge of north or south. They counted themselves lucky to have been able to return to us."

I shrugged. "We've just travelled that land. No problem within it is insurmountable, and we'd lead you. The part of the journey that worries me most is the path leading to the stone circles. It's a stream. The end near the stones is easy enough. It's wide and quite shallow, but where we enter at the northern end, the water is deep and the flow is strong. It takes two full days to travel it. I wonder how the young and the elderly would cope and what about your possessions."

Wind Runner nodded. "The carts we haul them in can float, so the things on them will be safe. Now for the children and elderly, could we perhaps take along some of our boats?"

I felt my eyes widen. "You have boats? I didn't realise. You're so far from the sea."

Wind Runner laughed. "We live by a river, and occasionally when it floods, it's one of the few ways we can leave the fortress. The boats are small, but each will hold three or four people and some packs."

I felt stupid.

Through the afternoon we discussed the logistics of the trip and just before the sun set, Wind Runner took me to look at the boats.

Wind Runners people had experimented over time to build a huge variety of craft. They were small vessels, propelled with paddles rather than the sail's we used. The smaller and lighter craft were made of willow withies wrapped with animal skin. A number were covered with the inner membrane of a tree I didn't recognise and some were made from hollowed logs. Not all would be needed on the trip, and I looked speculatively at those they planned to leave behind.

Arriving back at the fortress, I searched out the big map that showed the surrounding land and then went to find Wind Runner and Storm.

"When everyone leaves here, I'd like to take a small group to explore the river south of here. We could use some of the boats you're not taking and meet you closer to home."

Wind Runner went pale. "I forbid it."

Storm objected strenuously. "Absolutely not! It's far too hazardous," he said. "Once you're into the southern ravine, there's no way back. The rift is even worse. Even with the

The Fortress of Faltryn

lightest boats, you can't paddle against the flow. I'll not allow you to put yourself in danger. No one has ever come back from that trip."

"Someone must have."

He stared at me, mystified.

"Well, otherwise," I said, "you'd not know about the southern lake. There must be a way back. Anyway, I don't intend to return here. The map is wrong. This river doesn't enter our lake. It must go straight to the sea. We could climb over the western hill and enter The Green Valley that way or follow the coast eastward to our land.

"Well, you've certainly thought it through," said Storm. "But I still forbid it."

29

Kirym Speaks

The tunnel to the pool of Faltryn's tears seemed shorter. A large group of people joined me as I took the tokens to the cave. The storage areas were empty now. Everything had been taken to be packed on the large transport carts.

With so many people, the noise of the water was less obvious, but as Starshine and I lit lamps and placed them around the chamber, the awe took over and everyone stopped talking.

"It sings differently now, Kirym," said Starshine quietly.

"The people and the tokens alter things."

"Will it affect the ceremony?"

I shrugged. "Without them there is no ceremony, so any difference must be right."

With more light, I could see the size of the cave, much larger than I'd realised. I opened my pack, took out the wrapped tokens, and sat them on a flat rock. When everyone was quiet, I stepped to the head of the pool. It rose and

The Fortress of Faltryn

fell, gurgling and trilling. Already there seemed to be a tune rising from the water.

"Mekrar, I want you to choose a token," I said. "Leave it wrapped and select someone to hold it."

"Sis! Wait!" called Mekroe, frowning. "It's not the way it's done. You can't change the ceremony"

Bokum mumbled an agreement.

"Tell me, Mek. How would you fashion this ceremony for this cave, on this occasion?" I turned to include everyone. "Each ceremony is different, and each cave is different. If anyone knows more than I do, then please help me."

The silence lengthened.

"She's right, Mekroe," said Mekrar. "We are guided by those with knowledge. Wasn't there a story Zelriff told? Remember the big spring storm? Our eighth or ninth I think. A big snow storm, and it lasted for ages. Everyone told stories until we ran out of them. Then Zelriff told a new one, except she said it was very very old. Something to do with many large tokens, and it was weird because many of us hadn't even seen one of them. I don't remember the details, but I think Kirym does. Just let her guide us."

He frowned, thinking, nodded shortly and stepped back beside Bokum.

Mekrar chose a token and turned to face everyone. She closed her eyes, and concentrated. Then, with a deep breath and a surprised look, she handed it to Teema.

He accepted it silently and walked around the pool to stand beside me.

"Your turn, Lyndym."

Lyndym handed the token she chose to Willow, the young healer. Slowly one by one, the tokens chose holders for the ceremony. Bildon, Starshine, Mekrar and Arbreu were chosen. They stood around the pool, unsure of their positions in the ceremony.

180

Kirym Speaks

I asked the others to find places around the pool between the token holders and the circle widened to include them. Wind Runner and Findlow stood, one each side of me, the elders of the families with Sundas and Storm beside them.

One by one the covers were removed from the tokens. I was interested to see who each token had chosen.

Arbreu stood to my right, holding the green token he'd brought with him when he crossed the gorge. Teema held the blue token, Bildon the yellow, Willow the orange.

When Mekrar unwrapped the red token, there was a collective intake of breath from those who had seen the others, along with a few querying looks from those who had been with me in Faltryn's cave. Starshine held the rainbow token.

I sprinkled herbs and flower petals on the water and stepped back into the circle. The sounds in the cave changed. The lamps dimmed and the tokens lit up.

Those who had never seen the ceremonies before were wide eyed and awed by the sight. Each of those without tokens reached to hold the hand of the person next to them, enclosing the token holders within their circle.

Slowly, the sounds of the cave dimmed and the stones began to sing. The sound seemed to vibrate through me. I was unsure how long we stood listening. My tokens throbbed in time to the music, lit up and shot beams to Teema's and Arbreu's stones. From them, light arched back and forth across the circle connecting all of the stones we wore. The rays of light grew to surround us all in a warm cocoon of colour.

My tokens throbbed again, and this time connected with each of the large tokens. The sounds seemed to spiral upward, taking us all with it.

I closed my eyes and saw the lake, a lot higher than it had been and lapping the foundations of the dwelling built nearest it.

The washing area had been moved nearer to the large winter hall we had started building in the middle of last summer. The building progress was phenomenal: three of the walls were finished and they had begun to thatch the roof.

Around me I felt the message of our return with new people. Acceptance and news from the family returned to us, Harnita had given Peet another daughter, Zhins was pregnant, Cuthian and Harlumba wanted to marry, Tant had fallen out of a tree trying to rescue Parlansho. He broke his leg, Parlansho reached the ground alone. I saw Trayum, wide eyed and alert, and felt Bokum's pride and sorrow at having missed his life so far.

"We'll be home soon," I whispered.

"And you'll all be welcome," said Papa.

As the serenity of the thoughts from home washed over us, there was a violent crash.

Cold water splashed over my feet and legs.

The air smelt different. I opened my eyes carefully. There was no dust, but now there was no pool. The tokens still glowed, showing that the stalactite had detached from the ceiling, spearing straight into the pool and blocking it completely.

The top of the stalactite sat at shoulder height. In the silence that followed, the tokens continued to sing. This was different though. The sound was gentle and plaintive, a farewell.

The cave suddenly got very cold, almost as if Faltryn had breathed through the hole in the roof where the stalactite had sat. More than one person glanced up, fear in their eyes. The glow of the tokens expanded again and we were enveloped again in warmth. The lights died slowly into blackness.

Kirym Speaks

Now the tokens seemed to be laughing, and I was reminded of the sounds I heard when I first came to visit the pool with Starshine. When the light returned, there were two tiny white tokens sitting on the top of the fallen stalactite.

I stared at them, trying to comprehend their presence. I couldn't understand who they would belong to, although obviously if there were tokens, there had to be people for them.

I looked from them to each person in the room, trying to see a connection. Why two and not one for each of those new to the ceremony? The sounds of the tokens filled my head, trying to block my thoughts.

"Don't fight it, Kirym. Listen to the tokens."

I didn't know who spoke, but when I opened my eyes, I was lying on the ground with Teema, Arbreu and Bokum kneeling over me. A sea of concerned faces hovered above them. Teema's tokens connected to mine and I felt my strength returning. I struggled to sit.

Wind Runner knelt and took my hand. "You said the tokens couldn't hurt you, Kirym."

"They didn't," said Mekrar. "She tried to fight them. Did anyone else hear what they were saying?"

Oak's voice came from the back of the crowd. "They said the tokens were for Kirym." He looked nervous. "Well, that's what I heard — I think."

Others mumbled agreement.

"Why did you fight it?" asked Mekrar. "It's not like you."

"It doesn't make sense," I said. "Tokens are given for a reason, birth, family connections and joining. Why should I get these? No one is given two at once."

"Up until now," said Arbreu. He brushed my hair off my face. "You've always said the tokens do what they do, and the reasons become obvious when we need to know. This is different, but when you gave me my token, that was different

183

too. A lot of people thought it was wrong. The reasons will for this decision will become obvious, I guarantee it."

He helped me up and I went to look at the two tokens. They sat on the top of the stalactite, surrounded by the large tokens. They were tiny; I'd never seen any so small, and had never seen white tokens before. The large stones connected to them and then to those I wore.

I felt at peace and reached out to stroke them. They warmed to my touch and I didn't want to let them go. I slipped them into my token holder between the two I already wore. They connected to the blue and green, and then to the tokens worn by the others.

As the light dimmed, I collected the large tokens, wrapping them and putting them into the pocket I carried them in.

We started back to the fortress.

The light faded as I left the cave, the others ahead of me in the tunnel. It was peaceful here, and for the first time the cave was silent. It was no longer needed. Faltryn's tears would never run through it again.

I walked away, but at the point where the tunnel curved away, I turned back for one last look. Something in the cave glowed. There was a flicker — a flash of shadows moving around the cave. Then Faltryn roared his farewell.

I heard a shout from behind me and I spun around as Teema, Arbreu, Oak and Storm raced back around the corner. Storm held his lamp high and they all stared past me, mouths open.

I turned back. The cave was blocked. A large rock had fallen across the entrance. No one would ever enter again.

Now, it was truly sealed.

"The rock falling sounded like a dragon's roar," said Oak,

Kirym Speaks

laughing uneasily.

I nodded. "The tunnels echo. That distorts the noise."

"Was that Faltryn? Did we really see him in the ice cave?" Teema asked.

"I don't know what you saw," I said. "There were lots of shadows and the light was bad. I reached out to touch something as the ice wall collapsed. It disappeared and I held the token."

Teema caught my eye, with a questioning look.

I smiled sweetly and turned away to talk to Oak. There were things I wasn't ready to tell anyone.

Starshine was still distressed. "Have we left Faltryn buried or trapped in the cave?"

"I don't think so," Teema said. "There were lots of tunnels in the caves. Perhaps we let our imaginations run rife, or maybe the stuff we breathed affected the way we thought or saw things."

"But we all saw the same thing, didn't we?" said Arbreu.

"When I think of Faltryn," I interrupted, "I feel no distress. Wherever the dragon is, he's safe."

"If there is a dragon," muttered Storm.

He looked up, realising everyone had heard him. "Well," he said defensively. "Who saw him? In the cave it could have been shadows and everyone's desire to see one, or the fumes. That could be where the land hid the token when it was stolen."

I smiled. "Who stole it?"

"Falt ..." Storm looked nonplussed, paused and then laughed. "All right, between the myths and the facts, I'm a bit mixed up."

I laughed with him. "You could be right though. We don't know what we saw. We do know we have tokens and we know we have to leave here. So let's get on and do it."

30

Kirym Speaks

The culture at Faltryn was very old, and had evolved over time to a complex structure. They had a series of guilds that oversaw the day to day running of the community. Guild representatives answered to Wind Runner. Families took pride in belonging to a guild and some traced their affiliation back many generations, although personal wishes and talent often meant a person could belong to and work within a different guild.

There were five Guilds: Rulers, Carers, Protectors, Crafters and Entertainers. Wind Runner belonged to all, and I discovered over time, had talent enough to hold her head high in any of them.

The Carers were made up of healers, cooks, gardeners, farmers and cleaners.

Guards, hunters, carpenters, builders, boat builders, river men and stone masons were members of the Protectors Guild.

Kirym Speaks

The Crafters Guild included embroiderers, weavers, seamstresses, tailors, cobblers, jewellers, thatchers, and artists.

Teachers, story tellers, historians, bards and minstrels were in the Entertainers Guild.

The smallest guild was the Ruler's Guild. It was made up of the present ruler, her successors and two advisors from each of the other guilds.

The Guilds met to make decisions and, while they were guided by Wind Runner, they by no means gave in easily if they felt their arguments for something were valid. The Guild leaders were among the group we met on the first night of our visit here.

Once these men and women were convinced of the danger to the fortress, they leaped into action and began to organise the move away from Faltryn.

My days were full of meetings. Decisions were needed on what to take on the carts, what people should carry, shelter, food for the trip, water and a hundred and one other things.

Clothes were again a problem for me. Many of these meetings were formal, and my garments had suffered horribly during my time in the cave and the trip back to the fortress. Dust and soot from the cave had created stains I couldn't wash out. Even the tabard made for me, although it worked well, was looking drab and bedraggled.

I sewed sleeves into my dress and bartered some pretty stones I'd found for some material to make loose trousers for under the tabard. It was different to Faltryn fashion, but accepted and the style was quickly copied.

After a number of days of fine weather and hard work, the dawn brought rain, and I was able to enjoy a lazy morning. I had been up late the night before trying to calculate the best way to get the groups from the avenue of standing stones

The Fortress of Faltryn

to the three circles. I knew it would be impossible to have them all go in just one or even two groups. The stream would be one of the two most difficult parts of the journey, the other being the trip through the forest.

With some time off, I was attempting to finish one of the books from Wind Runner's shelves when Mekrar bounced in to the room, carrying a large guild basket and a folded parchment sealed with wax.

"This was left outside the door," she said. "It has your name on it."

I broke the seal on the parchment and read out the contents.

Kirym of The Green Valley
is hereby Summoned
to bring all who
belong to her
to the Great Hall
as the Sun touches the Meridian
for the Faltryn Spring Celebration

"Something's happening at midday, and we're invited," I said. I opened the basket and tipped the contents onto the set.

"Oh! My! Stars!"

Mekrar's exclamation echoed in my head. In front of me was the most beautiful outfit I had ever seen. It was exquisite: feathered, bejewelled and embroidered. Gorgeous, but far too much. I could not accept it.

"There are ten more at the door," said Mekrar. "One for each of us."

"Don't open them," I said. I quickly changed into my old dress, washed my face and hands and brushed my hair. Taking the basket, I walked up to Wind Runner's office.

She wasn't there, nor was she in her rooms. I asked for her,

Kirym Speaks

but no one seemed to know where she was.

I looked for Starshine and Storm. Again, they were not in the places they usually were, and the few people I did find had no idea where I should look. I tried not to panic. I didn't want to insult the guild members, but I felt very uncomfortable with this excessive offering.

I sat on the floor at the door to Wind Runner's office and wondered what to do. When it became obvious that she was not returning before the celebration started, I returned to our rooms to discuss our response.

"We cannot accept them," I said. "It's too much."

"So what happens when we return them in front of everyone?" asked Arbreu.

I shrugged. "I'd expect them to understand how we feel. What's the worst they can do? Send us on our way? More likely it will be a stand-off. We have to hold out, let them know it's too much. If we accept these, it alters the balance of everything we do. We'll start to be wary of helping them, and they'll eventually feel they have to pay for everything. The Guild leaders are reasonable people. They must accept our refusal."

Bildon interrupted. "But if we don't accept the gifts, will they refuse to come south with us?"

"It won't come to that. It can't. They have no other options. If they try to use that as an argument, we have to quietly let them know it's not about them."

I explained how I wanted to handle the rest of the day.

Despite feelings of unease, we trouped up to the hall. There was a strange feeling about the fortress, and we were almost at the hall before I realised what it was. "There's no one around. They must already be in there waiting for us."

Findlow stopped walking. "That implies a confrontation, doesn't it? What if they ahhh, insist?"

"We have weapons," said Mekroe.

The Fortress of Faltryn

"Hold on," I gasped. "This is not going to be a battle. We will not need to fight our way out, and if you think there is any chance of you using your knife for anything other than cutting your meat, then take it out now and leave it somewhere safe. Do not pre-empt anything."

There were three ways into the hall. The main entrance was through the huge double doors off the main lobby. A second way was by a door onto the raised dais where Wind Runner sat on formal occasions. The third was through a smaller door in the back of the room that also accessed the latticed floor above the hall.

As we walked, we discussed the best entrance to use. There were arguments for all three, but in the end, my reasoning for using the big doors won over. "We would normally enter by that door. Act naturally, but be prepared for anything. Don't be embarrassed about your clothes, and don't impute bad motive on their part. They are our friends," I said.

Mekroe and Tarjin hauled the big doors open. I walked in, Arbreu and Teema at my shoulders, the rest ranging behind.

In some ways our entry was a bit of a let-down. It looked like any other celebration we had been to. No one was concentrating on the door or us, and if our entrance was expected, it was not unusually so.

On formal occasions, the guild leaders would congregate at the top of the hall, but on this occasion, they were mingling with the rest of the families. Some were dressed up, some weren't. We wouldn't have been out of place if we had worn the gifts, but we also weren't dressed the way we were, although yet again, my clothes were the most ragged there.

Wind Runner was on the far side of the hall, and I slowly made my way over to her, stopping to chat to people on the way.

No one stared nor made comment about the baskets we

Kirym Speaks

carried. Everything was extraordinarily normal. That worried me more than if someone had pointedly asked why we weren't wearing the gifts.

There was an air in the room though, a feeling that something would happen. This wasn't unusual. Often when the family gathered, there would be a surprise of some sort, a play, a special song, dance, or a display. Today was different though, and I couldn't put my finger on it.

Teema and Arbreu stepped closer to me. They were aware of it too.

Wind Runner turned and smiled as I approached. Nothing in her face gave away her thoughts or feelings.

I quietly handed her the basket and explained.

She nodded. "As much as I hoped, I honestly didn't think you'd accept them. You do realise how much we appreciate all you've done for us? You've put your lives at risk for us, and nothing we can offer you or do will repay that."

"There is something," I said.

She looked at me, her eyes narrowing as she concentrated on our conversation.

"You've become our friends, and our family. Now you'll be our neighbours. Life in The Green Valley will no longer be lonely as it was before."

It wasn't quite what I wanted to say, and yet she smiled, nodded and guided me over to the laden tables for a drink.

The afternoon progressed with the usual assortment of entertainments. Mekroe and Tarjin joined the musicians. They had obviously been practising, both were playing instruments new to me, and from what I could hear, they were doing well.

I casually watched everyone. There was a lot of movement around the room. As we mixed and mingled, we were separated and surrounded by Wind Runner's family. Something just seemed wrong.

31

Teema Speaks

"Teema." Splinter slapped me on the back. "Just blooded a new hunter. Come an' meet him." He threw his arm around my shoulder, guiding me towards a group of young men on the far side of the hall.

I glanced back at Kirym. She was talking to Wind Runner, and Arbreu and Sundas were nearby keeping an eye on her.

As we approached a group of hunters, Splinter picked up an arrow and handed it to me. It was nicely fletched, the end wrapping cleverly done. I studied it closely.

"Good workmanship," I said. "Whose is it?"

A young lad I hadn't met before was pushed to the front of the group, bright red with the embarrassment of being singled out. I hunkered down beside him.

"You're doing well," I said. I pointed to a tied off thread. "If you smear it with bees wax, it'll hold the knot end close to the shaft, and the arrow will be more accurate when you shoot it."

Teema Speaks

Splinter squeezed the boy's shoulder. "My youngest brother, Lichen. He's not a bad shot. Not as good as me at that age, of course."

"Ah, that's true," laughed Limb. "Splinter got a high-flying bird with his first shot, Teema. Mind you, he was aiming at a pig. Not many of us are that good."

I relaxed, accepted a drink, and joined in the laughter and conversation.

Twig flicked my tunic. "Wondered if you'd be all dressed up tonight. Why not?"

"I like to be relaxed." I shrugged. "And I can't quite imagine mixing with you guys dressed like that."

Twig nodded. "I thought it was wrong. Guild leaders can dress up, but it's not for the rest of us." He lowered his voice. "Would you accept a small gift from us, my family, I mean? Droplet made it with a bit of help from Running Bird."

I glanced across the table at Droplet, sitting with her grandmother. The little girl's eyes glowed with excitement. I really didn't want to upset her. She had had such a hard time since her mama died during the last winter. More than once, her family had helped me when I was lost in the massive fortress, or unsure of what to do or how to cope with something.

I scanned the crowd looking for Kirym, hoping to get her attention. Her back was to me and I wasn't at all sure what to do. It seemed churlish to refuse, and it was only a small thing.

I smiled my agreement.

The sound of the panel being swung away from the window was bad enough, but on top of that, the light was blinding.

The Fortress of Faltryn

My head throbbed. My mouth felt dry and sour. "Shut that," I moaned, pulling the rug over my eyes.

"Kirym left you some powders and a tisane. You'll feel better when you've taken them."

I pried open one eye and stared blearily at Mekrar. "Only dying could make me feel better," I muttered.

She laughed quietly. "I know how you feel, but this really does help. She left a message too. Drink lots of fluid, get some fresh air, and rest."

I struggled up onto one elbow, accepted the flask of fluid and took a mouthful. Mekrar handed me a small platter, watching as I emptied ten seeds and a small pile of something ground into my mouth. I washed them down with another mouthful of the liquid.

I pulled the rug around me as I sat up, shivering involuntarily as the cool morning air from the window washed over me. I closed my eyes tight as my stomach threatened to rebel. I opened them and really wished I hadn't.

Mekrar was holding a tunic. My tunic! I remembered Droplet's excitement as she handed it to me, her happy kiss on my cheek, the tentative hug, and I felt nauseous again. "Kirym will kill me," I said.

Mekrar laughed quietly. "Probably. I haven't seen her this morning. She was gone before I woke. She left powders for all of us, and a message that she would talk to us later. You'd best get up. You'll feel better for it. At this stage, you can't change anything, but come on through and we'll figure out what to do."

A short time later, dressed and feeling a little better, I walked through to talk to Mekrar. At the door, I stopped, shocked. Our reception area was piled with items. My friends sat amongst them looking despondent. Everyone was there except Kirym.

Along with my tunic were trousers, jackets, boots, and

Teema Speaks

cloaks. More clothes than I'd ever owned, more than we'd ever owned.

"Oh no," I groaned. "I hoped it was a bad dream."

Mekrar grimaced. "We all did."

"We're all to blame, not just you," said Bildon. "Kirym can't kill us all, but she must be furious."

"How do we explain this, after all she said to us?" Arbreu leaned forward to pick up his flask.

"Personally," said Tarjin, "I'm going to blame that drink they dished up. We've never had it before, but it must have been that. It has the same effect as your stuff, Findlow, for all it tasted so different. Skafarhn tastes strong. Theirs didn't, but it was vicious."

Sundas snorted. "It tasted sweet and grassy. Do you think it was poisoned?"

Mekrar laughed quietly. "When I saw all of this, I wished it had been. I'm at a loss to know how it happened though. We knew not to accept their gifts."

"Initially, it was only a tunic from Droplet," I explained. "Then the cloak from Lavender. How could I say no to such lovely little girls? After that, I don't really remember."

"Pretty much the same for me," said Findlow.

32

Kirym Speaks

"You were all conned," I said. "They knew we'd decline such a large number of gifts. So they offered something particularly excessive, and politely accepted our refusal. Then they separated us and you were each offered something small by someone you couldn't say no to. You all fell for it, and although that drink certainly helped, you accepted the first gifts before it affected you. After the first item, they just kept it up, one small offering followed by another until they'd given you pretty much everything they originally planned to. It was very clever."

"So what now? Do you want us to return everything, Kirym?" Teema asked.

I picked up a tunic and held it up. "If I could think of a way of you doing it without hurting Droplet's feelings, I'd make you. But I'm not that mean, and if you can't return everything, then you have to accept it all."

"How did you know it came from Droplet?" asked Teema.

Kirym Speaks

I smiled. "Her adoration of you is transparent. But I saw her stitching it before we went to Faltryn's cave. She was so proud of her work."

"So what happens now?" asked Findlow. "Where have you been this morning?"

"Yelling at Wind Runner."

"You shouted at her?" said Findlow in awe. "Wow, I imagine that's not been done in a long time. How did she react?"

I laughed. "Quite well really, all things considered. She expected a reaction. She acknowledged it was deliberate and it worked out exactly as they planned. She apologised, but suggested we just accept it."

"And?" Teema sipped his tisane. He grimaced and closed his eyes.

"As reluctant as I am to allow them to get away with this, I have no choice. Not that I gave in easily, but it seems now you all have new clothes and a number of other gifts. Wear them proudly, but do occasionally use your old clothes. As worn as they are, they are a reminder of who you are and where you come from. Anyway, they'll make good work clothes, and there's a lot of work to do in the days to come."

Teema was obviously still in pain from the effects of his overindulgence. Everyone looked tired and they were still suffering from the night before.

I collected an assortment of seeds and powders from my healing pouch, ground them together and added some honey, with a little of skarfarhn, a drink Findlow made out of grains in which I'd steeped the bark of three trees. I shared the mixture between them.

"Oh no!"

We all looked up at Mekrar's exclamation.

"What?" I asked.

She looked sheepish. "Well, our new clothes will make yours look even worse. I mean, yours were the most worn when we got here. This won't exactly improve their look."

"Could we barter for some material, and make Kirym something?" asked Lyndym.

Mekroe snorted and winced, holding his head. "It's not like we have anything else to do, is it," he said sarcastically.

"We have to do something," snapped Mekrar, and suddenly they were bickering as they used to when they were younger, stopping only when Sundas groaned loudly.

"Kill each other quietly, or wait until I'm dead," he begged. "After that I don't care."

Mekrar looked guilty, and while she and Mekroe tried to look chastened, she giggled. It was infectious, and we all laughed, painful as it was for some.

Mekrar finally stopped, wiping her eyes with her sleeve. "What can we do, Kirym? There must be something."

"Wind Runner beat you to it. She made the same points you did."

"And?"

"I resent being manipulated," I yelled. I looked out of the window, and down to the river far below, wondering how I could resolve this in a way that allowed everyone to walk away with dignity. "You would object if part of the conditions for living in The Green Valley was that you lose everything that made you different from us," I said icily. "We are proud of our traditions and our clothes." I drew myself up to my full height, and lowered my voice. "I will happily and proudly wear my rags until they fall off me."

Wind Runner's lips twitched. She recognised what I was doing, because it was a ploy she frequently used. "I admit I was wrong, but I could see no other way." She drew a deep breath. "Everything was made by people who love

Kirym Speaks

you. Whether we're being good hosts to honoured guests, or welcoming to new family members, it doesn't matter. For us to become part of your family, you must become part of ours, and we have either an obligation to care for you or a right to. We think it's our right. And you need to let us."

And with that she had me, and I knew it as well as she did. I would have used the same argument had the situation been reversed and indeed, had used it last night.

Suddenly I found myself with more clothing than I'd ever owned before.

33

Kirym Speaks

The work of emptying the fortress and taking everything to the carts waiting beneath the walls was immense. The big furniture was lowered over the battlements with ropes, while smaller items were packed into containers and carried down. It was long, hard work, and the excitement wore off long before the job was finished.

A few days after the spring celebration, we found a strange guard at our doors at night. Oak, and the guards we were used to, had disappeared.

I expected to see them working at the battlements or loading the carts on the river flats. When I realised they were in neither place, I asked after them. The only answer I got was: herding squilute. It meant nothing, and then other things took my attention.

The community owned a huge number of carts, and I wondered how they would be moved. Although there were a lot of men in Faltryn, I doubted if they could adequately

Kirym Speaks

cope with the distance we would travel. I tried to calculate how long it would take to drag them down the river flats and then overland to the stream and beyond. *Maybe we are looking at many seasons after all*, I thought.

Five days before we planned to leave the fortress, Oak and the others arrived up the river flats with a large herd of animals.

Squilute! I had seen them close up only once before. One early dawn, when we were travelling to the canyon soon after we arrived in this land, I spied a small herd of them drinking at the lake. The mist allowed me to get close, but two guards exchanging a quiet comment sent them melting into the trees. I had later checked and memorised their prints in the damp soil. However, they proved to be very illusive, fleeing at sight or sound of us. There were representations of them carved on the poles at the three circles.

These with Oak, though, were tame; eager for human touch. The adults were the size of a large deer, with short legs, solid bodies, long necks, beady black eyes with gorgeous eyelashes, huge ears and thick fluffy fleece. I discovered they had a sense of humour, that was both endearing and sometimes exasperating, and an ability to lick, bite and kick if annoyed.

"They're friendly enough if we get them early," said Oak, "and once domesticated, they'll come when called. We try to herd them in every spring, mainly so we can cut their fleece before they shed it. It's good to give the young ones a bit of attention and get them used to us."

He brought a large black one with a tiny foal over for me to pet. She was beautiful. She accepted my rubbing her forehead, but was happier when Oak took over. I had a better time with her foal. She nuzzled me, licking my fingers and happily eating some honeyed oats Oak gave me.

"Her chest is vibrating. Is she all right?"

The Fortress of Faltryn

He nodded. "They do that when they're contented. The mamas do it when they give birth. It's the nicest sound when you're in the centre of a group of them. Not many are born as black as she is." He pointed out the various colours. "The males are mottled, the females a single colour only. Generally they're brown, but that can range from pale gold to dark like good soil. Only a few are black or white. Most of the herd belongs to the community, but this one's mine. I went out and caught her myself," he said, scratching the head of the dam. "That wasn't easy. Her dam was wild and very wary of me. I lived with the herd for four seasons and even then I couldn't get close enough to touch her. I only managed to get to this one first because her dam dropped two foals and was concentrating on her firstborn. After that, Soot was mine. What would you call the young one?"

"Her fleece is slightly different to her dam, isn't it? Will it change as she gets older?"

He shook his head.

"Why don't you call her Midnight? That would suit her. Up to you though."

"Well, no, it's your choice," said Oak. "She chose you, not me."

I was pleased and annoyed. Annoyed because, although she was gorgeous, I felt I'd been tricked into accepting yet another gift.

"Oak, I can't accept her. She's too valuable. You need her if you want to build up a herd, and I have no chance of caring for her now. When we leave here, I'm not travelling overland."

"That's all right. Soot'll care for her, and I'll keep an eye on them both. I didn't actually plan it, Kirym. She was born this morning. She chose you."

Despite arguments, Oak prevailed. I was the proud owner of a very black squilute.

Kirym Speaks

I was intrigued by them. The younger ones were mischievous. They were adept at grabbing anything left unattended, and more than one pocket, scarf or wrap was proudly carried off and investigated. Baskets of food vanished quickly when left unattended.

Soon after Midnight became mine, a group of women descended on the herd to cut the thick fleece from the adults. The fibres were long, and I discovered they were easy to spin and weave or knit. The fibres were vaguely reminiscent of the wool we used when our hunters captured sheep. This was the fibre used to make the clothing I now wore.

The squilute fibres had huge possibilities for us in The Green Valley. We more often used linen and cotton. Our winter clothes were padded and quilted for warmth. Animal fibres were only used when we found them, or when such an animal was killed for food, and they were highly valued. The thought of herding these animals was foreign to us, but the idea had huge possibilities.

"Oh, just watch this." Oak guided me back towards the cliff and pointed to the herd. A group of boys, Mekroe and Tarjin amongst them, had started a game of flicking the animal's large ears backwards. The squilute would then nod its head back and forth until the ears righted themselves. The boys had managed to get a large part of the herd nodding and some of them banged heads as they tried to right their ears. It did look amusing, and the boys wandered through the group flicking ear after ear.

A few of the older boys backed off after a short time, but the rest continued to annoy the animals. Mekroe was concentrating on a particularly long eared beast when another slipped in behind him and slapped a long slimy green tongue around Mek's neck.

His look of shock was priceless. The rest of the boys tried to slip out of the flock, but most of them carried the imprint

The Fortress of Faltryn

of teeth or hoof before they escaped. It seemed that Mekroe had got away with less of a punishment than most, until he started to walk towards us.

Oak grabbed me and backed away fast. Then the stench wafted in our direction, and we turned and ran.

"They have a gland under their tongue. They have to be very annoyed to use it," gasped Oak between guffaws of laughter. "Mek's lucky it had seen fewer than four seasons. If he'd annoyed an older beast, he would have to walk downwind of us for the best part of two moons."

As Storm bawled the boys out for teasing the squilute and for not taking care of their visitors, Oak drew me further along the cliff edge.

"Let's get out of Storm's sight. He does have a tendency to include everyone he sees in his tongue lashing. We could be punished for allowing it to happen." He looked at me and laughed. "Well, I could anyway."

We slipped around the rocks and followed a narrow path up to a wide ledge, where we could sit in the warm late morning sun.

"How long will the smell last?" I asked.

"Left to wear off naturally, it'd take twenty to thirty days. But Storm'll herd the boys into the river and they'll scrub the worst off. Even so, for two or three days close proximity will be less than pleasant." He laughed. "They won't be allowed into the fortress until we leave. They'll all be bedding down with the boats. That's a punishment in itself. Elm is always a bit sour when his space is invaded. No parties down there, he'll have them in bed as soon as the sun goes down, and up at dawn to start scrubbing again."

Oak spread his cloak on the ground for us to sit on, opened his shoulder pack and laid out some food and drink. "I wanted to talk to you," he said. "I was going to approach you at the spring celebration, but you seemed always to be engaged in conversation with one person or another."

Yes, kept occupied, I thought.

"There was something I wanted to show you. Are you up for a small adventure?" he asked, his eyes shining.

The path up the cliff was steep, and left me gasping for breath. "How often do you come up here?" I asked when we stopped for a brief rest.

"At least once every season, just to be sure it's as I left it. This'll be the last time, I guess."

While the climb was hard, Oak stopped often to explain the various safeguards he had on the steep path. In the middle of the afternoon, we stopped again for a breather and looked at the scene below us. The river looked small from up here, the people like so many ants scurrying around on the ground below us. The boys were still in the river, probably blue with cold after all this time, and as we watched, they waded towards shore only to be driven back by someone, probably Storm by the colour of the cloak.

"Not far now," said Oak, "and it's easier from here on. No more climbing."

There was no path here. The narrow ledge that stretched across the cliff was riddled with gaps and fissures. "We're over the fortress now," he said. "Directly below us is the Protectors Guild area. This path is the reason. The path looks more dangerous than it is, and that's its safeguard."

"You don't live in the protector's area, do you?"

He shook his head. "My family are stalwarts of the Crafters. I love the work, it's great and I'll go back to it when I'm a bit older, but working with the squilute is brilliant. To do that properly, I had to learn how to guard the fortress and be an effective hunter. It's a bit convoluted, but in fact, it all works in together. The Guilds encourage us to learn all aspects of our trade." He paused. "This is it."

He stepped sideways across a long fissure, into a narrow crevice and disappeared. I followed. The gap was deeper than it looked; once in it I found a narrow channel to my right. Oak was nowhere to be seen.

I could hear him ahead of me, although I couldn't see him. The tunnel continued, lit by cracks and slits in the rock above me. I followed it for just over 200 steps before I saw him again. Ahead, the tunnel darkened.

"I used to have a lamp here, but I've learnt to do it by touch." He led me on to a dead end. "It's a bit of a squeeze though."

I'd never have found the crevice by myself. It was in the darkest part of the far corner, behind a pillar of rock.

"Come through," Oak called. "There are steps here. Come down backwards, it's safer."

It was pitch black and the steps down were more like a ladder than stairs. I felt Oak's hand on my waist as I reached the bottom. He lit a small lamp. The door in front of me was obvious only because of the handle.

"The handle detaches and we keep it there." He pointed to a ledge above my head. "It just looks like another rock." He slotted it on, turned it, and put his shoulder to the door. It slowly opened and we stepped into a small room.

He put the handle back on the ledge, pushing the door closed behind him.

I looked around. "So this is the top of the guard's area."

He nodded. "The battlements are a great security, but if they were ever breached, then escape would be difficult. This is our bolthole. We've never needed it, but I use it when coming and going at night, early morning or when I don't want anyone to know I've left the fortress."

The next door, literally, was the wall. It pivoted in the

Kirym Speaks

centre and clicked shut, successfully hidden. Oak showed me how to open it from the fortress side, and then led the way through a number of rooms, along two passages and down some stairs.

"Oh, I know where we are, I said. I pointed to my right. "Wind Runner's rooms are just along there."

Oak nodded. "Even if this wasn't the pick of the rooms, it's where I'd have Wind Runner living. It's the safest place." He pushed open the door.

The rooms seemed bigger now they were empty. Our voices echoed as we walked through the suite. Everything had been taken away and packed, nothing left except the stone ceiling to floor shelves.

"I'll miss this room," he said, looking around. "A lot of my best memories come from here." Smiling, he pointed to a small black circle on the ceiling. "O for Oak. I climbed up the shelves to put that there. It was my second summer. I'd just learnt to write my name. I was in such trouble. I thought Storm would kill me, he was so incensed I'd climbed with ill regard for Wind Runner's possessions. She told me off, but she kept it there. She was quite proud of the achievement." He looked around speculatively. "It's changed though. It's as if the heart has gone from it."

The cosy braziers had been taken away, along with the furniture, the wall hangings, floor coverings and window panels.

"It's so desolate in here," I said shivering. "Advising everyone to leave was easy, but I feel I've killed something vital and alive."

"You didn't," said Oak emphatically. "The fortress was dying anyway. Few talked about it openly and it would have taken some time yet, but many of us knew we'd have to leave, and sooner rather than later. It's ironic really. Our biggest problem here is fuel. We've run out. It snows heavily in winter. We need fires through autumn, winter and spring, otherwise we'd freeze. The floor, wall and window coverings weren't just to look good. They insulate us from the cold stone. Each summer and autumn we've had to travel further and further to get wood, work harder to get it back here. Thirty springs ago, we made the decision to plant trees every season cycle, but trees grow slowly and the supply isn't keeping up with our demand. I'd say we had another twelve or fourteen comfortable winters, but already it's not sustainable. You've given us peace of mind, Kirym. Don't feel bad."

Despite Oak's reassurances, I did. The change in the rooms was so marked. The cold seemed to eat into me. I rubbed my arms trying to stop shivering.

Oak, instantly concerned, guided me over to the window to claim a little warmth from the setting sun. He put his arm around me, hugging me close.

"Wear this," he said. He shook out a black cloak that had been left sitting on one side of the deep windowsill.

I pulled the warm silky material around me. "Wind Runner must have been very distracted to leave this," I said. "You'll have to take it back to her."

"She didn't leave it here. I did. It's for you."

I looked down at the cloak. "I can't accept this, Oak. It's — it's wonderful, but it's just too much."

"Kirym, it cost me nothing except some time. The fleece came from Soot and I wove it myself." He saw the question in my face. "I told you my family were crafters. Papa was a master weaver. Mama still is. I grew up spinning and weaving. I've had the fleece spun and ready to weave for a number of seasons. I started to make it for you the morning after you arrived. I finished it just before I went to get the squilute." He settled it around my shoulders. It felt marvellous.

Kirym Speaks

I was surprised to see two guards walking the passages as I returned to the great hall. Although the passages and tunnels were checked through the day and night, generally only a single guard did this now. I nodded as I passed them. They turned and followed me back. I reached the landing above the entrance hall, and glanced over. The hall was packed with guards.

Twig glanced up as I looked down. He looked relieved as he bounded up the stairs. "Ah, there you are, Mam. Can you come with me please?"

Mystified, I followed him. He took me to the room we were first taken to when we arrived at Faltryn. Guards stood at that door also.

Since the decision had been made to leave Faltryn, we had moved to the great hall along with everyone else. We had helped pack the furniture on to the carts, but someone had brought a brazier, seats and some low tables back in.

All of my family, except Tarjin and Mekroe, were there with Wind Runner, Starshine and a number of the Guild leaders. They looked quite worried.

"What's happened?" I asked, as the door shut behind me.

"Where have you been?" exploded Teema.

"Teema!" said Mekrar sharply.

"We were worried about you, Kirym. The guards couldn't remember you coming in, and no one has seen you since mid-morning." Wind Runner guided me over to one of the seats. She rubbed her hand over my cloaked shoulder and smiled. "But you're fine, so we all need to call the guards back in and enjoy a meal. Then get everyone settled for the night."

Starshine's mouth dropped open and she and Mekrar exchanged shocked glances.

"Where have you been?" asked Teema again. "Everyone's been worried sick,"

"I'm sorry, I was exploring the fortress," I said. "I didn't realise it was so late, and suddenly the light was almost gone and ..."

"And perhaps I overreacted, Teema," said Wind Runner quickly. "Kirym is safe, and we've let our imaginations run away with us. There is no rule here that says one cannot have time to oneself. We've asked a lot of her lately. She no doubt needed to get away and think." She turned to Starshine and two of the Guild leaders. "Can you bring in some food, please?"

Platters of food were placed on the table. It was warm in here with all of the people and the brazier. I slipped my cloak off and hung it over a seat.

Mekrar picked it up. "It's gorgeous," she gushed. "Where did you get it?"

"It was a gift," I said.

"Oh, Kirym." Wind Runner raised her voice, gesturing me to her side. "You've missed all of the excitement." She patted the seat next to her.

"But ..."

"Oh, yes," said Mekrar, nudging Teema hard in the ribs.

Lyndym giggled. "Storm stood on the river bank for the morning, yelling at the boys for teasing the squilute. When he was told ..." She paused.

"He was so angry at them, he picked up a large rock," interrupted Bildon, with a glance at Mekrar, "and threw it against the bank. It hit so hard, it broke. One of the squilute took exception to that and licked him."

Now everyone apart from Teema was laughing.

Kirym Speaks

"He had to join the boys in the river," smiled Wind Runner. "He's not well pleased. He hates the dampness of the boat house. I must admit I personally had not noticed it was damp —"

"Harrummph," coughed Mole, the head of the Protectors Guild. "You haven't fallen out of the boat you were sleeping in, while a little worse for wear, Mam."

Everyone laughed again, and even Teema smiled. The evening was relaxed and when Wind Runner eventually stood, indicating the meal was over, we were all ready to sleep.

Wind Runner hugged me as I left. "I hope you had a lovely day, my dear," she said quietly.

"So where were you?" asked Mekrar spreading her rug over her knees.

"I told you, exploring the fortress. I realised it would be the only chance I'd get."

Mekrar's eyes reflected the dim lamplight. "Mek saw you walk around the south cliff. When Twig checked, you'd disappeared. No one saw you come back. They thought Danth may have managed to grab you. Wind Runner called all of the guards out." Her eyes narrowed in the dim lamplight. "By mid-afternoon she was beyond concern. Yet she suddenly changed. Tell me. What does she know that I don't?"

I laughed dryly. "She told you. She overreacted."

Mekrar put her face close to mine. "So where did the cloak come from? It wasn't with the things Wind Runner gave you. I'd have remembered it. It's sooo gorgeous."

"It wasn't finished then, but with all of the other gifts we'd accepted, it seemed impolite to refuse it when it was offered."

The Fortress of Faltryn

"Who?" she asked. "You'll have to tell me. You always tell me things."

"Well, not always," I said, "but it's not a big thing. Oak gave it to me."

"Oh yes. His mama's a weaver, isn't she? That's so nice of her." She picked it up and rubbed it on her face. "Do you think she's trying to entice you to join her family?" she giggled.

"You are an idiot," I whispered. "Go to sleep."

I turned on my side and pulled my rugs over my shoulders.

"Did he kiss you?" she whispered.

34

Teema Speaks

Leaving Faltryn for the last time was chaotic. The final journey down the river valley was slow; it took four days to reach the standing stone at the beginning of the massive river flats.

"At this rate it may very well take eight seasons to get to the valley," I said to Kirym, only half in jest.

She smiled. "They'll speed up once they leave the river. They're saying goodbye. It would be wrong to rush them. They know they can never come back."

The first mid-afternoon stop was confused, as we dealt with setting up camp, caring for the squilute, cooking and feeding everyone. By the third day, the routine was set and everything went smoother.

I was one of the ten people who kept pace with the carts in four small boats. This was a time of learning for some of us. We had no expectation of speed at this time, but the days were exhausting as Kirym, Arbreu, Mekrar, Mekroe and I learned to paddle upstream and down, zigzag around rocks, over small waterfalls and cope with eddies and shallow water.

Elm, and a slightly malodourous Storm, taught us how to turn the boats around rocks, shift our weight to alter direction and how to back paddle to slow down. We also practised falling out of the boats and getting back in.

When we all reached the standing stone at the mouth of the valley, camp was set up together for the last time.

This was different, though. After the usual chores were done, everyone was in celebration mood and the stories and songs began before the meal was fully cooked. With everyone moving around, it was a while before I realised Kirym was missing.

I found her and Oak playing with a little back squilute. They returned to the fire with me, but Oak slipped his arm around Kirym's waist and took her off into the shadows between the standing stone and the cliff as everyone settled down to eat. When I saw him kissing her, I went and talked to Mekrar.

"Is that a problem?" she asked.

"She's too young and Oak should know better," I said, wondering if she was taking this seriously enough.

"It's only a kiss and, well, everyone is doing it. We'll be going in different directions tomorrow. Everyone is saying goodbye."

She was right, kissing was rampant tonight.

"Everyone has changed since they left the fortress," I said. I was surprised at how indignant I sounded.

"They're leaving their home, and for some of us, it's goodbye for a while." She patted my arm, frowning at something behind me. I turned to look but all I saw was Arbreu chatting to one of Mole's nieces.

"Even if everyone else is doing it, Kirym is still too young to be kissed."

"Kirym is older than Halse was when you first kissed her, Teema. She's grown up and she doesn't need you to be her parent." She squeezed my arm. "She won't see Oak for well over a season. You'll see her every day. A lot can happen, but nothing will change unless you accept she's an adult. Let her know how you feel about her. If you don't, you'll have no chance at all. She won't wait for you, especially if you continue to treat her like a child." With a strange smile, she walked away.

I didn't know what to think.

With a fire to sit around and the sun setting on the western hill, the Faltryners sang songs and told stories of their history. Once or twice, they asked for something from our land, but mainly they reminisced, some with the feeling that they'd lose this as they left the land. There was laughter and tears.

In the morning we would separate. Bokum, Findlow, Tarjin, Sundas, Bildon and Lyndym would lead the Faltryners towards the stone circles, while the rest of us joined Storm, Elm, Starshine, Granite and Willow in the four boats to follow the river.

The boats travelled easily with the current. Even at the fortress, where the water was relatively shallow and sluggish as it crossed the stony river bed, no one needed to use the paddles. It was really a case of sitting and watching the scenery go past.

"You know, we travel much faster on water," I said to Kirym. "That means we'll do the trip really fast, even though we stop earlier in the day. I figure we could cut a third or more off the time we took to get to Faltryn, all going well."

"Aye, well, that's it, lad," interrupted Storm. "All going

well. So we'll be taking it slow for a bit. If we rush into this, we may find it impossible to extract ourselves. We may regret it before very long."

Seven days after leaving the family at the standing stone, we made camp opposite the start of the eastern ridge that held the fountainhead and ended at the canyon far to the south. Here, the river narrowed and the water flow increased in depth and speed.

Kirym shot a large bird during the afternoon and Mekroe and Storm caught three good size fish. While these were cooking, Kirym and Mekrar scavenged along the river bank, adding early summer fruits and herbs to the meal. The fire burned brightly as the moon rose over the eastern plains.

"We have to reassess our safety strategy from here on," said Kirym.

"Now you're seeing sense, Kirym. The safest thing is to turn back," said Storm. "This is as far as I'm happy to go. From here, the current takes over and there's no chance to change your mind. Once we're into the ravine, well, we can't return. And the rift is worse, much worse than anything you could imagine."

Kirym shrugged. "Not a lot of point going back. Everyone has already left the fortress."

"Oh, we'd soon catch up with them, I think," he said dryly.

"You don't have to go on, Storm. No one has to. If you want to join Wind Runner, go east. You'd catch up with them at the creek."

There was a short silence.

"I'm with you, Kirym," I said. "We need to do this."

She nodded and there were other sounds of acknowledgement and agreement.

"Oh well," sighed Storm. "I guess that's it. I hope it doesn't end in tears. Even when the river seems benign, there are hazards. The rocks and white water just make it more dangerous. Are you absolutely sure?"

Kirym nodded. "And because of the nature of the water ahead, we have to accept that if someone falls out of a boat and is not picked up immediately, then they have to save themselves."

Each day we were generally ashore by mid-afternoon, soon after the sun left the water. Storm refused to consider the possibility of us being in the boats after dark. Most days, we travelled no further than we would have had we been walking, and often less distance than that. A few of the places we stopped were little more than a space for us to lie down out of the water. On two occasions, there was no driftwood and we were unable to light a fire. Those nights were uncomfortable, although we carried enough rugs to ensure no one was cold. Despite the summer advancing, the area between the cliffs saw sun for less than half the day, and even on the hottest days, the damp air in the ravine was cool.

On the tenth day, we rested. By Storm's estimation the roughest part of the river was just ahead, and in the morning he wanted to be on the water as soon as it was light enough to see.

"We will stop as soon as we can, even if the sun is still rising," he said. "If we can find somewhere to stop, it means I've got it wrong, and the rift is further away than I thought. We'll need the whole day to get through, and the stories say there is nowhere to stop in there."

The Fortress of Faltryn

I woke early, joining Kirym and Storm who were guarding the camp. There was a feeling of excitement in the air, a sense of new adventure. I walked through the silent camp, watching the sky as it faded from black to grey. It was cold. I built up the fire and heated water to give everyone a hot drink when they woke, taking flasks to Storm and Kirym. "How do you think the boats will hold up?" I asked.

"There's been no problem so far," said Kirym.

"They're good for the river," interjected Storm. "Elm and I chose carefully."

I frowned. "Are you sure this trip's been done before?"

Storm shrugged.

Kirym laughed quietly. "It's surprisingly well mapped and documented, for all they say it hasn't. There were a number of books in the libraries and five good maps. Mind you, the maps were all wrong."

"What?" I gasped. "Did they make them up?"

Kirym shook her head. "When people travel a long way, they can get aspects of the trip wrong. They mix them up, especially if the maps are drawn long after they return. That's why Papa taught us all how to make notes during a trip. It doesn't come naturally. This part of the gorge, for instance. We're going south now, but over the last eight days, we've travelled west far more than south. And yet the maps show the river as going south only. That has repercussions when we reach the end of the river."

"In what way?" asked Storm.

"The oldest map at the fortress showed the river emptying into our inlet just to the west of Tarjin's path, but there's no river there, so I suspect this particular path will go right to the sea. The maps show the small hill between the river and The Green Valley. On the western side of The Green Valley, there are a number of hilly ranges. The nearest one is quite small, but further on they're much larger. I'm unsure which

Teema Speaks

hills will be between the river and the valley. But this is what exploration is all about."

I thought about that as we prepared a meal. This meal was larger than usual, made with the knowledge we'd not stop until we were through the narrowest part of the rift. Storm thought that would be early in the evening. There would be no meal until then, although we carried food in the boats in case we got the chance to eat it.

We held paddles, not to move ahead, but to assist slight changes of direction, ensuring our boats went around and between the rocks and hopefully not over or into them.

Everything we had, including our cloaks and boots, was packed in waterproof containers. Storm checked each of them to make sure they were properly closed. Anything that fell out of the boats might be retrieved — if it didn't smash against the rocks.

None of the boats held the full number of people they could. Storm reckoned that in the event of one or even two of them overturning in the maelstrom ahead, there would be room in the others for everyone to travel safely — hopefully. He was worried. We all knew that, and it was a little unsettling.

Kirym had tried to reassure him, but wasn't really successful. "When it comes down to it," she said, "we have no choice. We have to go ahead."

We were in the boats and on the river as soon as it was light. A mist clung to the water, changing the sounds around us. Very quickly, the cliffs drew in and towered above us.

The water moved very fast and the scenery raced past at a dizzying speed. Little time passed before I heard the roar of the first rock-strewn waterfall. There were a lot of rocks. The paddlers had to be very alert; small mistakes were likely to cause big disasters.

"We're facing this for the rest of the day," yelled Storm,

The Fortress of Faltryn

as our boat slipped between two waves, deftly avoided three rocks and sank into a small hollow in the water. We rocketed out and into smooth water beyond, exhilarated and breathless.

Kirym turned to look back at me, her grin as wide as mine. I could hear the others coming through behind us, screams and whoops of excitement. We raced ahead and all too soon, the roar of the next rough water was heard.

It was exciting and terrifying at the same time. Again and again, I watched Kirym tense, holding tightly to the sides of the boat as Storm and I dug the paddles in to drag the boat around rocks or between them, over or through the waves.

The sun was now overhead and the air between the rock walls was hot, highlighting the icy nature of the water. Insects buzzed around us and we could see and hear the birds that swooped down from their nests in the cliff walls that towered above us. With the sun directly overhead, we enjoyed the occasional shade from the trees clinging to the rock face.

The gap between the cliffs narrowed again and the speed of the water increased, pushing the boats to a dizzying speed. The wind raced past us.

A rock loomed ahead and I dug my paddle in to turn the boat, shifting it to the right and powering through a standing wave. I watched the rocks ahead, and felt Storm's powerful strokes altering the direction again to allow us to slip around a stone pillar, following the path taken by Arbreu and Willow in the boat ahead of us. More boulders loomed, the craft swayed to and fro as we swerved to avoid danger.

The speed we travelled at was breath-taking, but the problem with speed was we had less time to react to any change ahead. Rocks loomed up at a shocking pace.

White water highlighted rocks sitting above the surface,

Teema Speaks

but often sharp points just under the water were masked by the smooth rushing liquid. The cliffs seemed so close, although I was aware that the swiftness of the current exacerbated the illusion of a narrow passage.

The boat in front slipped into a channel that took them close to a line of rocks, needing a sharp controlled turn at the bottom to avoid a crash. It was a dangerous path and I knew Storm would want to avoid it if possible. I tensed for his yell of 'Left', to avoid the route.

It didn't come, but I had already dug the paddle in for the turn. The boat slewed and too late I saw the drop ahead.

With no choice, I paddled on and we powered between two humps of water, hoping for the best. The drop was higher than I thought. The water disappeared and the boat shot into thin air and fell.

Everything seemed to move in slow motion. The craft swung sideways, dropped, slammed into a large rock and split across the centre.

35

Kirym Speaks

I was pulled under, the water buffeting me into a number of rocks. My lungs hurt — I was fast running out of air. Something came up behind me and hit the back of my head, shocking me into gulping a mouthful of water. I flailed out at it, my hands entangling with something long and sinuous. I grabbed hold, kicking hard to get to the surface. I was beginning to see stars when I emerged and gasped, taking in a mouthful of water and air.

The force of the water slammed me onto a large rock, still far from the bank. It pushed me up onto the rock and held me there, safe enough for the time being, but the cold water was chilling me to the bone.

Getting to another boat quickly — our rule on falling into the water — wasn't possible. I couldn't follow the boats. The water was too rough, there were too many rocks.

Something tugged at my hands and I looked to see what I had grabbed while underwater. I held a length of rope, the end edging back into the maelstrom. I grabbed it and pulled it in, wrapping it over my shoulder. The other end came into view, tangled with two of the watertight containers from the boat. I dragged them to me and untangled the rope, tying the containers securely together. I'd need all the help I could get when I left the rock. They floated well, although I knew I couldn't rely on them.

I inched higher on the rock, trying to see the route ahead. It was obvious that all of the boats had gone through. I hoped they'd pick Teema and Storm up further downstream.

If I went to the left when I vacated the rock, I would slip into choppy water culminating, at the far end of my vision, in a standing wave. To go right would take me onto another rock. If I went left from there, I'd slip into a fast deep water race and, hopefully, be washed safely downstream. There was no choice, already I was beginning to chill in the ice-cold water.

I took a deep breath and, clinging to the floating packs, launched myself back into the water. I hit the rock I was aiming at, but the force of the water took me to the right of it instead of the left. I was buffeted into a group of rocks and pulled underwater again, losing hold of the packs, although I still had the rope clutched in one hand.

I struggled against the force of water, kicking towards the surface. I came to an abrupt halt, slammed into another rock, and I clawed up it to get my head above water.

I had been pushed towards the cliffs, and just ahead I saw a stony ledge thrusting out at right angles into the water. I lunged towards it, worried I would miss it, and more concerned because of the roar of rapids that now came to me from around the bend.

The Fortress of Faltryn

I crawled out of the water and lay there fighting to get my breath back, coughing and spewing river water from my stomach and lungs. I felt the rope slipping through my chilled fingers. The force of the water was pulling the containers back into the flow. The thought of losing them spurred me into action. I needed those containers. The contents could make the difference between life and death in the coming days.

Once they were safe, I assessed my situation. The ledge was narrow, and all it did was keep me out of the water. I couldn't stay there — I knew no one could return. Survival was up to me.

Further downstream against the cliff was a narrow stony shelf. It was slightly bigger than the ledge I was on, and the cliff, although steep, was my only escape route. The water between me and the shelf seemed calm, the ledge I was on redirecting the main flow of the water. I gathered the packs and rope together and plunged back into the water.

The current was more powerful than I realised, and I was pushed further south than I wanted. I was almost past the shelf before my feet touched the river bed. I took a step towards the bank, relieved to be safe.

Then my knees buckled and I was again under water, trying not to panic as I realised I didn't have the energy to stand and keep my head above the surface.

I crawled towards the bank, fearful of being washed further downstream. Breathless, I struggled to the surface, took a breath and sank, crawling closer to the cliff. I realised that every time I surfaced, I was being pushed further and further downstream. I was beginning to wonder if I would make it or be washed away.

My head broke the surface again. I was against the cliff, but past the shelf. I grabbed hold of a low bush growing out of the cliff face and pulled myself back towards the safety

Kirym Speaks

of the shelf. It was hard work, and seemed to take forever before I struggled onto dry stony land.

I lay on the ground, exhausted and aching.

The cold brought me back to reality. The shadows from the trees above me were growing, the sun no longer shining into the ravine. It was still early in the afternoon, but already the chill at the bottom of the gorge indicated the danger of staying there overnight.

I inspected the cliff above me. It was a daunting climb. As I explored, I found goat droppings on the bank around me.

Oh well, I thought, *if goats can get up and down, so can I.* I put aside the idea that they may very well have fallen down and been washed away.

I realised immediately that the tabard I wore over my trousers would get in the way as I climbed. Short of climbing topless or naked, I would have to adapt. I tied the two ends of the tabard over one shoulder, hoping it would stay there.

The containers were still tied to the end of the rope. I wound it around my waist and tied it securely, so they hung behind and below me. Then I started to climb.

It was difficult. The cliff was overgrown, but many of the plants had only a tenuous foothold in thin soil. Grasping the thin tree trunks was no safer. Until I put my weight on one, I really didn't know if it would hold. My progress was slow, but steady. Every step and every handhold had to be carefully checked. More than once, what looked like a solid hold pulled away and fell onto the bank below. Before I reached the top, two largish trees and quite a few smaller saplings and bushes had fallen onto the ledge below me.

Occasionally the containers snagged and the only way to unhook them was to climb back down to them. The tabard kept slipping off my shoulder, restricting my attempts to reach higher. Eventually, I resorted to holding the end of the knot between my teeth to keep it in place.

When I reached the top of the cliff, I faced a different problem. The edge was crumbly, and every time I put my weight on it, it fell away. I was almost crying with frustration and exhaustion when I finally managed to roll over the edge and crawl to more stable ground.

After a short rest, I pulled the containers up. The sun was low in the western sky. I was tired, damp, dirty and very thirsty.

I walked away from the cliff top, checking the area. Once through the fringe of trees at the cliff edge, the land was arid, rocky scrubland. This was the desert of Wind Runner's map.

There were a few trees though, and over to my left was a line of them where a trickle of water flowed towards the cliff. Not a lot of water, but it would have to do.

After deciding on a place to camp, I checked the containers, finding two thick cloaks: Storm's and one given to me by Starshine. My pouch of medicinal herbs was there; the tokens, my old dress, shift, petticoats and boots and some of Starshine's clothing. There were packs of travelling food, a small platter, a skin pot, two flasks, a knife and a flint.

I was relieved to find the knife and flint. The trees supplied deadfall and twigs, and a fire was more than just heat. Although I'd not seen any animals, there were signs of them, droppings and large prints in the soil.

As I collected wood, I foraged for food, finding herbs, mushrooms, roots and a little wild fruit. With some dried meat from my stores, it would make a satisfying meal.

At the stream, I built a small dam to give me enough water to fill the flasks and wash my feet and hands.

While collecting wood, I discovered a soap-nut tree and collected a handful of the nuts. They would make washing

Kirym Speaks

easier. I warmed some water, added a mixture of dried lavender and calendula from my herb pouch, and as the sun set, I took the mixture back to the stream.

On the far side of the small dam was a wide concave rock. I poured the warm water in, added the herbs and soap mixture, stripped off my clothes and washed them and myself in the lukewarm water.

I was surprised at how extensive my bruises were. I seemed to be black and blue from my shoulders to my ankles. I had a wide rope burn around my waist. My cheek felt swollen and I had a number of painful lumps on my head.

I slipped into my old dress, pleased I had brought it with me, and thankful I'd replaced the tattered sleeves. They didn't match the dress, but they were warm and comfortable. I hung my wet clothing over a tree branch near the fire to dry. I pulled the tangles from my damp hair while waiting for a hot drink.

As the sun set, I heard the roar of large cats in the distance. I was relieved I had the fire to protect me overnight.

Having no weapons other than the knife, I collected some long thin branches. As the food cooked, I stripped them of bark, sharpened the ends and carefully hardened them in the fire. As spears, they weren't as good as I'd like, but I felt better having something else to defend myself with. I wished I had a bow, but they took time to make and I had no feathers for fletching arrows.

I ate, and wrapped the remaining food for morning. I knew I was too tired to wake through the night to feed the fire, but I wanted to be able to build it quickly if the need arose. I had added a slow burning log earlier and the coals were glowing brightly. I built up a mixture of hot soil and ashes around it to reduce the amount of air getting to the embers. By damping it down this way, I should find glowing coals in the morning. I had a pile of twigs and smaller pieces

The Fortress of Faltryn

of wood handy, to build up the fire in a hurry if needed. A number of reasonable sized lengths of branch wrapped in long dried leaves also sat close by. Thrust into the coals, they would fire immediately if I were in any danger. They would give me time to build up the fire, as well as being weapons in their own right.

Wrapping myself in my cloak, my thoughts finally turned to those in the boats. Deep down, I knew that Teema and Arbreu were safe, and I sent a message letting them know I was too.

I could get no information about Storm, although I tried. Teema was blocking me. I was concerned, but too tired and sore to delve deeper into the reasons why. I hoped it wasn't because the news was bad, but there was nothing I could do about it anyway.

Morning saw me awake and aching all over. My shoulder, where I had been thrown into the rocks, throbbed and my hips, elbows, knees and ankles felt strangely weak from the battering they'd taken. The wide rope burn around my waist along with a few other wounds still oozed, and my clothing had stuck to them. My face felt stiff, and my hair caught in the still weeping grazes on my cheek. Even my throat was sore.

It was cold, and moving was painful. I really wanted to spend the day sleeping in the sun, but I had a long trip ahead of me if I wanted to catch up with the others. I checked over my herbs and medicines, but other than taking a small dose of harkii and an herb to stop my headache, I decided to wait and see what I could find as I travelled. I had seen the berries and roots I preferred to use for these types of injuries closer to the fortress, and I was sure I could find them and make up a remedy rather than using my valuable stores.

I ate the remains of the meal I'd prepared the night before, washing it down with a hot drink. While waiting for the

Kirym Speaks

water to boil, I collected more soap-nuts. I filled the flasks with clean water and packed the containers, tying them to my back.

My shoulders hurt where I'd been thrown into the rocks, but I needed the contents of the containers and there was no one else to carry them. The clothes I had washed the night before were still damp. I decided to carry them draped over the packs for a while until they had fully dried.

After carefully dousing the fire, and with the river on my left, I walked south.

36

Kirym Speaks

The terrain was difficult. Much of the stony ground was covered with spiky bushes. More than once I was brought to a sudden stop as my skirts caught, and by mid-morning was getting frustrated. Finally, I stopped and reassessed my clothes. The skirts of my dress and the petticoats were the main problem, so I cut them off the top. Although it was still summer, the day was cloudy and there was a cool breeze. I felt chilled — possibly reaction from the stress of the situation I was in — so I needed the top to keep warm. I still wore my shift which fell straight to my ankles, covering the top of my boots. It was loose enough for me to run if necessary, while being narrow enough to avoid being caught too often. The change made travelling much easier.

My feet were very tender. I would have walked without boots, but for the sharp spikes dropped by the surrounding plants. I discovered them the hard way, when two pierced my heel while walking from the fire to the stream. They

Kirym Speaks

were painful and difficult to remove.

I stayed fairly much to the path I'd set, wanting to travel as far and fast as I could. However, there were some things that had to be checked, and I made a mental map as I travelled. When I got home, I would add this information to the maps we relied on.

The land looked bleak, covered with dusty green plants I associated with arid desert-like areas. Despite that, I crossed a myriad of small water courses, most of them not much more than a hand span across, and there were stands of trees along some of them. I saw evidence of animals and birds and I was able to forage widely as I travelled, which was good because I didn't want to rely on the dried food I carried.

I was pleased to find the root and berries I was looking for to help relieve the pain from my bruises. When I stopped at midday, I scraped the root, mixing it with the berry juice, and spreading a thin layer on a hot stone in front of a fire to dry out.

My legs stiffened when I stopped, and it was hard to get going again. The bruises and abrasions I had received while in the river made stretching and bending difficult. I decided that eating while travelling may be less painful over the next few days.

I carried a few stones, trying to fell some small game as I travelled, but the abrasions on my elbows and shoulders took away the force I usually had and affected my accuracy.

I was relieved when evening approached and I could stop and rest. I hadn't gone nearly as far as I had hoped, but I knew this would change as time passed and I healed.

Soon after dawn I was again travelling south. With the cloud cover gone, it was a hot day, and I intended to travel as far and as fast as I could.

It was harder. There were fewer trees and more spiky

bushes, and I found no water until late in the afternoon. I decided to stop there for the night. I was still very sore, and couldn't settle for the first part of the night.

I was shocked to see the sun well above the horizon when I woke. I quickly ate a cold meal, and moved on, walking southwest now and following the grain of the land. I still felt exhausted.

Early in the afternoon, I heard a high-pitched kee-ik of a bird coming from somewhere to my right. I was reluctant to take time from my travel, but the thought of meat or possibly eggs for my next meal was too enticing. I had to keep my strength up. Leaving the packs, I started to search. Rounding a large rock, I spied the agitated bird and raised my spear, but in the moments it took to aim, I heard the muted call of chicks.

The brown speckled little owl, peered up at me, looking for all the world as if it were frowning. A small pile of worms sat beside a large, partly buried, off-white rock. Despite my proximity, which should have sent it running for cover, it continued to bob up and down, calling as it had before. It looked so funny, I laughed, but even that didn't scare the wee owl away.

"Well now, where are they?" I asked, enjoying the sound of my voice after three days of silence.

The chick calls were indistinct. This was a ground burrowing bird, and yet there was no obvious hole for the nest. I checked the area, ending up back where the bird still jumped about beside the strange coloured stone.

Yes, the sounds came from beneath it.

"How did that happen?" I asked the distraught little owl. I knelt down, grimacing in pain, and grabbed the rock. It was spongy, strange, not at all rock-like. Shocked, I instinctively pulled my fingers away.

This was just wrong.

Kirym Speaks

I leaned in to get a better grip. The tiny limp figure came out: a wee baby. I was shocked beyond belief.

The owl had no such problem. Still squawking with annoyance, she grabbed a mouthful of worm and dived down the hole.

I sat back looking at the tiny body. Why had she not been buried properly?

Then her little chest rose and fell.

I was galvanized into action. I grabbed her and raced back to the packs. Pulling one open, I wrapped the cold wee babe in one of my petticoats, trying to think of the best thing to do.

Ahead was another watercourse, this one much bigger than the others I'd crossed. I grabbed the packs and jogged towards it, struggling to work out what to do next.

At the trees, I pulled together the makings of a fire and lit it, putting water on to heat. The wee girl, the tiniest living baby I'd ever seen, was newly born, probably arriving during the night.

I couldn't feed her what nature intended her to have, but I wasn't going to give up without a fight. I opened my herb pouch, grabbed a harkii nut, ground it to a paste and added warm water until it was at a consistency she could cope with. I ripped a small square of material off one my petticoats and soaked a twist of it in the liquid. I squeezed it into her mouth. She sucked hungrily, and objected with a tiny bleat when the small amount had gone. Another scoop, and on until her little belly was full.

While feeding her, I got my first really good look at her. She had the sweetest triangular face, with a remarkable amount of dark hair that stuck up all over the place. Her eyes were dark, although I knew that could change as she got older. I was still amazed at how tiny she was. She was still covered with the residue of her birth, and I heated

The Fortress of Faltryn

more water with the intention of bathing her once she was otherwise cared for.

I knew I'd go no further today. Wood was readily available, and leaving the baby for a short time, I gathered a pile together. Wading into the stream, I scooped more water from the stream and with a lucky thrust, managed to spear a fish. Back at the camp, I checked the food I had collected during the day. There was enough for a couple of meals.

The baby was fretful. The petticoat I'd wrapped her in was soiled and wet and I knew I had limited resources for replacing it. I hauled all of my clothes out of the packs and starting with the petticoats, ripped them into useable lengths. The skirts of my dress followed. I replaced the swaddling around the babe and washed the soiled petticoat, ripping it into strips also and hanging them over a bush to dry.

"Where did you come from?" I asked gently as I rocked her. "Are there other people near here? Why were you discarded like that?"

As the wee girl settled, I walked back to where the owl had her nest. The worms and insects had disappeared and the chicks were now silent. I carefully checked the ground around the nesting hole. The prints of the owl were clear in the sand beside the nest, but the rest of the ground was stony and even my own prints were hidden. With the ground otherwise clear of footprints, I wondered if whoever had dumped the baby had chosen this place because they couldn't be followed. No one at the fortress had mentioned people living on this side of the river; indeed Wind Runner told me there had been no one over here in living memory. Obviously that was wrong, and I wondered what other incorrect information had been given me.

So far as I knew only Rabbit and Danth had not gone south with the family, but there had been no suggestion that

Kirym Speaks

they'd crossed to this side of the river and this was a most unlikely direction for them to go. Wind Runner said her people rarely came west. There were a lot of dangers here and the barren land wasn't conducive to survival. Rabbit knew that, and from comments made, I knew she liked to be comfortable. This was not an easy land. Storm had made a comment about strange things happening over here. I wished I had insisted on answers to my questions at the time, but the subject had changed and I'd never gone back to it.

I cast about further from the nesting site and finally found some clumps of tussock grass that were flattened, though these were quite a distance from the nest. Taking a line from the nest to the tussock, I searched further, but found only prints of the large cats I'd heard earlier. No signs of people. I wasn't even sure what flattened the grass. It appeared more in keeping with a large animal or bird than a person. I just didn't know, and to put more energy into the search would be a waste.

I foraged as I walked back to my camp, adding mushrooms, fruit and root vegetables to my store of food. I fed the baby again, changed the cloths wrapping her and washed her and them. I didn't have the oils I would have liked to rub over her skin, but I added dried lavender and calendula to the water I bathed her in. It was the best I could do.

I collected big leaves to wrap the fish in and set it in the hot ashes of the fire, heating water and adding chopped roots and herbs for my own meal.

My grazes were healing as time passed, but the scabs on them tended to crack when I moved; they oozed, and my clothes stuck to them. I still felt the bruises too. Despite that, I slept well, even though I had to wake a number of times through the night for the baby.

Having to care for her meant more stops were needed and

The Fortress of Faltryn

I travelled less distance than I had planned. I made sure my only stops were to tend her or to forage for food. To relieve the strain of carrying her, I cut a strip off the bottom of my shift and used it as a sling.

I appreciated how hard it had been for Zeprah travelling with Trayum, although there had been more people to share the chores and guard the camp. My workload increased dramatically, and I had the added worry of supplies, not for myself, but for the baby.

Although I carried a large number of harkii nuts, I had no chance of replacing them before meeting up with Mekrar. Even then, I'd have to get home before I could be sure of a new supply. I had found none growing wild in this land. Mama, Jorlenta and I had planted as many as we could over the last two season cycles. They had grown well and now we had a good supply in the Green Valley.

37

Kirym Speaks

For five days, I started walking as soon as the sun rose and kept going until dusk, stopping only to care for the wee girl. The land changed, with more open areas and fewer plants. It was harder to find food, although I didn't go hungry. After the full moon there were sudden heavy showers and the clouds built up, getting thicker as evening approached.

In the afternoon of the fifth day it began to rain heavily and I was caught out in the open. There was nothing I could do but trudge towards the nearest shelter, trying to protect the baby from the weather. By the time I got to the trees I was soaked and she, tucked in under my cloak, was damp and fretful. I pushed on looking for somewhere sheltered to spend the night.

The watercourse was deeper than anything I'd seen over the last few days. The level was rising quickly and I suspected it had been raining heavily in the north and west. I searched for a safe place to cross, knowing that if I couldn't find one,

I'd be stuck here without shelter for days.

A tree had fallen across the water, its roots washed out by the flow. It made the ideal bridge, although it was awkward to use. It rocked with each step. I couldn't rush — if I fell, the torrent would wash me back into the gorge.

I tucked the baby into the sling close to my body, allowing me the ability to use both hands for balancing and pushing branches aside to get across the tree. The poor wee thing was damp, cold and grizzling, but nothing would get better until I found shelter.

As I pushed through the middle branches, the tree twisted and pulled free of the bank. I was stuck. The water was too deep and the flow too strong for me to attempt to leave the tree. The branches and roots caught on the stream bed, slowing it down, but it floated clear of the banks and was making steady progress towards the gorge.

A great surge of water swung the tree in circles. Ahead I could hear the roar of a waterfall tumbling over the edge of the cliff. I'd have to do something quickly or I'd be back where I started.

The rain grew heavier and the baby screamed her protest. Intent on getting us to safety, I could do nothing for her. She wriggled and squirmed, arching her back, uncomfortable and angry. I felt her slipping out of the sling. In desperation I pushed on her damp bottom to try to manoeuvre her back into it. That didn't work, and now I had to hold her to ensure she didn't fall.

Nearer the gorge, the stream narrowed and deepened. The tree sped up swinging from side to side as the water surged. It twisted sideways and hit a bulge on the southern bank, jolting to a stop so sudden, I almost lost my grip on the branch I was holding. The tree swung around dipping from side to side as I worked my way towards solid ground. Holding the baby, I was unable to move as fast along the

Kirym Speaks

trunk as I'd wish. I was terrified it would again float away. I could feel the pull of the flow, the roots slipping away from the bank as the water gobbled chunks of the soil.

The river deepened again and debris lodged against the trunk, pushing it further out into the flow. I leapt through the roots, splodging down into the sodden mud of the bank. I sank up to my ankles and nearly overbalanced — held by the viscous mud. I pulled one foot loose, then the other, and struggled up the bank away from the rising water.

Behind me, I could hear the roar of the torrent. The sound of the branches and roots cracking and popping as the water pulled at the tree, followed me as I climbed above the flood of water.

I turned as I reached the top of the bank in time to see a huge log crash into the tree I'd been on. It gave up its tenuous grip on the land and lurched out of sight, speeding up as the water deepened. A surge of rubbish, branches and broken tree trunks filled the muddy water following it.

I climbed down the far side of the bank, swinging my sodden cloak around me as the rain got heavier. Lightning flashed and the accompanying thunder shook the ground. I ignored the frightened screams from the baby, it was more important to find shelter. The trees swayed as the wind rose, showering me with water. A bank to climb and then another and another and as I reached the top, I spied an ancient tree, its massive twisted trunk leaning against the side of the slope. The next flash of lightning showed its huge roots arching out of the ground, the branches creating a thick roof, keeping out the now heavily falling rain.

I slid down the incline and inspected the tree, digging out some of the debris from beneath a thick root. I pushed the crying baby into the small shelter, dropped the packs and started collecting wood for a fire. It was darker under the tree and there was little light anyway, except for the

The Fortress of Faltryn

occasional flashes of lightning. The fire was important for light, heating and protection. I hoped that as the tree had avoided lightning for so long, it would do so tonight also. Either way, I had no choice. This was a forest.

It was almost fully dark when I figured I had enough wood to keep me going. I cleared a circle of dry leaves from the ground, piled them up with twigs and a couple of bigger branches, and lit it.

The baby was now beyond crying. Her little chest heaved as she gulped in air. She was wet, cold and hungry. With water heating, I quickly washed her, replaced her damp clothes and pulled off my wet things, wrapping us both in Storm's thick, dry cloak. I held her close as I pounded some harkii and thinned it with warm water. She settled as I fed her, still hiccupping as she fell asleep. I hugged her close and we slowly warmed up.

I changed into Starshine's spare clothing wrapping the extra width and length around me. I was still chilled, but the dry clothes and the heat of the fire slowly helped me thaw out. I ate my meal, damped the fire in the usual way and curled up under the roots with the baby. We were dry here and protected.

The rain continued heavily through the night and all of the next day. It was a relief to have an excuse to rest. Had I been by myself, I would probably have continued on, but having to think of the baby was good for me.

When the rain eased slightly, late on the following morning, I took the dirty washing and the flasks to the river. The water almost reached the top of the bank, shockingly high and very dirty. It raced past me at huge speed and I could hear the roar ahead where it plunged over the cliff. During the storm, I hadn't realised just how close I was to the gorge, now I felt sick as I understood how lucky I'd been.

I rinsed the swaddling clothes and carried them back to

the huge tree, hanging them to dry, although I'd have to rinse them in clean water before they could be used. The water from the river was undrinkable. I needed to find a source of clean water.

The tree looked easy to climb. It was big and old and I hoped it would rise above the trees around it, giving a view of the surrounding area. Having fed and settled the baby I started climbing.

The tree was home to many animals and birds. A squirrel's nest gave me a supply of nuts and further up, I found seeds, rosehips and eggs. As I got near the top of the tree, I felt the rain again. Going further would be uncomfortable, but I had come this far and I needed to see what I could.

The view was magnificent. The sky in the west showed patches of blue, the worst of the weather had passed. The trees extended south for as far as I could see, but to the west, they stopped and the land opened up. Far to the south of the open area, lines of strange rock formations rose from the ground looking like chimneys towering above the land.

Within the trees I could see others as big as the one I was in. They were spaced through the wooded area, thrusting high above the canopy. A short distant to the south was a clearing with a pool, and the braches of nearby trees were bright with fruit.

I climbed down and stored the food I'd collected. I checked the fire, added a slow burning log to keep it going and put the baby into her sling. Taking the water flasks, one of the packs which I emptied, and the washing, I walked to the pool to fill the flasks, rinse the washing and collect what fruit I could.

I was still very tired and rather sore, although the day of enforced rest had done me a huge amount of good. My back hurt from the load I was carrying, aggravated again by the heavy waterproof containers.

The Fortress of Faltryn

Along with the baby and other possessions I hauled with me each day, my aches and pains were not healing as well as I'd hoped. I had sorted through my possessions, but there was nothing I could happily leave behind.

I sat back and looked around the wooded area that made up my shelter. It was a few moments before the sight of a nearby willow tree registered, and I mentally kicked myself. I routinely collected the bark for pain relief, but now I realised there were good lengths that were only seeing their second summer of growth around the base. I cut two long poles, a stack of willow withies and a large armful of long rushes. Back at the fire, I began weaving and tying them together, making a triangular hauling frame and a basket for the baby. I enjoyed working with my hands, finding it relaxing after so many days of hard travel. Once I'd figured the way to work the canes and rushes, my mind ranged freely over the information I'd gathered at the top of the tree. I watched the baby, curled in a nest of moss and leaves.

"You know, I've been a bit silly," I told her. "I have tools I've not used, and I could have made things a little easier." She gurgled back at me as I tied off a rush and picked up the pouch of tokens. "Well, little girl, which one should I use?" I closed my eyes, thinking of Teema, and pulled out one of the tokens. I brought it to my forehead. There was a flash of blue.

Where are you?

We've come to a large lake. We arrived just before a huge rain storm.

A lake?

He nodded. *The hills around it are really rugged. The next part of the journey will be hard. Are you close?*

Days away, I think. There are tall red rock formations south of me. Can you get to them?

I felt him nod.

Kirym Speaks

They're about two days north. We can meet you there. We'll leave at first light.

I felt good. I was beginning to act rather than react. Knowing I was about four days from the lake, gave me a definite goal.

The rainbow token continued to glow, unusual in the circumstances. The radiance grew, expanding out to envelop us both. The baby watched — her eyes wide with wonder. She reached out to the token and a beam of light illuminated her face. I felt my tokens begin to pulse. The two smaller stones were positively buzzing as I leaned over to touch her forehead with them. The beam of light intensified and one of the small tokens dropped onto her forehead, just below her hairline. It glowed brightly, seeming to be more alive now than it had before. The beam of light connected it to my three.

I didn't know what it meant. Did this make her mine? The token was obviously hers — I'd only held it until she arrived. Tokens generally came with names, and I wondered if this meant I could name her? There was no cave here and now I questioned the need for one, except to give the stones.

I had no answers, except that the token belonged to her. I made a holder as names ran through my mind. None made sense. If she had come from Faltryn's Fortress, then she should be named for something connected to her birth.

Owl, River, Flood? Desert, Torrent? Nothing seemed right. Then again, she probably wasn't a Faltryner. She didn't come from The Green Valley and although I toyed with using my deceased sister Halse's name, I knew that wasn't right either. It just didn't suit her. I felt her name was tied up with the tokens, and with that thought I accepted the need for patience.

"Your name has to be right, so I'll wait to be told." I smiled at her. "It'll be something beautiful." I slipped the token into a holder and clicked it to my tokens, first the white, then the blue and the green, and placed it on her forehead.

Her token connected to mine and as I watched, colours swirled through it, red, orange, yellow, green, blue and purple and black before returning to white. I had no idea what it meant.

It rained heavily again through the night, but in the morning, a light wind blew the heaviest clouds away and the sun shone. I walked across the open plain towards the strange peaks I'd seen from the tree. They were a natural landmark and I wanted to know more about them. The rain had washed the air clean and the resulting clarity made them appear so close I felt I could reach out and touch them. They towered above everything around them.

It took me two full days to get there.

38

Kirym Speaks

The peaks sat on the edge of the plateau I'd been travelling on. Just past them the land dropped away and there was a wide tree covered lowland that ended at the lake. It was a huge body of water, stretching into the distance towards the west, although part of my view was cut off by the plateau that swept across the lowland towards the shore ending, as a rough finger of rock, far out in the lake.

Dotted across the water in front of me were five small islands. I could see where the river current washed into the lake by the difference in colour. To the south, the distant hills Teema had talked about enclosed the lake.

To the east beyond a line of small hills, the massive snow clad heights I had seen from The Green Valley glowered over the landscape.

The rock formations were unusual. They were red, in a land where the soil and stone was various shades of yellow, and they looked like giant building blocks stacked on top of each other. If it hadn't been for the number and immense size of them, I would have assumed they were man made.

The area teemed with birdlife, many of them nesting in and around the great pillars. I arrived there as the sun was setting and searched for a protected place to set up camp.

The eastern end of the formation was far more weathered than the others and the most exposed column had leaned sideways onto its neighbour, dropping slabs of rock from the top to litter the ground around the base. Some of them stacked against and on top of each other creating holes and hollows. Finding shelter was easy, although finding shelter that was unused was a little harder.

It was almost dark when I found it. Not quite a cave, but the ground was free of animal tracks and debris. I could wedge the end of the triangular frame over the entrance to give extra protection against the elements. I lit the fire to one side of the entry, delighted that the smoke drifted up and disappeared through minute cracks in the stones above. It was a relief to be in such a protected area and I fell asleep soon after I'd eaten. I was tired and knew I'd be awake through the night to feed the baby.

Kirym! Kirym!

Teema called me, but I couldn't answer. He came closer and closer, leaning over me.

KIRYM!

I'm awake. I sat up, looking around the empty shelter. *Where are you?*

Why are you asleep? It's mid-morning.

I shook my head, as much to get rid of a question I wasn't about to answer. It was dim in the shelter, the lack of light and my tiredness allowing me to sleep long past my normal waking time. Next to me, the baby woke and gurgled at me. I reached for a platter and a harkii nut, crushing it as I gave my attention back to Teema.

Where are you? he asked.

At the eastern end of the tall red rocks. Are you near?

I can see them. I'll make a smoky fire. Let me know how far away you are.

I nodded. *I'll eat, and then it should be visible.*

I closed him off, but not before I registered his surprise and disapproval for my not acting instantly.

I built up the fire, putting water on to heat as I changed and washed the baby. I mixed her food and fed her, nibbling at a handful of fruit as I did so. I put her in the sling and walked to the southern side of the rocks.

A thin pall of smoke rose above the trees to the southwest. I estimated Teema was half a day away. The trees he was in were thick. It was difficult terrain — easy to get lost in.

Teema, you should come to me. It'll take you about half a day.

Again I felt his surprise that I wasn't already on the trail towards him, but it would be easier for them to find me. The terrain between us was thick and overgrown. Once he was here, there was an easier path to the lake that we couldn't get to if I went to them.

While waiting for him to arrive, I explored the rocks. They were inspiring, obviously shaped by wind and rain. There were lines of them, generally joined at the base. But every now and again there was a gap and I was able to slip between them and investigate.

There were a lot of creatures living amongst the columns. I found nests and dens everywhere I looked and the calls of birds and animals echoed around the peaks.

It was early afternoon when I returned to my packs and built up the fire. High above, two crows were attacking a

The Fortress of Faltryn

young hawk. The aerial fight was exciting. The hawk easily avoided the crows, but they managed to keep him away from the cliff where his nest was. He held something in his claws that sparkled as the sun caught it. It was too rigid to be food although I couldn't identify it from the ground. It restricted his flight.

After a while the crows began to co-ordinate their attack. Realising they were no match for him in battle, they were intent now on tiring him. They swooped and soared around each other until the hawk, with a scream of defiance, dropped what he carried. The crows were distracted by the object and as their attention was momentarily diverted, the hawk took the opportunity to fly to the safety of the cliff.

The object flashed as it plummeted towards the ground, straight towards the basket holding the baby. I dived towards it.

39

Teema Speaks

She's done it again, Arbreu. Each time I contact her, she cuts me short. Now we have to go to her. It'd be quicker for her to come here."

"Would it?"

I turned to stare at Arbreu. "What do you mean? This'll add a day to the trip, and it's time we can ill afford."

Arbreu shrugged. "She's by herself and she could be injured."

"Then she should've told me," I said crossly. "How can I do what's best if I don't know what's going on. She's never done this before. I hate not knowing."

Arbreu laughed. "That's what's really bugging you, isn't it? Perhaps she doesn't want to worry you, or maybe she's too tired to give you more. We really do expect a lot from her. She's been travelling by herself for twelve days without help. The land's unknown, and there could be other things we don't know about," he paused. "Anyway, have you told her everything?"

"Well, I didn't want to worry her," I mumbled. "I've tried to contact Mekrar, but I don't have the connections. I can't even contact Bokum now. So I'm wondering if there's a problem there too."

"Don't worry about Bokum. He has enough people to sort out anything that could happen there. If you'd told Kirym about Storm, she may have given us some advice."

The terrain was difficult and I was annoyed I'd have to travel the land twice. The trees were massive and the undergrowth thick, and Arbreu and I finally resorted to cutting a path to make headway.

Arbreu cut through another of the thick vines that looped across our path. "Well, at least we won't have to cut a path on the way back," he said brightly.

Sometimes he was so annoying.

Soon after midday, we climbed the rise to the base of the columns. The thickness of the trees and undergrowth dictated our path, taking us to the west of where we thought Kirym probably was and we turned towards the river and her camp. To the east, the raucous cries of three fighting birds distracted us. We stood watching while we caught our breath. The hawk dropped something and flew to the cliff, ending the fight. We heard the shrill scream of a wounded animal, and then the usual sounds of nature took over.

I hoisted my pack onto my shoulder and continued searching for Kirym. From a distance, the pillars appeared to be a solid line, but closer, we found there were groups of them joined at the base, and the paths in between were jumbled and maze-like.

Kirym's camp, when we finally reached it, was between the final two clusters of pillars. A triangular frame stood against the rock, a fire blazing nearby. Kirym knelt beside it wearing just her shift — ripped off above her knees — and her boots.

Teema Speaks

Her herb pouch was open on the ground beside her and there were an assortment of containers lying around.

Kirym glanced up as I stepped from the shelter of the rocks, her knife in her hand. She looked tired, her face sporting a number of grazes and fading bruises. I regretted my previous feeling of annoyance, particularly as she was so pleased to see us.

Arbreu darted past me and hugged her, clicking his token to hers. I felt a strange pang, wishing I'd done that first. He held her at arm's length, looking her up and down. "We've been so worried about you. I wish we'd come to help you sooner."

"You could scarcely do that," she said. "You had to get to the lake first." She sighed contentedly. Blood dripped from her fingers, splattering blackly into the dusty soil. She picked up a pad of dried moss and pressed it against the deep cut on her arm.

I grabbed a strip of linen from Kirym's herb pouch and following her direction, sprinkled calendula, lavender petals and a few pinches of other powdered herbs onto it. I warmed it on a hot stone, added a few drops of healing oil from my pouch and carefully covered the long wound, tying it off as she explained about the hawk, the crows and something that sliced though her arm.

There was a strange cry, reminiscent of a wounded animal. It sounded shockingly close. I looked around in alarm, slowly realising it came from the basket beside the frame. By then, Kirym had picked up a bundle and cradled it in her arms, jiggling it and making hushing sounds. Arbreu leaned forward and took the baby from her.

I stared in shock.

Kirym knelt and rummaged distractedly through the moss in the basket, almost missing Arbreu's question: "What's its name?"

The Fortress of Faltryn

"An amethyst," she said, looking at the stone she had found.

"Oh, that's sweet," he said.

"What?"

"The name, it suits it. The same colour as its eyes."

"Where did you get it?" I interrupted. "Didn't you have enough to do without adding that?" Kirym stiffened at my tone, and I immediately regretted the way I sounded.

"She was dumped! Dropped in a hole." She glared at me angrily. "What would you have me do? Leave her? They left no tracks, and anyone who could do that wouldn't take her back anyway."

I felt myself turn red at her reproach. "I'm sorry, I didn't mean it like that," I said. "But it complicates things."

"Why? It needn't concern you at all," she said stiffly. "I'll care for her. I've managed so far."

I took the baby from Arbreu. "I didn't mean it like that." I hugged Kirym close and kissed her on her nose. "Of course we'll help with her. She was obviously meant to be with you, the token shows that. It just makes things complicated. You always take on too much. "

Arbreu interrupted. "Amethyst. How did you choose her name?" he asked.

Kirym smiled slowly. "I didn't. You did." She explained how the hawk evaded the crows by dropping the stone. "It fell towards her basket. I tried to protect her and it sliced though my arm." She looked up at Arbreu. "You're right though, Amethyst suits her and I hadn't been able to think of anything. Perhaps we needed to do it together."

"Normally no one knows the name until the naming ceremony." said Arbreu. "Why the change, do you think?"

I laughed dryly. "Not exactly, Arb. Close family know it, obviously someone has to. Our family rule ensured the naming ceremony wasn't put off and gave the naming

Teema Speaks

an air of mystery and surprise. Beyond that perhaps this means you and Kirym needed to do it together. As for a naming ceremony, people are needed, and we're here. The tokens make those decisions." I touched Amethyst's token to Arbreu's, and handed her to Kirym. She reached up and touched the baby's token to mine. Amethyst's stone changed from creamy white to a blue based white. Our green stones now each had a small white inclusion.

I wondered what this meant. I assumed the connection was between Arbreu, Kirym and Amethyst, and I was happier about that than I'd felt in quite a while. But if my token was affected also, it may not make them a family. Where did I fit in?

She settled Amethyst back in her basket. "What's your news? You never said."

I winced. "Umm, we lost Storm."

"What? As in, he wandered off on another path? Or did he not come out of the river?"

My silence gave her the answer.

She scrambled to her feet and started packing the frame. "Let's go find him. If he got up the cliff, he'd do what I'm doing and walk south towards the lake. On the far bank, he'd have the choice of going south or east, but he'd go south if he could." She tucked Amethyst into her sling and lifted the frame.

Arbreu rushed forward. "We'll pull that," he said. "You've enough to do with the babe — with Amethyst."

She smiled her thanks. "What are the others doing while they wait for us?" she asked, dousing the fire.

I scowled. "Mekroe and Granite are searching the river's current into the lake."

"What? Why are they assuming he's dead?" she asked, shaking her head.

"Elm is sure he drowned," I said. "He's looking for the

The Fortress of Faltryn

body, and that's why he's searching the lake. He said if Storm had survived, he'd have contacted us somehow, or we'd have seen him. Elm checked every floating thing we came across. That's why we took so long getting to the lake. We found the remains of the boat soon after we picked Teema up. There were just pieces of it left. No matter what we said, Elm wouldn't change his mind."

"The rift changed drastically a short distance downstream from the accident," said Arbreu. "The cliffs became steeper and there was no growth on them. They arched in and almost met at the top. The thing is, it would have been impossible to climb them. So unless Storm got to safety before then, he had no chance. They were just too sheer."

"Elm reckoned Storm would have been washed to the middle of the flow and battered to death against the rocks just downstream from where the boat capsized. Mind you, he thought those rocks got you too." I sighed deeply. "Nothing we said would convince him otherwise. He thinks our journey to find you is an excuse to desert the group."

40

Teema Speaks

Late in the afternoon, Kirym, Arbreu and I breasted the last small rise before reaching the shore. The lake spread out in front of us, burnished to a deep copper by the setting sun. It was larger than the inlet we entered after going through Kirym's Arch. The hills around the south and west of the water were blued by distance. Around the shore were clusters of ducks, geese and swans, their evening calls echoing across the water. A black shape moved away from the closest island towards the shore.

I pointed it out. "That'll be Mekroe and Granite returning from their search of the lake." I swung my finger further west. "The camp is on the far side of those trees. There's a stream there. It's still a long way. We can stay here for the night."

Kirym shook her head as she started down the hill. "Let's get there. I want to talk to Mekroe before he leaves in the morning. It's silly to hunt for a dead body in the water when there's every chance Storm is alive on land. We need to start a proper search tomorrow, otherwise ..." She shook her head.

It had been a fast trip and we needed a rest, but Kirym pushed us on. We had travelled until dark last night and Kirym woke us before dawn to start as soon as it was light enough to see. She'd had been like this since learning Storm was missing. I knew that had Kirym not been pushing me, I'd have made camp, planning to start again very early in the morning.

We reached the shore before the light went. Kirym agreed to a short stop just after dark, although I felt that if Amethyst hadn't needed warm food, she wouldn't have let us stop, but eat as we walked. When the moon rose, we moved on. With moon dark approaching, there was little light and she agreed to a hooded lamp, but only because it was on the top of the frame and we didn't have to search for it.

"We could leave the frame here and come back for it in the morning?" Arbreu suggested, as we hauled it over deadfall. "I'll carry Amethyst. We'll be able to move faster that way."

"If I knew Storm was safe, I'd agree, but there are things on it we need and it'd take too long to sort them out," she said. "It really won't hold us up too much. There's a grassy strip above the shore from here on, and it'll be easier now."

We were all tired when we finally approached the camp. Even so, Kirym was cautious, searching for the guard before approaching. Unable to see anyone obviously awake anywhere within the camp area, she handed Amethyst to me and the now fully shuttered lamp to Arbreu. "Wait here while I check," she murmured. She slipped away through the trees.

The fire was a single glowing coal, not damped down as was usual overnight. If left, it would soon be out. The moon provided little light, but I could see dark shadows dotted

Teema Speaks

around the fire. I knew there'd be no sign of Kirym until she returned, so while waiting, I tried to identify each of the shapes in the camp. It was impossible.

I jumped when Kirym materialised at my shoulder. "There are only five people there," she said quietly, "and they have no guard. Either they haven't organised one, or the guard has slipped off to sleep elsewhere.

"Well, we can do guard duty for the night, and sort it out in the morning." I said.

Kirym shook her head. "Everything is all right here, but nothing is right. I'd have expected better of almost everyone here." She frowned to herself and then motioned us away from the camp. When we were far enough away to talk freely, she set her packs on the ground. "I want to talk to one person without disturbing the others. Arbreu, can you go in and get Mekroe. You've woken him often enough for guard duty that he'll wake and not alert everyone else."

Arbreu disappeared, returning a short time later with Mekroe in tow.

Mekroe's eyes widened and he grinned with pleasure when he saw Kirym. He hugged her closely, clicking her token. "You've been in the camp?" Kirym nodded. "I'm pleased you're here. Things aren't good." He glanced guiltily at his feet. "I've been slack too, sis," he said, "but I've been so tired when I got back from the search I didn't have the energy for an argument. This is the worst it's been, but everything fell to pieces after Teema and Arbreu left."

"It's not just your responsibility, Mek. What's happening here?"

"Mekrar's sick. I don't know what's wrong. She won't take any remedy, not even harkii. She said it wouldn't work anyway, and you needed them and you would sort it out when you got here." He put his hand on Kirym's arm as she started to rise. "Wait, she'll last a while yet. You need to know what to expect. Elm took charge when Storm disappeared. When Teema and Arbreu left, he became irrational. He's not a leader, but he explodes if anyone challenges his decisions."

"What about Starshine? She should have coped with that."

"She's scared of him — I know I am — and he's blaming her for Storm's death. He said Storm wouldn't have made such an idiotic trip if she hadn't insisted on coming along. He makes her feel guilty, and he pushes it every chance he gets. He let me know in no uncertain terms that he's in charge. We argued, but he's older and he has more people and ..." He shrugged. "He said I had no right challenging his authority. This is their land and he said only Faltryners should be here. He isn't making sense over the search, either. I've been ordered to search the same place, the flow from the river to the island, day after day. He checks on me. The morning Teema left, I decided to explore one of the further islands out there. Elm was furious. We had a huge argument when I got back the next afternoon. I thought he was going to thump me. Today Granite and I went to see if Storm could have swum to one of the other islands. If I didn't think he may be alive, I wouldn't have done it. It just wouldn't have been worth it." Mekroe looked troubled. "Elm accused Teema and Arbreu of deserting us. He said they wouldn't return, they'd be walking back to Faltryn, and we should do the same. He's decided you're dead too, Kirym. I told him you weren't, but he said it was wishful thinking and it got to a stage where it was easier not to argue. I talked it over with Mekrar, but she said just to wait for you to arrive and sort it out."

Kirym nodded. "So we need to step carefully around Elm. All right. Priorities now are wood for the fire, guard duty and Mekrar. Is there any food in camp?"

Mekroe shook his head. "Not a lot. The food we had has

Teema Speaks

gone quickly and no one has foraged. Granite and I are on the water most of the time and Mekrar can't forage."

"Where is her herb pouch?"

"It's safe. She's sleeping on it."

"Elm isn't in camp. Where is he?" asked Kirym.

Mekroe shook his head. "He disappears at dusk. I couldn't see the point in searching. If I found him, there was nothing I could say or do."

I built up the fire as Mekroe collected water and put it on to heat. Arbreu disappeared to find more wood. Kirym checked on Mekrar, feeling her forehead. "She's burning up and quite dehydrated."

I had a sudden deep feeling of dread. "What if she's infectious? I'll nurse her," I said. "If you catch something, Amethyst may get it too."

She beckoned Mekroe to her. "Who has been nursing her?"

"Willow."

"Is she or anyone else sick, even a little feverish?"

He shook his head.

"Let's find out what's wrong first, Teema. It's unlikely to be contagious."

As Kirym sponged Mekrar's face, she woke and smiled, recognising her sister. "I knew you'd find us," she whispered, her eyes burning with fever.

"Are you in pain?"

"My foot hurts. I stepped on something," she mumbled.

Kirym lifted the rug. I was shocked at the red swollen limb. She inspected it carefully, eventually finding a small puncture wound just above Mekrar's instep with a dark red line running up her leg. "Possibly a bite," she said. "Mekroe, when did this happen?"

He shook his head. "I dunno, maybe three — four days ago. It was when I spent the night on the far island. She was feverish when I got back.

I handed Kirym a bowl of boiled water. She cleaned the wound and opened her pouch of healing herbs.

"It needs a poultice," she said. "Mekroe, is there any onion or garlic?"

"We had some with last night's meal, I'll check with Starshine."

Moments later, Starshine rushed to Kirym and hugged her. "Can you help her?" she asked, handing Kirym a handful of wild onion. "There's plenty out there, and garlic. I'll get more in the morning." Kirym set her to chopping the onion finely.

As the fire blazed, I noted Starshine's red eyes and puffed face. She'd obviously been crying, still distraught over the loss of Storm.

"This'll do for now. We'll have another look when it's light," said Kirym. She infused some herbs and willow bark in hot water and prepared the poultice, wrapping it around the wound. "Something bit you, Mekrar. Where did it happen?"

"In the lake. I was looking for shellfish. I thought I'd stepped on a stone or something. It didn't really hurt too much until dark."

Kirym encouraged Mekrar to drink the herb infused fluid. She reached up and stroked Kirym's face. "You've lost a token, one of your little ones," she said sadly.

Kirym shook her head. "Not lost, it's safe." She smiled. "It found a new home."

Mekrar's eyes closed. Kirym tucked her rug around her and turned to look over the camp.

"Get some rest. Tomorrow will be here soon enough. I'll take first guard duty."

"You should sleep," said Arbreu.

"I'm not going to do it all," she said. "No one should.

Teema Speaks

Teema can help for now, and we'll wake you later. I need to watch Mekrar and feed Amethyst. So I …"

"Feed what?" interrupted Starshine.

I picked Amethyst up out of her basket and handed her to Starshine.

Starshine's eyes widened and she carefully opened the cloak Kirym had wrapped around Amethyst. "Where …" She paused and frowned. "I need to talk to Wind Runner," she whispered. "I wish Storm was here." She brushed a tear off her cheek.

Kirym hugged her. "We will find him. I'm sure he's alive." Amethyst stirred, and took a breath, preparing to cry. Kirym took her and slipped her finger into Amethyst's mouth; it was too soon for her to be fed again. "Are you rested enough to help us with guard duty, Starshine?" She nodded.

With Amethyst settled in her basket, and Mekrar, Arbreu and Mekroe asleep, I checked the perimeter of the camp while Starshine prepared a hot drink for us. We sat together listening to the night sounds.

Kirym sipped her drink. "What do you know about Amethyst's people?"

"Oh! I hoped you wouldn't ask. It's not a story I ever liked." Starshine's face was pale. "Do you remember the beginning of the story I told you when you first arrived at the fortress? The one about the Faltryn and the tokens."

Kirym closed her eyes, remembering. "The dwellers of the desert attacked the cave people." she quoted. "There was a lot of death, wasn't there. You were the cave people?"

Starshine nodded. "We were, and the land on this side of the river is where the desert people lived."

"I thought it belonged to your people," I said. "I'm sure Wind Runner said so."

"Yes she did, and it's true, sort of. We've tried to care for the land and people for hundreds of seasons. The problem was we rarely saw the people and whenever we had contact with them, there were problems." Starshine sighed deeply. "When we found Faltryn living in our caves, we looked for ways to protect ourselves. Partly, we were concerned he might attack us, but also we had no idea if the Desert People had survived and returned to their land. So we built fortifications and avoided them. There was a general prohibition declared, no one was allowed to cross the river. Somehow the suggestion grew that the land over here was haunted. Despite that, many young men have ignored the ban seeing it as a challenge. When they were found out, there were repercussions for their disobedience.

Of course, those involved maintained there was no indication of people here, and that led to arguments within the families. Many felt it would be sensible to expand our settlement to this side of the river. Most Guild leaders argued against it simply because the land wasn't ours. For a long time some of our people were very resentful.

When Moon, Wind Runner's great-grandmamma was matriarch, things came to a head. A boat sank and the man using it was marooned on this side of the river. No one knew he had taken a craft and as he often wandered off alone, he wasn't missed and therefore not searched for. Days later, he arrived opposite the fortress screaming for help, terrified beyond reason. Moon sent men over to collect him. He was exhausted and almost out of his mind. He was carried up to the fortress and told his tale.

He said he was washed to the far bank and had started to walk back towards the fortress. When darkness fell he found a sheltered place to spend the night and ate the food he had foraged for through the day. The last of the light left the sky, and the wind moaned through the trees. He said the clouds dissolved into disembodied eyeless faces. They swooped down to snatch at his hair and clothes, and hovered

Teema Speaks

above him, screeching and wailing mournfully. Fires sprang up all around him and the wraiths plunged through them, changing them to all of the colours of the rainbow.

He screamed at them to leave him alone and finally he raced away from his shelter and along the river bank. But the wraiths followed him and he blundered through the thorns and cacti, eventually falling down in fear and exhaustion.

He told Moon that he hid his head in his arms, but all through the night, the wraiths floated above him, clawing at him, whispering threats and eventually pinning him to the ground. In the morning, he managed to break the ties binding him and run for safety. The wraiths followed, and he was scared they would shadow him into the fortress.

He had long scratches on his arms and body, and strange dried vines knotted around his wrists. That implied there was a portion of fact in his story. But whatever the whole truth was, Moon had no idea. She had to sedate him to settle him down. He never fully recovered.

Moon listened to his story, troubled for him and the land. As evening approached, she wandered out to the battlements overlooking the river, a place she went for contemplation. To her amazement, the western bank was lined with children. She immediately sent food over, a feast for them as an offering of friendship. As the laden boats neared the shore, the children disappeared. When Moon checked in the morning, the food was gone.

Over the next few days, food, clothing and play things were taken over. Moon had a shelter erected for them, ensuring everyone returned to the fortress in the afternoon and leaving the children to enjoy the gifts, and hoping their parents would appear.

They stayed for ten days and then disappeared.

Day after day Moon checked, but they'd gone. They took nothing with them. When they were there food was eaten, and the dwelling used. But suddenly it was as if they'd never even existed.

Eventually Moon had what was perishable taken back to the fortress, and she had everything else secured. Her people left the land to its people and life returned to normal.

Four seasons passed. As the sun set one evening, the guards reported seeing the children again. Once more, Moon took over food and made sure everything was usable.

They stayed for ten days.

They always came at the end of winter, and now that Moon was aware of them, she ruled that the land was absolutely off limits to us. It belonged to them. Then she made sure the dwelling was prepared in advance of them coming. As time passed, they occasionally took a few things with them when they left. Moon was hopeful this was a sign of friendship and trust.

On the fifth day of their eleventh visit, Moon woke to see a large stone edifice on the river bank. Mystified, she went over to see what it was, hoping to find a sign that they would talk to her. What she found was horrifying. A baby had been placed on the cairn with an arrow through her heart. They'd wrapped her in clothing we'd sent over.

A line of pictures were drawn on the split skin of a young goat. It showed hunters with bows and arrows. An arrow hit its mark, but not an animal. The hunter was depicted as one of us.

Moon was aghast. She wove a basket, filling it with soft moss to settle the baby on. She surrounded it with flowers and herbs. In tears, she laid the basket on the prepared cairn and began to cover it with other stones lying around on the ground. Two tiny girls approached and helped her. The cairn rose higher and higher, and as the last stone was placed on it, the children removed all of the clothing we had provided and left. Moon called to them, but they didn't

Teema Speaks

even look back. Everything they had taken previously was left in a pile.

Moon took the skin pictures back to the fortress and questioned everyone. She discovered a group of young men had been going over to hunt, but full of superstitions they had panicked when they saw pale figures in the moonlight. They claimed they had fired at ghosts in the treetops but swore their arrows hit nothing but air.

Of course, Moon had seen the evidence. It was a direct hit from close quarters and it didn't matter if they had been in the trees or on the ground as depicted in the picture. The men should not have been over there at all.

They refused to say who had fired the fatal arrow, but as each of the hunters decorated their own shafts, Moon knew who was responsible. Nevertheless, all were charged with the death. She felt they were all accountable for it.

Before Moon could decide what to do, strange accidents happened to each of the hunters. One fell from the battlements, two drowned when their boat capsized. One managed to shoot himself while trying out a new type of bow and one was buried in an avalanche of rocks. That added to the superstitions.

A group, mainly the families of the young men, accused the desert people of actually killing the men. They wanted Moon to take an army and exact vengeance for the deaths of their boys, even though many of the accidents had been witnessed. In the end most people saw sense. The fault was ours.

After that, no one wanted to cross the river. But Moon began to check the land, leaving caches of food and clothing. Only women and children were allowed to help, and she insisted no weapon ever cross the river again. Over the seasons, she left messages, but there was no indication they had ever been found. Wind Runner continued as Moon had, but the supplies have never been touched.

We always wondered what happened to them. Many people thought they must have died out. Winters here are harsh, and we found no indication they built shelters for themselves. Lately a group has been pushing again for us to build on this side of the river. Wind Runner has had some heated arguments about it."

"Why did you only see the children?" I asked.

"Moon believed the winters were so hard, they needed help, and although unable to approach for themselves, realised we would have compassion for their young ones." Starshine smiled, looking at the sleeping baby. "She's clearly one of them. Moon sketched them in the record she wrote about the incident. Amethyst has the same distinctive face and eye shape. They had the same thick dark hair too. When she's older, it will grow past her waist." She paused. "I always wondered what happened to that first hunter. What did he really see?"

"Conceivably, when he foraged for food," Kirym said, "he collected some of the fruit or mushrooms one shouldn't eat. They would certainly affect his mind and explain all you've told me."

Starshine nodded. "It's possible. Many young men feel that foraging is work for women and children. Some of the dangerous fruits are similar to others we commonly eat, so he may not have known what he collected. What about the vines on his wrists? Moon didn't recognise them as anything she had seen before."

"There are many possibilities. Perhaps the desert dwellers realised what he'd eaten and tried to help him. Maybe he was taken prisoner, although I can't imagine why they would do that. I guess we'll never know. I saw the cairn across the river. One of the guards told Mekroe it marked the spot where the midsummer moon sets. I thought it was a strange

Teema Speaks

angle from the obvious points in the fortress. I should have asked," Kirym said.

"You'd not receive an honest answer; well, not unless you asked Wind Runner or me. Many people are still very superstitious about it, and some would prefer the reminder not be over there. There have been some strange stories told, although if Wind Runner hears them, she ensures the true version is voiced. However, the lies still persist. I think they are repeated by the families of the men who were responsible for the death, although Moon and Wind Runner have never been able to prove it. The stories have caused trouble over the seasons. Even recently it looked as if some families would leave the fortress and build a new home. The only thing keeping them with us was Wind Runner's strength — that and the knowledge that those who left us would have to travel north far into mountains to find a place to build. It would be a harsh existence.

"This is an indication these people still exist," I said. "But what would make them leave Amethyst like that?"

41

Teema Speaks

Dawn had lightened the sky when Elm walked into camp. As the meal was dished, Kirym asked what had been done in the search for Storm. Mekroe answered easily enough, but the air of resentment was so obvious, soon even he resorted to mumbling.

Kirym frowned. "What is the problem here?"

"You!" said Elm angrily. "You're the last to arrive, and already you're trying to take over. We were managing quite well and we don't need you sticking your nose in. Anyway, you're not even from this land."

Kirym raised an eyebrow and looked at him. He looked away.

"It isn't our land either, Elm," said Granite. "And we weren't coping. Whatever we were doing wasn't working and it was disjointed. Last night proved the point: three people walked into our camp and helped us. You haven't thanked them, but had they been of a mind, they could have killed us all."

Teema Speaks

"Not me," said Elm. "I wasn't here."

"That's the whole point, Elm," said Willow. Elm opened his mouth to interject, but saw her face and thought better of it.

"If you claim leadership, Elm, you have to practise it," Granite said. "You didn't make decisions, but you wouldn't let anyone else make them. A leader has to be here to lead and to take responsibility."

"We shouldn't argue over what's been done," interrupted Kirym. "It's what we do now. What do you suggest, Elm?"

He pursed his lips tightly. "Find Storm's body and take it back to the fortress. It must be out there in the lake."

"Where else have you looked?"

There was a long silence.

"If he's alive, he'll be on land," said Kirym.

"He can't be alive!" yelled Elm. "No one could survive that river." There was an awkward silence as everyone looked pointedly at Kirym and Teema. "Well, it couldn't happen again," Elm snarled.

"Is it that you don't want him to have survived?" asked Granite.

Elm swung around, his face flushed with anger. "How dare you. I've spent longer than any of you searching. Where do you think I was last night while you all slept comfortably in camp? I've been off searching."

"And what did you find out there in the dark?" Granite's disbelief was obvious. Elm went red, then turned and stamped off towards the lake.

Kirym sighed deeply. "If we don't assume Storm's alive, he may not be for long. We need to search the shore, to the east and west, one boat in each direction. If we don't find him in a few days, we have to accept he hasn't made it here or that he's given up on being found and made other decisions. Then we need to go home."

269

Starshine was pale. "Do you think he's dead?"

"No, I don't, and that's why we'll keep searching. But we can't look forever. Storm knows we won't and after a while, if he can't find us, he will make other plans."

"East or west? Which direction do you want, Kirym?" I asked.

"Neither. I'll stay here and care for Mekrar and Amethyst. Can you take Willow and go west?"

Granite looked up. "I'll go with Teema. We get on well and ..."

"No," said Kirym. "I need you here. Willow is a healer and she is quite capable in the boats. Mekroe, you and Arbreu go east. You both have enough healing knowledge so if you find Storm, you will manage until you get him back here. Paddle for at least three days. We need to be sure. Stay near the shore and listen. Storm will yell if he sees you. He probably doesn't have a flint, so don't expect to see a fire. Anyway, good fires don't smoke that much unless it's planned. But keep your eyes open for anything unusual. Do you think Elm will go with you?"

Mekroe shook his head. "I've asked him before. I don't know why, but he's always refused."

"I think he is so terrified of finding Storms body, he won't even get in the boat," said Granite.

"He'll go," said Willow, getting up and following Elm's path. "I'll make him."

Despite all of my misgivings, Willow was an excellent companion. She knew much more about the craft than I did and was happy to pass on her knowledge. She taught me to read the water and recognise areas where rocks were hidden beneath the surface, where roots and driftwood hid ready to

Teema Speaks

entangle our paddles and hole the boat.

Our route took us out around an outcrop of rock. It started as a ridge high in the hills north of the lake.

"Why come past here?" Willow asked. "Storm wouldn't climb that. Surely he'd stay beside the river and then follow the lake shore to where we are. What if he went east and aimed for your land by himself? It's only over the hill."

"Storm wouldn't go east unless that was his only choice and if he's on this side of the river that's an impossible option. He knows we'll look for him, so he'd aim for the lake." I paused thoughtfully. "The map at the fortress showed the river going south to The Green Valley. But the map was wrong. Kirym said the river went more west than south and she told Storm that. So there are probably a couple of hills between here and there, at least two. They're fairly rugged, so the river may turn out to be one of the easier parts of the trip."

By mid-afternoon, we had rounded the jagged line of rocks. I stared up at them, tracing their line far ashore. "If Storm followed the western side of that," I said pointing, "he may have thought it was the edge of the gorge, and in that case he'd have gone west looking for us."

"But he'd have to walk west for days to get here. Why would he do that?" asked Willow.

I shrugged. "When there are no paths, the terrain can dictate where you go. All sorts of things alter your direction, and unless you are experienced, you may not even realise. Storm may have taken an easier path down a hill or maybe he saw something he had to investigate. Kirym did, but she's experienced in travelling across unknown land. I think Storm's hunting experience has more often been in land he has known and travelled many times."

The shore remained wild and rocky for some distance and then opened up to rock enclosed grassy bays. Flocks of swans dotted the water, gliding towards us, objecting to our presence.

We paddled on, pausing to listen for a response to our calls. The air was full of noise and so many of them sounded human. Each had to be checked out. As the evening approached, we looked for a place to spend the night.

A small stream cascaded over the hills and into the water, the ideal place to stop. I left Willow to set up camp and returned to the lake to catch dinner. I rather think I overdid it, arriving back with a string of gutted fish and a swan, plucked and ready to roast, the feathers in a roughly woven basket.

Willow had erected a shelter and set the fire. She wrapped the fish in leaves ready to settle into the hot ashes, while I spitted the swan. As darkness fell, we piled wood on to the fire from a massive heap we had collected.

The night passed without incident and for the next three days, we continued west, finally accepting that we were beyond an area it was reasonable to search. We turned back, lingering over our trip in the hope of seeing some sign of Storm. Finally we were back where we had spent our first night. I added to the pile of wood we'd left from our previous visit.

"Let's not bother with a big fire tonight?" Willow said tiredly. "If Storm was here, he'd have come last time."

"He may not have made it to the lake then. Kirym travels fast. Those first days after the boat capsized were vital. Kirym salvaged equipment. We know Storm didn't have the same luck because everything else from the boat was recovered. His trip would have been a lot harder. He'd have been cold and wet, with no fire and probably no knife. He'd have nothing to help with any injuries he may have sustained. All of that could have held him up."

Moon dark had passed while we were travelling west, but

what little light there was, was barely seen through the thick cloud. I taught Willow to weave panels of willow withies and vines, daubing them with clay to provide added protection against the coming wind and rain. I slept soon after dark. With only two of us, we split the night-watch in half to ensure the fire was kept burning.

I woke with a start. My feet were cold and wet. The rain bucketed down. The fire had burned low and was sizzling as the raindrops hit it. Willow was asleep in the back of the shelter.

I quickly moved two panels to protect the fire from the downpour and added extra wood, carefully building up a blaze. As I placed water on to heat, the torrent increased and thunder echoed across the lake. Concentrating on the fire, I didn't notice the flash of lightning, but I looked up in response to the noise, in time to see the next flash light up our camp. The wind whipped around the fire, blowing part away into the night. I frantically scraped what was left further into the protection of the shelter, and set about shielding the flame.

Most of the wood was piled under a tree, and although it would get slightly wet, I knew I'd have no problem getting it blazing when I no longer had to battle the rain and wind. Again, lightning flashed across the sky, followed quickly by the rumble of thunder. Using the flashes of lightning, I moved what equipment I could into the protection of the shelter.

The storm quickly blew away to the east, the thunder fading into the distance. In the silence that followed the cacophony, I built the fire again, carefully nurturing it until it took hold.

The Fortress of Faltryn

I smiled at Willow, still asleep in the back of the shelter. I understood her exhaustion: the strain of Storm being missing and the arguments with Elm had taken it out of her. She hadn't been sleeping well, and had put her all into paddling each day and racing ashore to check a myriad of sights and sounds for evidence of Storm.

I put more water on to heat, feeling chilled from the downpour. Above the roar of the disappearing storm, I heard noises of night animals beginning their hunt for food, the hoot of owls as they flew through the branches above me and the snuffling of hedgehogs and the like. With a hot drink in hand, I sat back and watched the sky. It was clear now, but thick clouds welled up from the west covering those stars. Another storm front was approaching. Figuring it would be as bad as the first, I built a stone wall around the fire to ensure it wouldn't again be blown away. I tied the shelter down and hauled in more wood. Finally, I raced down to look at the lake, worried the water may rise and invade our camp. No danger there, although the water was much rougher than before. I pulled the boat higher and retied it, to ensure it couldn't float or be whipped up and away by the wind.

As I ducked back into the shelter, I heard a strange noise from up in the hills. It reminded me a little of the noise I had heard above the sea cliffs of The Land Between the Gorges. This was different though, far more inconsistent. First it sort of screeched. Next it wavered up and down, a sort of low pitched monotone, followed by a series of huffs that sounded similar to the large cats I'd seen when hunting. The rest was variations on those, sometimes quite tuneful.

A second series of long wavering notes disturbed Willow. She was on her feet with a spear in her hand before she was fully awake. "What in Faltryn's name is that?"

I shrugged. "Well, it could be Faltryn himself, although

Teema Speaks

why he'd leave his nice warm cave on a night like this is beyond me. It could be the wind blowing through something. It's more likely to be Storm though."

The noise came again.

"How could Storm make a noise like that?"

I added more wood to the fire. "I'm not sure, but if he wanted to attract our attention, it worked."

She sat down, her back against the large tree I had tied the shelter to. "There are other people in this land. It could be them. Maybe they're warning us to leave."

"Kirym saw nothing of them even when she found Amethyst. Nah, that doesn't make sense."

"Well, I think they're more tolerant of women than men. There's a long history there. Every time there's contact between them and us, someone dies. Sometimes lots o' people die."

I tried not to let her see me smile. "No one would be out in this weather unless they had to be. The sound points to Storm, but whatever it is, we'll have to wait and see."

"Oh, no!"

I glanced up at her exclamation. "What?"

"I fell asleep. We could have been killed."

Now I did laugh. "It's a problem with only two of us. Sometimes, it's more dangerous to stay awake than to sleep. You get too tired to react when something does happen. It's worse when you're by yourself, you have no choice but sleep." I paused, noting the distraught look on her face. "Look, the chances of something happening are fairly remote and there's a limit to what we can do. It's easier to stay awake when you've got company. That's why Kirym doubles and sometimes triples the guards."

She nodded. "At Faltryn it's even easier. There are so many men to share the work and the walls make an attack unlikely. The men spend less than a quarter of the night on guard, and

The Fortress of Faltryn

they work only a few nights before they have time off." She jumped visibly at the sound from the hill. "What happens at your settlement?"

Before I could answer, the wind rose and the first splattering of rain hit us. Again the storm was short and vicious, but we were more protected this time and sat companionably through the tempest.

The strange noise wasn't heard once the rain started again, but I wasn't sure if that was because the noise of the storm drowned it out or because it had stopped. As the storm passed, I suggested Willow sleep again, promising to waken her towards morning. However, as she settled, the noise started again and she was suddenly wide awake.

"We can leave at first light," she said.

"Somehow, we need to check if that's Storm. It'd be horrid to leave him behind because we're scared."

"What if it's not him? I mean, that's just the weirdest noise. If it's the desert people and they don't want us here ..." She paused, looking very uncertain.

"Just sleep for now. We'll sort something out." I was concerned. She was obviously scared, and yet I didn't want to leave without being sure of the source of the noise.

The wind rose again and the rain began to fall. After feeding the fire, I settled back and tried to concentrate on Kirym. I wasn't used to this type of communication, although I had been part of it when Kirym needed me to be. In the past though, she had always initiated the contacts.

I stared into the fire, thinking. *There's something in the hills. It may be Storm — or not. Do we leave? Willow is very scared.*

I was surprised to get an answer. *Get Willow into the boat at first light. Have her paddle offshore. Then wait. See what turns up. At first sign of danger — swim.*

I smiled. It was simple and effective, if it worked.

Teema Speaks

It was a miserable morning. After the weather fronts had passed, the rain set in to a steady downpour which did not let up.

At dawn Willow was in the boat and paddling out into the lake. Despite the weather, she seemed relieved, although I knew she'd regret it before long. She was wrapped in her cloak, and with the hood up she'd stay reasonably dry. But over time, I knew the rain would seep through any thickness of felted material. I was relieved to have two cloaks with me, and tried to ensure that one was always dry.

The noises from the hill had stopped later in the night, but began again once it was light. There was a rhythm to the noises, and they couldn't be a natural occurrence, they changed to often. It was almost like a tune, albeit still a bit of a monotone. There was enough variation in it for me to be sure it was man-made, although how was a mystery.

Anyway, I thought, *we didn't hear it the first night we stopped here.*

Soon after light, the sound appeared to move west along the top of the hill. I wasn't sure why until late morning when the rain and cloud lifted for a short time. The hill above us dropped too steeply to be climbed down. Whoever was up there would have to travel west to find a safer place.

I kept the fire burning brightly, pleased to rest and keep warm and dry. Willow had declined my suggestion of returning for meals, taking the cold remains of last night's dinner with her.

I had caught a couple of birds and found some eggs when I was helping her into the boat. I hated taking birds from a nest, but I had no choice. I didn't want to go off hunting, and anyway, hunting in the rain was a thankless and often useless task. I wanted to have hot food ready for Willow

The Fortress of Faltryn

when she returned. Before midday the rain set in again and the wind rose.

Willow lasted until mid-afternoon. She returned, wet and depressed, thankfully accepting dry clothes and hot food.

"I felt quite good at the start," she said. "Then the rain got heavier and the wind rose. It kept blowing me east and I had to paddle back. It's impossible to keep your cloak closed when you're paddling. The rain dribbled into my boots. Even my back is wet. I couldn't hear anything on shore. Every time I drifted, I kept expecting to see you rushing through the shallows, assuming I'd left and cursing me. Then I thought of you sitting over a blazing fire, and well, I finally decided that I didn't care if it was the Desert People. If they're out watching us in this weather, they must have pretty miserable lives." She drank deeply from the flask I handed her. "That is so good. What's the stuff you put in it?"

"Skarfarhn. Findlow makes it from fermented grain. It's a speciality where he came from. It's great for warming you up in wet weather like this. It's a good pain killer too. It knocks you out if you drink enough, but there's a nasty price to pay next day. It's a bit like that stuff you all gave us at the Spring Festival." She looked quite cute when she blushed.

Evening came fast. The clouds had hidden the tops of the hills for most of the day and now they sank lower drifting over the lake and reducing vision to less than a boat length.

I had collected wood from under the trees whenever I had the chance during the day, and now I brought in my last armful, pleased not to need more. "Even the fire's hard to see in this weather. I doubt Storm will make it tonight."

"If it was Storm," said Willow. "Surely he'd be here by now."

"The terrain will be harder to traverse in the rain. He'll get here."

Teema Speaks

Despite the rain, Mekroe challenged us before we'd put a foot on land. He grabbed the boat and hauled it ashore, helping us out and lending a hand to carry our packs up a well-used path.

Ten days away meant huge changes here. I hardly recognised the clearing. The area had been swept clean and a shelter with a basic stone oven attached to one end, had been erected. Firewood was piled under a lean-to against the eastern wall. Nearby, a small pool had been created by damming the stream. A stone-lined channel diverted water across the corner of the dwelling, giving access to fresh running water inside. A food store hung from a tree. I saw Kirym's hand in everything I looked at.

Mekroe pulled open the door — effectively a panel of the wall — and ushered us in. We were swooped on, hugged, kissed and generally fussed over. It was a while before we extricated ourselves. Kirym indicated dry clothing and the nearly prepared meal. She seemed especially pleased to see me, although maybe her pleasure was directed equally at the three of us.

I handed over two swans and a duck. I hadn't fished, knowing Mekroe would have, and with more expertise than I had. I gave Kirym the feathers I had collected on the trip, suggesting she make something for Amethyst. Mekrar was up and walking again, looking a lot healthier. I was surprised at how pleased I felt when I held Amethyst. She was still tiny, but more alert than I remembered. She smiled at me. Then she blurped over Storm when he took her.

I looked around the dwelling, taking in a weaving frame leaning against the wall and rough-woven reed mats scattered across the floor. It had all of the hallmarks of busy industry while we were away.

Everyone was shocked at Storm's injuries, although he laughed them off. He explained that most of the recent wounds were due to slipping down a small cliff in his eagerness to get to the fire he'd seen from the top.

His clothing was ripped and he was thin. His hands showed new and old cuts. His face was grazed and still oozed, blood coagulated in his beard. His face, knees and shoulder showed the fading remains of bruises.

He had joined the edges of the shoulder wound with long thorn spikes. They joined the lips of the cut successfully, but the punctures caused by the thorns had begun to fester.

Willow had started to treat his injuries, but when she tried to remove the thorns, the wounds threatened to rip again. She left them for Kirym to deal with.

Kirym removed them and washed the holes with boiled water. "I want to sterilise the wound," she said, picking up a flask of Findlow's drink. "This will hurt a bit."

"Can't be worse than falling down the cliff," Storm boasted.

It was. Once he had caught his breath and wiped his eyes, Kirym questioned Willow on the meals he had consumed since his return, nodding her agreement at the broth and mashed vegetables he'd been given. Despite objections from a pale faced Storm, she mixed him a meal of egg and meat broth, insisting that after the extended time with little or no food, he work his way up to more solid foods. His arguments were half-hearted.

Questions waited until everyone was dry, had eaten and was sitting comfortably with a hot drink. Kirym started. "How did you make that noise, Storm?"

Willow and I roared with laughter as Storm leaned over to the weapons we had placed in the corner when we entered. He pulled out a length of hollow branch, put it to his mouth and blew. The sound still made me shiver.

Teema Speaks

"Found a fruit tree," he said, "but it was really spiky, impossible to climb. I used this to dislodge the fruit. It worked well until one got stuck inside. I blew in the other end and when it shot out, it made this noise. It was fun and useful, so I kept it. It saved my life then, without the fruit, I'd not have made it. Did it again later when one of those large cats took a bit of an interest in me. It followed me for a few days and was getting far too bold. I was at a stage where I was reluctant to even sleep. Then I had an idea. I put one of those spiky-ball-things from the cactus plants into it. I let the cat get close and turned this on it. It got it on the nose with the cactus, and then the noise scared it further. It leapt into the air and took off fast. It didn't come back.

There are a lot of those cats there now, far more than I thought there'd be. Some of them are huge, although I only saw them from a distance, and I made sure I kept quiet and upwind of them. I could hear them fighting through the night. I saw two of the big ones attack a band of smaller cats. Annihilated them. They're vicious. You know, Kirym, if you hadn't found the baby, I'd have sworn there were no people in the land. Without fortifications, they must be in great danger. Of course they may have built something on the other side of the desert, but living on this side of the river is really unsafe now. "She's lucky," he said, nodding at Amethyst. "Without you, she'd have been cat food within a very short time. Anyway, I had to go west to get around a flooded watercourse. It took a while and then I worked my way back to get to the gorge. I followed a ridge towards the lake and saw a fire, but only two people sat at it. I wondered if everyone else had already gone east. I was scared they'd leave in the morning. I yelled, but I was too far away to be heard and the wind was in the wrong direction anyway. I figured this," he hefted the branch, "would encourage them to wait or scare them off. As it turned out, the weather was so bad, they'd have stayed put anyway. The cliff was sheer and I had to go west again. I was terrified they'd leave without me."

"It was touch and go," laughed Willow. "When I heard that noise, I wanted to leave immediately, regardless of the rain and wind. Fortunately Teema was more sensible. As it was, he had two drowned rats to care for and not enough dry clothes to go around. That's why we travelled today in spite of the rain. Teema felt it'd be easier to deal with Storm's wounds here."

Storm was already dozing and Kirym suggested the rest of the news could wait. One by one, we settled down to sleep.

Just after midnight, I woke to Amethyst gurgling and cooing. I changed her soiled wrappings as Starshine prepared her meal. It was nice to sit and watch her being fed. "Where's Kirym?" I asked.

"Guard duty," said Starshine.

I leaned over and grasped her arm. "In our family, we don't lie to each other. Kirym took her turn just on dark. She should be back now. Anyway, our policy has always been that those with babies don't do guard duty."

Starshine flinched and pulled away from me. "We all care for Amethyst. Mekrar has done a lot of it because Kirym wouldn't let her do guard duty. Kirym insisted on doing her share and more."

"I accept that, but there's no need for any doubling up now. I could have done a turn." I looked around. "The numbers don't add up, Starshine. There are too many people out there. What is going on?"

Starshine looked uncomfortable. "Elm didn't return at the end of his guard duty. Kirym went to find him. She thought

Teema Speaks

he might have fallen asleep somewhere. We're all tired."

I was halfway to the door, when she grabbed my shoulder. "You'll make things more difficult if you follow her. Let her sort it out. If she can't, Storm will have to, but it's better if she does."

42

Kirym Speaks

I stepped away from the dwelling and waited for the noises around to settle to normality. Rain pattered onto the leaves above and I could hear the small night animals snuffling their way through the nearby undergrowth. Further away, I heard the sleepy protest of an alert duck. I pulled my cloak around me and set off towards the lake.

The smell of crushed lavender pinpointed Elm's whereabouts. The fragrant plants had a foothold under a small overhang, giving them a little protection from the westerly winds. I slipped under the ledge beside him.

"Come to gloat, have you?" he asked bitterly. "You were right, I was wrong."

"It's nothing to do with right or wrong," I said. "I had a different view of the land."

"But I thought ..." He paused. "I made a right mess of things."

"Elm, the hardest thing in the world is making the right

Kirym Speaks

decision when all of them could be wrong. Our fears get in the way."

"You got it right first time."

"I knew more. I saw the land from above. I knew Storm may have been forced further west by the flooding and the terrain. When he got near the coast, he may have thought he was nearer the river because of the landscape."

"So you sent me east knowing I'd fail," he said accusingly.

"If he'd been washed to the eastern side of the river and climbed the cliff there, he still would have tried to get to the lake. I asked you to cross the river because you were the only person I trusted to do it safely and get into those unknown rocky bays. Arbreu and Mekroe didn't have the experience and Starshine and Willow didn't have the strength."

He glanced at me, distrust etched across his face. "But …"

"No buts," I interrupted. "You did what you were best at and you did it brilliantly. Arbreu and Mek told us just how difficult it was."

Despite now all being together, the continuing inclement weather stopped us from continuing our trip. I was pleased, as it gave Storm and Mekrar a chance to continue healing. Other than foraging for food and guard duty, there was little we needed to do apart from rest.

We spent our days mending clothing and gear, telling tales of previous journeys and family histories. Storm listened intently to the tale of my climb from the gorge. His was somewhat different.

"I just walked out," he boasted.

"That easy?" asked Arbreu sceptically.

"Well, I was washed over a small waterfall." He was

The Fortress of Faltryn

suddenly serious. "You know, the weight of the water rolled me over and pushed me down. It kept me there. I really didn't think I'd get out. It took me all of my willpower not to panic, and it was a close thing. I managed to grab hold of a rock and pull myself towards the surface. I cut my hands and shoulder doing it, and I almost gave up," he paused, looking grave. "It was terrifying. I got my head up and edged along the rock. Then the force of the water pushed me under again and held me there. I couldn't swim out, because the water kept rolling me back towards the rocks. I was lucky that the rocks weren't smooth. I could grab them and crawl forward.

Like Kirym, I guess I just kept going. When I got to the cliff, I grabbed hold of what I could and pulled myself up. Half way up the cliff, I ran out of steam. I'd swallowed a lot of water, and I was exhausted. I wedged myself in for a short rest. It was dark when I woke and I was stuck for the night. In the morning I was so cold I had trouble getting to the top and when I finally did, I found some sunshine and fell asleep. It was late when I woke. I foraged, but I had to stay there for the night. Next morning, I followed the river.

It was good for a few days, I travelled relatively fast, but then it rained and streams that had been a step across suddenly grew to be almost impassable. Even so, I crossed a lot of them, but one was really deep and wide. Full of broken trees and stuff. I followed it upstream to find a way over. That took a few days, and I was going northwest most of the time. I figured I'd have more chance of getting across it if I had more room. I held on to a log to help me. Even so, it took a long time.

I figured I'd been washed almost back to the river by the time I got over. I'd try to get a line on the sun each day, but of course it moves, and some days were cloudy. I was travelling almost east when I got to the lake, and I saw the ridge and thought it was the edge of the gorge. I realised my mistake after Teema explained the terrain."

Everyone knew the reality was much more serious then he implied. We had all been extremely lucky.

"What now, Kirym?" asked Storm. "How long will it take us to climb the hill?"

"Too long. I think there's an easier way." She pointed to the water. "It's not a lake, it's the ocean. I think we can go south and east and get to the arch."

A shocked silence followed.

"But — but we can't go on the ocean. It's far too dangerous," gasped Willow.

Mekroe laughed. "No more than a river and you coped with that quite well."

"Hold on," said Storm. "There are hills all the way round. Now I may never have seen the ocean, but I'd have sworn you can't see the other side."

With only three boats, Storm and Elm took charge and organised the seating to best cope with crossing the river mouth. They ensured there were strong paddlers in each craft. Amethyst and I went with Storm and Elm. They were the most experienced with the small craft, and they coped with the extra movement I made while caring for Amethyst.

The current from the river was strong and we were occasionally hit by unexpected waves. However, we did it with no problems, which said more about the expertise of Elm and the other paddlers than anything else.

Elm, Arbreu and Mekroe had described the land we'd pass, massive towering cliffs with the waves thundering into them. There were few places we could stop, and each day we started to look for a place soon after midday. Paddling past the rocks into a grassy bay on the first day was frightening. The clean water was narrow, and the rocks were extremely close, both under water and to the sides. The area we could use to camp in was horrifyingly small, and I realised that if the wind changed and blew straight in, the wash of the tide would cover the dry land. Still, the worst didn't happen, but I ensured the guards were aware of the possibilities and I checked every time a new guard started, watching the sky to see if there was any change in the weather.

Elm knew the coast for the first three days, but after that, we could only hope to find somewhere safe to stop. The violence of the water hitting the cliffs meant we had to take the boats quite a distance from shore each day. That made it difficult to see if the inlets along this coast were negotiable. Teema and Granite each took turns to paddle closer to shore to check them out.

The camps were variable, two being generous and comfortable, and one being scarcely more than a stony strip with no wood for a fire. Fresh water was scarce. We managed, although there was one day when what fresh water we had was kept aside for Amethyst and the rest of us went without until evening. It took six fraught days to get to the southern end of the bay. There we found a wide channel going east.

I knew there was a lot of doubt about this being a connection with the sea. With rugged hills all around us, the water appeared to be landlocked. The hills to the south of us were simply massive jagged rocks, teeming with birds. Lizards and a few swimming animals climbed the lower walls and basked in the sun.

We found the exit late on the seventh day after we left the camp. It was narrow, really just a break in the massive jagged southern rocks, with cliffs towering high on either side. The water boiled through, rising the height of two tall

Kirym Speaks

trees with each swell. The cliff opposite the gap was sheer for the most part, but a couple of ledges offered a refuge above the water. They would give us a chance to watch and decide the best way to get safely though the gap.

Getting onto a ledge was difficult, the water rose and fell dramatically and our timing had to be perfect. Mekroe and Teema took their boat in first, Teema climbing ashore holding a rope attached to the craft. On the next swell, he lifted Starshine bodily from the vessel. Then Mekroe scrambled out and he and Teema lifted the boat from the water onto the ledge. It seemed, from a distance, to be quite simple.

Storm and Elm took Amethyst and me in. They timed our approach perfectly, and we sat just out from the cliff as the water rose. The cliff raced past us, the impression of speed intensified by the close proximity of the jagged rock.

As the water peaked, I handed Amethyst over to Teema, my heart in my mouth at the moment I had to let her go. However he had a firm grip, and when I next had the opportunity to look, she was safely in Starshine's arms. Then it was my turn.

Having manoeuvred in once, it seemed the second time would be easier, but our timing was out, and it wasn't until the third rush of the tide that Teema managed to grab me under my arms and dump me unceremoniously onto the rock beside him. I had expected it, but I was it was a strange feeling to find myself hanging in mid-air as the boat disappeared from beneath me. I was shocked by the speed of it.

Then it was Storm's turn.

Teema altered his plan this time, because Storm was so much bigger than Starshine or me. He needed Mekroe's help to haul Storm out. Their timing wasn't as good as it had been previously. The boat sat beside the ledge as before, but Storm tried to be too helpful, hindering Teema and Mekroe's attempt to grab him. As the water reached its peak, he slipped from their grasp. Elm had been watching carefully, and dug his paddle in, swinging the back of the boat towards Storm. The water began to recede, but Storm felt the boat below him and pushed up, propelling his top half onto the ledge where he was grabbed by Teema and hauled over the edge.

We were sobered by the closeness to disaster we had come. Two boats sat out from the cliff as we discussed the best way to cope with the thrust of the tide.

"Generally, it worked well before Storm," I said, "and the problem with him was his extra weight and his desire to help you. We have ropes on each boat, so let's also get a rope around the chest of the person coming in, as an added precaution. It'll take a little longer, but in the end it'll be safer."

It worked to get Elm in, and with the extra people ashore, the boat was quickly hauled in. Ropes were then thrown to the last boat, and Mekrar was followed by a terrified Willow, Arbreu and finally Granite.

The front of the ledge was clear of debris where the tide had washed across it, but beyond that was a pile of driftwood and room to set up a shelter.

Watching the narrow exit out of the bay caused grave doubts. The tide raced in and out with equal strength and speed. It came in with a massive surge, and we could feel the vibrations as the water thundered into the cliff below us. The speed with which the water left the bay on an outgoing tide was unbelievable.

Elm was pale as we sat at eating our meal around the fire at dusk the next day. "We can't do it. The water goes through too fast. We can't see what happens out there when it meets the incoming surge. It could create waves big enough to

Kirym Speaks

swamp us. Maybe we should take another look at the hill."

"We need to stop deluding ourselves," I said. "This one is a hill, but beyond that is a mountain. There's snow on the top of it, for goodness sake, and we're not equipped to cross it. We don't have the clothing, the shelters or enough rope. As dangerous as the channel seems, it is do-able. It's not that different from the sea arch. We'll handle this the same way we did that. We go through at the turn of the tide. That's the only time the water is still. If we go on the high tide, it'll be easier to get off the ledge. We'll have some time after the tide turns, and the outgoing flow could assist us on the other side. When we get through the gap, we must keep going straight out to sea. Once we're away from land, we can look at the coast and assess the best way to continue. We need to be ready at daybreak tomorrow."

The fire glowed brightly as everyone thought about the coming trip. Arbreu broke the silence. "Kirym, how did you know this wasn't a lake? It sure looked like one."

"The fish we've been eating taste like ocean fish," I said.

Storm turned thoughtfully. "They do taste different. I've only ever tasted those we caught in the river, so I imagined the change was because they were from a large body of water. I should have asked."

43

Kirym Speaks

Elm and Storm paddled into the gap. In the misty light, the water was eerily calm. Sounds travelled a long way, and once between the cliffs, the slight wash of water echoed noisily. The comments of those sitting at the entrance were surprisingly loud. They seemed to reverberate between the walls of the gap. Shards of rock constantly fell off the cliff, splashing into the water beside us. We hadn't seen this from the ledge, the distance had been too great.

Willow screamed with fright when a bigger shard fell. Then a large rock detached from the cliff high above, grazing the wall of the boat beside me as it splashed into the water. I frantically checked to see if it had breached the skin, but other than scraping the surface, the boat seemed intact.

"You all right?" called Granite, and more rocks slithered off the cliff. The boat bucked and rolled as the waves from the stones hit it. I wasn't sure what was worse, the rocks or the waves.

Kirym Speaks

"Fine," called Storm. More rocks splashed into the water.

"Storm," I said quietly. "Any noise makes the rock fall. Keep quiet."

We slipped out of the narrow gap and Storm turned and called back to the others. "Don't make a noise when you come through. It brings ..." His instructions were drowned as an avalanche of rock plummeted into the water.

The two boats back paddled away from the gap, and those in them gesticulated wildly. There was obviously an argument going on between them. Willow started to sob hysterically, and more rock shale splashed into the water.

"Faltryn's oath!" screamed Elm. "Shut! Up!"

Everyone was shocked into silence, but two huge rocks sent a large wave out towards the boats. Teema's boat turned and shot into the gap, he and Mekroe paddling steadily towards the open sea. Willow whimpered, her terror overcoming sense, and more rocks hit the water.

I watched, my heart in my mouth, willing Willow to gain control and keep quiet. Mekrar turned and hugged her, burying Willow's face in her shoulder. Teema made it through safely. Arbreu and Granite paused for a few moments and then dug their paddles in, starting their trip through the gap. Willow's terrified sobs were muffled, but even that caused small avalanches as they travelled through the gap.

After long, heart stopping moments, they drew alongside the other two vessels, everyone still embarrassed by Elm's outburst.

"Let's go," I said shortly, and we paddled on out to sea.

Once beyond the narrow gap, the cliffs widened funnel-like towards the open sea. I now understood why so much water was pushed into the gap and why it left with such speed and force.

The water was choppy, and more so the further we went

towards open sea. Finally we were beyond the protection of the land, and we turned east towards the arch that would gain us entry into our inlet.

The coast was treacherous with strong currents and deadly rips that could take us far from shore very quickly, or worse, straight towards the rocks that littered the coast. We had to be constantly vigilant. A moment's inattention could mean disaster.

We all knew something about reading the water after our time on the river, but this was new for all of us. Teema, Arbreu, the twins and I had a little open ocean experience from fishing excursions near the arch Papa named after me, but this was a far different experience and much more dangerous. Then, we had a much bigger boat, one of those we had used to escape the blighted land we had lived in. Those boats had a larger crew and facilities for us to sleep and prepare food on board. We'd used sails, and had anchors that could keep us securely in one place when the need arose. We also had Armos, our boat expert and although he had passed on his expertise, we had relied on him to make the important decisions. We had used smaller boats on the lake of The Land Between the Gorges, but they also had sails and were used on perfect days when the wind was right. It was difficult to transfer that knowledge to these small, paddle-propelled boats.

The coast continued to be rocky, and I was concerned we would not find somewhere to spend the night. The thought of having to paddle in open sea in the dark was frightening. However, late in the afternoon, we spied the entrance to a small bay that, unlike the others we'd seen, was free of rocks.

Kirym Speaks

I spent the days of travel carrying Amethyst in a sling. It held her in my lap, leaving my hands free to help the paddlers as needed. An amiable baby, she slept a lot and gurgled and cooed to me and the others when she woke to be changed and fed. At the end of each day, my back hurt from the weight and along with everyone else, I was tired of sitting for so long.

It was a relief to reach land each day, but then clothes needed to be washed and dried, food prepared and a fire and shelter built. Amethyst needed to be cared for and played with, and while this wasn't a chore, it made for long days.

There was always a slight reluctance to get back into the boats at the beginning of each day, but the knowledge we were a few short days away from The Green Valley kept us going.

44

Kirym Speaks

The freak wave caught us unawares. It was mid-afternoon on our ninth day at sea and we had just spied a bay we could enter safely. Elm was leading us into shallow water when we were hit.

I didn't hear the huge wave until it was almost on top of us. My scream of, "Keep straight!" was almost lost in the roar of water.

Elm and Storm struggled to keep the boat on line, riding the wave into the small cove and up onto the beach. As the water receded a second wave followed, crashing into the ebbing wave and slewing the craft sideways, tipping it over.

In the resulting chaos, I was thrown out onto the sand. I landed on my knees, and as the water boiled past my waist I struggled to keep Amethyst's head above the surface. The pull of the water as the wave ebbed began to drag me back into the bay. Just as I lost my footing, Storm grabbed me, lifted me above the water, and struggled towards shore. Then

Kirym Speaks

the water receded, and he put me down.

As a third wave pushed the boat onto the sand, I fumbled with the baby sling and thrust a now protesting Amethyst into Storm's arms

"Hold her," I screamed. I raced back to the water, grabbed the boat and hauled it into the swirling maelstrom. Elm sprinted after me, picking up an extra paddle as he came. Together we searched for a glimpse of the others. As we paddled into deeper water, I saw Mekrar struggling towards shore. I glanced behind to see Storm racing towards her, vaguely aware of Amethyst's now strident scream of discomfort. Then I turned my attention to the water.

Near the entrance to the bay was a body, lying face down in the water. I secured my paddle and dived in. I got to Starshine moments after Arbreu reached her. We turned her over and wiped her hair off her face. With Arbreu's help, I got her to the side of the boat, relieved when she took a deep breath and started to cough. We heaved her over the side into the craft, where she promptly vomited on Elm's feet.

Elm shouted, pointing behind us. I turned. The other boat and two waterproof containers floated nearby. The boat was dangerously close to the rocks at the entrance of the bay. I acted instinctively, attempting to push it away from the rocks and towards shore. Lacking the strength to cope with the long craft, I felt myself being pulled into the choppy water swirling towards the majestic rock that guarded the western end of the bay.

Arbreu surfaced alongside me, adding his strong stroke to mine. It seemed to take forever, but slowly we edged away from danger. We had to keep swimming strongly, the tide threatened to pull us back towards the rocks.

Away from the cacophony of the breaking surf, I was aware of something banging against the inside of the boat. Aware that the skin of the craft could be breached under stress, I

297

ducked under the side to secure whatever was loose.

I surfaced in a pocket of air and brushed the water from my eyes. With one arm over one of the seats, Teema struggled to hold Granite's inert body high enough to keep his head above water.

"We're in the bay," I said. "Can you hold on until I get help?" He nodded, and I ducked back under the side. Moments later the water heaved as Arbreu and I surfaced beside them.

Somehow we got Granite out from under the boat. Teema and Arbreu heaved him over the inverted craft, and swam it to shore. With my help not needed, I kept pace, collecting two oars and another floating container as I went.

Storm waded into the water to help carry Granite out, settling him beside the spluttering beginnings of a fire. The men took the boats back out into the bay and beyond to search for Mekroe and Willow.

Starshine and Mekrar were awake. Both had swallowed water and were in shock. Starshine had a weeping graze on her forehead, the edges darkening into an ugly bruise. She was very listless, seemingly not aware of the questions asked her. Mekrar had lost her token. She appeared healthy enough, but sad and very distant.

Granite had a large lump on the back of his head. I checked him carefully. His breathing was strong and his heart beat was regular. I could only roll him onto his side wrap him in dry rugs and keep him warm. Storm was concerned he may have swallowed water, but he showed no signs of having done so. There was nothing we could do but wait. He stayed asleep long into the night.

Four containers holding possessions we sorely needed had

Kirym Speaks

disappeared. As much of a disaster as that was, it was minor compared to the loss of Willow and Mekroe. Teema climbed a tree to see if there was anything floating in the water. The only thing he saw proved to be a sodden cloak tangled in driftwood. Elm brought it to shore, where it was washed and hung to dry.

Teema, Storm, Arbreu and Elm searched the waters in and around the bay for as long as the light allowed. They were guided back to shore by the fire Mekrar had lit. As night fell, it helped them dry off, and we kept it burning high, hoping Willow and Mekroe would see it and be guided to us.

I cooked a meal, but no one had any appetite. Mekrar sat listlessly staring at the fire until I placed Amethyst in her lap, insisting she care for her. "I need to watch Starshine and Granite," I said. "Starshine swallowed a lot of water, and both have head wounds." Amethyst obligingly cried pitifully, bringing Mekrar out of her lethargy, although she didn't have the spark she normally had.

Out of Mekrar's hearing, I explained my subterfuge to an increasingly worried Storm and Teema. "She needs something to take her mind off Mekroe's disappearance. Amethyst is the best solution."

As the moon started back towards the horizon, Storm joined me in guarding the camp and keeping the fire high. "Where did the wave come from, Kirym?"

"I don't know, but when we left our home, there was an earthquake and the cliff collapsed into the sea. It created a big wave. Then again, large waves were described in the journals we found on our boats. They called them rogue waves and said they're just much bigger than normal waves. There's no way of predicting them. This was small compared to the ones they wrote about. Arbreu was telling me about mountains that explode, and they can create huge waves if they're near the sea. Whichever it was, we were lucky."

I glanced up at his gasp. "If the bay hadn't been here," I explained. "We'd all have been washed onto the rocks ..."

"And we'd all have died," he finished. "What now? How long do we search?"

I shook my head. "Honestly, the chance of them surviving is zero. Had they been within the bay, they'd have been washed ashore. If they survive the wave out there, the cold will get them. We search tomorrow and then we have to leave."

He looked grave. "There'll be arguments. Willow is special and ..."

"Mekroe's my brother," I said softly, "but the longer we stay, the more we jeopardise everyone else. We've had good weather, but it'll not last. This coast is vulnerable to storms from the south and west. If you looked at the cliffs before the light went, you'll have seen where the water washed them. It was way above our heads. If we're here when the next one hits, there's every chance we'll all drown. Even searching for a day could be a day too long, but we owe Willow and Mekroe that much at least."

As the moon approached the western horizon, Granite woke up, groggy and nauseous, with a massive headache. I was sure that would go, but I was concerned when he saw two of everything. He spent the day lying in the shade with a damp cloth over his eyes, and by late-afternoon he was sitting up, feeling better, and seeing straight most of the time.

Starshine had different problems. She was pale and listless; I suspected she had inhaled water. She had emptied her stomach, but that didn't help her lungs. She didn't respond to anything I did, and seemed far too sleepy. I was very worried.

While the men investigated the bay, the rocks around the entrance, and the coast east and west for signs of Willow or Mekroe, I searched for inspiration. Nothing I gave her seemed to work. I'd have been delighted to find wild onion or garlic, but there were none in this little cove. Eventually, I spied a mass of lush greenery in a tree some way up the cliff. I returned with a large number of wild pumpkins. I chopped, boiled, and mashed them. I spread them onto pieces of my petticoat and wrapped Starshine's chest and back with the hot poultices. Then I covered her with every warm rug and cloak I could spare. I spent the day replacing the compresses, and late in the afternoon my perseverance paid off. Starshine managed to cough the sea water out of her lungs. She brightened noticeably after that, although she was still weak.

Again the men searched until there was no light left, dropping exhausted when they returned.

Morning brought the argument Storm had foretold. Elm point blank refused to leave.

I explained the dangers of staying.

"I won't go without my daughter," he said woodenly.

I was stunned. I had no idea they were even related.

"They were estranged," explained Storm. "Wind Runner sent Willow along with us in the hope that this trip would bring them together."

In the silence that followed, Mekrar laid Amethyst in Elm's arms. "One daughter is enough," she said stonily. Elm stared up at her. She picked up an oar. "Let's do a final check of the bay and the rocks just outside. The others can pack up while we do it." She walked towards the boats.

"We can cut down to two boats," said Storm, as we packed the containers. "It'll be a squeeze, but that way we'll only need four people paddling.

The Fortress of Faltryn

I shook my head. "What if something happens to one boat? We need to keep every resource we've got. Besides, we'd have to leave some of the containers behind, and we can ill afford to do that. Anyway I want to keep Starshine alert, and caring for Amethyst will be good for her. If I'm not needed for paddling, I can't ask her to do it."

It was still early when we left. Elm sat stony faced in the rear of his boat, not talking to anyone. I put him and Mekrar in the same craft. They had both had a huge loss and I hoped her bubbly personality would come to the fore and jog him out of his depression.

The seating in the boats had changed. Storm and I paddled, with Starshine caring for Amethyst, while Teema and Arbreu helped Granite. There was none of the laughter and antics that normally issued from the boats.

After an uneventful day, we stepped onto a narrow strip of driftwood covered gravel in the late-afternoon.

It was an uncomfortable night. The only plus, other than driftwood, was a small pool of fresh water near the cliff. There was no stream to it, the water oozed through cracks in the rock. With the need to get water for drinking, cooking, cleaning and washing, Mekrar and I worked late into the night before we could rest.

Teema took over Mekroe's fishing lines and brought in three fish and a basket of shellfish. No one was hungry, but the savoury smells brought us all around and there was little left by the time the sun set. He fossicked again for the morning meal, and a tasty broth of shellfish with wild onion and mushroom, cooked slowly overnight and thickened with some of the root vegetables I had dug up while we were waiting for Storm to be found. A good meal and the smells cheered everyone up. We set off mostly feeling a little lighter in spirit.

I watched the sky with trepidation. Bright red in the

morning, the clouds began to gather soon after.

Elm, deep in depression, didn't respond to anyone and was generally too dispirited even to paddle. Again and again, we waited for him and Mekrar to catch up. Neither Storm nor I was happy. Mekrar had to paddle the boat by herself, and she was tiring fast.

As the clouds gathered, I lost patience with Elm and pointed out the dangers. "We need two people paddling," I said. "If not, we won't make it."

"I'll paddle," said Starshine.

"You can't do that and care for Amethyst." I turned to Elm. "Elm, you have a choice. Either care for Amethyst or take one of the paddles." I waited, but there was no response from him.

"Elm, if you don't help, none of us will make it. We need you." I handed Amethyst to him. He let her slip to the bottom of the boat. The wee girl whimpered.

I leaned over, speaking quietly so only he heard. "Willow loved you. She admired your strength and she was proud of you. Don't let her down now."

He looked miserable. "I yelled at her," he whispered. "I ignored her. I didn't deserve her."

"She knew you were scared for her and she understood."

He looked up, his face streaked with tears. "She despised me," he said sourly. "Perhaps she was right."

Mekrar thrust a paddle into his hand. "Amethyst deserves better than this, Elm. We all do. Yours isn't the only loss. Kirym has lost her brother and Mek was the other part of me."

He sighed deeply. "I'll paddle. Well, I've no experience with babies." He handed Amethyst back to Starshine. "Mekrar's

The Fortress of Faltryn

right, I shouldn't keep making the same mistakes."

We made far better time after that, but the storm still overtook us. Initially, the heavy rain deadened the sea, and although it was uncomfortable we made good time. Then the wind rose and the water became choppy. Visibility reduced and we paddled nearer the shore, watching the cliffs in the hope of finding somewhere safe to land. By mid-afternoon we were all cold and wet. Even Amethyst, protected by wraps and Starshine's cloak, was damp and miserable.

Lookout was normally a job shared by us all. It was a thankless task in bad weather, as one constantly had a face full of rain and sea spray. Over the last few days, only Mekrar, Teema and Arbreu and I had done it, as those from Faltryn wouldn't recognise the coast or the arches, especially from the direction we were approaching. The rock formations only looked like an arch when approached from the east.

Arbreu spied the towering pillars late in the afternoon. We peered through the sleet as he called out. The tall formations were quite different from the west, and those from Faltryn couldn't understand the name.

I was ecstatic. "Our luck is turning," I said. "Our timing couldn't be better. The tide's going in, so it should be easy. The boats are small and there'll be plenty of room." Nevertheless, I was still cautious. Visibility was low and there were many things that could go wrong. Storm, Starshine and I went first, to be followed at a distance by Mekrar and Elm, with Teema, Granite and Arbreu in the rear.

Closer to the arch, I called a halt. "There's something on the rocks," I called back to Storm. "Can you blow your noise stick? That direction," I said, pointing.

Storm pulled it out and put it to his lips. After a few false starts, he got a resounding blast out of it.

"Keep going!" I said. "Louder!" I knelt up in the boat, straining to see ahead. I stared through the rain and spray.

Kirym Speaks

I knew that there were strange currents at the arch, and the exploring I'd done since arriving at The Green Valley had taught me to expect the unusual here, but this was the strangest creature. It looked like nothing I had ever seen before. The large amorphous lump rested on rocks well above the wash of the water, not the easiest perch to get to. Its position implied possession.

I thought about the sea creatures described in the journals Papa found with the boats, and others we had seen in our travels. I could think of nothing that looked like this, although I was sure the list wasn't inclusive. This creature was almost black, and was very still, possibly asleep.

Wild animals often attack if woken and faced with something new and unknown. Awake and watching they may be wary, but possibly more accepting of something or someone passing through their territory. For that reason if no other, I wanted it awake. The arch wasn't a large area for a territorial animal.

Storm continued to blast on the stick. The sound echoed forlornly across the water. Starshine and I back paddled constantly, fighting against the tide.

"It's moving," gasped Starshine, grabbing my arm. The creature climbed higher, putting distance between itself and the water. Atop the rock, it turned ponderously.

Behind us, Mekrar screamed.

A faint cry drifted from the rock. "Yoohoo-hoo! I knew you'd find me!"

It seemed simple. "We'll skim through and pick him up on the way," said Storm.

But not so simple. The tide was a problem. It flowed swiftly through, giving little chance to stop mid arch, and

The Fortress of Faltryn

there were rocks just beneath the surface of the water all around the area where Mekroe was.

The three boats grouped south of the rocks as we discussed the logistics. I listened to all of the suggestions, turning one idea after another over in my mind. Eventually, I realised there was only one solution.

"Starshine, I want you and Amethyst in the boat with Mekrar and Elm. Storm and I will pick Mekroe up."

"I should do this," said Elm. "I've the most experience, and Storm would be best to help me. We can change places, Kirym. Getting to the rocks is one thing, but holding still so that two people can get aboard is harder."

I knew that although we hadn't seen Willow, it didn't mean she wasn't there. She could be in a more sheltered part of the arch. Elm obviously assumed that if Mekroe was here, Willow must be. I hoped he was right.

"This boat is the only one big enough to take four people," I pointed out. "I know the rocks. Anyway, Elm, we need your experience on the other side if there's a problem. I want you all through the arch now while the tide is running strong. If something goes wrong and our boat hits the rocks or something, you all need to get to shore as quickly as possible. Get Armos to bring Dragon Quest back to rescue us."

Elm continued to argue. "I should be here helping with Willow and Mekroe. Teema can lead the boats. Where's the nearest land?" he asked.

I pointed north. The shore was hidden by distance and the misty rain. "Teema doesn't have the experience. It'll take until tomorrow afternoon to get there, and it may take longer. There's no place to rest until you reach land. There needs to be two of you who can lead. They need you as well as Teema." I turned to Teema and Arbreu. "Aim for the rock path. If you find the boat cave, go there, but don't

306

Kirym Speaks

even think of using the cave at night. The path is safer." I handed over some rope. "Tie the boats together, front and back. When we come through, we'll hook on beside you. You must stay together."

If you don't go now," I said, "you will have to wait until the next tide change. That will be early tomorrow morning, and it'll mean we are in the boats for an extra day. Teema, tell Mek what's happening as you go through."

Elm again tried to change places with Storm or me, but Starshine took his paddle and she and Mekrar paddled after Teema.

I wanted the other boats to go through with the push of the current, but I needed the still water at the turn to pick Mekroe up. Once we rescued him, we'd have to move fast, or we'd be pulled out with the outgoing tide and have to wait until it turned again, not something I wanted to do with the storm increasing in ferocity as night drew in.

As we waited, the rain got heavier and thick fog rolled in. Visibility was going to be a problem. The wind did strange things, thickening and thinning the fog. Occasionally, we'd get a view of the whole of the arch, but generally all we could see was the nearest rocks, and sometimes they disappeared too.

45

Kirym Speaks

The two boats had disappeared into the fog as they went through the arch and I hoped that Mekrar and Starshine could cope with Elm until after they were through the arch. I could do without him doing anything idiotic at this stage.

Storm and I continued to back-paddle, the tide was still too strong for us to make a rescue attempt.

We didn't have long to wait. The water slowed, and we powered forward. The arch suddenly appeared to jump closer.

It was eerily quiet as we approached the outer pillar, and the sound of the water slapping against the rocks seemed startlingly loud. The mist thickened.

"I hope Mekroe doesn't think we missed him in the fog," said Storm. "Time waiting always seems so long, and he is a bit impatient."

I shook my head. "Teema will have told him what we planned. Mek'll know these rocks. He'll have checked them

Kirym Speaks

thoroughly to find the safest place for the boats. That's where he'll be waiting."

The first pillar of the arch slipped past. The channel narrowed, but it seemed massive when I compared it to going through in Dragon Quest. This time, though, far from sticking to the clear water in the centre, we wanted to go close to the rocks, just not too close. Noises echoed here; it was uncanny. The second arm of the arch came into view. We edged closer, wondering where Mekroe was. There were strange movements in the fog. Something dark materialised and disappeared. Storm's sharp intake of breath was followed by a whispered, "Monsters."

I thought of sea creatures again, but then realised Mekroe was twirling his cloak to get our attention, the movement made bizarre by the thickening fog. He had climbed to the northern end of the arch. We paddled tentatively forward. I called to him.

"Hey Sis. Be careful. Go north past the rock that looks like a toadstool. A boat length beyond that is a narrow channel. Come in backwards, but take it slow, there are rocks near the surface."

We spotted the toadstool rock and edged our way into a channel that was so narrow, we could touch the jagged rocks on each side. Mek loomed out of the fog and stepped into the boat in front of me. He pulled two containers in with him, took my paddle and pushed off. We edged our way back past the rocks and into the channel again.

Mekroe looked back at us, his eyes glowing with merriment. "Did you hear that noise?" he asked. "I always reckoned there were monsters out here. That proves it. Can we call it Mekroe's monster?"

"Only if Storm wants a name change," I giggled, relieved we were safe.

We were clear of the arch now and paddling into the bay.

309

The tide was still slack and I wanted us as far from the arch as possible before it turned. I leaned forward, talking to Mekroe quietly. "Mek, did you see Willow?"

He stopped paddling and turned back to me, suddenly tense. "The boat sank and the wave took us out to sea. She was face down, but I got to her fast. I remembered what you taught us about breathing for someone, but ..." He shook his head. "She'd hit the rocks. She must have been slammed straight into them. It would have been quick." He swallowed convulsively. "I wouldn't have known her, except for her clothes and the thing she wore around her neck. A real mess." He leaned back and laid his head on my shoulder, turning his face into my neck and stifling a sob. "It was horrible," he whispered.

I put my arms around him and rubbed his hair with my cheek. "When the others ask, just say she was face down in the water. They'll make their own assumptions. She was Elm's daughter."

His head left my shoulder and he turned to look at me. He was pale. "I would have done that anyway. No one else needs to know. Poor Elm. Why did they hide it? She was lovely." Ever cheerful, he brightened. "How's Mekrar? Did she miss me?"

Storm laughed stiffly. "Nah, lad. She was enjoying being the remaining half of a twin. Counting up all the sympathy she'd get. You really messed up, returning like this. She'll never forgive you."

"Oh, I think she will," he laughed. "I've got her token. That's why the wave got me. I saw her token fall and went for it instead of going for the shore."

The arch had disappeared into the mist and we could see nothing but the water around the boat. I had no idea where the others were.

Storm pulled out his noise stick and blew it. Teema called

Kirym Speaks

out, but we couldn't tell where the call came from. "Keep calling," Storm yelled.

We paddled into the tide, knowing that we had to be travelling north this close to the arch. Later, as we got further away, we would probably veer slightly to the east or west. Teema called intermittently, but as the mist thickened, his voice distorted and we couldn't work out what direction to go in.

"Go north," Storm yelled. "We'll catch up later."

Their acknowledgement died in the thick mist. It was lonely. It felt like the world had disappeared. The daylight died quickly.

Over the days of paddling, we had often needed to empty water out of the boat. It dripped off the paddles and splashed in with the waves. The heavy rain added to the problem. I picked up the dried gourd we used for bailing out and started yet again. It had been at a constant throughout the day, but I realised it was deeper in the boat than ever. I drained the water out, and then surreptitiously checked the bottom of the boat, wondering if we had scraped over one of the rocks by the arch.

The bottom was intact, but there seemed to be a crease in the side of the boat. It wasn't that it leaked, it just oozed. I carefully felt the outside of the skin. One narrow strip felt smoother and I remembered going through the gap to get to open ocean, a large rock grazing the surface beside me. What appeared to be minor then had become a fatal flaw with all of the stresses of the last few days. I again emptied the boat of water, then quietly told Mekroe and Storm what I had found.

"We'll live with it for now," said Storm. "We mustn't stress the skin any more than we need to. So we sit as still as possible and do the minimum we need to do to get to land safely."

I nodded. "You two paddle, I'll bail. If the worst happens, we need to be as far away from the arch as possible. How did you survive, Mek?"

"I tied myself to those," he said, indicating the waterproof containers. Then I kicked against the tide taking me away from land and tried to go east. I counted. I'd kick for a hundred and then rest for a hundred. If I lost count, I'd start kicking."

We paddled on. Storm taught Mekroe to take slow, deliberate strokes.

I made plans. "We need to stay with the boat as long as possible, tie ourselves to it if need be. The boat, even partially submerged, will be easier to see than a person. Above all, we must stay together, and we must keep alert."

We took turns to rest. We were all extremely tired, but I found though that my mind was too active for me to sleep. Storm and Mekroe were likewise affected. I was worried we would all fall asleep at the same time. That could be a disaster.

We told stories to keep ourselves alert. While Storm pretended to snooze, Mekroe told me about his trip to the arch. He had been very lucky with the tides. When Storm gave up all pretence of sleeping, I asked him about Elm and Willow.

"She was a foundling. We didn't have many of those, generally we knew when a baby was due and it was always a reason to celebrate. Wind Runner discovered her. She returned one morning from visiting Faltryn's pool, and the basket was in the middle of the tunnel. No one saw who put it there. There were all sorts of stories of course, that Faltryn had stolen her from a distant land or possibly from

Kirym Speaks

the Desert people, or she was the dragon in disguise, us being under Faltryn's spell and unable to see it. Well, lots of them, each stranger than the last, but Wind Runner put a quick stop to that. She found someone to care for the baby, and talked to every single person in the fortress. She got no answers.

The basket was made of willow, hence her name. Wind Runner found the pendant under the blanket she was wrapped in. It was so unusual, but no one had seen anything similar, and although it was work to be proud of, none were ever made for barter. Wind Runner made sure Willow was well cared for, taking a personal interest in her through the seasons. She told her the story of her beginnings early on, so she wouldn't be affected by any of the silly stories. Wind Runner taught her to ignore them and personally guided her in her choices — she was talented in healing even as a child.

Eleven springs passed and one of our seamstresses, Gazania, got very sick. Willow was doing her apprenticeship and nursed her. Wind Runner attended her just before she died, and she admitted that Willow was hers and that Elm was her papa. He didn't know; she had never told him. She had a pendant similar to the one left with Willow.

Wind Runner talked to Elm and discovered he owned a pendant also, a gift, he said, although he wouldn't say who gave it. All three pendants were obviously made by the same hand. When Wind Runner told Elm what she knew, he denied all knowledge of Gazania, threw the pendant at Wind Runner and walked away. That's when he took over the boats. He stayed down there with them and never again entered the fortress.

Wind Runner gave the pendants to Willow and told her the story. She explained how Elm must feel and gave her advice on how to handle it. Two springs passed and

The Fortress of Faltryn

Willow approached Elm and tried to get to know him. It was difficult. He either ignored her or kicked her out of the shelter. She persevered, and in her fourteenth summer started taking lessons in the boats. Elm had to teach her, that was his job. She had a bad time. She was terrified of water, but she refused to give up. Elm was a hard task master, harder on her too. He stuck to his attitude though, and I told him it would end in tears. I wish I'd been wrong."

I thought about what I knew of Willow. She had been very quiet, almost invisible during the early part of the trip. She'd worked hard and done all we asked of her. She hated the boats, but she'd stuck to it. Although she was young, she was a gifted healer and had recognised the value of the cave of tears, joining us there when she could. On occasion she had shown great strength of character. I now understood how she had managed Elm when he'd been at his most stubborn. I wished I'd been told about her background. It may have helped.

By midnight, Storm and Mekroe were sleeping fitfully. After emptying the boat yet again, I sat still and concentrated on Teema.

Where are you? he asked.

Mid bay, I answered. *You?*

We'll get to land mid to late-afternoon as you predicted. It'll be near the stone path. You?

Not too sure, further south and west, I think. When you get to land, rest there overnight. Are you all still together?

He nodded.

46

Teema Speaks

We reached shore late in the afternoon. I couldn't quite believe we had done it. The boat slid onto the sand and we just sat there, shocked and exhausted. No one moved. No one had the energy. I felt I could go to sleep right there and never wake up.

It had been a fight from the moment we lost touch with Kirym. Elm wanted to return to the arch. He was certain Willow was still there, waiting for him. He would attempt to turn the boat, and I had to be constantly watching. Eventually Granite cottoned on to it too, and took Elm's paddle off him. "You'll kill us all, you moron," he gasped. "Honestly, if we were at the arch, I'd leave you there. You know the rules. You've yelled them enough times. The safety of those in the boat is paramount. Nothing endangers that. Anyway, if she was there, she won't be now. Kirym and Storm will have picked her up."

Elm sulked from then on, refusing to help with anything,

so the workload increased for the rest of us. I had hoped to allow Mekrar a rest, but now, she had to paddle as well. I was livid.

Still, it was over. We were safe.

Amethyst cried, and Mekrar leaned over Starshine, struggling to pick her up and comfort her. Cold and damp, she had been grizzly since yesterday when the rain finally soaked her through. There had been nothing we could do for her; there were no dry cloths left. We were as damp and miserable as she was, our skin irritated from the constant rubbing of the water-laden clothes we wore.

The sky glowered blackly; rain wasn't far off. Nor was night for that matter. We needed shelter, hot food and dry clothes. The shelters were just a short distance up the beach, near and yet almost unattainable. So close, and yet I hadn't the energy to get out of the boat.

Mekrar jogged me into action. With Amethyst cold, wet and hungry, now protesting loudly in her arms, she gingerly stood, attempting to climb out of the boat. It tilted alarmingly and she almost fell.

"Hold on, Mekrar. Let me get out first." It was harder than I thought it'd be. We had sat in the boat for two days and a night with almost no sleep. My legs had seized up and when I finally managed to stand, my head felt strangely disconnected from my body. I had the feeling I was watching everything from a great distance.

Once upright, I staggered around the boat and took Amethyst so that Mekrar could climb out. She had the same problems I did, but she collapsed, suddenly sitting waist deep in water. I looked at her stupidly, wondering if I had the energy to help her up.

She giggled. Soon it was an eye-watering roar of laughter, and it was infectious. Shortly we were all laughing, except Elm, who sat in sullen silence, and Amethyst, who responded

Teema Speaks

to the sound by screaming in protest.

"Come on," said Mekrar, struggling to her feet. "Let's clean her up and feed her."

By the time we were on dry land, I was feeling better, although still light headed and detached from reality. The climb up the beach to the storage shed was exhausting, but I felt better when I hauled open the door and saw the supplies stored there. I grabbed a handful of dried fruit, and poured some water into a bowl. I drank deeply and handed it to Mekrar when she reached me. Then I hauled out the things we'd need for the night. Mekrar grabbed a soft rug and sat on the ground, removing Amethyst's damp clothing and wrapping her warmly.

Arbreu was the first to join us, the others still struggling out of the boat. I handed him a flint. "Can you light a fire and heat some water? Then we can sort out a meal of sorts." I took a large armful of wood over to the dwelling and opened the door. It was basic, used only in an emergency, but it seemed the height of luxury after the camps we had had since leaving Faltryn's Fortress.

Now everyone was out of the boat, and they dragged themselves up the beach and into the shelter. The air was damp, struggling to become raindrops. I was glad we had a roof over us for the night.

The fire looked cheery. Mekrar was heating water to give Amethyst a warm bath. She had found some clothes for her, the first she would wear other than swaddling cloth. She was wrapped in a rug and Mekrar was feeding her as the water heated.

Starshine teased dried meat into a pot of water. A large bowl of dried vegetables sat next to her, waiting to be added.

Arbreu crouched beside her, skinning root vegetables to add to the stew. It already smelt wonderful.

With the basics sorted, I checked the stores for clean dry clothing for all of us. Plenty for the men, but I was somewhat mystified by the things the women had stored there. Eventually, I took a couple of items off each pile and added them to the stack I had and took them through to the dwelling.

Amethyst was splashing in her warm bath, the sweet oils and herbs in the water struggling against the damp mouldy body smells emitting from the rest of us. I slipped out to the storage shed again and brought back two more large flasks of fresh water. "We could all do with a clean-up," I declared to everyone and no one.

Starshine looked up and smiled appreciatively. "Oh, that sounds like bliss. We'll need large bowls, towels and clean clothes." She stood, waited for her head to clear and started to sort out the clothes I had brought in. She held something up to Mekrar and they both roared with laughter.

I left them to it.

Night had fallen. We were well fed, warm, dry and very sleepy. I vaguely thought about guards, but knew I'd not manage to stay awake and wouldn't ask others to do what I couldn't. I thought briefly of Kirym, wondering if she had gone to the boat cave, or if they'd had the energy to walk through the ravine to the settlement. I smiled thinking of Loul fussing around them, the rest of the family hoping they'd have enough energy to tell some of their adventure before sleeping. I was envious. We still had a good half day walk to get to the settlement, a little less if we paddled down past the boat cave and took Tarjin's path through the ravine.

Teema Speaks

I woke with a start soon after midnight. Mekrar was changing Amethyst's wrappings and Arbreu was grinding harkii and steeping it in warm water.

I slipped out of the dwelling to get a breath of fresh air. It was strange being inside after so long without real shelter. The rain had stopped, but the clouds were heavy in the sky. There would be another deluge before morning. I watched the waves surge onto the beach, pushing and pulling the boats about. I wandered down to secure them. The water was cold. I felt unsettled and wondered why. I looked around the bay, seeing nothing in the blackness. I missed Kirym. Still tired, I returned to the shelter. Everything was settled, Mekrar curled up asleep, but Arbreu walked the room with Amethyst in his arms.

"Is everything all right out there?" he asked. I nodded. "I'm worried about Kirym," he said softly. "Can we search for her tomorrow? Mekrar can take everyone to the settlement and we can take a boat."

I felt as if I had been hit in the belly, the one thing I'd known, but not admitted to myself. Kirym wasn't yet safe. "How could I not realise?"

"Ach, you've been concentrating on getting us here," said Arbreu. "Anyway, she'll have made sure we knew nothing. She wouldn't want us to worry. Can we go look for her?"

I nodded. "We'll go in the morning. As much as I'd like to start now, it's too dark and I'm too tired."

I was shocked to find it was almost mid-morning when I woke. I panicked, refusing a platter of food as I frantically stuffed things into a pack. I was still tired.

Mekrar stood over me, insisting I eat; I hastily gulped a mouthful of what she offered.

The Fortress of Faltryn

My suggestion for them all to go to the settlement while Arbreu helped me search was met with icy silence, followed by a barrage of objections.

"It's easier if you go together," I shouted. "It'll relieve Veld and Loul to know you're all safe, and it'll be better for Amethyst."

Mekrar snorted. "Kirym and Mek are their favourites. They'll never forgive me if I go home without them. I'm going with you." She wiped her eyes. "I want to see Mekroe. I need to see him."

"I'm going too. I have to apologise to Willow," said Elm.

Starshine joined in. "I have to see Storm."

Exasperated, I turned to Granite. "And you?" I snapped.

"Aye, well, lad," he said, nodding gravely in his best imitation of Storm, "I need to check the noise stick is safe."

There was a moment of silence and Mekrar started to giggle.

When they'd all finished, I shook my head. "I'm not sure why I think I'm the leader. No respect at all."

"Ah, lad, be assured you are," said Granite, sounding again like Storm at his most serious. "I intend following you, 'cause I'm assuming you know vaguely where they are."

"Mmmphm, until we find Kirym." I muttered. "Then all I'll see is your backs."

"Well, you could take Amethyst home and we'll catch up with you later," suggested Mekrar.

"If I thought you'd all follow me there, I would," I snapped. "All right, let's get going." I picked up the pack I'd put together.

"Hold on," said Mekrar. "We'll need extra food, clothes, some rugs, water, a medicine pouch and a shelter."

Arbreu frowned. "It's a lot to carry, and it's not necessary?"

Teema Speaks

"Yes, it is. The chances are they are at home, but if they're not, they'll have been out all night. They'll be cold and hungry. They could be hurt. We need to be prepared."

She hauled open the shed door and started to pull the items out. The extra supplies made for a heavy load. I hauled out a triangular frame to pack it on to. Mekrar looked at me as if I was an idiot. "There's not much use packing that. It won't float."

"I didn't think any of you would want to get back in the boats again."

"We don't," said Mekrar, "but they're faster and speed may be of the essence. Anyway, they'll be needed if we have to search the bay."

"I'm fairly sure," I said tentatively, "they've made it ashore."

"There are islands down there," she snapped. "They could be on one of them."

Once we got moving, it was easy. We fell into the rhythm of paddling very quickly. Elm was now eager to help and the coast raced past. With the boats still tied together, there were plenty of fresh paddlers. Those not paddling kept a careful look out.

"Boat cave first?" asked Mekrar.

"There's not much point," I said. "If they made it that far, they'll have walked through to the settlement by now. They'll leave a message at the path."

Mekrar snorted. "Why would they go along the shore? If they got to the cave, they would probably take the direct route through to the path."

"Well if they have been there, their boat will be at the entrance, "I snapped, "and we'll see it from the water."

They weren't at the cave. Even from quite a distance it was obvious no one had been there. The sand at the entrance was pristine, no tracks at all. I was pleased we had no reason to stop. We paddled further, stopping at the beginning of Tarjin's path, the narrow track through the hills. There, Granite and I searched the sand for footprints.

"The overnight wind and rain may have washed any signs of them away," said Granite.

"We always leave a note, and Kirym wouldn't forget." I pointed to the sheltered spot where the messages were engraved. "Armos was here last." I frowned. "These are old. Look, late winter then very early spring. I remember the winter trip, there was a short break in the weather and he had a good catch. I wonder why he hasn't come through since spring."

"Maybe he just fished in that lake you told me about," said Granite.

West of the path, the coast was rougher and we had to go into deeper water to avoid the rocks. Some small bays were hard to get to, even with the boats separated.

While Arbreu, Granite and Elm paddled out to check out some floating debris, Mekrar, Starshine and I followed a narrow channel into a watery cave. We knew this cave, and although it was always at least knee deep in water, there were ledges above high tide, and more than one meal had been cooked here in the middle of past summers.

Kirym wasn't there.

I was devastated. This was the last really safe place I knew, and I desperately wanted her to be here.

"Well, it was unlikely," said Mekrar. "It'd be easy enough to get into when it was light, but if they could have, they'd have paddled or walked back towards the path. Anyway, they probably came ashore after dark. We only just made it to the stone path in daylight."

Teema Speaks

We paddled out of the cave and back into the bay. Arbreu was still quite a distance from shore, but not paddling anywhere.

"Why's he stopped? We'll never find Kirym at this rate." I whipped the boat about and paddled furiously towards him, ready to berate him for wasting time. As we came nearer, I realised it wasn't how it had looked. Elm was in the water, but only above the surface because Arbreu had a firm hold of his tunic.

"We found part of the boat, and Elm wants to dive for them," Arbreu gasped as we approached.

"Where is it?" asked Mekrar. Arbreu pointed southeast, and she rose in her seat to locate it. "With a current like this," she said, "there's no way they'll be here, even if it sank just before you found it."

Mekrar dug her paddle in and manoeuvred herself close to Elm. In one quick movement she leaned over, grasped his tunic and bodily lifted him up the side of our boat, thrusting her face close to his. "While you waste time diving for the dead, they could be on shore needing us. If my brother or sister dies because of your selfishness, I'll make you wish you were dead too." She thrust him towards Arbreu's boat. "If he doesn't get aboard," she snarled, "leave him here."

She dug her paddle in and spun the boat around, barely missing Elm as he clung to the side of Arbreu's craft. Without a backward glance, she powered towards the shore.

I was impressed. I looked back, wondering if Arbreu would need help, but he and Granite were hauling Elm over the side. A short time later, they were paddling their way towards the coast.

47

Kirym Speaks

The wind rose. In some ways it was good because it blew the fog away, but the water became very choppy. There was a lot of cloud, I still didn't know what direction land was in. I worked on the premise that most of the winds and storms here came from the south. That meant we were probably being pushed towards land, although the effect of the tide was unknown.

Dawn was pearly grey and tranquil. The sun rose, hidden behind thick cloud. As the day brightened, we finally saw land. I thought we were over half way, but the low hills were blue with distance and there was a large expanse of empty water to cross before we got there.

For a while we shared the paddling, although the person not paddling needed to bail out. Eventually, the job became mine alone. It was easier. In the few spare moments I had, I organised food and water, checking to see if there was anything else I could do. Mekroe and Storm continued their

Kirym Speaks

steady strokes towards land.

Late in the morning, we realised that the water was pouring into the boat faster than I could bail it out. Mekroe had lost his boots when he was first washed out to sea, but I packed Storm's and mine into the waterproof containers along with everything else I could fit in. I took off my cloak, cutting the hood away so I had a covering for my head. I then did the same for Mekroe and Storm. I made them tie their hoods on; wearing them would lessen the amount of heat we lost in the water and would hopefully keep the sun off us as the day progressed.

First Storm and then Mekroe slipped over the side. They insisted I stay aboard. The boat was more buoyant with less weight, and I was able to cope with the bailing out. I handed the waterproof containers over to Mekroe, and he and Storm sorted them out, tying them together and to themselves. Then they started to swim, pushing the boat with them. I continued to bail.

We made good time this way, but the waves got larger and eventually, with a resounding crack, the boat broke in half, dumping me unceremoniously in the water. It wasn't the entry I had intended. The plans I'd made to stay with the craft were gone. It sank straight away.

48

Teema Speaks

Just before dusk Mekrar spotted the small bay and suggested we spend the night there and continue the search in the morning. The entrance was narrow and the rocks around it limited our view of the beach. We had to enter now, or it would be too late, the clear water was so constricted I doubted it could be negotiated at night.

We paddled towards the stony shore, rounding the rocks and eventually able to see the beach. Three bodies were partially hidden by the rocks. There was no movement, even when I called.

My heart was heavy in my mouth. Mekrar and Starshine were both pale as we powered the boat onto the shore. I was out and running up the beach before we were properly beached. Mekrar was right behind me. Kirym's knife sat on the sand beside her, the blade black with blood.

49

Kirym Speaks

The containers float well," said Mekroe. "Two held me up even when I slept. One should hold you, Kirym."

"I wish we had one more. Then Storm could have three," I said as we retied them in a line.

"Are you saying I'm fat, lass?" laughed Storm. "If we keep them together, they'll be enough. You get in the middle. Land can't be too far away, we'll be there before nightfall."

I didn't argue. I knew it would take longer, but I hoped we would get to land before exhaustion set in enough for us to need to sleep.

The water was chilly to start with, but I soon got used to it. Mekroe and Storm tied a rope around my waist to hold me between them on the floating containers. I twisted a loop of the rope around my left hand to give me something to grasp. With the boat gone the wind affected us less, and coming from behind, I hoped it was pushing us towards shore. However, we had no protection from the sun and were constantly pummelled by the waves. Soon my eyes were red and sore. The salty water made my tongue feel thick.

We kicked on. Being so low in the water, I had no idea if we were making any headway at all. We used Mekroe's technique of counting, kicking and resting. We needed to pace ourselves so we wouldn't run out of energy. I was surprised at how often we lost count.

The hoods couldn't protect our faces from the sun's reflection on the water. Our noses, cheeks and lips peeled, and I felt my face glowing like a flame. Although the hoods stopped us from getting too chilled from the water, the sun heated the damp cloth. Before long, we all had headaches.

Late in the afternoon, the sky darkened and it began to rain heavily again. As had happened yesterday, the rain deadened the waves. It was a wonderful respite from the heat but I knew it meant we had a heightened chance of getting too cold. The rain washed the salt from our faces and we lapped up what we could, despite it still being tainted with salt. In the lull, I handed Storm and Mekroe two harkii each to chew, and slipped the last I had into my mouth. I had put five into the pouch around my neck, leaving Mekrar enough for Amethyst's meals. Now I was pleased I had. I knew there was a good supply at home, and they were kept in the storage shed for emergencies also.

The fog rolled in just before dark. It was thick and damp. We kicked on.

I was running out of energy and more and more often I found myself dozing. The cold always wakened me. As I began to doze, Mekroe or Storm would hitch me higher onto the containers. It kept me out of the water, but the air was colder, and I would soon be shivering and eager to slip back into the ocean's warm blanket. It was a dangerous haven. The water also drained our heat, and I knew the cold would take over eventually.

Kirym Speaks

I would suddenly find myself not kicking and I'd wonder if I had slept or just lost count. Occasionally I would hear Mekroe or Storm begin to count out loud, and I would join in and we would kick in unison. Then, as the salt affected our throats, our voices faded away.

I dreamed, heard voices, and would jerk awake and peer through the darkness for the speaker, only to realise it was the thrum and echo of the containers as the water lapped against them. It also glugged hypnotically through Storm's noise stick and when he lifted it clear of the waves, it moaned as the wind whistled through it.

The rope had tightened, biting into my waist. It rubbed me raw very quickly and the salt water made it sting. My hand and wrist were similarly chafed by the hairy rope. Movement was so uncomfortable it was easy to lie still and rest, letting the wound settle, the water warm around my body. Eventually, I woke enough to haul the water flasks towards me. I shook Mekroe and Storm and handed one to each of them, encouraging them to drink. After a mouthful, Storm handed his back, but I urged him to finish it. "I have some in the other flask," I said, opening it and tipping it to my lips. Despite being empty, there was one tiny drop, not nearly enough, but wonderfully sweet.

I knew we had to reach land soon or it would be too late. I took a deep breath and hauled myself higher on the container, peering through the darkness. The wind had blown the clouds away, and the crescent moon sat low in the sky. My mind was fuzzy and it took me a while to make sense of it. If the moon was low after most of the night had passed, it must sit in the western sky, which meant we were facing north.

Land was to the north.

"Kick," I croaked, nudging Mekroe. "We're going north. We have to kick." I poked Storm. He groaned and turned

The Fortress of Faltryn

his head away. I elbowed him in the ribs.

"Doon'," he moaned.

"Kick!" I screeched. "Kick! We're nearly there." I started kicking with all of the energy I had. "Help me," I begged.

Mekroe began to snore. As he breathed in, he swallowed water and coughed violently, waking himself up. His head came up as he took a deep breath.

"Help me," I gasped.

As he started kicking, he put his arm over me and shook Storm's shoulder. "C'mon, mate. Let's get to shore. Then we can sleep."

Storm lurched awake, leaning on the container we shared. My hand got caught in the rope holding them together. Something cracked, and pain raced up my arm. Someone screamed. I realised it was me.

"What's up?" croaked Mekroe.

I didn't have to energy to tell him. "Just kick," I whispered.

For the first time in ages, we all kicked together. The water felt cold as it rushed past us. We kicked for a long time. The moon went down and it got very dark. I was no longer cold, but I wasn't warm either. My jaw ached, my hand ached, my whole body ached. I had been shivering earlier, but now I couldn't even do that. Storm and Mekroe must have had similar problems, not the hand of course, but I knew the dangers of feeling the way we did.

My ears ached. An irritating drumming sound reverberated through my head. I tied to shake it away. It wouldn't go. My hood had disappeared — I didn't remember losing it. I knew I was colder than I could afford to be.

Storm and Mekroe were flagging, their kicking less coordinated, and they occasionally stopped for a while.

The drumming was still there. It was annoying, and I wondered if it was simply the water in my ears.

330

Then I recognised it. Surf!

We had to be close to shore. I strained to see ahead. The sky wasn't quite as black, dawn was close. Ahead, I could see white where the waves broke against the rocks. It was too dark to see exactly where we were.

"Land!" I screamed, although it sounded more like a croak.

Both Mekroe and Storm stirred.

The surf washed us forward and back, and when I finally felt solid earth under my feet, I was too exhausted to stand. The containers stopped us from sinking, but an incoming wave tipped us over in a mass of limbs, sand and water.

The wave rolled me over and the containers floated above me, holding me under the surface. I was dragged backwards into deeper water and I couldn't get my head up to breath. I started to panic. The next wave thrust me back up the seabed until I lodged fast, but still under water. I pushed myself up, inadvertently using my injured hand. The jolt of pain was almost my undoing. I took a breath, but still underwater, swallowed liquid and started to lose consciousness.

The weight of water lessened and the container settled on my stomach. The wave had gone out, and with small lights flickering at the peripheral of my vision, I knew I had but one chance to save myself. I pushed with all my strength, despite the pain, and was relieved when my head broke the surface. I spat out a mouth full of water and sand, coughing and choking.

The rope tying the containers together had broken with the strain and I lost contact with Mekroe and Storm. They drifted away as I crawled towards the shore, my knees scraping against the rough stones and shells on the sea

The Fortress of Faltryn

bed. A wave came up behind me and rolled me over, before retreating.

Suddenly I was clear of the water. I lay on stony sand fighting for breath. I struggled to my knees and fell on my face. I had no energy to move. The waves broke over me, rushing up past my waist. I was achingly cold now, but beyond shivering. I struggled to open my eyes to look at the beach. The sky was grey. In the time it took for me to be washed ashore, dawn had broken. I pushed myself up, knocking my hand again, the pain so bad I almost passed out. I ached all over.

I struggled to my knees, looking over the small beach for Storm and Mekroe. Both were still in the water, being washed to and fro like so much flotsam. With each wash of the tide, they were being dragged back into the bay. Suddenly, Mekroe was floating away.

I panicked. It got me to my feet. Wading into the water, I grabbed the rope holding him along with the containers. While he floated, he was easy to move, but I didn't have the energy to pull him ashore. I coordinated towing him with the surge of the water and eventually he was free of the tide.

Then I staggered back in to haul Storm out. He had settled across three containers, moving to and fro with the wash of the tide. I grabbed the ropes and pulled him to shore. However, I couldn't get him out of the water, he weighed too much. Every time I lodged him near the beach, a wave would drag him back.

I struggled back to Mekroe and shook him. "Help me."

Opening one bleary eye, he struggled stand, but he was tangled in the rope. He felt for his knife. It was gone.

Mine was still safely tied to my thigh under my shift. It seemed to take forever to cut the ropes around Mekroe. I was numb with cold, and could scarcely feel the knife in my

Kirym Speaks

hand. Mek took it off me and slashed at the ropes, so cold that he didn't notice when he cut into his own leg. I hauled the debris away and helped him to his feet.

We waded back into the water. Mekroe grabbed one of the ropes wrapped around Storm, I another. We hauled him above the wash of the tide and onto the beach.

Mekroe collapsed on the sand beside Storm and leaned over, lifting his head, shaking him awake. "Land, mate. Wake up! Kirym got us here."

I looked around, trying to take in the three tall figures on the beach above me. I walked towards them.

The wind whistled around me. They waved.

My vision clouded. I felt shell and sand on my cheek. Everything went black.

50

Teema Speaks

I raced up the beach, turned Kirym over and checked her pulse. She was so cold. *I'm too late*, I thought. *She's dead.* Her left hand was black and swollen, the bruises reaching up her arm. Her face was raw with abrasions, her wet clothes ripped and stained.

There were only three bodies. It was obvious who was missing.

Elm stood back, his face ashen. "Willow's a healer. She'd have gone for help or to search for healing stuff," he said.

Then Kirym moaned and her eyes flicked open. She smiled weakly. "We made it," she whispered.

Mekrar and Arbreu checked Storm and Mekroe. Both felt frozen, but they were breathing. Mekrar hauled Mekroe into the dying sunshine. "Quick, we need shelter, a fire and hot food." She galvanised us all into action; the only allowance she would make was permitting Starshine to care for Amethyst.

Teema Speaks

Arbreu dragged Elm off to collect driftwood. Granite emptied the boats, while Mekrar helped me to strip wet clothing away and wrap Kirym, Mekroe and Storm in blankets. By the time Granite and I had erected a shelter it was fully dark, the fire was burning brightly and a meal was cooking. Kirym, Storm and Mekroe, sat against the grassy bank wrapped in rugs and cloaks, their wounds cleaned and bandaged.

Mekrar and Starshine handed out hot drinks while Mekroe told everyone about finding Willow. Elm took it badly. When Mek brought out the pendants he had taken from Willow's neck, Elm dashed them from his hand and stamped off down the beach. He refused to listen to either Storm or Starshine when they tried to talk to him.

"Just give him time to adjust," said Kirym. She picked up the pendants and put them safely away. "For when he's ready to hold them," she said.

Once the meal was finished, Mekroe frowned as he fidgeted with the small pocket he had carried Willow's pendants in. "You know, Mekrar, it's not the same when you don't have a token. I've never seen you without it. You don't look like my sister at all. I don't think we can have the same relationship as we did."

She looked hurt, close to tears, and then saw the sparkle in his eyes. "You monster," she screeched, leaping on him and thumping him on the shoulder. He winced with pain. "Where is it?" she demanded. "How did you get it?"

He opened the pocket and took out her token. It looked quite dull for a moment, but then it brightened, and when he placed it on her forehead, it flashed and connected to his.

The Fortress of Faltryn

She smiled contentedly. "You know, Mek," she said, "Papa likes me more than you. Mama too. They told me. They were quite disappointed when you were born."

Kirym summoned the energy to separate them, sending Mekroe to help tidy up the belongings and Mekrar to preparing food for the next meal.

Life appeared to be back to normal.

51

Kirym Speaks

Teema wouldn't let me do guard duty through the night, but I cared for Amethyst when she woke. I was still feeding her when he woke for his watch.

"You should be sleeping," he scolded softly. "Any one of us could have cared for her." He glowered at Mekrar as she handed us both hot drinks.

I patted the grass beside me. "I needed to spend time with her. She is my responsibility."

"I'll take over, Mekrar," he said. "Can you nudge Granite, please?"

"Don't wake Granite." I said. "I'll help Teema." Before he could explode, I pulled him down beside me and leaned against him. "I was awake anyway, and everyone's done so much. They'd paddled all day, and it seems silly to have three people awake when we only need two."

He had to accept it, but still argued. "You'll never recover fully if you don't rest. It's not just being awake. It's being able to respond if something goes wrong. In your condition, you'd be of no use at all."

"We're safe, Teema. There is no reason to think anything untoward could happen. We're surrounded by cliffs on the land side, and it's unlikely anyone would manage the sea entrance at night. It's too dangerous."

"You did," he grumped. He stepped away from the fire, allowed his eyes time to adjust to the darkness and checked along the shore and around the cliffs. "You're right," he begrudgingly admitted when he returned. "But you need to let others help. You're not the only one who can be responsible." He looked back at the cliffs. "I almost fell over Elm over there."

I nodded. "He went off soon after dark and looked for a way out. He's so sure Willow has gone for help. He won't accept what happened."

"What can you do?" he asked.

"Hope that given time and common sense he'll sort it out. It's just feelings of guilt for not having made the right decisions and now not being able to change those he did make."

He handed me a warm drink laced with herbs. "I was so scared I'd lost you. I don't think I would have wanted to live if you'd died." He pulled me close, his arm around my shoulder.

I leaned against him. "I'm so glad I don't have that on my conscience. It's nice to sit here and watch the stars, knowing we're safe." He kissed the top of my head, and then when I turned to look up at him, gently kissed my lips.

Morning dawned bright and although there were still heavy clouds racing across the sky, the worst of the bad weather

Kirym Speaks

had obviously passed. Everyone eagerly devoured the hot meal Mekrar and Starshine had prepared overnight. While they ate, Storm, Mekroe and I told the rest of our story. Mekroe embroidered his tale excessively and hilariously. When he began describing a battle with sea goblins who had tried to kill him because he was on their rocks at the arch, I shut him down.

Mekrar, every bit the story teller her brother was, told us about their trip.

"It certainly sounds better than I remember it," murmured Teema.

By mid-morning, we were ready to leave. With only two boats remaining, Teema, Amethyst and I waited for Granite to drop Starshine and Storm off at Tarjin's path before returning for us. It was peaceful waiting in the sunshine with Teema.

I looked around the cliffs and laughed quietly to myself.

"What's so funny?" Teema asked.

"When I was washed ashore, I thought I saw people up there. Next thing I heard your voice. I was relieved we had come ashore where you were. It wasn't until late last night I realised a whole day had passed, that it was almost dark when you arrived. So it couldn't have been you. I've just realised I was looking at those trees up there."

The boats suddenly rounded the rocks, and Granite called out to us.

"That was a quick turnaround. I hope everything is all right." muttered Teema. "That was quick," he called. "I thought you'd eat before you returned."

"I left them cooking. Elm tried to take the boats. He said Willow was still out at the arch and he wanted to go collect her. I left him to Storm and Mekrar."

Again the clouds were closing in, misty now over the sea and coming closer to shore.

Teema piled the last of the possessions in in front of Granite, helped me into the second boat, and climbed in behind me. We manoeuvred out past the rocks.

"Oh, by the way ..." said Teema, and he told me about the absence of visits to the big boats since we'd been away.

"That's not usual," I said, untying the ropes holding the boats together. "But even if he didn't fish, he always checked on them every moon, and he always made a note of that."

With Amethyst asleep in her carrier, I untied the rope holding the boats together and picked up the spare paddle. "Granite, can you go back to the path? Tell Mekrar we're just going to check the big boats. We won't be long."

He nodded, but already we had powered ahead. "Are you really worried?" asked Teema.

"I don't know. I just feel I have to check, and it's easier to do it now, than go through to the path and then come back."

The cave looked as it usually did, except for a trail of strange prints across the sand. I paused for a few moments, carefully taking in every detail. Then a small wave pushed us up onto the beach and we climbed out onto the sand. Dragon Quest's prow was just visible in the gloom of the cave. As we walked up the beach a huge shadow drifted across the sand.

We both glanced up. Nothing there; the mist was drifting closer and we couldn't see far at all. My token pulsed and I felt the big tokens throb, too. At the entrance of the cave I reached into my pocket and pulled out a token. The red one.

A narrow beam of sunshine burst through the cloud, hit the token and reflected onto the prow of the boat. In the shadows it looked like a dragon's head with a blood-red eye, almost a reflection of the dragon we had seen in the ice cave.

Beside me, Teema gulped. Then the beam of light disappeared and we saw the boat as we had always known it.

Teema laughed shakily. "I could have sworn ... Umm, silly what you think you see, isn't it?" He put his arm around my shoulder. "This has been the weirdest trip, Kirym. It'll be nice to settle down to normality with our new neighbours." He shook his head. "You know, I can't understand why Wind Runner's people stayed on at Faltryn. I know what she said about land ownership, but you'd think they would have moved across the plains nearer to the forest. Faltryn had such a harsh climate, and all that really kept them there was a tenuous story about a non-existent dragon."

"Who said it didn't exist?"

He stared at me, his eyes narrow. "I thought you said ..." He paused. "No, perhaps you didn't. You believe Faltryn's real?"

"Mention of the dragon is a constant thread in their history, and it's mentioned in ours too."

"Since when?" He was flabbergasted. "It's not in the memory book, or you'd have told me."

"Our boat. It's called Dragon Quest. Did you ever wonder why?"

"Are you saying we ..." He paused. "Why isn't it mentioned in the memory book?"

"For some reason, our written history at the settlement started once we were settled there."

"Perhaps they didn't keep records before then," he said.

I shook my head. "The notes are detailed and consistent from the beginning. I'd guess there were — or are — more of them somewhere. Notes, that is. Something happened to stop us learning the past. Those recollections probably include dragons. There is something more here though, a connection between the boats and the tokens. It's something big. Perhaps we need all of the tokens though."

"You think there are more?" he asked.

"I'd say so, but even if there aren't, I need more information. When we first found the token cave here and in the cave of tears, the tokens sat together and sang, but each time it was as if it wasn't a complete sound. This is so much bigger than I thought."

"Where do the boats come into it?"

"I don't know, but the one thing we have from before settling in The Land Between the Gorges is the boats, so they might be significant. Perhaps —" I said slowly, "we — need to follow the invitation on the boats."

"What?"

"A quest. Our next one. Let's find the dragon."

"The dragon's quest?" He laughed. "Well, that'll do for another day. Right now, all I want to do is sit on the gathering porch and listen to the twins tell about our adventures," he said.

I laughed with him. "We may even recognise some of them. Yes, we've plenty of time to plan a new adventure."

Back in the boat, we paddled slowly towards the path. On shore, the waves washed against the rocks, now scarcely visible in the thickening fog. Something splashed into the water behind us and sent waves towards the boat. It kicked and bucked as they hit us. Amethyst cooed and gurgled, unaffected by the turbulence. The boat rocked, and then lurched sideways. Something under the water was bumping us. Something raced towards us, but underwater enough so I couldn't identify it. The boat was picked up and suddenly

Kirym Speaks

we were racing out to sea, scarily fast.

Both Teema and I held tight to the sides of the boat as it swayed and rocked. Then we slowed as what had taken us sank below the surface. It was quiet; the only sounds I heard were the waves lapping against the side of the boat and Amethyst cooing and giggling.

"What was that?" Teema's voice was unnaturally loud. "Where's land?"

I glanced around. The coast had disappeared in the fog, and I could no longer hear the waves wash against the rocky outcrops.

"It's that way, I think," I said, pointing.

Teema dug his paddle in and turned the boat around.

The water beside us heaved, and something huge and black rose out of the water. I was briefly aware of a large black eye and long slim horns, and then it turned front-on and slowly climbed, towering above us. It had massive wings that flexed, wrapping around the boat, closing tighter and tighter, cutting out what little light there was. The boat flexed and creaked.

I touched the glistening membrane. It felt different to anything else I had felt before. Then, with a crack, the wings opened and the beast shot up. It was gigantic, dwarfing the boat. As its great wingspan flicked again, we were showered with water. Then it disappeared into the fog above us, its thick, sinuous tail rubbing along the side of the boat.

At that moment, Amethyst reached out and touched the tail. The beast paused.

I grabbed her hand and in doing so, I too brushed against its skin. I could feel it flexing beneath my fingers.

It knew we were touching it.

We let go and the tail shot skyward. Drops of water showered onto us as it flew overhead, now just an indistinct shadow in the sky.

Teema grabbed me, pulling me back to him and wrapping his arms around Amethyst and me. "What in heavens was that? Are you all right?" His voice shook. "What ... what was it?" I could feel his heart hammering against my back.

"I don't know, Teema. Oh my stars, that was ..." I took a breath, shocked to hear how ragged and choked I sounded. "I'm fine, and so is Amethyst. Whatever it was, it's gone."

I looked around.

The fog thinned, and land appeared, grey in the distance.

I wriggled back into my seat and picked up a paddle.

"Let's go home."

If you have enjoyed The Fortress of Faltryn, please leave a review on the website of the seller you purchased it from. Good reviews are the life blood of independently-published authors, so please take a few moments to let others know what you thought of the book.

Thank you for reading.

Do look for further adventures as
The Token Bearer's series continues.

www.wordlypress.com

Made in the USA
Charleston, SC
18 March 2016